MY MOTHER, THE WITCH

"How is it that you know so much about—well, *things*?" I asked my mother.

"Because for eight years I was privileged to sit at the feet of a man who was both wise and good."

And who had died, I remembered, at the hands of men who had hidden their faces. But she had unmasked them! I felt a small tremor of excitement. "Where you really a witch?" I asked.

She smiled gently. "You know perfectly well there are no witches."

"Then how did you make all those things happen?"

"It just happened to be a bad year, Nubbin. Some of those things happen every year without people taking much note of them, and there's a drought every three or four summers. It was more exciting, of course, to blame the witch for everything."

"But you must have done something to the preacher. Everybody says you did."

She smiled modestly. "I hoped to give him *something*," she admitted, "and I may have just mentioned to God that if He was ever going to lend me a hand, then was the time. He responded beautifully, too."

"I won't ever tell a soul," I promised.

"They wouldn't believe you anyway. These people *need* their witch, Nubbin. If I wasn't here, they'd invent me, or something like me."

YASMINA'S DAUGHTER

Corinne Childs

LEISURE BOOKS NEW YORK CITY

To my mother

A LEISURE BOOK

Published by

Nordon Publications, Inc.
Two Park Avenue
New York, N.Y. 10016

I

She came striding into the kitchen, her every nerve and sinew attuned to some compelling purpose. Snatching the shotgun from the corner by the door and, in one continuous motion, reaching with the other hand for shells on top of the kitchen cabinet, she broke the barrel, jammed the ammunition home, then stalked out as purposefully as she had come.

The two shots came so close together they reverberated into one, shattering the earth with their sound. Silence thundered in to fill the yawning void.

In the kitchen three jaws went slack; three pairs of eyes, two blue and one brown, filled with dreadful apprehension, then slowly slid away from one another to peer fearfully out the open door into the backyard. There was a pounding of booted feet across the front verandah, the slamming of a screen door, and then a man's voice—harsh, quavering, scared. "What in the name of tunket, Minnie!"

"There!" she announced vehemently, tossing aside the gun and dusting her hands together to indicate her satisfaction at a job well done. Then, without another word, she went marching off around the house.

Papa stared from the gun to the mess on the stump to us, then shrugged hopelessly like a man trapped in the middle of a giant spider web. "Would any of you," he inquired in a voice he was trying, without success, to make authoritative, "want to tell me what's going on here?"

"The bread wouldn't rise," explained Margaret.

"So often it doesn't," put in Justine, rather spitefully it seemed to me. "She poured it over the stump."

"In the sun," amplified Margaret, "and then it did. Rise."

"So she shot it," I said, not to be done out of my thirty cents' worth.

Papa sat down heavily on the cistern cover. "Things like that could be dangerous," he protested inadequately.

"You couldn't really blame her," said Margaret. "The bread was being sneaky."

Papa stared at her, started to reprimand her for her frivolous attitude, then gave it up. "I got to get back to work," he muttered under his breath, and hastily departed.

Margaret was right, though. You couldn't really blame her. This was only the latest skirmish in the running battle she and light bread had been carrying on for nearly seven years; and according to Mama the bread didn't play fair. She had a tolerable hand with soda biscuits and quick breads but remained inherently suspicious of anything you had to coddle along in a Mason jar from one baking to the next, such as starter yeast. It paid her off by being unreliable. I hoped she had now succeeded in teaching it the error of its ways.

"At times like this," remarked Justine, "I'm so glad she isn't my real mother."

"Fudge!" I said, ready to take up the cudgels in Mama's defense, but Margaret whispered, "Hush. Here she comes."

She entered through the front door, now apparently in the finest of humors. She was a big woman, tall and well-fleshed, her face still flushed from her recent triumph. "Time to start dinner, girls," she sang out cheerfully, then her eyes fell on me. "Poor little Nubbin," she crooned, ruffling my hair and patting my cheek. Then she picked me up, swung me over her head, hugged me quickly on the way down, and let me slide to the floor. "I didn't scare my Nubbin, did I?"

"No," I said.

"Good." She spoke with immense satisfaction. She didn't mind terrifying the daylights out of us now and then but she never wanted us feeling scared.

'Are you going to make some more bread?" I asked.

"Tomorrow," she replied, as serenely as if she expected all her tomorrows to be ringed with rainbows. "Tomorrow I shall borrow somebody's yeast and start all over again."

Then she sighed deeply and added the inevitable postlude: "We never made light bread in the wagon."

II

There were numerous other chores they hadn't needed to perform in the wagon, such as mopping floors, making crops, planting gardens, and tending chickens and children. Yasmina and Dr. Modesta had, like migratory creatures of the air, spent the long leisurely days following the seasons, north in summer, south in winter, taking their meals at farmhouses along their route or cooking simple repasts over a campfire. Evenings they would stop in some pleasant clearing, stake the horses out to graze, and after supper Dr. Modesta would read aloud from one or another of the books he had brought with him or picked up along the way, while the Princess Yasmina busied her hands with sewing or mending, likely as not adding a few pieces to one of the quilts she was always in the process of making.

Now and then they would pause for a day or more beside some pleasant country stream where Dr. Modesta would concoct another batch of his Magical Elixir to fill the bottles they had picked up at the last railroad depot they'd passed. On Saturday afternoon they would pull into one of the country towns along the way and start setting up for a show that night.

It isn't just the things you have experienced yourself that become a part of you. Even now I have only to lean back and close my eyes to see the big black wagon come rolling down the street and read the white and gold lettering emblazoned across its side:

DR. MODESTA'S WONDERFUL CARAVAN
STARRING
PRINCESS YASMINA
DANCING DELIGHT OF THE ORIENT

The wagon is drawn by four spirited horses black as midnight, decked out in red leather harness with white and red plumes on their heads. On the high seat of the wagon, holding the reins, sits the princess herself, resplendent in blue silk with gold and silver embroidery, magnificent paste jewels winking from the high crown of her hair. Dr. Modesta, sitting beside her, is rendering a spirited air on one of his two instruments, banjo or accordion.

That was how they came to Springhill one summer afternoon. Neither of them was ever to leave it again.

"You have never *seen* such a man," Yasmina would tell us, an incandescence beginning somewhere in the bottomless darkness of her eyes. "An educated man, with such a voice as you've never heard."

It was that mellifluous voice, according to her, which had trumpeted his doom. "They were always jealous of him," she would explain. "No, not the doctors, they never minded. Had their hands full anyway with broken bones and babies getting born and such."

It was the preachers, she said, who were always stirring up trouble. "Riffraff," was Yasmina's opinion of the Fundamentalist clergy. "No more sense than you could cram into a thimble," she would sniff, "and no education worth speaking of. Too shiftless to earn an honest living was why they took to preaching."

Dr. Modesta, she would invariably assert at that point, had been a finer preacher than the whole kit and kaboodle of them together. Certainly he had hewed to a kindlier message. "It isn't medicine we're selling, my dear," he would remind Yasmina. "It's hope. Hope for better health and better lives. The finest medicine in the world can't cure a man who doesn't believe it's going to."

That's what they had been about that Saturday night in Springhill, peddling hope well preserved in Dr. Modesta's

Magical Elixir.

Yasmina would bring it all back to life there in our kitchen as we prepared the evening meal and later washed the dishes. At the first strumming of the doctor's banjo, all the people in town would start hurrying toward the medicine wagon to group themselves around the back panel which had been let down into a platform. In addition to the townspeople, there were the farmers, still in their overalls, the sweat of their week's toil upon them, along with a week's growth of whiskers awaiting Sunday morning application of the razor. All had one thing in common; a yearning for some entertainment to leaven their workaday loaf.

I can hear the music clearly, sense the excitement, smell the kerosene lantern, marvel at the grace and beauty of the dancing princess in her royal gown, feel my toes set tapping to the clicking of her castanets. I watch the doctor rise and stand, majestic in his long black robe, his hair a silver glory that seems to ripple a little in the summer breeze. The voice I hear is that of God delivering to Moses the Ten Commandments.

The lantern light flickers over the faces of women in faded calico and the wide-eyed children they clutch by the hand. Presently a middle-aged farmer starts to dig deep into an overall pocket for the few coins to hand over in exchange for one of the magic bottles, and there is something in his face that had not been there before.

I do not see, refuse to ever see, what happened later that night.

"An accident, ma'am," insisted the Sheriff. "Rowdy young blades feeling their oats like they do on a Saturday night. Didn't mean to hurt the old fellow."

"Murderers," returned Yasmina implacably. It had been no accident, had it, that after the show had closed down for the night, but before the occupants of the caravan had gone to bed, bandana-masked men had come sneaking out of the night and set fire to the wagon? No accident that they had roughly dragged her and the doctor outside, all the while speaking among themselves of tarring and feathering and other primitive pastimes. When they saw that the old man was dead, however, they had melted away as speedily as they had come. "Like the cowards they are," said Yasmina.

"Hard to prove, ma'am," the Sheriff pointed out, "with no witnesses."

"Witnesses!" sniffed Yasmina.

"Hardly to be expected in a case such as this," interjected Dr. Armstrong, gallantly if ill-advisedly assuming the role of intermediary. "There's no doubt in my own mind that the unexpected—excitement brought on Dr. Modesta's heart attack. In a court of law, however, it would be most helpful to have a description of at least one of the—cowards involved."

"There are other ways of dealing with vermin," said Yasmina, looking every inch a princess in the metallic-embroidered silk she'd been wearing since the night before; had, in fact, no choice, since all her other garments had gone up in the fire. She had been able to salvage nothing except a large but undeniably shabby black leather handbag and her best quilt, made entirely of silk blocks, which she had spread over the doctor's body until the undertaker arrived.

"It was not his time to die," she continued. "They shall pay dearly for each of his days that they stole."

"I don't suppose," pursued Dr. Armstrong, "you happened to get any kind of look at all at even one of their faces?"

Yasmina smiled then. In Springhill they will still tell you about that smile, that it was a terrifying thing to see. They knew right then, some of them would maintain to their dying day, that the heathen woman was a witch, and that something dreadful was going to happen in Springhill.

"Don't reckon you happened to get much of a look at any of them," remarked Mrs. Tabitha Threlkeld later that day, after having made the Princess Yasmina welcome in her home as long as she cared to stay.

Leisurely and unblinkingly Yasmina took the other woman's measure. "Might have," she conceded at length.

"Should you be planning to stay around for awhile, you might happen on them again."

"Might," said Yasmina.

"I've lived in this town all my life," remarked Tabitha. "Reckon I know most everybody around these parts, and all their goods and bads. Might come in handy, was somebody interested in that sort of thing."

"Might," said Yasmina again, and grinned.

There wasn't the slightest doubt in Mrs. Threlkeld's mind then that Yasmina was a witch. It takes one to know one, doesn't it? "Been lonesome as hell," she rambled on companionably, "since Dan died, rattling around in this big house all by myself."

Yasmina's dark-browed scrutiny never wavered. "I am a woman of means," she said finally, "should you ever consider letting a room."

"Make yourself right to home, Princess," urged Tabitha happily. "Anything you want, all you got to do is ask."

So with many swishings and secret whisperings, the silken quilt settled gently over the bed in Mrs. Threlkeld's upstairs front room, and Yasmina started brewing up an elixir of her own, potent enough to keep all of Springhill hopping for a good long time.

First, however, came the matter of getting the medicine man decently interred. Not feeling altogether comfortable about the circumstances surrounding his death, Springhill was inclined to bend over backward about his burial. A free gravesite was offered in the hallowed ground of Springhill Cemetery which, with a notable lack of appreciation, Yasmina declined. The doctor had paid his own way in life, she informed them; he would continue to do so in death. She would *buy* a lot for him and she would choose which one.

Nobody believed, of course, that the dead man's real name was Primus Modesta, or that he had the slightest claim to the 'Dr.' which preceded it, but that was what went on the death certificate all the same, and on the tombstone that was eventually set at the head of his grave. The princess was equally insistent that her own name was simply Yasmina, just that and nothing more. Under considerable pressure she finally seemed to remember that at one time or another she may have been called Jezzy.

"For Jessamine perhaps?" they asked hopefully.

Yasmina looked honestly puzzled, then pained. "Jezebel," she said.

Mrs. Threlkeld covered her face with her apron and went into a choking fit. The others decided somewhat precipitately that Yasmina was quite a suitable name after all, but there really must be a last name to go with it. Modesta perhaps?

That brought forth another dark brown stare, an almost imperceptible twitching of the very tip of her nose, the slightest possible curling of her upper lip, and not a single word. Not that anybody was really surprised. They'd never imagined she was actually married to the man who had called himself Dr. Modesta. People like that simply didn't bother.

At that point Tabitha Threlkeld intervened and said to quit pestering the poor bereaved creature, one name was plenty for anybody. Look at *her*, she said, christened with three names, no less, and another tacked on when she got married, and who had ever called her anything but Tabitha? It was already becoming manifest to even the most unobserving that Mrs. Threlkeld and the Princess Yasmina were witches off the same broomstick.

When Tabitha thoughtfully offered her guest the loan of a black dress for the funeral, however, Yasmina thanked her politely but declined. She found black depressing, she explained. Dr. Modesta had never liked her to wear it. Tabitha said the blue dress was certainly handsome enough for any occasion, whereupon Yasmina modestly acknowledged that she'd made it herself from a length of silk the doctor had ordered all the way from New York City. It seemed only fitting, therefore, that she should wear it to see him off on his final journey.

Except for her flamboyant attire, Yasmina's conduct remained exemplary until near the end of the graveside services, whereupon she decided the time had come to start separating the sheep from the goats. After sprinkling half the traditional handful of earth over the coffin, she turned to scan the assemblage behind her, settled on a face and, after muttering under her breath what was taken to be a heathen curse, flung the rest of the dirt forcibly into it. The face belonged to Brother Philemon Nestor, pastor of New Hope Baptist Church. Before the week was out the unhappy man came down with erysipelas and nearly died. Yasmina's reputation as a witch was now firmly rooted in fertile soil. She would tend it faithfully and watch it grow.

Not for a moment did Springhill believe that the hand of vengeance had erred in its falling. Had not old Nestor been shouting himself apoplectic all these years, calling down fireballs and brimstone on medicine shows in general and Dr. Modesta's Wonderful Caravan in particular? Was not his own wife's well-known addiction to Dr. Modesta's Magical Elixir a long-festering thorn in the preacher's side? Nestor had never been greatly loved and the consensus was that he had only got his just deserts. The vexing thing was not being able to figure out how the princess had spotted him and how soon she might decide to take care of his cohorts.

Springhill began to sleep uneasily at night and shiver through the noonday heat. Wherever people gathered to whisper among themselves, they began to eye one another with suspicion, reluctant to be counted as friend of one who might have accompanied Nestor on the ill-omened nocturnal mission.

If, they murmured uneasily, the Indian girl would only finish up her business and get out of town, maybe the dust would settle. That was what she had become to them by then, and would long remain: the Indian girl. American variety at that since, despite Dr. Modesta's eloquent evangelizing on the oriental heritage of his princess, nobody in Springhill, with the possible exceptions of Dr. Armstrong and Tabitha Threlkeld, considered seriously that the fabled Orient might actually exist.

Not that they were much better versed regarding Indians,

American variety, beyond the fact that they were well known to be ignorant, cruel, and filthy to an abominable degree, and heathens to boot. Dr. Modesta would undoubtedly have found the situation highly amusing. Yasmina was overjoyed. Since it allowed her plenty of scope for acting inscrutable and lapsing into meaningless gutturals when she wasn't inclined to answer bothersome questions, she was only too glad to indulge Springhill in its ignorance. What she didn't appear inclined to do was pack up and leave.

She had stayed on after the funeral to sell the horses which, having been stabled at the local livery barn, had escaped the fire. She got an excellent price for them too, more than they were worth, simply because nobody dared risk offending her by offering less. Even after that she lingered on. She and Tabitha Threlkeld seemed to be hitting it off like a house afire. And while they rocked and fanned themselves and talked the summer away on Mrs. Threlkeld's vine-shaded front verandah, a season of pestilence descended upon Springhill.

Sickness without a name afflicted guilty and innocent alike, inflaming the brow and draining the body juices, then hung on and on. Horses bolted, bones got broken, dogs went mad, hens stopped laying, milk curdled in the pails, cows went dry and so did wells; corn fields which had been flooded out in April and replanted in May shriveled and died under the unrelenting sun of August. Strawstacks mysteriously caught on fire, children woke screaming in the night, and mothers wept in despair. A baby was born with a caul.

By fall, however, things seemed to be settling down a little. The pestilence lifted. Preacher Nestor had folded his tents and slipped out of Springhill. So had Yasmina, in a manner of speaking. She had packed up her silked quilt, her blue silk dress, and the new wardrobe she and Tabitha had sewed during the summer, and gone of to keep house for one of the local farmers, a widower with several children. Six months later she married him and, in due course, gave birth to me, Julia Victoria Broadbent.

Springhill was both astonished and dismayed by these events. They knew then that they would never be rid of the witch as long as she lived.

III

Oliver Broadbent's first wife had borne him two sons and seven daughters, an inequity he never quite stopped holding against her and the Almighty, both of whom might have been expected to take into account that, while sons were an asset to a farmer, daughters were an unrelieved expense from the day they were born. Until he got them married off, that is, as he had succeeded in doing with the four older girls before Yasmina arrived on the scene. The other three were still at home, as were the boys, Kenneth and Wilbur, then in their late teens.

That was the kind of household in which Yasmina found herself. It was a far cry from life in the medicine wagon, but nobody has incontrovertibly proved that an orchid set down in an Indiana cornfield can't flourish there. Yasmina would have tried anyway because it simply wouldn't have occurred to her to do anything else.

It soon became evident, however, that she had brought with her a number of radical ideas, such as that pretty dresses cost no more than plain ones. She started the two youngest girls off to school that fall in bright new plaid gingham frocks she'd sewed herself instead of the drab browns and grays the first Mrs. Broadbent seemed to have favored. To Oliver Broadbent's inevitable objections she replied serenely that the little girls were too pretty to be spoiled by ugly dresses, and that *she* would do the worrying about the washing and ironing, thank you. She said on a farm you were always working anyway; if you weren't washing and ironing pretty dresses, you'd only be doing something else. Margaret was enchanted with both the new dresses and her stepmother's show of independence. Justine, characteristically, as Mama would learn to her sorrow, dragged her heels.

But that was another thing about Yasmina, she never held Justine's attitude against her. She never interfered in Papa's handling of his nearly grown sons, but she would go cheerfully to bat for all three girls whenever she felt it necessary.

Not that Oliver Broadbent had ever physically abused a child. When they were small, he had been an indulgent and loving father, as he would be with me. Somewhere around the age of ten, however, he would arbitrarily consider their childhood at an end and henceforth expect adult behavior of them.

He had his own ideas too about how a good Christian wife should conduct herself. She was to work hard without complaint, bear as many children as the good Lord sent, dress economically and modestly without unseemly adornment in the form of ribbons and jewelry, and teach her daughters to do likewise. Last, but far from least, she was to be absolutely subservient to her husband.

All these mandates Yasmina was prepared to good-humoredly ignore, but there was worse to come. Oscar Broadbent was known throughout the community to be a 'close man with a dollar.'

"Tight as the bark on a beech tree," was Yasmina's more trenchant version, "and a domestic tyrant to boot." For she understood at once that to him money, even the trickle of silver that found its way into a farmer's pocket, represented authority. He would dole out a dime to a child for a school tablet or a nickel for a pencil as if the coin were his own heart being squeezed of its lifeblood, always with the stern admonition that the article in question must be used sparingly and made to last. No child of his had ever been allowed to have money to spend for what he categorized indiscriminately as 'all that trash people put in their stomachs,' which included store-bought ice cream, candy, cracker jack and soda pop; in other words, anything that cost money that came out of *his* pocket.

Most farm wives are allowed the chicken and egg money for their personal handling, but not the first Mrs. Broadbent, much less an ignorant Indian girl who didn't know the first thing about the value of money. She'd proved that, hadn't she, by the way she'd blown in her housekeeper's wages, which he had, as was proper, discontinued as soon as they were married? He'd pointed that out to her, kindly enough because he had no wish to hurt her feelings; told her when she needed money for anything, she should ask for it.

At that moment Yasmina's whole spine must have taken on an unprecedented rigidity, but she spoke calmly. "Is that your final word?"

A more intuitive man might have detected something in her voice or manner to warn him. Papa didn't. "Yes," he said without even hesitating.

"Very well."

It must have been the quietest battle he had ever fought but the echo of his defeat would resound in his ears to the last day he lived. His punishment began almost at once, for despite his own stinginess, it soon became apparent that Yasmina *had* money and *spent* money. No great sum at any one time but always a little. On Sunday mornings she would dig down into the big leather handbag she always carried and drop a shiny half dollar rather grandly into the collection plate. Before the little girls left for Springhill with their father on a Saturday afternoon, she'd slip them a dime or two to fritter away on some of that 'trash' he so abhorred. More than likely she would return from her weekly visit to Mrs. Threlkeld with a fold of cloth or something for Mildred's hope chest.

At first Papa suspected his new wife of a practice not uncommon among rural women, that of slipping eggs and a fat hen or two out to the huckster wagon behind his back; but spy on her as he would, he was never able to catch her in the act. It seemed impossible that she could be getting the money from anywhere else for the woman seldom left the house except to attend church with the family. And, of course, to visit Tabitha Threlkeld.

For the trips into town she drove Nellie Maude hitched to the buggy. After one hair-raising experience at the wheel of Mr. Ford's pride and joy, she had categorically declined to be responsible for any form of conveyance that had no idea which way it was headed or how to stop when it got there. Papa was just as pleased; gasoline cost money whereas Nellie Maude had to be fed whether she was driven or not.

Frustrated in his previous attempts to ascertain the source of his wife's affluence, Papa took to rolling out the buggy for her and hitching up Nellie Maude, taking advantage of those occasions to inspect both buggy and wife for any indication of contraband. He also made a point of searching her handbag, which she ordinarily left hanging on the bed-post when she wasn't carrying it, when he imagined himself unobserved, but never found it to contain more than a dollar or two in change. He practically scraped the walls of their bedroom closet, even examined the mattress and springs of their bed for possible places of concealment. The little girls, questioned repeatedly, professed themselves as mystified as he. Approached personally on the matter, Yasmina simply drifted into her inscrutable savage role and stayed with it until the heat went off.

In sheer desperation Papa even dared tackle Aunt Tabitha Threlkeld, a foolish decision which left him with a pair of badly singed ears and nothing more. The first Mrs. Broad-bent had been Dan Threlkeld's sister; and while Tabitha had always considered her sister-in-law a poor-spirited creature, she didn't figure that excused Ollie Broadbent's tight-fisted tyranny. She did finally unbend sufficiently to suggest that Yasmina might still have a few dollars left from the sale of the horses.

Papa took hope. After deducting Dr. Modesta's funeral expenses, including the marble headstone, from the selling price of the horses—no man, woman, or child in Springhill was ignorant of those figures—he satisfied himself there couldn't be more than a few dollars left.

He resolved to put the matter out of his mind and might have succeeded to a degree if things hadn't kept popping up to aggravate his curiosity. Such as his three girls stepping out to church one Sunday in fine new frocks he hadn't been asked to provide. That was what really scalded him—that the woman actually had the gall to parade *his own children* in public wearing dresses she'd bought for them with *her own money.* That episode, in fact, unnerved him so much that he finally told Yasmina she could have the egg money if she'd tend the chickens. It didn't amount to much, especially as she'd been taking care of the chickens all along, but it was a moral victory all the same, and as such she accepted it. Never one to gloat over the fallen, she even made him apple dumplings—his favorite dessert—for supper. She hadn't a mean bone in her body, anybody could see that.

As a matter of fact, except for the money problem which kept cropping up now and then, they seemed to get along as well as most married people. They seldom quarreled, and they always seemed to have plenty to talk about. Yasmina enjoyed living on a farm and she was quick to learn—anything she wanted to learn, that is.

She disliked housework and did it sketchily, but anything she stuck in the ground grew and flourished. She tended the chickens more conscientiously, now that they were hers, but never stopped believing them by far the stupidest of all God's creatures, undoubtedly created by Him late in the afternoon when He was tired.

She cooked adequately for our needs, canned fruit and vegetables in season; but except for bread, which she eventually managed to gain the upper hand of, she seldom bothered with baking. She sewed beautifully and enjoyed it as long as it was pretty.

By the time my memory begins, she and Papa seemed to me just like other children's parents—or maybe not quite. Strangers inquired now and then if Oliver Broadbent was my grandfather, which he could well have been in point of age. He had grandchildren several years older than I.

And Yasmina? Well, Yasmina wasn't quite like any other mother in the world. A few days before I entered first grade I heard her calling me one afternoon, crawled out from my current hideaway under the snowball bush, and asked her what in the name of tunket she wanted.

"I must make you ready for school," she explained.

I reminded her that I already had my tablet and pencil, as well as a new Primer and dinner bucket and three spanking new gingham dresses, so what else could possibly be required?

"Hold out your hand."

I started to comply, then remembered the current state of my hand and drew it hastily behind me.

"A little dirt won't matter," she assured me kindly, then let me see what she was holding in *her* hand. A huge squirming fishing worm with some of the earth still clinging to him.

"I don't like worms," I protested, the understatement of a lifetime.

"This kind won't hurt you, and you only have to hold it a minute."

"Why?"

"When you go to school, sometimes at noon and recess the boys will tease you with bugs and worms. If you scream and run, they'll pester the life out of you. Stand your ground just once and show them you're not afraid, and they won't bother you any more."

"He's all dirty," I pointed out.

Generously overlooking the fact that I often carried a greater amount of dirt on my own person without even noticing, she said, "Not very, and it's nice clean dirt. He won't bite you, Nubbin, and you only have to hold him long enough to prove you're not scared."

"O.K.," I said, holding out a grimy paw and squinching my eyes. I hardly felt anything at all; but when I dared open my eyes, I felt my stomach uptilting. "He hasn't even got a head!" I croaked.

"If he were cut in two, both pieces would crawl away."

"Ugh," I said, and tipped the repulsive thing onto the grass.

"You'll remember, won't you, when the teacher asks for your name, to tell her it's Victoria Broadbent?"

"When you call me that it sounds like you don't love me."

She knelt in front of me, bringing her face on a level with mine, her eyes wide and dark and eloquent with emotion. "I'll always love my Nubbin," she assured me, holding me close, "no matter what I call her."

"As much as Julie?"

"More. More than anybody else in the whole world."

"Why do they?" I asked after a moment. "Why do boys be like that?"

"Because they're boys," said Mama, and stood up.

"I'll fix 'em," I promised.

She grinned widely. "I'll bet you will," she said, "but not right away maybe, so best you remember you're not afraid of worms."

IV

Never keep the school bus waiting. That was the first rule to be impressed upon my malleable young mind. Horse-drawn and presided over by a crotchety little man in his sixties, the school bus was generally spoken of as an entity whose every whim had to be gratified. If you weren't right there waiting to get on the minute it stopped in front of your house, likely as not it would drive on without you, although that was not quite the calamity it might seem since the school building was less than a mile away by road, and not much more than half that as the rural child prefers to travel, over fences and through fields.

Although I would have preferred to walk, Mama decided that I must ride the school bus at least in the mornings; so five minutes early, properly turned out and with my lunch pail on my lap, I would be established on a chair by a bedroom window to watch until the wagon hove into view around a curve in the road, then hurry outside to get aboard.

Each year there were usually twenty-five or thirty children in school, distributed randomly through eight grades. Boys were no longer kept at home to work in the fields during busy seasons, school laws having recently been tightened up on that score; but since temporary teaching certificates were available to high school graduates who had been able to pack in a six weeks 'normal course' during the summer, it was nothing out of the ordinary for there to be a few students in the upper grades not much younger than the teacher.

An experienced teacher was, of course, preferable. If a beginner was all that could be had, a man was preferred because of disciplinary problems with the older boys. That, however, was likely to precipitate another problem, in that the older girls fell in love with the teacher and spent the rest of the term in sentimental vaporings and not-always-lady-like rivalries.

Occasionally an older boy would get a crush on a young woman teacher, but this did not happen often. There was something about her being a school teacher that seemed to put the boys off.

Our teacher that year was Miss Waterman, a veteran of some dozen years in country schools, the preceding three of them in ours. Mama, I remembered, had seemed pleased when she learned that Miss Waterman was planning to stay on.

With eight grades to be taught their three R's as well as certain embellishments in the way of grammar, history, geography, and physiology in the upper grades, Miss Waterman was kept on the run throughout the day, with fifteen-minute classes one after the other. That first morning, having hastily block-printed an A, a B, and a C at the top of a sheet of paper for each of us four first graders and instructed us to copy them, she had swept along to other chores.

Mama had warned me never to leave my seat without permission; but when I spotted a bookcase in one corner of the room and satisfied myself that Miss Waterman's attention was engaged elsewhere, I tiptoed over and squatted down in front of it. Presently, as I became more absorbed in my investigation of what constituted, as I was to learn, the school's entire library, I sat down on the pine floor which, as was the custom, had recently been treated with a liberal coating of oil.

"Victoria, dear, did you ask permission to take a book?"

She looked nine feet tall standing there over me, but since the Nemesis I was used to at home topped her by a few inches, I didn't feel particularly intimidated.

"You'll ruin your clothes sitting on the floor like that. Go back to your desk and practice your letters like the other children."

I stood up, clinging stubbornly to my book.

"You've got your Primer, haven't you, dear? Why don't you look at that?"

"I read it last night," I explained, and saw her mouth tighten. In addition to being a disobedient child, Victoria Broadbent was also a liar. Speaking quite sternly now, she said, "Put the book back, Victoria, and return to your desk at once."

"Oh fudge," I said, but there was nothing to do but comply. By the time I reached my desk she was holding my ABC paper, now become an A-to-Z paper solidly inscribed front and back.

"So you already know the whole shootin' match," she remarked in a voice carefully devoid of expression. "Where's your Primer?"

I produced it.

"Read me a few lines, Victoria, if you will be so kind."

I started off quite willingly but it didn't take much to satisfy her. "That's plenty," she said. "I can see already this is going to be one of those years."

Mama seemed glad to see me that evening but was displeased about my ruined bloomers. She was afraid the oil stain would never come out. So my very first day in school I had learned two important facts: Never be late for the school bus, and don't sit on the schoolhouse floor with your white bloomers on.

It must have been a week or two before Miss Waterman got around to paying me any more personal attention. One day she asked, "Who taught you to read, Victoria?"

"Nobody," I said.

As far as I knew, nobody had. I'd spent quite a lot of my young life sitting on laps, sharing companionably in whatever was being read at the time. Papa favored the Bible and *the Indianapolis Star*. Margaret leaned more toward the love stories she was able to borrow from a neighbor.

As for Mama, she read like some people ate, everything she could get her hands on, including the newspaper, *Comfort Magazine*, *Ladies Home Journal*, *Prairie Farmer*, the books Aunt Tabitha borrowed for her from the Springhill Public Library, and every other scrap of printed matter she could beg or borrow. It was nothing uncommon to come across her squatted down on the kitchen floor happily perusing the newspaper she'd just spread to protect her newly mopped linoleum. She claimed items seemed to kind of jump out at her then that she'd overlooked before.

So although it was true that nobody had actively tried to teach me to read, the tightly curled bud of my infant curiosity had responded famously to all this enthusiasm for the printed page. My "What it say, Mama?" in due course unfolded to "Where it say that?" and finally burst into radiant blossom with the discovery that I could make out a few words myself.

I had never considered my accomplishment particularly remarkable, nor I believe had Mama until Miss Waterman called it to her attention, along with the fact that something had to be done about Victoria Broadbent's troublesome habit of supplying answers to the second grade's arithmetic problems—aloud. Receiving a note to that effect gave Mama an excuse to do what she'd been dying to do anyway, get her nose inside the schoolhouse door. I advanced to second grade and Mama invited Miss Waterman to supper. That was only the beginning; soon they became fast friends.

Maybe it finally got through to Mama that nothing so hampers a school child's acceptance by her peers as having teacher and mother chummy with each other. In any case she started courting the opposition, showing up nearly every Friday afternoon with a big stone crock full of fresh sugar doughnuts or a pillow slip filled with popcorn balls.

Such largesse, however, did not account for the fact that boys didn't chase me with worms. Somewhat to my disappointment, they never so much as tried. "They say I'm a witch's kid," I reported to Mama one evening.

"Don't tell me they're still beating that same old drum," she said, but she didn't seem at all dismayed.

"Could you really turn a boy into a toad?" I asked, hanging somewhat fearfully on her answer.

She frowned, then looked contemplative for a long moment. "I don't know," she said finally, but with what appeared to be a quickening of interest. "I never tried."

V

Of all my father's first family, Margaret was the only one I ever felt close to. The older girls were married with families of their own. Mildred had got married when I was two. To Justine I was simply another item in her catalog of complaints, and the boys paid practically no attention to me at all.

Margaret had liked Mama from the first and been grateful for her presence. Justine, on the other hand, never forgave Mama for marrying her father or having me. Oddly enough, she never held these lapses against her father, any more than she nourished grudges against him for his stinginess. In both cases she somehow managed to twist the facts around in her mind until Mama was to blame.

In the same way, she always blamed Mama because she didn't get to go to high school, although she and everybody else knew Mama had been on her side all the way.

Papa considered himself pretty liberal in the matter of education, insisting that all his children finish grade school, no matter if it took them past their fourteenth birthday, which was as long as the law required children to be kept in school. At that point his views shifted abruptly into reverse but were equally inflexible. He said high school was a luxury farm boys and girls were better off without. Furthermore, since his farm and Springhill High School were in adjoining townships, he would have to pay both transportation costs and tuition.

What he did not understand, and would have refused to understand had it been pointed out to him, was that Justine was in desperate need of ego boosting. She deeply resented the fact that Margaret was popular with young people while she was not. Margaret was allowed to date while she was still too young. She had been the baby of the family for eleven years and although by then an adult by Oscar Broadbent's peculiar method of reckoning, had been put out of countenance by my birth. The fact that a majority of farm girls never started high school, and that hardly any of them finished, was the very reason she wanted to go. She spoke of it as if she were anticipating a four-year tour of all the exciting places in the world.

Mama, understanding all that, did as much as she could to further Justine's cause, even offering to pay her tuition, which had the unfortunate effect of reinforcing Papa's opposition. On top of that she piled another tactical error. She told Justine if she would study harder and make better grades during her eighth year, Papa might be more kindly disposed. This, of course, was not at all what Justine had in mind. Papa must prove his favoritism for her by sending her to high school no matter what kind of grades she made.

Nevertheless, she did seem to be making an effort and, during the first half of the year, her grades improved. She had also conceived an enormous passion for her teacher, a young man named Darrel Fuster. In an incident that occurred during the last month of the term, she had engaged in a hair-pulling contest with some eighth-grade rivals for the teacher's hand and, during the fracas, had fallen down the basement stairs and sprained her ankle. It was just the excuse Papa had been looking for. No high school for Justine.

Justine reacted by starting through what in earlier years would probably have been referred to as a 'decline.' Papa said it was lucky she'd never started high school; with her health turning out so bad, she'd never have been able to finish.

Shocked out of her vapors, she almost immediately acquired a virulent case of religion, during which she walked through the house with her eyes toward heaven and dropped into genuflection whenever the spirit took her. In this phase she was, unfortunately as Mama saw it, encouraged by the current pastor of Whipley Corners United Brethren Church which all the Broadbents attended. This went on until one day I carelessly tailgated into one of the genuflections and got whacked on the nose with her elbow. Mama instructed her that subsequent raptures would have to be confined to her bedroom. A rapture unobserved being no rapture at all, Justine soon began to lose interest.

She began looking forward with more impatience than ever to her sixteenth birthday, when she would be allowed to begin dating, thus bringing to an end Margaret's exclusive use of the Broadbent parlor.

That was the first of Justine's yearnings I was able to understand because the parlor was the only really elegant room in our whole house. Five Broadbent young ladies had already become affianced to their young men in the muted glow of the kerosene lamp with pink roses in its global shade. The rug was green with more pink roses, and the best rocking chairs were kept in there as well as a green plush divan. The wall paper repeated the rose motif, and the white lace curtains were starched until they could have stood without hanging. The organ was there too, although I'd never heard anyone play it but Mama.

"Just like the parlor of that other house," I would say, somewhat wistfully.

"Very much like," she would agree.

"Except we haven't got any of those beds."

In "The Girls' " rooms there had been canopied beds with red velvet hangings to match the carpets.

"Nobody has beds like that now," she would say.

"And no chandelier."

"Our parlor is too small for a chandelier, Nubbin."

The other house had, of course, been much larger, and a hundred times more magnificent. The Girls—Francine, Louise and Julie, and Mama of course—had worked at a garment factory and boarded and roomed in the big house owned by Aunt Bessie.

Mama spoke of all the girls with affection but there was never any doubt that Julie had been her favorite. Once she had told us about the terrible things that had happened to Julie, but after that she would never speak of them again.

When only seventeen and an orphan, Julie had fallen in love with a young stranger in town named Gordon Trover, who only pretended to be in love with her. Instead of marrying her as he had promised, he took her to a house of ill fame and kept her prisoner there.

I hadn't, of course, the slightest idea what a house of ill fame might be and somehow I hadn't dared to ask. I was glad, though, that Julie had finally got away. She had waited until Gordon Trover was asleep, then put a pillow over his face and held it there until he was dead. Afterward she had put on his clothes and walked right out of that place with nobody trying to stop her.

I don't recall being particularly frightened by this harrowing tale. After all, it was pretty much on a par with Hansel and Gretel cooking the witch in her own oven, the wolf swallowing grandmother, and the woodsman slitting the wolf right down his middle to let grandma out. All Mama's stories, whether fact or fable or something she just made up out of her own head, were pretty realistic. It may have been an advantage never to be sure which was which.

That had been Mama's Third Life, the one with Aunt Bessie and The Girls. Before that had been the First Life with The Papa, then had come the Second, with Aunt Hortense Braithwaite in the Alamo Hotel. After The Girls had come the Fourth Life on the medicine wagon, and now she was living her Fifth one with us. "Will you have some more lives?" I asked her once.

"No," she said. "This is my very last one."

"Will I, Mama? Will I have a lot of lives?"

She looked very solemn then, and was silent for so long I began to wonder if she was going to answer. Then she said, "You're having your first one now, child. Maybe there'll be another when you grow up and go to college; and another when you marry and have children. If you're one of the lucky ones, Victoria, that will be all."

I no longer felt a lack of love when she called me Victoria; rather it had come to serve as a signal that what she was saying was one more thing I needed to remember, like being on time for the school bus and not sitting on the schoolhouse floor in my white bloomers.

"Tell me about The Papa," I said. Even when she was feeling sad, she could almost always be induced to talk about *him*.

The Papa. *Her* Papa, that nobody in that small Indiana town had ever laid eyes on until, a few months after the Civil War had ended, Dr. Lemmon brought him there. The doctor said the twelve-year-old boy's name was John Smith, and that he'd found him sick and homeless in New Orleans. The doctor and his wife finished raising the boy, then tried to set him up in a general store, but he wasn't much interested in that. He preferred to get off by himself somewhere and read and write poems. Sometimes he would play the parlor organ and sing songs in a language he said was French. When he was twenty he married a girl two years younger and sired three children, but only one of them lived. He was a failure in business and a disappointment to his foster parents and his young wife, but to his daughter he was everything in the world.

He insisted on naming the baby for his mother and began at once to mold the infant clay into his mother's image.

He supervised the little girl's education and deportment, selected her clothes and taught her how to wear them. He taught her to play the parlor organ and sing a fair soprano to accompany his own excellent tenor; taught her some of the French songs too and a number of hymns as well. Most of all, he was able to talk to her as he never had to anyone else, and to her he handed down the first twelve years of his life. He told her about the small but perfect house with its walled garden where his mother spent long summer afternoons reading or entertaining friends; where, when there were evening parties, beautiful ladies in elegant gowns strolled in the moonlight with their courtly gentlemen, pausing to embrace in the fragrant shadows of the spreading mimosa. The little girl began to dream that she might stroll with her own courtly gentleman—who would, of course, look exactly like Papa—when she grew up.

He spent eleven years filling his daughter with delight and enchantment, and then he died in a gushing of blood over a white coverlet, leaving her to face alone a world which placed no commercial value on ladylike accomplishments.

"He made me feel beautiful," Mama would say. "A girl has to feel beautiful before she can ever expect to be that way."

I wondered aloud if that would help Justine, who was now spending most of her time in front of a mirror. "It would be easier," I said, "than pinching her cheeks and sneaking out the cake coloring to put on her lips."

"Don't you be making fun of Justine," she admonished. "All girls go through that stage. At least she's over religion."

I considered mentioning that, although Justine seemed to have recovered, I had not. My nose had been bleeding at intervals ever since. I remembered in time, however, that Mama disapproved of complaining about one's ills.

VI

You'd think Papa would have given up after seven years of nothing but failure; but like the molten mass inside Vesuvius, the thought of Mama's secret horde seemed to simmer and bubble inside him until he simply had to do something about it.

One of the most peculiar things about the situation was that Mama never seemed particularly interested in money, and even her bitterest detractors could scarcely have accused her of being a spendthrift. The years in the wagon with so little storage space available may have contributed to her habits in that respect.

For each season she liked having one 'nice' dress, with the previous 'nice' dress relegated to less illustrious occasions. She had a winter coat and a spring one, a felt hat for winter and a straw for spring and summer, and two or three pairs of shoes. That, with a few house dresses and a suitable supply of underwear and nightgowns, comprised her modest wardrobe. She wanted each of the girls to have three dresses for school and one or two for Sunday, as well as coats, hats, shoes, and underwear equal in quality and quantity to her own. She spent a little money on the house but not much, leaving it pretty well the way she'd found it. And she liked just *having* a little money with her in case she wanted to buy some trifle.

Even taking into account the modesty of her expenditures, however, Papa knew the egg money couldn't begin to cover them, and he felt sure she must have spent what was left of the horse money at least a dozen times over, so he started probing and prying again. On one occasion, I remember, he even tried patriotism. He said if anybody had any money just lying around, seemed like they ought to be putting it in Liberty Bonds. Yasmina smiled at him in a vague sort of way and said, "Please pass the potatoes, Ollie."

He made sporadic appeals for her confidence, as her husband, the father of her child, her natural protector and adviser. Then, as a last resort he took his problem to the one place in the world from which, as he should have realized, Yasmina would brook no interference. Brother Colvin Purdygood.

Although she had attended church regularly since her marriage, she always made it clear to Papa she did so only to spare him the embarrassment of having people think he had a heathen wife. Not, she insisted, that she had anything against the church as long as it didn't get in the way of her personal relationship with God.

The preachers were quite another matter, her longstanding opinion of *them* having been painfully reinforced by the manner of Dr. Modesta's death. Furthermore, she didn't consider Purdygood a particularly outstanding specimen of his breed, besides which she blamed him for encouraging Justine in her religious fervor.

How *he* ever found the courage to challenge *her*, and on her home ground at that, remains a mystery to me even to this day. I've wondered if Papa might not have promised him a little something for himself if his efforts were successful, or maybe he simply figured any farm woman who blithely dropped a half dolllar into the collection plate every Sunday was worth a little extra evangelizing.

A naturally friendly woman, besides being uncommonly curious, Mama made him welcome. That afternoon she was working on her silken quilt which, like Penelope's mantle, never seemed to get quite finished. It had looked finished for years, but every now and then you'd see her ripping out a few blocks she'd say were worn or soiled or not the proper color, and replacing them with new ones which she would neatly featherstitch in place.

So there she sat, diligently cutting and measuring and stitching, the very picture of placid domesticity. "Perhaps," the preacher suggested, "the child should go out to play."

"No, no, she's all right." Mama tipped me a wink, snapped another length of thread, and reached for her needle.

With a sigh of resignation Brother Purdygood transferred his complete attention to Mama and launched into his oration. It seemed to have something to do with a wife cleaving unto her husband, forsaking all others.

"But what about the little children?" Mama wondered, carefully knotting her thread.

"I wonder, dear lady, if you understand the seriousness of your position. I beg of you for your own soul's salvation—"

As he warmed to his theme, Mama stopped her needle in mid-thrust and regarded him with such rapt attention he must have considered it all over but the shouting—which he promptly began to supply.

"You have read your Bible, my good woman. You know what it says about man being the head of the family and woman's duty to obey. If you have money which you have been withholding from your own loved ones, you must put it into your husband's hands."

His good woman's eyes narrowed and I noticed that she seemed to be expanding a little in all dimensions. "Are you implying," she demanded, "that Mr. Broadbent is too sorry a farmer to support his family? Must I sit here and be deafened while you insult my husband in his own house?"

"Mrs. Broadbent," he exhorted earnestly, but Yasmina was on her feet now, waving the quilt around her like a banner. "Silence!" she cried. "Victoria! Find your father at once! Tell him to come and deal with this creature."

She knew perfectly well I couldn't have moved if the house had been burning down.

"Mrs. Broadbent," screamed the preacher, "it was your

husband who asked me to talk to you!"

"Fudge," sid Mama. "My husband and I have our disagreements same as everybody else, but the one subject on which we have total understanding is money."

Brother Purdygood looked so much as if he were going to cry, I suppose she thought it a shame not to give him something to cry about. "Speaking of money," she said, "expect no more half dollars from me."

That finished him. He went tearing out the front door like a turpentined cat.

As far as I was concerned, it had been dandy entertainment, but I was getting old enough to be developing a little curiosity of my own. "Where *does* the money come from?" I asked her.

"Well, you see, Nubbin, I've just got it, that's all."

What could be plainer than that? It was quite awhile before I so much as thought about it again.

Papa didn't mention it either, at least not in my hearing. I suppose he must have had a report from Purdygood, probably etched in some of that brimstone he was always calling down on sinners. The story that finally began to make the rounds was that Mama had come out of the burning wagon with that leather handbag of hers stuffed full of gold pieces which she'd buried somewhere around Aunt Tabitha's place for safekeeping. Aunt Tabitha got her garden dug up for free that year, said it had never been so flourishing.

Papa didn't protest as much as he might have ben expected to when Mama told him she wasn't going to church any more. He insisted, however, that the child, meaning me, ought to be in Sunday School. She said it would probably do me no harm; I could go with him and the others.

I had already observed that Mama's own dealings with the Almighty were conducted on a considerably more informal level. Apparently she judged Him powerful enough to handle most situations unaided, but since He couldn't be expected to be everywhere at once even if the Bible did say so, it wasn't a bad idea to call things to His attention when they came to yours. "You don't have to scare me half to death," she would remind him equably when a dropped butcher knife embedded itself in the kitchen floor a fraction of an inch from her toe.

"Rain's fine," she would observe mildly, "and goodness knows we needed it there a spell back, but best You let up a little now so we can get the hay in."

When Justine came home from a trip to Springhill crying her eyes out because Papa had refused *in public* to give her money for a new ribbon sash, Yasmina besought, "Please forgive them both, although You know and I know it wasn't necessary."

I agreed. Justine should have known better than to ask. Yasmina would certainly have given her the money if she had mentioned it to *her*.

Mama never spoke a word against Papa though, not to us or anybody else. She would, on the contrary, frequently play up his better points, calling to our attention that he'd ben orphaned young, then batted around from pillar to post by relatives who tolerated his presence only for the work he could do. "So when he got a family of his own," she would go on to explain, "he was determined to be everything in the world to them. Because he was so poor, every penny had to count; and he thought the only way he could be sure of that was to handle all the money himself."

Misguided, she implied, and that was a pity, but good in other ways. Certainly he was an honest man, hardworking and respected.

As I would understand when I was older, he was also confused. His sons had never challenged his principles. Until recently none of his daughters had openly questioned his judgment. Now Justine was moping herself into weeklong headaches because she hadn't been sent to high school. Even worse, Minnie had taken Justine's part in the matter, and was putting even more dangerous ideas into the young one's head. Ideas the woman had got from heaven knows where.

Heaven knew and I knew. Those ideas had come straight down from a gentleman named John Smith. If Papa had really listened to those stories Mama was always telling, and realized how completely I had fallen under their spell, he would have been even more disturbed than he was.

VII

Although she had acceded willingly enough, in fact not without evidence of maternal pride, to my advancement to second grade, Mama put her foot down when, around Thanksgiving of that first year Miss Waterman proposed promoting me to third. She mentioned somewhat cryptically that I was already past the danger point and added that it might make me a little peculiar being in a class with children so much older than I.

Miss Waterman tactfully forebore to mention that in her estimation I was more than a little peculiar already. She didn't belabor the point at all except to remark that I was becoming bored with school and something ought to be done about it. Mama said she'd been thinking about giving me music lessons to take up some of my time but I was too little to pump the organ, and no hope of Papa buying a piano. Before long, however, there *was* a piano, bought by somebody.

It was a repossessed instrument somebody had failed to make payments on, but Mama pronounced it good as new except for needing tuning. She immediately called in the piano tuner, a gentleman named Huckstep, who also gave music lessons and led the band at the summer concerts in Springhill.

Mr. Huckstep would have come to the house for lessons but for some reason—perhaps to provide herself another weekly outing—she decided upon a Mrs. Jarman, who lived about four miles away.

Nellie Maude, being elderly and set in her ways, could be expected to clip along briskly when headed for the home stable, but outward bound she exhibited all the enthusiasm of a sickly snail. As if, Mama would comment, she was afraid she'd get so far from home she'd never be able to find her way back. Thus there was time to kill, nothing to kill it with but conversation, and nobody to talk to but each other. I would chatter unreservedly about my schoolgirl experiences, and Mama would tell me stories about her childhood that had long since ended in a gushing of bright blood across a white coverlet.

Some of the stories about a little boy living in New Orleans with his mother, she hadn't told me before. She told me how it had been when the little boy's father who had seemed taller and handsomer than any other father in the world in his gray and gold uniform, had prepared to ride away to war for the last time. After kissing the boy's mother, he had turned to his son and held out his hand. "My son, I'm depending on you to take care of your mother while I'm gone."

"Yes, sir," the boy had promised manfully; but when she had needed him most he had lain dazed and bleeding, struck down by a Yankee soldier's sword. He heard her piteous pleas, then her screams, then nothing more.

He did not know how long it was after that before the Yankee doctor had found him, but they had nursed each other back to health and become fond of each other. After learning that his father too was dead, he had raised no objection when Dr. Lemmon proposed carrying him back to that little Indiana town where he would be forever lost and lonely until, in the flesh of his flesh, he found a kindred soul.

"He was your grandfather, Nubbin," Mama would tell me, but the term had no real meaning to me because I had never known grandparents of my own.

"Was Dr. Modesta a grandfather too?" I asked her once.

"Perhaps he was in a kind of way," she said.

"What was the other one, the soldier one? Was he a John Smith too?"

"Perhaps he was, at least a part of the time." Her smile seemed to grow distant and a little sad. And then she said the thing that will always remain in my memory. "Nellie Maude is pretty smart for a horse. The saddest thing in the world is never being able to go back home."

Hardy fare for a seven-year-old? Maybe, but she had to talk to somebody, didn't she, and who else was there? Margaret loved Mama dearly but didn't more than half believe some of her tales. Justine didn't believe them at all. Maybe she talked to Tabitha Threlkeld on those weekly visits. I like to believe that she did, and that Aunt Tabitha listened, and believed, and understood.

Although Papa must have known when he married her that she was no more Indian, oriental or otherwise, than he was, he'd have had no patience whatsoever with that other papa, who in his opinion shouldn't have been putting all those outlandish notions into his little girl's head. All Mama had was a moppet of seven who never doubted a thing she said. If she'd told me that during the night Papa was going to grow a purple horn in the middle of his forehead, I'd have got out of bed next morning expecting to see it there.

Another thing that began to happen on those trips to my music teacher was that Mama started making brief calls at houses along the way. "I need to see Mrs. Mullican a minute," she'd say, as if she'd just that moment thought of it. "Whoa, Nellie Maude. Here, Nubbin, you hold the lines. Mama'll be right back."

She would be too, in hardly longer than it took her to walk to the door and back, I don't remember being the least bit curious. Adults being impossible to understand anyway, why bother your head trying?

"Hey, Vicki," Paul Ziegler hailed me at school one day. "My mom wants you to tell your mom she's out."

"Out where?" I asked.

"I dunno. Just tell her, will you?"

"Mrs. Ziegler says tell you she's out," I faithfully relayed to Mama that evening.

She looked slightly puzzled for a moment, then nodded her head. "All right," she said. "I'll take care of it."

No curiosity at all. Soon forgotten. Margaret's marriage that winter may have had something to do with that. I loved Margaret and didn't take at all to the idea of her leaving home.

As it turned out, she didn't leave, not right away. Most young couples started out on a rented farm, those rentals running from March to March. Those who got married at other times of the year usually lived with the groom's parents until the following March, but Bob Marsh's parents already had a full house so he and Margaret would live with us until they could move to their own place. That was how Mama happened to be on hand when the shivareers came.

Shivareeing was an old country custom that had fallen into disfavor for a time but had recently been resurrected in our community, with few embellishments that did nothing to enhance the practice. One bridegroom of the year before had been forced to spend the night alone in a locked corncrib to which no key could be found. Another luckless pair had been left in the woods to find their way home in a driving rain. The bride had contracted pneumonia and almost died.

These excesses were said to be due to the influx of some hooligans from outside the township. Everything bad that ever happened around Whipley Corners was laid to 'hooligans' and 'outsiders,' the terms having become almost synonymous.

After the uproar over the girl with pneumonia, shivareeing had evidently been abandoned; there hadn't been one in our community in more than a year. Nevertheless Margaret voiced misgivings. Bob, however, thought the shivareers had learned their lesson and there wouldn't be any more trouble with them. He seemed to be right too, until almost two weeks after the wedding.

I must have been asleep for at least an hour that night when suddenly I was awakened by what I felt certain must be a warmup for Judgment Day. Once awake, however, even my unattuned ear perceived that the instruments in use were of no celestial variety. Mama got me out of bed and led me over to the window where Papa was trying to assess the situation.

"Church folks mostly," he announced presently. "Young crowd, out to have a little fun. I'll build a fire in the cook-stove, Minnie, you make some coffee and get out whatever we've got for them to eat."

The others were coming out of their rooms by then. Justine was in her bathrobe but Bob and Margaret had dressed. There was shouting and some coarse laughter when the young couple appeared on the front verandah, but nothing threatening began to happen until the crowd had finished the coffee with the doughnuts Mama had made that morning, and the apples Papa had brought up from the cellar. Then as if on cue a couple of big boys rolled the buggy out of the barn and invited Margaret and Bob to go for a ride.

"Don't hurt anybody now," Papa cautioned; and Bob said, "O. K., folks, we'll play along." You could see, however, that both they and Margaret were uneasy. Bob had already spotted a pair of known troublemakers in the crowd, Carl and Wimpy Adams, who lived somewhere on the other side of Springhill.

Mama had heard about the Adamses too and didn't like the situation at all, especially when she saw they were taking the buggy out on the road. "Can't go far, pulling it themselves," Papa said, but he spoke as if it was himself he was trying to convince.

They didn't go far, however. They just pulled the buggy up and down the road for awhile to the accompaniment of some shouted remarks and occasional bursts of laughter. I got tired watching, sat down on the bottom stairstep, and went to sleep.

I was wakened by a piercing scream and people shouting. The house was quiet now; they had all gone somewhere and left me there alone.I went outside.

Mama had put my bedroom slippers on me; but as I made

my way across the front yard to the barnyard gate, the October wind whistled right through my flannel nightgown, cutting into my small body like a million tiny knives. There was a great deal of running about and shouting in the barnlot, and most of the people had by that time gathered around the big stock tank down by the barn.

Then, in the light of the lanterns which some of them were holding aloft, I saw Wimpy Adams walk toward the trough with Margaret struggling to get out of his arms, and Bob trying to go to her rescue but the other Adams boy was fighting him off. As I watched, Papa appeared in the circle of light. I saw his lips move, and he put his hand on Carl Adams' shoulder, whereupon Carl turned and pushed him so roughly that he fell to his knees.

With Margaret still in his arms, Wimpy Adams reached the tank and raised her frail body high above the almost-freezing water.

"Set that girl down! At once!"

There was Mama in her long-sleeved flannel nightgown, black hair loose and falling to her waist, but all anybody had eyes for was the double-barreled shotgun held steady as a rock in her hands.

"A little water never hurt nobody, missuz," brayed Wimpy Adams, and the crowd laughed obediently, but uneasily too.

"Let my daughter go or I will kill you." She was in excellent voice, and I never doubted for a moment that she meant exactly what she said.

The bully hesitated, then what little courage he possessed began to flicker out. He was simply too scared to move. Bob Marsh took Margaret's limp body out of his arms.

In a final attempt to save face and titillate his followers, Wimpy Adams turned back towards Mama and whimpered, "Honest, missus, we never meant no harm."

"Neither did Mrs. O'Leary's cow," she snapped, and walked a few steps toward him. He, and the crowd behind him, began to back away from her. "Get going now," she said. "All of you. Anybody not through that gate yonder by the time I count five is going to take home a rump full of buckshot."

"Mrs. Broadbent!" That was a feminine voice making itself heard.

"One," replied Mrs. Broadbent affably, and presently, "Two." I was the rock in the sea against which the waters were parting as the shivareers hurtled past me on either side.

"Three," I heard, then "Four," and braced myself for the inevitable. "Five!" she said, and then the gun spoke, once. All I could hear after that were people running down the gravel road, then that sound too died away.

"Did you kill anybody?" I called out in a voice so small I could scarcely hear it myself.

"Nubbin! Sweetheart! I thought—oh, Nubbin, baby, how scared you must have been!"

I suppose I had been, but with Yasmina for a mother I hadn't exactly been conditioned to a tranquil life. Enveloped in her arms, assured there were no corpses cluttering up the barnlot, carried to the house, cossetted and warmed and reassured, I soon forgot my fears.

Our side, in fact, had suffered no real casualties at all. Margaret, ginger tea warming her within and heated bricks without, was going to be all right. Papa's lip was cut, Bob would be sporting a black eye for a few days, and Justine had a skinned knee from being pushed down by the retreating revelers; but nobody was seriously hurt.

As I started back to bed I heard papa clear his throat and say "Minnie." I turned to see what was going on.

"Minnie," he said again, and couldn't seem to go on. "It should have been me done that, Minnie," he said finally. "You shouldn't have to—" He couldn't finish.

"Doesn't matter which one it was, Ollie, you or me. Our girl's safe, that's all that matters." She stood up, resting one hand on his shoulder; and as I watched, he put his own gnarled and workworn hand gently over hers. I would have sworn there were tears in his eyes. She said, "Come to bed now, Ollie. You need to get your rest."

It frightened me a little, and there was another feeling I

didn't begin to understand. I looked around for Justine and saw her standing in the doorway of her room staring at them, for once reduced to silence.

It was the only gesture of tenderness I ever saw pass between them. I pray with all my heart that there were more.

VIII

As Mama's aspiring young musician I was turning out to be a disaster. *She* had played the organ well and had shifted happily and apparently effortlessly to the piano when we got that. She sang as naturally as she breathed, always had, took it for granted anybody could do the same if she just opened her mouth and let fly. As she did frequently, and under a variety of circumstances.

No classicist she, but her touch was as true as her voice in such popular favorites as "Red Wing," "Swanee River" and "Till We Meet Again." During her churchgoing days she had sometimes substituted for the regular pianist. She played instrumental pieces too, some of which she'd learned as a child and long since forgotten the names of.

Good altos being scarcer than the proverbial hens' teeth, the church had inveigled her into a ladies' quartet while she was still Papa's housekeeper. They sang at weddings, funerals, and other special occasions at the church. Mama could sing soprano too, usually did around home; but her alto, being rarer, was most in demand. She had kept on with the quartet awhile after she quit going to church, apparently recognizing neither link nor barrier between warbling and worshipping.

Although there had been straws in the wind all along—I could scarcely manage to carry a tune, even in the nursery jingles which she'd taught me first—it had simply never occurred to her that little Nubbin wasn't going to toddle right along in Mama's musical footsteps. Now, however, she began to notice that I frequently struck wrong notes on the piano without seeming aware of it.

"Victoria, you're flatting that," she'd yell all the way from the kitchen when I was practising. She'd come to the parlor and show me that I was doing wrong but even then my ears could hardly detect the difference.

It was the custom in Springhill to have a piano tuned once a year. Less would have constituted neglect of a valuable instrument; more would have been construed as extravagance or, worse, vulgar ostentation. Months before tuning time, however, Mama would start complaining that "that piano doesn't hold a tune at all any more." Although I never openly disagreed, I did rather wonder how she could tell. *I* couldn't.

Still, I was only eight years old and, mechanically speaking, Mrs. Jarman professed herself pleased with my progress. So why worry when time was going to take care of everything?

Unfortunately, however, time does not turn all ugly ducklings into swans or transform all frogs into handsome princes. Some of them remain simply ducks and frogs. I enjoyed music lessons, particularly rousing marches and lilting melodies with a pronounced beat, but past a certain point I did not, seemingly could not, advance.

"Mama," I said one day, "I just don't hear notes the same way you do."

Her hands arrested in what she was doing, she looked at me for a long time. "I suppose that *could* be the answer," she said finally. "Do you hear other things, Victoria? Really well, I mean?"

"I guess so," I said.

"Some people are tone-deaf," conceded Mrs. Jarman. "You run across one every once in awhile, but I shouldn't have thought—Victoria."

Dr. Armstrong confirmed the dread suspicion. "Tone-deafness is what they call it anyway. Nothing to do with ordinary deafness, though, so you don't need to worry about that. Nothing to be done about it either. Due to heredity probably, thought to be anyway. Don't remember as any of the Broadbents ever turned out musical, maybe that's the reason."

"Aren't you going to give me a pill?" I asked. He had given me a pill almost every time I saw him when I was smaller.

"Oh yes, Victoria, I'm going to give you a pill. Indeed I am."

He brought a small white box out of his pocket, carefully extracted one fat pink tablet, and laid it in my hand. "Wait now till I bring you a glass of water."

I dutifully washed down the pill and waited, but nothing seemed to be happening. I was still tone-deaf. An eight-year-old catastrophe, but Mama would never show disappointment or let it matter in the least. In due course I was allowed to stop the piano lessons, but she and I kept right on singing together. After all, she could always drown me out if necessary.

"Got it from me probably," Papa commented when informed of the verdict. "I was never much for singin' anyway."

"Nothing to worry about," Mama replied serenely. "It's not as thought there was anything *serious* wrong with the child."

I wondered a little if Dr. Modesta's Magical Elixir would have helped me but forebore to mention it right then. I had long since learned that certain subjects were best referred to only when Mama and I were alone, as we were to be more and more as time went on.

Darrell Fuster, who had been Justine's eighth-grade teacher, was now clerking in a store in Springhill, and Justine was determined not to let him slip through her fingers a second time. She had neither eyes nor ears for anyone else in the world.

Margaret, almost two years married now, had a baby boy and a second child on the way. There was, in fact, a veritable thicket of Broadbent grandchildren sprouting up around me, to whom I was, I supposed, some kind of aunt. The older ones mostly ignored me, I was expected to play nicely with the ones around my own age on the infrequent occasions we were together, and occasionally to look after the smaller ones, all of whom I regarded with varying degress of affection or disinterest.

Mama got along quite well with her stepchildren and their families. Children were invariably drawn to her although she made no apparent effort to attract them. I would ultimately come to see that, lacking experience with children, she simply treated them the way she treated everybody else, with interest and respect, and they responded in kind.

My stepbrother Kenneth's wife, Orpha, was frequently spoken of as "such a good Christian woman." Mama said fudge, she was just the sort of sad sorry Christian who provided the worst advertisement in the world for the Christian faith. "And," continued Mama, "how she ever managed to lend herself to the procedure necessary to bear a child, I can't begin to imagine."

Having done so, however, and borne him, she must have immediately reverted to type. When she nursed the baby or changed him, she carried him off to another room, closed the door, and set a chair under the knob.

Having got little Robert toilet trained, she began to dress him in little striped cotton suits she sewed herself, with a drop seat aft and a slit in front large enough, but barely, to accommodate the member for which it was intended. Since, however, she thriftily made the suits big enough to be grown into, the slit seldom if ever fell conveniently adjacent to the member.

I'd encountered that little problem once or twice before and complained to Mama about it. Since she evidently didn't see fit to intevene, I thereafter tried not to be along with Robert, but came the afternoon I got stuck with him anyway. Sure enough, while we were playing down around the haystack back of the barn, Robert got the call.

Having seen a succession of babies in various degrees of undress over the years, infant male anatomy was hardly a complete mystery to me. It was this kid's oversize pants that put me off. I simply couldn't find the darn thing.

I started getting mad, mostly at Orpha, but since Robert was there and she wasn't he was the one who caught the blast. If she considered it indecent for a little girl to see a boy baby's equipment when he was being changed, what about making it necessary for that same little girl to go fishing around for it inside his pants? Through a skimpy hole that was some more of her bloomin' modesty! "*You* get it out!" I exploded.

He tried, poor tyke, but was hindered, as I had been, by seeking so small an object in so great a void. Also by not being able to get more than one finger at a time through the slit. In desperation I unbuttoned the seat. "Squat then," I commanded.

But squat he would not, and did not. Give him credit for knowing a little something; there were things you squatted for and things you didn't, and this wasn't a squatting occasion. "You'd better," I threatened. "If you wet your pants, your mother will tan you good."

"Help me!" he wailed.

I didn't like him much at the best of times, now less than ever, but I was sorry for him so I tried again. Eureka! There it was! But something truly dreadful had happened. It had grown, or the slit had shrunk in washing—there simply wasn't room.

"You've simply got to squat," I said, trying to push him down, but already a telltale wetness was staining the front of his pants. Then came the cascade.

"Come on," I said disgustedly, and took him by the hand.

He came docilely enough; in fact I was beginning to feel a twinge or two of sympathy for him until we stepped up on the back porch, whereupon he loosed an anguished howl which brought his mother on the run.

"It was *her* fault," he managed to blubber between wails. "She wouldn't—" Words failed him and he lapsed into damply incoherent gurgling.

"What happened, Victoria?" Mama was biting her lower lip the way she did when she was trying not to laugh.

"I couldn't find the damn thing," I said. "Why didn't she make the hole bigger?"

Orpha gasped, made some odd choking noises, and fled, towing her still-blubbering manchild off with her to be changed—in private.

"It wasn't his fault either, Victoria." Mama hadn't ever reprimanded me for swearing, sensing, I supposed, how much I'd been put upon already. "He can't help being a boy."

"I know," I said wearily, "but that wouldn't be so bad if she'd only make the hole big enough."

I was, at that stage of my development, working pretty hard at being fair-minded about the male element anyway. Most of the boys at school I had liked at least as well as the girls until the previous winter when I'd been treated to a new slant on one of the species.

There were always several pitch-in suppers during the winter months, constituting almost the only social activitiy around Whipley Corners. Following supper there were always dancing games for the adults—Skip to My Lou, Pig in the Parlor, and such. While our elders thus disported themselves, and the small children romped in the kitchen, we in-betweens played Spin the Bottle.

It seemed pretty silly to me, but I was already beginning to suspect that at least half the things other people warmed up to were going to leave me cold. You spun a bottle, or possibly a plate or even a potlid, to get a partner of the opposite sex, with whom you retired to another room, or weather permitting, outside the house. When you reappeared a few minutes later, everybody laughed and gave you sly looks.

Obviously I was missing the boat somewhere, because all that ever happened was that some boy and I went into another room, closed the door, and stood there in the dark for a minute or two, then came out.

Then came the night I found myself sitting on an enclosed

stairway—the chosen retirement spot for that evening—with a boy I hardly knew named Kenny Hill. Before I could say ABC, Kenny had one arm around me and the other hand was making an exploratory raid up the outside of my bloomers. In the ensuing imbroglio Kenny got his head banged against the wall and fell the rest of the way down the stairs. While he was still counting stars, I opened the door, stepped over him, and out. "If you die," I said, indulging in a popular pleasantry of the day, "I'll plant nettles on your grave."

"I wonder what happened to the Hill boy," Mama remarked on the way home.

"He hit his head on something," I said.

"Oh." She was like that. You seldom had to tell her everything. "I've been thinking, Victoria, some of you children are old enough now to join the dancing games. Next time I'll see to it."

I never played Spin the Bottle again in all my life.

A little at a time, in such quantity as I supposed she deemed digestible, Mama had tried to further what would later become known as sex education, and the birds and beasts of farm and field had collaborated famously to that end. I doubt that any great effort was made to keep farm children from finding out how pigs get born, and calves and lambs and kittens. Nor did Papa exactly embark on a secret mission when it was time to escort one of his milk cows to visit the neighbor's gentleman cow, as he was generally called. I had no idea, of course, nor much curiosity, as to what actually transpired during those encounters except that it had something to do with the cow 'coming fresh' and having a calf.

Dogs mated freely whenever and wherever the urge came upon them, cats invariably at night, often beneath our bedroom window. More than once Mama had got out of bed to throw a pitcher of water through the screen so we could get to sleep In short, sexual activity surrounded me like the Ancient Mariner's sea water but was just as unassimilable, cause and effect being still a long way from coming together in my mind. As for translating such bizarre behavior into human terms—well!

Mama had also explained about my monthly periods which she thought would be starting soon; made rather a thorough job of it, I've no doubt, but not much of it stayed with me except her speculation that it might stop my nosebleeds, which had been recurring at intervals since the application of Justine's elbow.

I might have expended a little more contemplation on the subject had not something else started claiming my attention about that time; something that should never have filtered down to a backwater like Springhill but eventually did, and changed our lives even more than we realized at the time. It was called the Ku Klux Klan.

IX

About all we knew about the Klan up to that memorable summer was the name, which for some reason seemed to strike the rural funnybone. Precocious toddlers were coached to greet visitors with lisped versions of "Hey there, you a Ku Klicker?" This generally elicited howls of appreciative laughter, thus spurring the tots on to even greater thespian efforts.

But even the lowly mole bides his time until you wake up one fine morning to find your nice front lawn tunnelled this way and that from his passing. It started with handbills which were tossed into all the front yards during the night. They were badly printed and full of terms like pure womanhood, native born Americans, white Protestants, and the like.

The mole moved in a little closer the night 'somebody' burned a cross outside Whipley Corners United Brethren Church. "Nobody we know," Papa asserted, and went on to speculate that it must have been 'somebody' from over Stringtown way, not even a Klansman likely as not.

Mama listened and looked troubled. Naturally she hadn't been in church that night but I had, and it had given me an eerie feeling to step outside the door and see the burning timbers that were lashed to a corner post of Mr. Plimpton's corn field. Mama said she hoped that was the last anybody around Springhill would ever see of the Klan, or hear of it either.

Papa said it probably was but from all he'd heard, the Klan might be a pretty good thing. Foreigners had no business in this country anyway.

"Foreigners," sniffed Mama goodhumoredly. "How do you reckon any of us got here? If your grandma's time had come on her a day earlier, your own father would have been born a foreigner."

Papa had always enjoyed telling the story about how his grandmother had, deliberately according to the family version, contrived to delay her child's emergence from her womb until after she had set foot in the new country. Now, however, he didn't seem to enjoy Mama referring to it. He said, "Best not go around talking about things like that, Minnie, with things the way they are now."

"Fudge," said Yasmina, but she kept on looking thoughtful.

During the days ahead it began to look as if Papa's admonition might have been in order. There were more cross burnings, some of them set dangerously close to people's homes. At the Brenners, after an elderly uncle came to live with them and it was noted his speech was liberally sprinkled with German words; at the Goldmans, for no reason at all anybody could figure until somebody remembered they'd always kind of wondered if the Goldmans weren't Jewish on account of the name. The grocer's new clerk, dark-eyed and handsome, disappeared after hooded Klansmen called at his boarding house and told him they "didn't need no Eyetalians around here taking jobs away from good Springhill boys." The clerk, as it turned out, was the grocer's cousin's boy, but he left Springhill on foot that same night and never came back.

Springhill hadn't been in such a dither since Parson Nestor and his midnight desperadoes had raided the medicine wagon. Most of the furor was about who might be and who probably were not Klan members. Certainly there were agitators and organizers about, although nobody admitted knowing who they were. The whole movement, in fact, was cloaked in unbelievable secrecy. A member was warned not to reveal that fact to anyone, even his own wife. Nonmembers maintained an equal secrecy to protect their families from possible retribution on that score.

Surely the Klan must have realized early on that they were wasting their powder on Springhill insofar as their announced objectives were concerned. Organized labor was just something we might read about now and then in the newspaper if we happened to be interested. Baptists might snipe at Presbyterians, and Presbyterians in their turn were not above taking an occasional verbal swipe at Methodists, but every winter they attended each other's revival meetings and were all good Protestants together. There wasn't a Catholic or a Jewish family within miles, and only three or four negro families living on small farms a few miles the other side of Springhill.

Our lone foreigner was the wizened Chinese laundryman, who as far as anybody could remember had simply appeared one day in his cubicle next door to the post office and had been there ever since. He washed and ironed men's white shirts and detachable collars. You wrote your name on a slip of paper when you left your laundry and thus identified it when you came to pick it up, paying the amount pencilled on the same slip. Not a word was ever exchanged; either the man was mute or didn't know enough English to communicate. Nobody even knew his name.

With no religious persecution in the cards, and foreigners present being in short supply, foreigners past must be made to fill the bill; hence the forays against the Brenners, the Goldmans, and the supposed 'Eyetalian' boy. Since everybody in the community had foreign ancestors not too far removed, this twentieth century witch hunt was swiftly assuming the proportions of a game called Point The Finger First.

That was when I started worrying about Mama. An American Indian wasn't exactly a foreigner but was frequently thought of as such. Anyway she wasn't one, but would the Klan be inclined to believe that? Especially when she *looked* so different from anybody else, and goodness knows her activities in the past could well have branded her as something of a fireball.

I tried to look her over at supper that evening as if I were seeing her for the first time. She was taller than most women, wide-hipped and deep-bosomed. Her back was straight as a poker and she carried herself like—well, like a princess. Her complexion had the appearance of a moderate suntan, even in midwinter, but it had none of the leathery harshness of skin exposed too long to the sun; it was smooth as silk to the touch. There was considerable color in her lips and cheeks, and her hair was long and lustrous, the kind of black that glinted blue in the sun instead of brownish like a lot of black hair. I wondered if she could possibly be an Indian and not know it.

There was just the three of us at table that evening. Justine had married Darrell Fuster a few weeks earlier and gone to live in Springhill. Papa cleared his throat and said, "A man got anything to hide, best he get into the Klan before they find out about it."

"You figuring to join?"

She had never countered him so directly before, and he wasn't prepared for it. "I didn't say that," he muttered, refusing to meet her eyes.

"Don't be an old fool, Ollie," she said, almost fondly. "Nothing you and all your ancestors have ever done could have been half as bad as joining the Klan would be."

"The Klan's all right!" he blared at her, as if she'd suddenly ground down a nerve. Then I could see he wished he'd left the words unsaid. "At least," he temporized, "they got some pretty good ideas. I been thinkin' that all along. All the church folks are joining up, even the preacher."

He could not possibly have waved a redder flag in her face but he was too caught up in himself to notice her expression. "Folks like us got to organize," he plowed on, "if we want to keep foreigners from coming over here and taking our jobs and ruining our womenfolk. I ain't sayin', mind you, I been asked to join, and I ain't sayin' I'd join if I was asked, but I *am* sayin' it's an organization any man would be proud to belong to."

"Is that why they hide their faces?" her voice was perfectly steady and unmistakably deadly. "Because they're so proud to be running around in bedsheets scaring innocent people half to death and burning their houses over their heads? Or is it because some high muckety-muck in Indianapolis is making big fools of them and they've not got sense enough to know it?"

"That's enough, Minnie!"

They had seldom quarreled before, and certainly never as they were quarreling now.

"What do they think they're doing, playing God in a nightgown? Where were all your fine upright protectors of home and country when there was a war on? I'll tell you where. Scuttling between the blankets with the first girl they could talk into marrying them, then using their patriotism trying to get her pregnant in time to save themselves from the draft. Cowards then, Ollie Broadbent, and cowards now; and if you join the Klan, you'll be a coward with them."

He had gone so pale I wondered if he was going to die then and there; but when he got to his feet trembling with rage, I wondered if he intended to kill her instead. He said—and his voice was trembling too—"What right you got to talk about anybody, after all you been and done?"

She drew herself up to her full height and seemed to be looking down on him, although he was slightly taller. She said, "You don't know the half of what I've been and done, Ollie Broadbent. You never will, and you wouldn't understand if you did. But I tell you this, I would go through it all over again, and I would rather see my daughter become all that I have been and more; I would wish her every sin and every pain, every heartache and every regret I have ever had in my life, rather than see her condemned to live in this benighted place for the rest of her life."

"She's my child too, woman!"

The way she looked I thought she might be going to tear

into him again, but she only said, very quietly, "Yes, Ollie, I know." Then she said, even more quietly, "But this Klan thing—it can't be allowed to go on."

"And just what do you think you're going to do about it?"

She smiled at him then as she must have smiled in Springhill that day they still remembered. She said, "Why, Ollie, I'm going to stop it, that's what I'm going to do."

For a long moment their rage and hate seemed to crackle through our kitchen like summer lightning, then he turned furiously and flung out of the room, slamming the screen door resoundingly behind him.

She sat there staring into her plate. She had hardly touched her food, and neither had I. Finally she raised her ead and began to speak.

"When we used to pass through this part of the country in the wagon, it seemed the most beautiful place in the world. People seemed to lead such pleasant tranquil lives, and the children always looked so healthy and happy. Dr. Modesta was always saying farmers were the salt of the earth, the backbone of the nation, stubborn and courageous and independent. One thing he was worried about, they're not independent at all. They're so eager for something to lean against they fall like rotten apples for any twister of words who makes them feel smarter and more important than they are."

"You always say Papa is a good man." Actually I was no longer sure of that; she may have been talking about *her* Papa or even Dr. Modesta. She regarded me fondly but sadly. "Even a good man becomes irresponsible when he hides behing a mask. Backed up by other men in masks, he will do things he wouldn't dream of doing, wouldn't have the courage to do, alone and in fear of being recognized. Do you understand at all what I'm saying, Victoria?"

"A little maybe, I don't know." I didn't want to know. I couldn't bear to think of Papa in a slit-eyed hood setting fire to a cross in the Goldman's front yard. "Are you sure Papa really belongs to the Klan?" I asked.

"Every man in the township belongs to the Klan who can rake up, beg, borrow or steal the initiation fees and dues. It isn't sense that keeps a man out, it's sheer poverty."

"Are you really going to stop it?" I asked. "Stop Papa anyway?"

"You can only stop a man *before* he leaps on a runaway train. After that you have to wreck the train." She paused and looked over at my plate. "Finish your supper now, Victoria, before it gets any colder."

"If I did," I said, "I'd throw up."

"Then don't," she said kindly. "You can have something later if you get hungry."

At bedtime Papa had still not returned. Mama got ready for bed as usual but told me she was going to sleep in Margaret's old room in case I wanted her for anything.

"Why crosses?" I asked, already half asleep.

"The devil prefers the guise of a Christian for doing his dirty work. Those burnings frighten people even more than they would otherwise because they see it as destruction of a Christian symbol."

If she'd been speaking Chinese, she couldn't have confused me more. "How is it that you know so much about—well, *things*?"

"Because for eight years I was privileged to sit at the feet of a man who was both wise and good."

And who had died, I remembered, at the hands of men who had hidden their faces. But she had unmasked them! I felt a small tremor of excitement. "Were you really a witch?" I asked. "Then?"

She smiled gently. "You know perfectly well there are no witches."

"Then how did you make all those things happen?"

"It just happened to be a bad year, Nubbin. Some of these things happen every year without people taking much note of them, and there's a drought every three or four summers. People who feel the need to be punished frequently bring accidents on themselves; and although only a few actually participated in the raid, they all felt guilty, about that or something else. It was more exciting, of course, to blame the witch for everything."

"But you must have done something to the preacher. Everybody says you did."

She smiled modestly. "I hoped to give him *something*," she admitted, "and I may have just mentioned to God that if he was ever going to lend me a hand, then was the time. He responded beautifully, too."

"How were you so sure it was the preacher?"

"We heard his bullfrog voice outside the door before they broke it down. Dr. Modesta was laughing himself sick, I remember, at the thought of the preacher calling in for a bottle of tonic. Besides, it was easy enough to spot him at the funeral. Just looking at his face was enough."

"I won't ever tell a soul," I promised.

"They wouldn't believe you anyway. These people *need* their witch, Nubbin. If I wasn't here, they'd invent me, or something like me."

There was something else that had been puzzling me. She talked about Dr. Modesta as if she'd been terribly fond of him, and she'd certainly gone to considerable trouble to avenge his death, but—"You've never once visited his grave," I said aloud.

"Dr. Modesta's? Of course not, because he isn't there. He never was."

"You mean he went to heaven?"

"Maybe there isn't a heaven, not the kind people talk about anyway, but there's *something*. God wouldn't spend sixty years developing a man like Dr. Modesta just to let him slip into nothingness. And he didn't. I have felt his presence with me ever since he died."

I could feel my scalp prickling and icy fingers start walking down my spine. I suppose it must have showed in my face for Mama said, "Victoria, you silly child, I'm not talking about ghosts." She paused. "He walks beside me. You won't understand that now but maybe you will some day."

It seemed to be my night for questions. There was one

more I needed an answer to. "Were you married to Dr. Modesta?" I finally dared to ask.

"Of course we were married. We'd been married for eight years. I'll tell you all about it some day. Just now you can stop chattering and let me go to bed."

X

Witch or not, as time went on people came to depend upon Mama more and more for advice about their health problems, on the premise, I suppose that she must have learned something about medicine from Dr. Modesta. Whenever she went abroad, the big leather handbag was likely to contain a bottle or two of something she had put together that was supposed to be good for some common ailment.

Sometimes I accompanied her on those trips, sometimes not. I was, as a matter of fact, becoming somewhat disenchanted with her method of transportation. "You could learn to drive the machine as well as not," I grumbled on one occasion.

I had decided she wasn't even listening when suddenly she chuckled and said, "Lysistrata."

"Lizzie who?" I said.

"Lysistrata," she corrected, taking more care to pronounce it carefully.

"Did she live in the boarding house too?"

"No, Nubbin. Lysistrata was a lady who lived and died hundreds of years ago. Then, like now, it was the men who ran things, and the women were getting pretty tired of them constantly waging war. It was Lysistrata who came up with a way to make them stop. She and the other women simply refused to live with their husbands until they all stopped fighting."

It didn't seem much of a story, certainly not up to her

usual standards. Where would the women have lived, I wondered, if not with their husbands?

The air had cleared at our house after that one cataclysmic episode, and Mama seemed more cheerful than she had in a long time. The fact that she had shifted her quilt to the bed in Margaret's old room, indicating she was in residence there, had nothing to do with Papa or the Lizzie-something-or-other she had mentioned. She wasn't sleeping well, she said, and it was a shame to keep Papa from his rest with her tossing and turning when he had to get up so early and work so hard.

The Klan hadn't been mentioned at home since that night either, and I didn't hear much about it elsewhere. It seemed to have slipped away as quietly as it had come; but once again the mole was simply biding his time. In August two cars full of robed and hooded Klansmen visited the negro families late one night and ordered them to pack up and leave. One of their houses was set on fire as a warning to the others of what would happen to them if they delayed.

It was reported that one of the negro men had got up courage enough to call the Sheriff. For all the good that would do, Mama said, the Sheriff likely as not belonging to the Klan himself. Papa set his jaw and said nothing.

"Papa was at home that night," I mentioned after he had left the house.

"They're all in the this thing together, Victoria, no matter whether they were all there or not. How can they be so brutal, so arrogant, so just plain stupid!"

"Are the ladies being stupid too?"

She threw me a look of approval and almost smiled. "Women have never been encouraged to use their brains," she said. "A lot of them do what their men tell them to do, even when they know it's wrong and they don't want to, simply to keep peace in the family. Some women like it that way, I suppose; think they do anyway, never having known anything different. A woman's life isn't easy, Victoria. Once she gets married and has children, there's no escape, no possible way for her to make enough money to take care of herself and the children if she leaves her husband. But women *can* think, Victoria, if they try. And they can *act* too, if they have a good enough reason."

Although she sounded serious enough, she spoke with none of her former fervor, and presently I heard her humming as she washed the dishes. Obviously not a cloud on her horizon.

School, when it took up again in September, was not nearly as tranquil. The kids were bad-tempered and edgy, not with anybody in particular but just in general. Even Paul Ziegler, easily the least inhibited child in school, kept his lip buttoned and went around looking as he'd been orphaned during the summer.

As luck would have it, we had a new teacher that year, a Mr. Banks, not more than twenty and appearing as bewildered about the situation as we were. He, poor fellow, had no way of knowing which children's fathers were Klan members and which were not, or how a Klansman might react to the chastisement of his child.

Then it started raining leaflets again, this time announcing a Klan parade in Springhill the first Saturday night in October. That, of course, inspired the children to even greater frenzies. Paul Ziegler maintained he could tell his father by his feet, no matter what kind of clothes he wore.

"Where does he keep his things?" I ventured to ask. "You know, the robe and things."

"Somewheres," he said glumly. "Most likely in the barn. If mom found it in the house she'd use it for a dust rag."

"He'd only buy another one. If," I added, remembering what Mama had said on the subject, "he had enough money."

"She'd do something to that one too. They been fussin' somethin' awful lately."

"So have mine," I said, mentally asking God to forgive this slight lapse from the truth since Paul seemed in need of comforting.

"I kind of wish your mom really was a witch, then maybe she could do something about it."

"Maybe she is," I said.

"Naw, she's a real nice lady. My mom says if it wasn't for your mom to talk to sometimes, she'd just go climb a tree."

When I conveyed this sentiment to Mama, she said everybody was up a tree these days. I suggested Mrs. Ziegler might help her do something about the Klan since she was so riled about it too, but Mama seemed to have lost interest.

I supposed she must have found it discouraging to have at last encountered something bigger than she was; but conditioned to more scintillating performances from her, I couldn't help feeling disappointed. So I'd shake her out of this mood, I would, or know the reason why. "You haven't made any Stuff lately," I said.

"There hasn't been much call for it."

"You mean nobody wants it any more."

"I believe it's more what you might call a temporary lull."

There had been more secrecy surrounding The Stuff than any of her other remedies. It certainly wasn't a subject on which she had heretofore encouraged my questions, but her continued serenity only inspired me to greater efforts. "Is it really to keep ladies from having babies?" I demanded.

She didn't turn a hair. She just said, "Allow me to remind you, Victoria, that, regardless of popular opinion, I am not a witch. The Stuff, if it does anything at all, only helps the ladies have their babies farther apart, which is better for everybody."

That I could well understand. Margaret had borne three babies within as many years of her marriage, and the third had been stillborn. She'd had no babies since, so maybe she was taking the Stuff too.

The first time I'd spied a batch of it cut into squares and cooling on the back porch table—I must have been six or seven then—I'd taken it for caramel fudge and helped myself to a piece, only to have my hand slapped down before it could connect with my mouth. And before I caught a good whiff of The Stuff, which would have discouraged my appetite in short order. "It smells awful," I said now, remembering that traumatic experience. "I don't see how the ladies ever manage to swallow it."

"Victoria," said Mama. Then she began chewing on her lower lip. "Never mind," she said finally, "we'll talk about it later."

But another question had popped to the surface, one I should have thought about asking before. "How much do they pay you for it?" I asked.

She smiled gently. She said, "There are some things you can't take money for, Victoria. Until you learn that, you haven't learned anything at all."

XI

About the only parades most of us had ever seen were the ones staged by the small circuses which came to Springhill for a day or two every summer. "It won't be like *that*," said Paul Ziegler. "The Klan ain't got no band even."

"How do you know?" I challenged.

"How do you reckon a man could toot a horn all done up in one of them hoods?" he retorted.

"*Those* hoods," I said.

"Them, those, who cares? You're gettin' worse'n a school teacher, Vicki. Anyway, there ain't goin' to be no band."

Mama verified that. She said that, among other considerations, the Klansmen couldn't tolerate anything that might distract attention from themselves.

"How many will there be?"

She had no idea. The leaflets hadn't said whether it would be just local members or whether outsiders would be coming in for a real show of force. She didn't, in fact, seem particularly interested.

"Are we going?" I asked.

"Certainly. Everybody's going."

"Then how in tunket are the men going to get all rigged out in those things without anybody seeing them?"

" 'The way of the transgressor is hard,' " she quoted, and grinned. "They've got a problem, Nubbin, and no mistake. No sense having a parade without people to watch, and that means getting the families there; otherwise I'm sure the men would be only too glad to dispense with their company on this occasion."

She was right. Saturday night was traditionally family night in Springhill. Weather permitting, the whole family rode into town after the chores were done, to shop, visit, and just amble around. For a man to come to town alone would, on this night of all nights, indicate domestic trouble of the most serious order or brand him irrevocably a Klan member and thus shatter his vow of secrecy. The only alternative seemed to be for the poor fellow to somehow transport himself and his regalia into town under the already curious eyes of his wife and children without them noticing it, then find a place he could wriggle into it in time for the parade.

I couldn't help feeling a little sorry for Papa that evening when I saw him load a gunny sack in the back of the car with the muttered explanation that he needed to get some corn ground if the mill was still open. It wouldn't be, of course; it closed at six and it was now almost seven. Besides, the contents of the sack had obviously been much too light for shelled corn.

Mama must have felt a little sorry for him too, because she told him to drop us off at Aunt Tabitha's and we'd walk downtown with her in time for the parade, which was scheduled for eight o'clock.

Main Street was the only street in town with street lights along the whole block of the business district. The marching men would emerge from the darkness at one end of the block and be swallowed up in similar darkness at the other. I knew in my bones that Papa was going to be one of those marchers but, unlike Paul Ziegler, I had no confidence at all I would be able to recognize him, by his shoes or any other way.

By ten to eight everybody was lined up along the two sides of Main Street. I shivered and pressed closer to Mama. She said, "There's nothing to be nervous about, Victoria."

I could have told her she was speaking entirely for herself. I knew beyond the shadow of a doubt that if I were to come face to face with one of those creatures in their slit-eyed hoods, I should promptly die of terror, even if he happened to be my own father. I also felt more than ever provoked with Mama. After all her inflammatory remarks in the beginning, she had simply sat back and not lifted a finger. It wasn't like her at all.

It was the quietest crowd I would ever be a part of. Everybody just stood there with their eyes glued to that patch of darkness beyond the first street lamp, waiting for the first shrouded marcher to appear. I wondered where the parade was forming and how the men could see to get into their regalia in the dark.

"Why don't they come?" I said, when it was ten past eight.

"Maybe they're having a meeting first," someone suggested.

It struck me as being a most inappropriate time for a meeting, but the Klan seemed funny in a lot of ways so they just might be having one while everybody stood and waited and half froze to death in the crisp October night.

The crowd was becoming more restive by the minute, peering up and down the street and muttering among themselves. There were a few men in the crowd but most of them were women and children. When somebody said it was eight-thirty, the lines started breaking up. "What can possibly have happened?" people kept saying to each other.

"Ask me," I heard a man say, "It was the witch's doing. Saw her standing over there, didn't you? Looked to me like she was putting a hex on something."

I turned to look at the speaker and found myself eye to eye with a man whose unshaven jowl was distorted by a huge wad of chewing tobacco. "I'm the witch's daughter," I said. "She won't like you saying things like that."

Behind me I heard Mama laugh as the man went scuttering away through the crowd, his hat pulled over his eyes. "Victoria, you're a sight," she said.

I felt rather pleased with myself, but another way I was feeling rather spoiled the effect. The wind had chilled me through and through; I was aching from head to foot and felt feverish. I'd probably caught a cold at their old parade, I thought, and it hadn't been worth it.

Aunt Tabitha announced her intention of walking home and left us. Mama and I walked around for awhile, pretending to look in store windows until, after what seemed a long time, Papa appeared behind us and said gruffly, "I'm ready to leave now if you are."

Since Main Street had been blocked off for the parade, we'd had to leave our car on a side street. We followed Papa there and got inside, as silently and solemnly as if were leaving the church after a funeral service. Nobody spoke a word all the way home.

Our comportment was more fitting than we knew, for insofar as Springhill was concerned, the Ku Klux Klan died that night, was in its death throes even as we rode silently home. Papa must have known that, and I feel certain now that he knew why, because, when he came into the house, I saw that his face was gray and drawn as I had seen it only once before, when Margaret's baby had been born dead. He went straight into his bedroom without speaking.

"He's not—hurt or anything, is he?" I asked.

"Not in the way you mean, child." She looked at me searchingly. "You don't look too well yourself, Victoria. Are you feeling sick?"

I wanted to ask her if she had really stopped the parade, and, if so, how. Then I decided I didn't want to know. The way I was feeling already, that might finish me altogether. "I'm freezing to death," I said. "Can I have a hot brick?"

I forebore to mention that my head felt as if someone had build a fire inside it, and my stomach was aching and churning. I might even be going to die. When I undressed and found out what was really happening to me, I was more certain than ever of the unlikelihood of my surviving the night. While we had stood there waiting for the parade that never came, I had become a woman.

Mama hovered over me with hot ginger tea and certain other necessities, and tucked me into bed with a couple of heated bricks. She promised I'd be as good as new by morning. Then she sat down on the edge of my bed as she had when I was small and frightened from a nightmare. For a long while she was silent. Then she said, "Sometimes you find yourself doing what you don't really want to do because there's no other way."

I felt I ought to make some response but I was by then getting warm and comfortable and hated to rouse myself. I fell asleep without answering.

Next morning I found that she had made a grievous mistake in at least one particular. I was nowhere near as good as new.

"You didn't say it would go on and on and on!"

I had supposed, when I thought about it at all, that it would all be gotten over quite speedily, probably during one quick trip to the outhose. Now I was stuck with *this*!

Mama lifted her eyes unto the hills, from which help almost never came but she still liked to give it a chance. "I *tried* to explain," she insisted.

So no doubt she had, but somewhere in the circuitry between her brain and mine there had obviously been a loose connection.

"How long *is* it going to take?" I demanded.

"Four or five days probably."

"Why did I have to be a girl anyway!"

"Count your blessings. At least you won't have to shave every morning."

"Well," I said in astonishment, "who does?"

Then she became truly exasperated. She said, "Springhill is not the world, Victoria, not by a long shot. I assure you there are places not too far distant where men shave every morning and put on clean shirts and underwear whether they're going anywhere or not. Some day, if you survive this little crisis, you will become acquainted with such men."

"I shan't survive it," I grumbled. "All I'm going to do is

die."

XII

With the Klan out of the way, Mr. Banks was finally able to get down to teaching school—and ogling the eighth grade girls. Including me, which couldn't have been much of a treat since my scrawny twelve-year-old frame hadn't yet got the word I had attained womanhood.

Papa *had* got the word he was going to be sending a Broadbent child to high school, and was alreay fuming about it. At first he claimed Mama had tricked him into it by getting Miss Waterman to skip me a grade, thus insuring at least one year in high school before my fourteenth birthday. This grievance became academic when the state legislature, allying itself on Mama's side, raised the compulsory school age to sixteen, which would see me through all but the final year.

"You should have let Miss Waterman skip me another grade," I said.

Mama said we shouldn't expect to have everything done for us, we had to help ourselves a little.

I didn't see why Papa should mind since it wasn't going to cost him anything. Parents no longer had to pay either tuition or transportation, and Mama would pay the rest of my expenses, as she had always done. Papa, however, didn't believe in sending children to high school, period. Especially girls, who were only going to get married and waste their education, double period.

If at that moment anyone had asked me if I loved my

father, I would have unhesitatingly answered "Yes." It is natural for children to love their fathers, and in earlier years mine had been good to me, and patient. If he was being less patient now, I tried to remember that it was because I was getting older, and so was he. But love is not a matter of age, or of impatience. I had no doubt that he loved me as I loved him, even if he was grumbling about high school.

Mama had seemed to be making a special effort to be nice to him since the debacle of the Klan parade, cooking the foods he most enjoyed and not giving him anything new to worry about. Presumably recovered from her bouts of sleeplessness, she eventually moved back into the big bedroom, carrying her quilt with her.

And I? Well, I was learning that a four-day menstrual period, while certainly inconvenient, wasn't necessarily fatal. It hadn't done a thing for my nosebleeds though, which still struck every few weeks without warning. I would feel a tickling inside my nose and then see that it had already dribbled on my dress.

I was at long last acquiring a bosom, of which I was alternately proud and self-conscious, sometimes resorting to hunching my shoulders to minimize the effect.

Mr. Banks noticed too. Although he was turning out to be a good teacher when he put his mind to it, he seemed more interested in joining the children at play, especially the older girls. Sometimes I caught him just looking at me in a way that made me squirm with embarrasment.

One evening he detained me in the cloakroom and, under guise of helping me into my coat, put his arms around me and tried to kiss me. "What do you think you're doing?" I demanded, and broke away.

He said, "Quit acting like a baby, Vicky. You're a big girl now."

I looked at him, wishing I could pulverize him on the spot, and that reminded me of something that had achieved most satisfactory results the first time I'd tried it. "I'll ask my mother about it," I said. "She's a witch, you know."

His face was even more interesting to watch than the

man's in Springhill had been. He said, "You'd better get along home before she starts wondering what happened to you."

"Oh, she knows," I said. "Witches know everything."

I never thought much of Mr. Banks as a teacher after that, but for years, with Mama's help, I'd been mostly educating myself, so that wasn't important.

I knew too by then that I would be going to high school. Papa might try to flout Mama's authority but never that of the law. She kept insisting that I must go to college too but that was too far in the future to think about, even if Papa would permit it, which I was sure he never would.

XIII

I went to high school and fell in love; not the expectable variety but the adoration a girl frequently conceives for an older girl or woman, in my case my English teacher, Miss Arlou Willison I talked about her so much at home that Mama said we must invite her to supper one evening.

I could have bitten off my own tongue. What there was about schoolteachers that fascinated Mama so I had never understood unless it was that she'd hoped to be one herself. She was always fretting about the single women teachers being hungry or sick or lonely or unhappy, and inviting them over for supper to cheer them up. Once she had even invited Mr. Banks to supper—and he had come! All my high school teachers being superior beings who'd been all the way through college, I'd thought she might stop trying to fraternize, carelessly overlooking the fact that she was as tone-deaf to educational and social barriers as I was to music.

"I don't suppose she'd come," I said.

"Why ever not, Victoria?"

I mentioned favoritism, not very convincingly probably, and then the whole horrible truth rolled over me and left me gasping for breath. "We haven't got a bathroom!" I wailed.

"Well," said Mama reasonably, "we never did have."

In that moment I was able to understand at least a little of what Justine must have suffered from what she considered the general backwardness of her family. "It never mattered so much until now," I said glumly.

"If more education is only going to make you ashamed of what you have, there doesn't seem much use going on with it."

"I'm not ashamed," I said, "and don't start telling me what you did in the wagon . . . what *did* you do anyway?"

She laughed until I was afraid she might never find her breath again.

"We did," she said, when she was able to speak again, "whatever we had to do at any given time. As people are still doing. There have to be sewage lines for bathrooms, Victoria. There aren't any except in towns."

I should have been able to figure that out for myself since the only bathroom I was at all familiar with was the one at Aunt Tabitha's. "I suppose," I said, "I wouldn't want to live in town just to have a bathroom."

Her face softened and her eyes became luminous. "I would like to give your Miss Willison a bedroom hung in silver stars with a bathroom done in pink marble and water spouting from golden lions' heads, just because you love her. Since we can't we must offer her the best we have, generously and cheerfully."

"I'll ask her," I said, "as soon as I get a chance."

Somehow, though, I kept putting it off until one day Miss Willison inquired about my mother. "We met the day you came in to register," she reminded me.

"She's fine," I said, then plunged on. "She's been wondering if you'd come to supper with us some evening soon."

"I'd be delighted, Victoria." She looked and sounded pleased. Then she said, "Your mother doesn't come from around here, does she, dear?"

If somebody hadn't already told her about the medicine wagon, somebody would soon enough, so I might as well do it myself, but there wasn't time right then. "How did you know?" I asked instead.

"She doesn't talk like the people around here. Nor do you."

I knew what she meant. It was the bane of every English teacher's existence the way children left what they had learned of correct grammar at the schoolhouse door each evening and picked it up there next morning, using the home variety in the interim. It was almost as if every child had two languages, with not much doubt as to which would stay with him after he left school.

Mama had always been strict about that; my language was hers, not that of Springhill. I supposed it fell in much the same category as brushing my teeth twice a day, keeping my nails clean and filed, brushing my hair its full hundred licks each night, and a few other refinements not usually enforced in our community. From the way Mama had been talking lately, I supposed it all had to do with my ultimate meeting with those men who shave every morning and put on clean shirts and underwear, but she had never said for sure.

"Your mother is an unusual woman," Miss Willison had remarked after her first visit to our home.

I wondered how she would feel if she knew exactly *how* unusual, how completely unpredictable, Mama's behavior could be, and that it was becoming more so all the time. That very evening when I got home she announced that she was going to learn to drive the automobile.

The Buick touring car Papa had bought a short time before, had a gear shift, which you'd think might have discouraged her completely, instead of which it seemed to offer her some reassurance. She reasoned, accurately enough, that Nellie Maude was getting too old for cross-country jaunts, that there would be school affairs at night I'd want to attend and somebody would have to take me. She said it was a pity I wasn't old enough to drive as I would undoubtedly be better at it than she was, but in the meantime she'd do the best she could.

So learn to drive she did, although she never got around to really trusting the infernal contraption. Grasping the wheel firmly with both hands, eyes trained unblinkingly on the road ahead, she'd keep a running commentary on just what was expected of the sneaky creature. "We're going to turn right at this corner up ahead. Can't see around it on account of the tall corn so I'll blow the horn in case anybody should happen to be on the other side. Then we'll slow down, like this, to make the turn. There we are. Straight ahead now until we get to the next corner."

At first I felt a little uncomfortable about going in to a party and leaving her outside in the car, but she insisted that, although I was too young for dates, the social life would be beneficial to me. She didn't, for that matter, entirely miss out on it herself. Usually when people noticed she was there, they'd invite her into the kitchen, where pretty soon they'd be enjoying themselves as much as the young people.

I found it a pleasant arrangement, once I got used to the idea. A year or two later, however, when certain glands which had just been fooling around swing into full production, and I began to develop hips and a creditable bosom, boys began to invite me out. That posed another problem. Young people living in town could walk to whatever was going on; in the country transportation had to be provided. Automobiles in the hands of sixteen-year-old boys were considered dangerous, as were fifteen-year-old girls. Papa said absolutely not; but after he and Mama talked it over, she told me I could have dates on Friday or Saturday night but not both.

Remembering Kenny Hill, I was taking no chances. Neither was Mama; she watched me like a hawk, and every time I came home from a date, she pounced. I could feel her drawing my brain right out of my head and fingering through it to see what had got into it since the last time she'd looked. "Don't you trust me?" I would protest.

"I don't trust anybody without a head, and a girl with two or three boys on the string doesn't have one. She's just a bundle of emotions. If she allows herself to reach a certain point with a boy, she won't be able to stop herself going the whole way."

"I don't reach *anywhere*, Mama. I hardly even *start*."

She shook herself, as a dog does on coming out of the water. "A goose walking over my grave," she said. "Somehow I always get thinking about what happened to Julie."

"Things like that don't happen nowadays, and it wasn't Julie's fault anyway."

"When a girl gets ruined, the world never stops to ask how it happened or whose fault it was, so she's just got to see that it doesn't happen at all."

"I'll bet you anything," I said, "there isn't a single white slaver in Springhill."

"There are other vermin. And you're not going to stay in Springhill forever. If a man ever tries to force you, Victoria, you fight him. Understand? Not the namby-pamby way girls usually fight but hit him *hard*, with your fists, in the stomach and in the face. Bite him, scratch his eyes. If you have to, get hold of it and twist it, as hard as you can. That'll stop him in a hurry."

"Mama!" I felt completely limp with astonishment and shock. All I could think about was Robert, with his poor childsize waterspout hidden away inside those oversize pants.

"So it isn't pretty, but a lot of things aren't pretty that a girl needs to learn. I didn't make the world, Victoria; I'm only trying to live in it and help you live in it, wherever you may be."

"I'll never be anywhere but here," I told her fervently. "I'm not going to college, in fact I may not even finish high school. And I won't be able to even look at another boy as long as I live."

"Nonsense, child. That's only the worst that can happen—and usually doesn't. Lots of nice things can happen too—and usually do."

XIV

I rode to and from high school on the bus except on Wednesday afternoons, when I met Mama after school at Aunt Tabitha's and rode home with her. Usually I would find the two of them in the living room chatting companionably under the identically framed photographs of Dan Threlkeld and Woodrow Wilson. Aunt Tabitha considered Wilson the greatest president who had ever lived.

That Wednesday the Best Husband in the World and the Greatest President in the World had the living room all to themselves. There didn't in fact seem to be a living creature anywhere in the house. They couldn't have gone far, I reasoned, since our car was still parked outside. Maybe they were in the basement.

Aunt Tabitha's basement was a big one. An enormous furnace squatted at one end of it, with a coal bin beside it. Cement shelves lined the other walls, and these were filled with canned fruits and vegetables. There were baskets of potatoes and onions and apples on the floor. The washing machine was down there, and lines were strung across for drying clothes in bad weather. Aunt Tabitha did her canning down there too, on the kerosene stove she used for heating wash water.

I heard their voices from the top of the stairs and started down. "What on earth are you canning this time of year?" I asked.

Aunt Tabitha turned from whatever she was stirring on

the stove and looked up at me. She said, "My goodness, Yasmina, the time has really got past us."

My mind hardly registered the consternation in her voice because it was too busy with something else. "What on earth do you can in medicine bottles?" I asked. And then the scent assailed me. It wasn't unpleasant at all, only a little unexpected. The two women were now standing close together, their backs to the oil stove, as if to shield it from attack. "Cats caught in the cream," I said. "What are you two up to anyway?"

Mama said, "I'm glad you discovered us, Victoria. I've been planning to tell you anyway." I heard the familiar undertones of laughter in her voice. "I hope you closed the door after you," she said.

I hadn't, but promptly moved to do so; moved slowly because my mind was moving so much faster now. All those sashays into people's houses on the way to my music lesson, always with the big black handbag swinging from her arm; Mrs. Ziegler sending word she was out; all those visits made every week by a woman who didn't really like to visit; all those bottles of tonic I had never seen her prepare in our own kitchen. How could I possibly have been so dense?

"Mama's money tree," I said.

Aunt Tabitha laughed delightedly. "The dandiest bootleg operation south of Chicago," she boasted.

"Dr. Modesta's Magical Elixir," I said.

"More," said Mama, "or less, although even in his day the formula was somewhat variable."

"How do you manage to find herbs in the dead of winter?"

"Oh, those," she said. "I wouldn't know what to gather anyway. Neither would Tabitha. Come to that, Dr. Modesta seldom bothered with them."

"Then, how—"

"Only two ingredients are needed, Nubbin, besides water, of course. One to pep you up and the other to make it taste like medicine."

"The worse it tastes, the more faith people have in it," chuckled Aunt Tabitha. "The perk-up stuff is quite easy to come by, although Dr. Modesta would spin in his grave if he knew the kind of stuff we have to put up with these days."

"Bootleg stuff," explained Mama. "They don't let it age long enough. We water it down considerably but even then it tastes almost bad enough all by itself. We have a friend who furnished an infusion to make it even nastier."

"Don't try to tell me it can cure anything," I said.

"Tonics never do," returned Aunt Tabitha blithely. "Of course, they mustn't hurt anybody either. Our product is as pure as the corn from which it was squeezed."

I sat down on the bottom step and wondered what Miss Willison would think about my mother making bootleg tonic with Aunt Tabitha in her basement, what the kids in school would think for that matter, and what Papa might *do* if he ever found out, and wondering how in the world they'd managed to keep it from him. I remembered those Wednesday afternoons before I'd started school when I'd been packed off to play with a neighbor's children across the street. "You've been doing this for a long time," I said.

"Where there's a demand for a product," explained Aunt Tabitha reasonably, "there's nothing to do but supply it. You've no idea how insistent people were, Victoria. You see, the other medicine shows gave Springhill a wide berth after they found out about Dr. Modesta."

"What are those tiny bottles for?" I asked.

"Cute, aren't they?"

They were indeed. Somebody had painted tiny pink and blue flowers all over them.

"Love philtres," said Mama. "There's always a demand for those."

"Did Dr. Modesta sell those too?"

"You might say that was my department, and very subtly handled if I may say so. Nobody would have been caught dead asking for one when there was anybody around to hear them."

How dull indeed must chicken and egg money have seemed to a woman accustomed to dealing in tonics and love potions. "It wasn't the tonic you thought old Nestor had come for," I said.

"No," she agreed, sobering, but then she smiled again. "That's why Dr. Modesta was laughing," she said. "He may have still been laughing when he died. If only I hadn't opened the door."

"Pshaw," said Aunt Tabitha, "they'd have burned you out anyway, that being what they came for. Not that the old hell-shouter would have been above swallowing a love potion if he'd thought it would do him the slightest good."

"You don't mean they actually work?"

"How could they?" asked Mama reasonably. "It's only the tonic put up in these tiny bottles."

"I just hope," I said with feeling, "Dr. Armstrong never finds out what you two are up to."

"As a matter of fact," returned Aunt Tabitha airily, "Dr. Armstrong found our bootlegger for us."

And probably was the 'friend' who'd furnished the dreadful-tasting infusion as well. I preferred not to think about it but there it was. And there *they* were; but try as I might, all I could see were two pleasant-faced ladies in cotton frocks and voluminous pink-checked aprons, looking for all the world like ordinary housewives cooking the family supper. I felt a bubbling start somewhere in the middle of my chest and push slowly upward until it started twanging my vocal cords. Then we were all laughing together. "Let's get on with it then," I said. "Tell me how I can help."

As we worked, they filled me in on the financial details of their operation. They charged the same amount for the love potions as for the tonic, sixty cents a bottle, knocking off a dime for the customers furnishing their own bottles, which most of them did, thus obviating the necessity for having suspicious-looking deliveries of new bottles to Aunt Tabitha's front door.

There was an outside stairway to the basement where the customers left their bottles on Tuesday with the money inside, picking up the filled bottles on Wednesday evening at the same place. Since Aunt Tabitha lived on a well-traveled street and had quite a few visitors anyway, the additional traffic either wasn't noticed or nobody cared. She and Mama split the profits down the middle.

"I live like a queen" Aunt Tabitha stated immoderately. "I've even finished paying off the mortgage."

"You must have quite a few customers then."

"Seems like," she said, "most everybody around here depends on one or the other."

Or on The Stuff, but nobody ever paid for that. What could be fairer, two for cash and one for free? I thought for a moment longer. Things did get connected occasionally, even in a mind like mine. "So that's how you stopped the Klan," I said.

"Yes," said Mama, but didn't seem inclined to go on. She started corking the bottles.

"Are you going to drive?" I asked as we walked out to the car a little later.

"What do you think I taught you for?"

She had, in fact, proved herself the perfect teacher, taking over after Papa had turned me and himself into raving maniacs, and run us into our own mail box, he was that nervous about it. *She* apparently hadn't a nerve in her whole body. She simply sat quietly beside me, coaching the Buick for me as she always had for herself. All I had to do was listen in.

"One," she would say, and I would shift into low and release the clutch. "Slowly now, don't let it jump."

"Two" was intermediate, "three" was high; reverse was simply "back."

Now that she considered me a competent driver, she simply sat back and enjoyed herself. She had never liked driving anyway, not because it made her nervous but because it distracted her mind from more agreeable pursuits.

"May I ask you something?" I said.

"Of course."

"When you said Lysistrata persuaded the other ladies not

to live with their husbands, you didn't exactly mean *live*, did you?"

"You were too young to understand it any other way at the time."

"Does that keep meaning so much to a man—even after he's married?"

She seemed to be having a little trouble finding an answer, besides which she was fingering her lower lip as if she might be starting a pimple. Finally she said, "Yes, Victoria, it does."

"I don't see why women put up with it since *they* don't like it, and especially after they have enough babies anyway."

"It is an act of love," she said firmly, "and women do enjoy it, or should, and would if they had no more to worry about than a man. Maybe some day they won't."

"About babies, you mean?"

"About babies, yes, but more about the kind of men they marry. The world is changing, Victoria. Your generation, young girls like you, will be able to go out into the world and earn a decent living for yourselves. You won't have to be in any hurry about getting married, or have to feel you should take the first man who asks you. You'll have more men to choose from, more different kinds of men, instead of having to take whoever happens to be available in your own little frogpond."

"And after we get married, we can use The Stuff."

She chuckled, then grew serious again. "The Stuff is only the beginning. I've heard there are better things even now, and there will be more. When women start becoming doctors, as they will, they'll be more understanding than men about that women need. Mostly it's fear, Victoria, that makes a woman shun married love; fear of unwanted pregnancy, and then a woman gets into the habit of being afraid. And the churches don't help. They act like we all came into the world by immaculate conception, and preachers are the worst hypocrites of the lot. Always have been, all the way back to those dreadful Puritans, who should have been dumped into Boston harbor instead of wasting a lot of nice tea. Always contending that, after the flood, God commanded Noah's family to repeople the earth. Suppose he did, he didn't say keep it up forever, did he? As far as I can see, the earth's repeopled as much as it needs to be so women can relax a little.

"The world's got so topsy turvy, hasn't it? But it will be better in your time, I know it will. When relations between a woman and her husband *can* be the way they were *meant* to be, then women will come into their own."

While she was talking, the car had come to rest at the barnlot gate, but she still had something on her mind. "You mentioned the Klan," she said. "You have a right to know what I did and why I did it, because it affects you too.

"Not that I wouldn't do the same thing again if necessary. People have a right to be judged for what they've made of themselves, not for what their folks were before them, or for the color of their skin or the slant of their eyes or the clothes they wear or the way they walk and talk or the church they go to. Once intolerance gets started—" Her voice trailed away but picked up again a little further on. "I had to work through the women, of course, and I wasn't sure that refusing to supply the tonic, or those silly love potions, would be enough to make them stand up to their men."

"So you threatened not to give them any more Stuff."

"Not just threatened. I stopped it cold the morning after the negroes' houses were burned, and I told the women that, until their men got out of the Klan, there wouldn't be any more of anything, ever, except the witch's curse."

I felt a little stunned in spite of myself. "Papa must know then. How could he not know?"

"He knows. I suspect he knew about the tonic long before that night, but as long as it saved him a few dollars, he wasn't going to do anything about it. It was my interference in what he considered strictly men's business that makes him feel as he does. Not that he will talk about it even now; and I've never been sure exactly what happened that night, whether the other men just didn't show up, or refused to march after they got there, or what they told your father."

"You'd think he'd be over it by now, whatever it was."

She smiled a little grimly and said, "There are two things in this world a man finds it mighty hard to forgive a woman: belittling him and being right. Ah well, it's over now. I only hope—why are we stopping here, Victoria?"

"We've been here for five minutes. We're home, Mama."

"I talk such an awful lot, don't I?" she asked cheerfully. "But mostly to you and Tabitha."

There was a little talking I would have liked to do myself if I could find the words. Here she was, my own mother, a self-confessed bottler and distributor of bogus tonic and worthless love potions, illicit purveyor of birth control material, Nemesis of the Ku Klux Klan, a threat to domestic tranquility, and for all I could prove a sorceress and a witch, and I had never loved her more. I'd had the feeling as I worked alongside her and Aunt Tabitha that afternoon that I was undergoing some sort of maturity rite and would never be a child again.

I searched my mind desperately for words to convey my feelings, and finally found them. "Yasmina," I said, "you are really the berries."

XV

I had gone to the Junior Prom with Don Morrissey, whom I had been dating for the past several months. After decanting another couple from the rumble seat, he drove me on home, stopped the car on our front lawn, and reached for me. He said, "Vicki, you're my favorite girl. You know that, don't you?"

"I don't think I'm ready to be anybody's favorite girl."

"Why not?"

Because I was Yasmina's hope for that lovelier world she glimpsed looming over the horizon. Because I was curious about all those men who shaved and put on clean underwear every morning whether they were going anywhere or not. Because I wanted to keep on learning, and visit strange places, and experience everything there was in the world before I had to settle down in one place for the rest of my life. Because, perhaps, I wasn't really in love. "I don't know," I said.

"You never let a guy get very far, do you?" he complained after a moment.

"I let you kiss me."

"You even cooperate, in case you hadn't noticed."

I pushed his hand away from my knee. "Don't," I said.

"I'm not going to *do* anything, Vicki."

"I just don't like being touched, not that way."

"You might, if you'd loosen up a little. Here. I've got just the thing for a girl like you." Whereupon he produced from a back pocket a flattish silver object such as I didn't remember seeing before.

"Pretty," I commented. "What's it for?"

He unscrewed the top and held it out to me. "Have a drink," he invited.

"Don Morrissey, don't you dare tell me you're a drinking man! Mama would have a fit."

"She doesn't have to know, does she? Just a little one?"

As I lifted the proffered flask to my lips, a surprisingly familiar smell assailed my nostrils. "It's that cheap bootleg stuff," I said disdainfully, handing it back.

"W-w-w-what?"

"It isn't aged properly these days," I said, "although I must say the bootleggers charge enough for it."

"Vicki Broadbent, what on earth do you know about bootleggers?"

"Fudge," I said, "everybody knows about bootleggers."

He stared at the flask as if it had suddenly turned into a hissing snake, replaced the cap, and returned it to his pocket.

"Movie Saturday night?" he said finally.

"If you want to," I said.

"I wouldn't say that exactly. It's just that, when I'm away from you more than a day or two, I start getting the feeling I've dreamed you."

With the coming of summer, Papa began to reassert his authority. It started off with what I could only think of as his incest phobia. It seemed he'd lost track of an older sister who'd married when he was small and moved, he thought, to a community several miles to the north of us. He didn't even know her married name, and wouldn't have recognized her or her children, or *their* children, if he'd met them on the street. It was not a matter which had caused him any particular grief, nor had he worried that his older daughters might perchance meet and marry one of their cousins, to some degree removed; but with young people running all over the country in automobiles these days, the danger was greater for Vicki.

Mama pointed out the unlikelihood of such a tragedy occurring, and said that in any case such cousins would be far removed from the danger point by now, and anyway, Vicki wasn't planning to marry anybody for a good long time.

Sweet reason, however, was always wasted on Papa, and never more so than when he was working up to a fine old ultimatum of his own. In the future, he announced, Vicki was not under any circumstances to leave the house in the company of any boy he himself had not previously approved. There was the Smithson boy, he pointed out. A fine young fellow from a fine family, no doubt about that.

"No doubt about his hot little hands either," I said.

"Vicki!" he roared.

"Ollie," placated Mama, "they're only children. Nobody's ready to get serious about anybody just yet. Vicki knows which boys treat her nice and which ones she wants to go with."

"Henry Morrissey's a hypocrite and a sinner," he flung at her, "and that boy of his is no better. Vicki's got no business running around with a town boy anyway."

So that was it, the Klan business all over again. "Papa, please," I said.

He ignored me. "You spoil the girl, Minnie, You always have. From now on she'll do as *I* say."

He turned to leave, hesitated, turned back to us. "There'll be no more of this high school foolishness either. Vicki's sixteen now."

"Papa!" I cried. It was an anguished wail.

"The others are agin it," he said, unmoved. "'Tain't fair you gittin' more'n they ever had."

"Not from you!" I cried. "You never—"

But Mama said, "Hush, Victoria. The child will finish high school, Ollie."

He tried to look at her, then dropped his head, unable to meet that somber appraisal. "You heard me," he muttered, and left the room.

"Mama—"

"Hush, child. He's angry now, and too stubborn to give an inch."

"He's never mentioned the others before. Why should they mind?"

"Small people have small ways, child. They see your father growing old, and they're afraid he might die and leave his little bit to me and you instead of them."

"Whatever it is," I said, "they can have it, but I'm going to finish high school. I'll sleep in the hallway and beg my food if I have to, but I'm going to finish."

"Behave yourself, Victoria. You know it isn't as bad as all that. You can stay with Aunt Tabitha if you need to. She'd be tickled to have you. You may, however, have to curtail your social life for the summer, at least until this blows over."

"What do you mean you can't go with me any more?" demanded Don Morrissey a few days later.

"Papa suspects you may be a cousin in disguise," I said.

"Holy jehosophat! What put that in his head?"

I explained as well as I could but it sounded even sillier without the background of Papa's indignation.

"You could slip out, couldn't you? No, I suppose you couldn't. I like your mother too, Vicki."

"The thing is, I've simply got to finish high school."

"We could get married."

"Gosh no! Then I'd have to stop school for sure."

I became aware then of Don's expression, and my lack of consideration for his feelings. "I'm sorry," I said, "but it isn't only high school. I'm going to college too."

"Because she wants you to?"

"I want it too," I said honestly. "You're going to college too, aren't you?"

"I guess so. That's what my folks say anyway."

Since Papa had not relented by September, I went to live with Aunt Tabitha. Word got around, of course, as it always did in Springhill, and Miss Willison asked if there was anything she could do for me.

"I'm fine," I said, "except that I miss my mother."

"Don't you get to see her at all?"

"Only on Wednesdays," I said. "She visits Aunt Tabitha then, the same as she always has, and now she stays for dinner."

Miss Willison nodded. "I'm sure the kindest thing you can do for her is get on with your education."

"That's what she says, only—why does he have to be so mean!"

She sighed and shook her head. "Unfortunately he isn't the only one. We're losing many of our most promising students when they reach sixteen, and in most cases it's the fathers who make them stop."

"My father acts like he hates me."

"I'm sure he doesn't. It's just that so many men seem to become frightened when they see authority slipping away from them, see their children getting more education than they ever had and growing away from them, or that's what they seem to think. The difference between you and some of the others lies in the mothers. Yours stands firm. As," she added after a moment, "did mine."

It was around the middle of October that, on her usual Wednesday visit, Mama announced that I was moving back home. She said, "He misses you, Victoria. He'd choke before he'd admit it, of course, but he does. And there are no restrictions, I saw to that. You can go out with any boy you want to."

"I'm not all that popular," I said. "I'll try to avoid the cousins anyway, although Miss Willison says some of the ancient royal families used to always marry their relatives because they didn't consider anybody else good enough for them."

"Trying to preserve the royal bloodlines," she said, "which might have been all right if they'd depended on more distant relationships. People claim that's what caused the Gladberry children to be the way they are, their parents being first cousins."

The Gladberrys were a large family and I'd seen only one or two of them, but they'd been pitifully deformed, with overlarge heads and short spindly legs horribly bowed.

"You'd think they'd have stopped after the first ones, when they saw how they were going to be," I said. "I suppose, though, Mrs. Gladberry didn't know about The Stuff."

"They should have stopped anyway," she said.

That reminded her again of Mrs. Rosetree, who had lately been much on her mind.

Up until then I had never known Mama to actively push her wares. She had simply, as Aunt Tabitha had claimed about the tonic, supplied a demand. It was an indication of how deeply she felt about the matter that she finally decided Mrs. Rosetree was due for a spot of proselytizing.

The Rosetrees were Whipley Corners' major charity program as well as its scourge and shame. Mr. Rosetree, short, plump and slothful, was dedicated to the opinion that, having expended *his* manly energies begetting a succession of sickly-appearing infants, it was no more than equitable to allow his neighbors to support them. Mrs. Rosetree, scarcely more than the proverbial rag, bone, and hank of hair, regarded both husband and children, as well as anybody else she happened to meet, with a peculiarly vapid smile which she seemed to have affixed to her face during a happier period and forgotten to remove.

Despite their apparently fragile grasp on the world, all but two of the first dozen frail infants had lived, making a total of twelve people in a house that would have been strained to bursting with half that number. The Rosetree boys were foul-mouthed, sexually precocious, and unfailingly impudent. The girls were pale and stringy but as impudent as the boys. All the children, male and female, were afflicted with permanently dripping noses, and all wet the bed well into their teens. At any given time, at least three-fourths of the tribe had seven-year-itch, with which they accommodatingly infected half the school every winter.

When Mrs. Rosetree was brought to bed with the birth of her thirteenth child, the neighbor women had, as usual, to take turns helping out. Yasmina came home from her stint looking as if she'd been dragged backward through a keyhole. "Such filth," she raged in her own inimitable style. "A pig sty. Worse. No respectable pig would live in such a place." So naturally she'd worn herself out swamping out the place, with the full knowledge that it wouldn't stay that way much longer than it took her to get home.

"Those children are stacked like cordwood into two tiny rooms. No beds, just mattresses on the floor, and those have been so constantly wet for so long only burning would ever get the stink out of them. And not half enough to eat. And still they keep on having babies! That woman's only thirty-three, Victoria! She could have a dozen more!"

"Didn't you tell her about The Stuff?"

"Of course I told her! I begged her, implored her. I explained over and over again until my tongue was hanging out. I even drew her pictures. And all the time she just lay there with that silly smile on her face. Then when I finished, do you know what she said?"

"All right, Mama. Tell me!"

"She said—" She seemed to be chewing on something so extraordinarily large and tough it wouldn't go down, but finally she pulled herself together. "She said, 'Oh no, Mrs. Broadbent, I couldn't do anything like that. Why, that's about all the pleasure Mr. Rosetree gets out of life and I wouldn't want to spoil it for him.' "

I felt a desperate urge to laugh but I knew I didn't dare. Instead I went over and put an arm around her shoulders. "Never mind," I comforted, "you did all you could."

"That poor stupid woman. And all those poor stinking itchy little children. She—"

She tried to go on, then gave it up.

"Don't take it so hard," I said.

"He ought to have it cut off!" she ground out viciously.

Then she stood up, yawned prodigiously, and grinned. She said, "Get the Flinch deck, Nubbin, and let's play a few games. Maybe it will settle my mind."

XVI

Papa had finally hit upon a way to turn my thirst for knowledge to his own account and at the same time keep me under his thumb for the rest of my life. He would finance me through two years of college—the minimum requirement by that time for a grade school teaching certificate—after which I was to get a job in the local schools and live at home. "No use paying board to strangers," he said, thereby making it clear I was to pay board to *him*. In case I might have misunderstood, he also made it clear that, until I repaid every penny he'd spent on my education, I would not be free to leave his roof even to marry.

I knew it was futile to point out that, even before those two years were up, it was likely that a bachelor's degree would be required to teach anywhere in the state. Although I had no intention of getting married for many years if ever, and would undoubtedly have tried to get a job in the local schools in order to be near Mama, I resented his highhanded assumption of prerogatives I regarded as exclusively mine and hers. I doubly resented his final dictum that I would go to college on his terms or not at all, recognizing it as an effort on his part to forestall Mama using her own funds to send me wherever I wanted to go.

"You'd think he doesn't care anything about me at all," I said.

"He does, child, in his own way. He's just never learned that love is helping people do what they want, not forcing them to do what you want." She smiled a little grimly. "If you were a boy, he might find your reaching for independence slightly more tolerable, but the one prospect in the world he finds it impossible to face is any female having money of her own to do with as she pleases instead of having to go down on her knees to some man every time she needs a package of pins."

"You've never talked like this before."

"I've tried not to, Victoria. You needed your father, and he needed you, and a home should not be a battleground. I have hoped in time he would come to recognize that a child has rights too, but he never has nor ever will. However, his present unpleasantness is not really directed as much against you as against me. All these years he has been festering inside about the Klan affair, determined to get even. Unable to bring me to my knees in any other way, he is now determined to do it through you, but I will not allow that."

Well, she had stopped the Klan, hadn't she? Papa shouldn't be holding that against her, but he was. I did not think he would ever give in. Neither did Mama. She said if it came to that, she would use her money is spite of him; but in the meantime we must try not to antagonize him.

What we should have both realized was that, in this crisis as in previous ones, he would turn to the preacher. Despite considerable evidence to the contrary (Brother Purdygood had capped an unillustrious ministry by eloping with a Sunday School teacher), Papa always looked up to the current incumbent of the Whipley Corners pulpit as the fount of all wisdom. The present occupant had several children, one already in college, another a senior in high school; and it had never been any secret that preachers received a discount on their own children's tuition for every student they induced to attend the church college. Papa knew all that as well as anyone else, but in no time at all the preacher had convinced him that no man who called himself a Christian would risk sending his innocent young daughter anywhere else.

"Not there!" I cried in honest dismay when Papa broke

the news.

"It doesn't even *look* like a college," I complained to Mama later. "It's just a bunch of buildings in the middle of a muddy field."

More to the point, she said, it wasn't fully accredited. She had asked Miss Willison to check on it for her. I wasn't altogether sure what lack of accreditation might mean in practical terms, and Papa certainly wouldn't know either, and wouldn't care if he did.

Once again, however, Mama advised letting it ride for the time being. The important thing, she pointed out, was for me to settle down and keep up my grades for the rest of the school year. That, however, proved more difficult than either of us had anticipated, for early in March Mama, who had never been sick a day in her life, was suddenly stricken.

What had seemed no more than a mild case of influenza soon developed into pneumonia. Dr. Armstrong brought in a nurse to take care of her, but Papa and I stayed by her bedside almost constantly for Dr. Armstrong had given us no real hope for her recovery.

Papa could not have been kinder or more considerate during that period; and one evening I came upon him in the barn where, believing he was alone, he was crying as if his heart would break, great wrenching sobs that shook his whole frame. I had never seen a man cry before, and it was a shattering experience. I crept away before he detected my presence, and went back to Mama's bedside.

Although Papa continued to stand by, and I understand now how much deeper must be his feeling for her than I had ever imagined, in her fevered delirium her thoughts were all for me. "Vic-tor—" she would cry out, too weak to finish my name, but trying again and again. "Vic-tor — Vic—"

"I'm here, Mama," I would say stroking her hand, but it was other voices than mine she was hearing, struggling to sit up in bed until the nurse would come to quiet her. At one of those times she opened her eyes, seemingly rational, but the words came from somewhere in the past. "You can't possibly imagine what he was like," she said, "the glory and wonder of him."

The Papa? Dr. Modesta? She had never mentioned a lover, but there could well have been one, or more than one, when she was young.

Finally, after all those days and nights of agonizing, she came back to us, thin and hollow-eyed and weak as a kitten, but otherwise herself. She immediately started worrying because I'd missed so much school. "I can make it up," I said, "with your help."

Her face brightened. "Of course you can," she said.

At the beginning of the following week the nurse was dismissed, Aunt Tabitha moved in for awhile, and I went back to school. I felt sure I would never be as young again, or as unthinking, as I had been before her illness; for having so nearly lost her, I had become as protective of her as she had once been of me.

In May I brought home a Latin contest medal and pinned it to her dress. "That's where it belongs," I said.

"I am so proud of you. Papa will be proud too."

And he was. That was another thing about him I found difficult to understand. Much as he grumbled about me going to school, he was always proud, even boastful on occasion, of my accomplishments.

By the time school was out Mama seemed pretty well recovered, although she continued to sleep in Margaret's room where she had lain during her illness. Often, however, she would get out of bed and wander around the house, sometimes murmuring to herself as if looking for something she'd misplaced during the day. Once when I'd gone to look for her, I'd found her in the front yard. She had seemed unaware of my presence but had not resisted me when I took her hand and led her into the house and back to bed. Her daytime mind, however, seemed to have regained all of its former acuity.

Apparently reassured by her seeming return to health, Papa, who had been so attentive to her during her illness, lost no time reverting to his former stance regarding my education.

"Is he really my father?" I said to Mama one day.

"Of course."

"You didn't love him," I said. "You can't ever have loved him."

She said, "Listen to me, Victoria. When I was a child I thought all men must be wonderful and good because of my father. Then when he died and I went to live with Aunt Hortense, I had to work in her hotel; what she called it anyway, although it was little more than a boarding house, down the street from the railroad station.

"All her boarders were men, the kind of men to whom a chambermaid, even a fourteen-year-old one, seemed fair game. I had to clean their rooms, carry their chamber pots, fight off their advances—and hate them—until I came to think of all men but my father as stinking and dirty and evil. Later I fell in love with a young man who was, seemed to me to be, as fine and good and wonderful as my father; but that didn't turn out well either, so I no longer believed in either love or goodness.

"Then one day Dr. Modesta and his wife Rose came to visit Aunt Bessie, who was Rose's cousin. They stayed for a week, and it was the first time in my life I had ever been around married people who loved and respected each other and enjoyed just being together. It impressed me so forcibly that I began to wonder if possibly now and then love within a marriage might not really be possible. All that winter I looked forward to the spring, when Dr. Modesta and Rose would visit us again.

"When spring came, however, Dr. Modesta came to us alone, for Rose had died during the winter. When he was ready to leave, he asked me to be his wife. We did not speak of love, either of us. He was still too full of grief and I of unbelief. He needed someone to be with him in the wagon; he said that he was fond of me and would be kind to me. Because I so desperately wanted to believe in the goodness I had so recently discovered, and because I was sorry for his loneliness, I went with him."

'And were you happy?"

"I became content. He was unfailingly kind to me, Victoria; a pleasant and stimulating companion, and completely fair to me in every way. He treated me as if I were indeed the princess he'd made up out of his own head. He gave me everything in the world that was his to give, everything any woman could possible dream of wanting, except a child.

"Then suddenly he was dead. I was bitter, angry, revengeful. It was only later, however, that I began to realize what I should have known a long time before—how very much, and in how very many ways, I had loved him.

"After he was gone, there was only one thing in the world I really wanted, a child of my own, and a child must have a father. So when another man I did not love but believed worthy of respect asked me to marry him, I accepted, hoping that once again love would come later.

"Tabitha warned me about his parsimony but I had not known a great many men, nor been financially dependent upon any man except Dr. Modesta, who was the very soul of generosity. I had no idea how horribly twisted the soul of a really stingy man could become. In any case," she went on with a slight smile, "I had my own source of income."

"You should have found yourself another wagon."

"For myself I have no regrets because my decision gave me you. My only regret is that I have failed to give you a loving and understanding father."

"It wasn't your fault," I said, "and I never meant to upset you like this."

"I'm not upset, child. Sometimes it does one good to talk about things."

"All right, but I don't want you worrying about me any more, or having any more trouble with Papa. I'll go to his silly college for two years if that's what he wants."

"When you are away from here, wherever you go, everything will seem so different to you. You can have such a wonderful life, Victoria." Her gaze had gone far away as if she were already seeing me in that wonderful life.

"We'll have it together," I said. "I'll teach bratty little kids their ABC's while you peddle love potions and Magical

Elixir. We'll have a black cat, and you can teach me to be a witch in your spare time."

I was relieved to see her face break into a smile. "The first prerequisite for a witch is to make people believe you're one." She chuckled contentedly. "Maybe that's the last thing, too."

The morning had been warm but that afternoon it began to rain, a cold rain such as sometimes falls even as late as June. That night I woke with a feeling that something was wrong and, unable to persuade myself back to sleep, got up and found Yasmina's bed empty. Papa had got up too, and a few minutes we found her in the yard, her thin summer night dress drenched and clinging to her shivering body. "He was calling," she said. "Didn't you hear him calling?"

"Nobody was calling, Minnie." Pap's voice was harsh and frightened.

Next morning, however, she seemed quite herself again, suffering no ill effects from her chilling. "What an old fool I'm getting to be," she said. "I must have had a dream."

"Maybe you dreamed you were a little girl again and heard the Papa calling you."

Her smile grew tender but it was turned inward. "His father was a wealthy planter," she said. "It was because of his other family that—" Her voice trailed off but presently resumed as if it had been following right along with her thinking. "They say that Creole girls are very beautiful. All the things I should have asked, and didn't, before it got to be too late."

It wasn't the first time she'd touched upon the subject of The Papa's possible illegitimacy, but the term Creole was new to me. Before I could question her, however, she had resumed speaking.

"But there, I'm dreaming again. In broad daylight at that. But I feel so well, Victoria."

So well, in fact, that she insisted on paying a visit to Aunt Tabitha that very afternoon. An old lady by then but still lively and bright, Aunt Tabitha had been carrying on the tonic business alone with what help I'd been able to give her. Mama felt sure she'd be able to lend a hand herself in another week of two.

As indeed she was, and for a few weeks after that, at the end of which time I had finally reached my own moment of truth, amazed that it should have eluded me for so long. "Would you be awfully disappointed if I didn't teach school?" I asked her one day.

Her look was immediately troubled. "Wouldn't *you?*" she countered.

"No," I said, "because I don't really want to. If I did, I guess I'd have jumped at the chance of getting to college anywhere at all."

"I haven't meant to force you into a decision, Nubbin."

Her old name for me, as usual, reduced me to tenderness. "You haven't," I said. "I thought that was what I wanted too, and maybe I was flattered that you and Miss Willison thought I could be, so I just let myself be carried along. I don't really like children that much, though, and I'm not a bit impartial the way a teacher ought to be. I'd hate not being fair to a child just because I didn't like him."

"Are you sure that's all, Victoria?"

"Not quite all. I suppose high school teaching might be better but—all right, I'm simply not willing to let Papa put us both through the grinder for four long years for something I don't really want anyway."

"What *do* you want, Victoria?"

"I thought I might go to business college," I said, "and learn shorthand and typing." The preacher wasn't the only one who'd been recruiting, there'd been representatives from the business colleges too.

'I'm afraid you're only trying to spare me, Victoria. Would it affect your decision to know there would be enough for college without your father's help."

"No," I said. "I'm just not cut out to be a schoolteacher."

"Well," said Mama thoughtfully, "it certainly isn't the only way for a girl to earn a living these days. Some women are doing quite well in business, I understand. And you can always study and learn, wherever you are. Dr. Modesta was studying right up to the day he died."

"Of course I may not be much good in business either."

"Of course you will be. All you have to do is make yourself indispensable. And I'm perfectly well now, Nubbin. You must start to this business college in September."

"There are classes starting every few weeks," I told her. "And you aren't to worry about me being alone in a big city because I'll be careful."

"You must find a nice room somewhere, all to yourself."

"You lived there," I reminded her. "You can go with me and help me find a place, and satisfy yourself there aren't any white slavers hiding under the bed."

She smiled at my teasing but I knew she wasn't convinced. For all she knew there was one lurking behind every bush and tree, ready to pounce. "Such deceitful creatures," she said. "They look and act just like anybody else. In fact, the men who seem the nicest often turn out to be the worst."

"You never did tell me what happened to Julie—after you married Dr. Modesta, I mean."

"She married a fine man who understood her. Julie was very fortunate, after all the bad things that happened to her. It doesn't happen like that very often."

I insisted I would break the news to Papa myself. It seemed to me he should be relieved, since I wasn't going to cost him any money; but his reactions being somewhat unpredictable, I intended to get him alone before I told him, and try to impress upon him that, however he felt, we were to hassle it out between ourselves without bothering Mama. After all, I would remind him, Dr. Armstrong had warned us that what she needed most was peace and quiet and freedom from worry.

Before an opportune moment arrived, the necessity for such a talk was rudely banished by Justine, who appeared at our door one afternoon with her child in her arms. Darrell Fuster had left the house saying he was going to the drugstore for cigarettes, instead of which he had got on the evening train. That had been more than a week ago, and there had been no word from him. Papa said he ought to be brought back and horsewhipped.

Mama, however, wasn't surprised at Darrell's defection, nor was I. Although I had considered him a rather poor stick I'd been sorry for him too. Any man's natural reaction to Justine's nagging and complaining would be to beat her or leave her. Darrell had chosen the latter course. "If he'd had any sense to speak of, he'd have done it sooner," was Aunt Tabitha's acrid comment, with which there was considerable agreement.

With Justine throwing tantrums all over the place, and her offspring following suit, I couldn't possibly consider leaving Mama alone to cope. I simply told Papa I wasn't going to college, and he appeared relieved. Later, when things quieted down a little, I could tell him about business college.

Things did not quiet down, however, and within the week Mama was beginning to show the effects of the strained situation. Still she remained insistent about my going to business college in September.

"It's so hot now," I said. "There's another class starting in a couple of months, and the weather should be better then. What can two months matter?"

"None, I suppose. It's just that I hate to see important things put off."

That afternoon she went to her room for her usual nap. She released her hair from its knot, lined her shoes up neatly beside the bed, lay down and pulled the silken quilt up over her, then closed her eyes for the last time.

Her heart had been bad for a long time, Dr. Armstrong told us. He had first discovered that when he attended her at my birth. It had, he said, been touch and go since then but she hadn't wanted anyone to know.

I felt so frozen inside I couldn't even cry. The shock of her going just when it seemed she was going to be completely well again was more than I could accept. I blamed Justine and Papa. I blamed myself.

Papa's other family started kicking up a storm almost at

once. It was *their* mother, they reminded him, who lay in the two-grave cemetery lot, with the other place waiting for him when he died.

"My mother was his wife too," I said. And then, speaking more gently, to Papa. "Perhaps an adjacent lot is for sale."

There was one, he said, but it was a two-grave lot. He refused to look at me, to say that the other grave space would be wasted, but the implication was clear enough.

"What do you want to do with her!" I blazed. "Bury her in the cornfield so she won't cost you anything? Even after she's dead?"

"I never said that!"

"You married her so you could stop paying her for keeping your house. Since then, except for the food we ate, neither of us has ever cost you a dime."

"Hush," said Margaret, and tried to lead me away but I shook her off.

"Never mind," I said. "There's room on the lot with Dr. Modesta. He'll be glad to have her back."

"How dare you mention that name to me!"

"He treated her better than you ever did."

"Hush child," said Margaret, and took my arm again. I let her lead me away.

"He'll do the right thing," she said, "if you'll just leave him alone."

"When did he ever?" I demanded bitterly.

"He will now. Mildred and I will see that everything is taken care of the way it ought to be."

I would remember nothing of the funeral services except, at the last, watching them lower into the grave on the new lot the box containing the chill clay that was no longer my mother Yasmina. I left the cemetery without once looking back, because there was nothing there to hold me. Or to hold onto. My mother Yasmina was lost to me forever.

But I was wrong. I found her again a few nights later as I walked alone in the side yard bordering her garden, where we had often walked and talked together. We didn't speak, nor did I cease my walking, but I knew why she was there and what it was I would have to do.

"He walks beside me," she had said, and now I understood. She was not in the grave, or in the house, or even by the garden, but beside me. To keep her there I would have to do as she directed.

The next day I told Papa I would be leaving for business college in two weeks, when the next term opened. He looked astonished at first, then a sly look came over his face. "You got to stay home now and take care of your old papa," he said. His smile was ghastly.

"You've got Justine for that."

"That poor girl ain't able to take care of herself proper, let alone anyone else." He sounded petulant now. I wanted to tell him many cruel and hurting things, but *she* had never stooped to that, nor would I now.

"Next year," he wheedled, "maybe you can go."

There was no mention now, as there had been on previous occasions, that I was his child too. No appeal on the grounds of love, no extension of simple kindness, only a wheedling demand that I become an unpaid flunkey for him and Justine.

"Justine can get up off her fanny and do some work for a change," I said coldly. "But whether she does or not, I'm leaving."

"And just what you aimin' to use for money?"

"I'll manage," I said.

A crafty look came over his face, a look that I remembered only too well. "That money of your mama's you got hid away, that ain't yours. It's mine. The law says so."

I looked at him without speaking.

"No decent girl would think about traipsing off to the city by herself."

I stopped myself just in time from telling him Yasmina would be with me. "So I'm not decent," I said instead.

"If you leave now, don't ever come back," he said pettishly.

For a moment his voice broke and I was sorry for him, but not sorry enough to make me change my mind. "I'm going to pack my things," I said. "If you won't drive me in to Aunt Tabitha's, I'll get someone else."

When I had finished packing the clothes I decided to take with me, I went into the room where my mother had died. the old leather purse she had been carrying for more years than I had been alive was hanging over the back of a chair, empty now except for a linen handkerchief, three dollar bills, and almost a dollar in change.

She had said, years ago, that sometime she would tell me more about her marriage to Dr. Modesta. Maybe she was trying to tell me then for, with my hand still inside the leather bag, I felt something that had slipped, or been slipped, under the lining.

The yellowing document told me that a year before my birth a woman named Yasmina Miller had married Oliver Daniel Broadbent. I realized then that until that moment I had never known Dr. Modesta's real name, nor had I quite given up hoping that he had been my father.

When I went back to the living room carrying my suitcase, Mama's blue silk dress in a box, and her quilt over my arm, Papa voiced further objections. I was to take nothing from his house except my clothes.

For the first and last time in her life, Justine served me well. She flicked the quilt contemptuously with a long polished fingernail. "Let her take the ratty old thing," she said. "It will save us having to burn it."

Papa and I rode all the way to Aunt Tabitha's without exchanging a word. I tried to tell him goodbye but he sat there staring straight ahead and, as soon as I was out of the car, drove stolidly away. I turned and walked toward the porch, where Aunt Tabitha was waiting.

XVII

"Of course you must go to school," agreed Aunt Tabitha. "Dr. Armstrong will take you there and get you settled in."

"Dr. Armstrong?"

"Yes, Vicki. He's very fond of you." She paused, then continued. "Very fond of *her* too, as it happened. If he had been free at the time she came here, I've no doubt he would have asked her to marry him."

Maybe I wasn't as surprised at that as I should have been. I had always known that Mama liked Dr. Armstrong and had a very high regard for his opinion. "It would have been better if he had," I said.

She nodded. "Ollie Broadbent's an old fool," she declared fiercely. "Always was, and always will be, I reckon. Cutting off his nose to spite his own face."

"Is there anything I can do for you?" I asked. "Are you going on with the tonic business by yourself?"

She shook her head. "It wouldn't be any fun any more. That's what it was, Vicki, fun. Oh, the money was nice, and we could both use it, but mainly it was doing something a little out of the way with somebody who had an ornery streak as wide as mine."

"Papa's still wondering about the money," I said. "He mentioned it again today."

"For all the good it did him, I hope."

"He didn't press the point. Justine had to get in her two cents' worth too by insulting Mama's quilt. She called it a ratty old thing, and said if I didn't take it along, they were going to burn it."

Aunt Tabitha laughed heartily. "Justine never did have much taste, poor girl. And now you must be hungry. What would you like to have for supper?"

A few days later Mama's quilt and I started on the last leg of our journey, leaving the gold-and-silver-embroidered dress in Aunt Tabitha's keeping. I kissed her withered cheek, promised to write her the minute I got settled, and come back and see her as often as I could. Then I walked out and got into Dr. Armstrong's car.

With what Aunt Tabitha had told me still fresh in my mind, I found myself a little uncomfortable with him for the first time in my life. In fact, I kept staring at him until he finally inquired, "Dirt on my chin, Victoria?"

"No," I said, abashed. "I was only thinking."

He shot me a quick glance and smiled. "Seems like only last night I helped your mother bring you into the world. She was so pleased with herself, and with you. I said, 'Being the only practicing witch hereabouts, seems you might be inclined to confer some special boon on the child.'

"She thought about that for a minute, then she said, 'May she always know the value of what she has while she still has it.' I've never forgotten that."

I had known *her* value, I thought, if nothing else. "Did you know Dr. Modesta, I mean really to talk to?"

"Oh, yes. That wasn't his first trip to Springhill, you know. He'd been making it on his rounds for a good many years, starting when his first wife was still living. It was after she died that he married your mother. Maybe they didn't think of it as a love match at the time but that's what it turned out to be. Dr. Modesta was exceedingly fond of his princess as well as being proud of her.

"He used to pay me a visit now and then when we both had the time to spare, told me a little about himself. He was the second son of the owner of a textile plant in New England. Shortly after he graduated from college, his father died and left the plant to the boys jointly. It seems they had widely divergent ideas as to how it should be run, and eventually the brother bought him out. Dr. Modesta then set forth to find his fortune elsewhere. Somewhere along the way he fell in with a medicine show and decided that was the life for him, so he got together his own outfit and started out.

"The life suited him perfectly, providing him a moderate income with plenty of time to read and study, and he brought a great deal of talent to his calling. He was a keen old fellow, with considerable insight into the trials and foibles of the human race. And he was a magnificent faker, enjoyed fooling people in a gentle sort of way that didn't hurt anybody at all.

Just as your mother did, once she got the hang of it. I liked the man, used to look forward to his visits."

Suddenly he chuckled. "Your mother went right on being a faker too, bless her. Every time I think of her and old Tabitha setting up shop and supplying the patent medicine trade, it sets me off. And those love potions!" Again he chuckled.

"You don't know the half of it," I said impulsively, then my hand flew to my mouth. But when he looked at me again, I saw by the merriment in his eyes that he *did* know. "It probably didn't work anyway," I muttered.

"On the contrary, I should say it worked uncommonly well, all things considered. Eternal vigilance is the price of more than one kind of freedom, but the women didn't always understand that, so sometimes they were careless or sick or just too tired to bother. Even so, I believe Yasmina eased the burden considerably and may even have saved a few lives."

"I used to think you would have a fit if you found out about it."

"She came to me before she started to make certain nothing she was going to use would hurt anybody. Fact is, she was doing exactly what I would have liked to do myself if I had dared; but for me to have recommended anything pertaining to birth control just once, much less supplied it, could well have cost me my license to practice."

"What would it have cost her?"

"I would never have let anything happen to her," he said, almost fiercely. "Not that anything was likely to. Nobody would ever have been able to prove it was anything but a home remedy she was sharing with friends. Your mama was every inch a princess, Victoria, and don't you ever forget it."

As if I could. I was feeling better though, the talk having cheered me immensely.

Dr. Armstrong professed leanings toward Mrs. Lee's Secretarial School, having heard good reports concerning it; but upon being advised they wouldn't have another class starting for almost a month, we decided to settle for City Central. When they suggested paying six months' tuition in advance, however, Dr. Armstrong turned cagey. He advised them that Miss Broadbent would pay a month at a time until she had an opportunity to evaluate the quality of their instruction, implying that if it wasn't up to snuff, Miss Broadbent would take her trade elsewhere.

"That'll keep them on their toes," he chuckled on our way out. "Let's find somewhere to have a bite of lunch, Vicki, and then we'll look for a place for you to stay. I don't suppose you know much about finding your way around here, do you?"

"I've never been here in all my life before."

"Oh. Well, in that case, we shall have the grand tour. But lunch first."

It was the first restaurant I had ever set foot in but I could hardly begin to do the meal justice because excitement was setting in. This was the city Yasmina had known, where she had lived when she met, and later married, Dr. Modesta.

"A penny for them," said Dr. Armstrong.

"I was just wondering if there was any chance of finding the house my mother used to live in, but I don't know what street it was on or even what part of town. It was a big house, but I suppose there must be lots of those."

"Quite a few, but a lot of the houses that were here

twenty-five years ago aren't around any more. Aren't you going to eat your dessert, Victoria?"

I obediently picked up my spoon. "I guess I'm too excited to be hungry," I said, "and I ought to be ashamed, with Mama—"

"You ought to be ashamed *not* to be excited," he said. "This is exactly what your mother would want for you."

By sundown I had viewed Yasmina's city from the top of the Soldiers' and Sailors' Monument and walked through more stores and gaped into more shop windows than I would have believed existed in the whole world. Dr. Armstrong insisted on buying me a present—a handbag, gloves, and three embroidered linen handkerchiefs—to commemorate the occasion. I had been settled into a pleasant upstairs bedroom, and Dr. Armstrong had prevailed upon my landlady, a Mrs. McCready, to furnish me breakfast and dinner as well.

"If you need anything, child, you'll call on me or your Aunt Tabitha, won't you?"

I promised that I would, and he kissed me on the forehead and took his leave. I couldn't help thinking how much happier my mother would have been married to him instead of Oscar Broadbent, how different my own life might have been, and might be now, with Dr. Armstrong for my father. Feeling stirrings of guilt, I tried to put the thought away but it was a long time before it would leave me entirely.

Mrs. McCready stopped by my room at bedtime to see that I had everything I needed, admired my quilt, fingered it, said she'd never seen a quilt so light and crisp and finely made. After promising to call me in plenty of time to eat breakfast and get to school, she left me.

I looked around my new domain. It was small but neat and cozy, and it suited me well. The few dresses I had brought with me were hung away in the closet, my underwear was neatly folded away in a drawer. I turned out the light, got into bed, and pulled the sheet up over me, then the quilt. Yasmina, I said, this is it.

XVIII

City Central Business College occupied the two top floors of a three-story building near downtown Indianapolis. I found that much of the classwork was simply a review of the basic grammar and arithmetic I had learned before. Only shorthand and typing were new to me.

I made no friends among the other students because everybody was in too much of a hurry. Some of the students had part time jobs; several of the girls were earning their board and room by household chores and baby tending. Mrs. McCready obligingly steered me to a branch library and, having nothing else to do, I usually read at night until I fell asleep.

One weekend a month I visited Aunt Tabitha, who was my only remaining link with home. Nothing had ever been heard from Darrell Fuster since he'd left, and Justine was still living with Papa.

Dr. Armstrong usually drove me back to Indianapolis on Sunday evening and frequently took me to a movie and to supper afterward. "Got to get my digs in," he would say, "before you have half a dozen boy friends crowding me out."

"I don't want boy friends," I would assure him. "At least not yet."

Not until the right one came along, that was what I meant. During my solitary walks and between the pages of the romantic novels I was currently devouring by the dozen, the kind of husband who would eventually find me was taking clear shape in my mind. Although I didn't analyze it then, he was a composite of The Papa, Dr. Armstrong, five or six popular movie idols, and a stage actor whose picture I'd cut out of a newspaper. He would be a little older than I, tall, dark and mysterious-looking, and very, very restrained, until finally we would discover in the same blinding instant how truly we loved each other, then the night would be studded with stars.

I didn't get homesick in the usual sense because, without Mama, the home I'd had no longer existed. I still missed *her*, achingly, and felt certain that I always would.

In February I passed all my typing and shorthand tests and was pronounced ready for the world of business. If only that world had been more receptive to me. The stock market hadn't crashed yet, and I had no idea what it was anyway, but there was considerable talk of recession and references to belt tightening, none of which fazed me in the least. On the farm there had been good seasons and bad but, unlike the usual farm wife, my mother had enjoyed a modest but steady and independent income.

City Central provided an employment service for its current as well as former graduates, and a number of the latter were now being regurgitated by the same business world that was proving so reluctant to swallow me. Every time I was sent out on an interview, I found myself outflanked and outclassed by more knowledgeable applicants with up to ten years' experience.

When I complained of this, however, Miss Flatz, the placement manager, assured me that all current graduates could benefit from the experience of being interviewed. She said my day would come, and forthwith sent me to an automobile agency for a week's vacation relief. I returned in disgrace. How was a simple country girl to know that city telephones cut off the calling party when you hung up the receiver?

"If I'd gone to Miss Lee's," I seized the opportunity to point out, "maybe they'd have taught me a few things like that."

Miss Flatz sighed, and a few days later sent me to Sylvester's Fine Shoes. Mrs. Weaver, a dear little lady in her fifties, who hadn't taken a proper vacation during the twenty-three years she'd been working there, was now off to Florida for six full weeks. She shared the tiny office on the mezzanine with the owner and his older brother, also Mr. Sylvester but usually addressed as Harry.

One little point was troubling me. Either by accident or design Miss Flatz hadn't mentioned to me that Mrs. Weaver served as both stenographer and bookkeeper, whereas I had only the most rudimentary grasp of, and practically no interest in, bookkeeping. I had no doubt Miss Flatz had also concealed my fatal flaw from Mrs. Weaver, but rather than confront that good lady with such depressing information on the very eve of her departure, I decided I would go to Mr. Harry Sylvester with any problems that might arise. I had already noticed that he never seemed especially busy, and appeared more than willing to offer advice even when it wasn't being asked for.

Even that slender prop, however, was knocked out from under me by Mrs. Weaver's parting admonition: "For heaven's sake, whatever you do, don't ask Harry anything. He gums up everything he touches."

So, I was sure, would Victoria. And so, even unto this day, I am sure Victoria did. It was years before I could find courage to even walk past the store again. But there was even worse to come.

When I reported back to City Central, Miss Flatz asked me if I used a deodorant. It sounded as if it might be something Yasmina had neglected to tell me about. Uncertain in this instance whether to deny or affirm, I kept silent. Miss Flatz went on to mention that Mr. Sylvester was a very fastidious gentleman.

I could have told her that Mr. Sylvester was also a snob. Except for dictation, he hadn't spoken ten words to me during the entire six weeks of my employment.

I supposed my continued silence must have conveyed the

awful truth to Miss Flatz, for she then undertook to explain at some length what a deodorant was.

"I take a bath every single night," I expostulated.

She explained some more. "Maybe it was your bad time of month," she suggested kindly.

Feeling as poor little Robert must have felt on that memorable occasion some years earlier, that my personal prerogatives were being encroached upon, I decided it was time for Yasmina's inscrutable look. Evidently it worked for Miss Flatz abandoned that tack and never got back to it again.

During the next couple of weeks what I continued to cover myself with was certainly not glory. Noting on my application that I was the youngest of ten children, an insurance agency supervisor declined to hire me on the grounds that youngest children in a family were invariably spoiled.

On the next application that came my way I thoughtfully lopped off my half-siblings, who had been little joy to me anyway, and acquired three full-siblings, all younger than myself. *That* supervisor said older girls in a family were inclined to be bossy and overbearing, and the other employees wouldn't put up with them.

Before I had an opportunity to insinuate myself into the middle of a well-disciplined family of three, I was hired, after the most painless of interviews, as a typist for the Freegate Company, captained and piloted by Mr. Freegate himself and dealing in—shades of Dr. Modesta!—the Freegate Remedy. It seemed to be one of the few enterprises in town that was still doing a flourishing business. Even, so far as I knew, without a sideline of love potions.

Whatever else the company may have lacked, it had standards. Nothing so crass as a form letter ever left its sacred precincts. Mr. Freegate had worked out an ingenious system of numbered paragraphs, combinations of which were, at his direction, incorporated into neatly typed letters, to which would then be affixed his personal signature. All day long as many as a dozen girls were employed typing those letters, explaining why the first bottle of Freegate Remedy might not have helped but the next one was bound to; or that, while no specific claims were made by the company for curing certain idiosyncrasies of the stomach, lungs, gall duct, and spinal column, many of our customers had voluntarily furnished unassailable testimonials that it had done so.

Unexciting, certainly, especially to an old hand in the patent medicine business, but I was making all of eighteen dollars a week, Mr. Freegate was a pleasant man to work for, and I made my first friends since coming to the city.

Dorothy Forest was a little older than I and had been working for Mr. Freegate nearly two years, but we shared the same rural background and got along easily together. We took to having lunch together and going window shopping afterward, and shortly learned that we were living in the same area of town.

"Another girl and I moved into a furnished apartment last month," she told me.

"An apartment!" I breathed, with all the reverence a statement of that kind deserved. "I'll never be able to afford anything like that."

Dorothy pointed out that in the long run they expected the apartment to cost each of them no more than the separate bedrooms they'd had before, plus taking all their meals at neighborhood restaurants. "It would be even less," she said, "if we could find another roommate. There's quite a comfortable daybed in the kitchen. How about you, Vicki?"

I was pretty comfortable in my snug little room at Mrs. McCready's but the idea of an apartment was tempting.

"Thirty dollars a month," she went on. "That would make it ten apiece, and groceries shouldn't cost as much as eating meals out."

Shortly after that I moved in with her and her roommate, a girl named Eunice Folke, on the upper floor of an old house which had been converted into light housekeeping apartments. There was a large bedroom, and even larger kitchen which also served as living and dining room. The bathroom, across the hall, was shared by two other tenants.

That fall was when the stock exchange went berserk and people started jumping out of windows. It seemed to me rather a drastic solution to their problems until I reflected that Papa might have taken some such action if he'd ever lost the farm, and could have found a window high enough to jump out of. It was the first time in months I'd thought about him at all. Maybe subconsciously I was holding such thoughts at arm's length because they could only be tinged with bitterness.

By the middle of the following year the general blight had spread to the Freegate Company so that in one fell swoop half the office force had to be dismissed. Last on, first off seemed equitable, even to me, although I was once again unemployed.

XIX

Reluctant to creep back to City Central again, especially since Miss Flatz didn't really approve of me and, more importantly, had no fine regard for my unique capabilities, I registered instead with a commercial employment agency and started answering ads in the newspaper. That still left me with a considerable amount of time on my hands, much of which I spent alone in the apartment trying to read while listening to our landlady sing to her own accompaniment on the piano.

Unlike me, Mrs. Walker wasn't in the least tone-deaf. When she struck a sour note, she knew it as soon as she heard it, and her fingers as well as her voice skipped back to make amends. Her rendition of her favorite aria was likely to run rather like this:

"Home, home on the—the range—range—range
Where the deer—the deer and the an—ante—antelope play play . . ."

Her other standby, "Rainbow Round My Shoulder," being more spirited, came out sounding like a piece of abortive ragtime. Mrs. Walker was a good soul and nobody held her musical peculiarities against her; but being a captive audience to her concerts could try the soul.

Eunice and Dorothy seemed even more concerned than I about my continuing jobless state. "If you're running a little short," Eunice told me one day, "don't worry about the rent until you find another job."

"Don't give up and go home, whatever you do," Dorothy put in. "Good roommates are hard to find."

I forebore mentioning that I no longer had a home to return to. I doubted that Papa would actually slam the door in my face but my life there would be intolerable without Mama. Nellie Maude might never have made it, I reflected, but I had definitely passed the point of no return. "I'll probably find a job any day now," I said, with considerably more confidence than I felt.

"What you need is a boy friend."

"That can wait."

"This friend of Fred's," Eunice began, then hesitated. I knew by now the reason for the hesitation. Eunice and her friend, Fred Currier, as well as most of their friends, worked at the PureSilk Hosiery Mill. Although Eunice was earning far more than Dorothy, and more than I had when I was working, she was sensitive about working in a factory.

"I'd be happy to go with Fred's friend," I said, "provided he's willing."

Ray Gillian turned out to be a pleasant-mannered young man and we got on well together. "We'll have to get Vicki a job at PureSilk," he would say, in an effort to be kind; but he wouldn't, couldn't, because things were slowing down there too.

I worked for nearly two months for a man named Streeter, who had conceived the ingenious idea of hosing out hog and cattle trucks, fitting them with canvas tops, and providing their drivers a cargo for the trip home. Christening his brainchild Pay Loads Inc., he rented office space, had letterheads printed, took out ads in the newspapers. Then we sat and watched it fold. Apparently people didn't take kindly to this makeshift arrangement for their shipments even if it did cost less. I was sorry because it *had* been a job and Mr. Streeter had been a nice man to work for.

After that I was out of work for several months, which would always seem to me like so many years. False hopes can sustain you only so long, then you begin getting scared. You have to lash yourself into appearing for an interview, always with the feeling it isn't going to do any good. Then you keep plodding on simply because you can't think of anything else to do. You try to arrange your features to reflect optimism, try to put a little hope in your voice, all the time convinced that you look a failure and sound a failure because you *are* a failure.

I did a lot of aimless trudging up and down streets that winter, killing time in department store restrooms, occasionally going to a matinee, but even movies were depressing in the daytime. I retreated more and more into my own limitless fog until one day, in a crowded elevator, an immensely obese man nudged my arm and whispered, "Looking for a job, girlie? Come by and see me, why don't you?"

Maybe it was the 'girlie' that did it, maybe it was just the appearance of something that I could vent my rage upon. I looked up into his gold-toothed leer and said, loudly and distinctily, "Take your fat paw off my arm or I'll slap you senseless."

There was a concerted gasp from the other occupants of the elevator, and my persecutor, scowling angrily, left the car at the next floor. He was probably one of *them*, I speculated to Yasmina, but I had no real feeling that she was sharing my life any more. During that dreary hopeless time I had not only lost my mother forever, I had come to realize why.

On a miserable day in January, armed with a newspaper advertisement, I entered a building, got on an elevator, stepped out into a long carpeted—carpeted?—corridor, walked along checking room numbers, finally pushed open a door.

A man sat writing at a large mahogany desk, on which sat a lamp providing the only light in the room. The door barely swished in closing, and my shoes made no sound on the carpet. Without looking up from his writing, the man jerked one dark-jacketed shoulder in the direction of a closed door. "Go in there," he directed, in a perfectly ordinary voice, "and take your clothes off. I'll be with you in a minute."

XX

There was only one thought left in my mind. *This* was *certainly* one of *them* and here I was, frozen to the floor, powerless to move a muscle.

The man's head jerked up impatiently, and he said, "Well?"

Then it was his turn to freeze. The pen dropped unheeded from his fingers, rolled slowly across the desk, and over the edge. Without moving, he said, "Where in the hell did *you* come from?"

It was the last question in the world I had expected and I ws totally unable to supply an answer. I simply stood and stared. If Mr. Sylvester had been a fastidious man, there was absolutely no name for this one. Just looking at him made me burningly aware of my own imperfections, from my unfashionable old brown cloche to the run up the side of my left stocking, not excluding a bra strap mended hastily with a safety pin so large it made a lump under my dress, or the chipped nail polish I'd meant to replace the night before. "I came about the ad," I finally managed to croak.

"What ad?" He stood up. He looked no more real than a manikin in a men's store window. The only creases in the black suit were the knife-sharp ones down the front of his trousers. His shirt cuffs, extending exactly the same breadth beyond each coat sleeve, were fastened with massive gold links; a diamond stickpin glittered wickedly from his tie. I was sure that if I could see his shoes, they would show absolutely no sign of ever having been walked in. He certainly didn't *look* like a white slaver, but then Yasmina had intimated those were the most dangerous kind.

"What ad?" he demanded again, this time with considerable impatience. "Cat got your tongue?"

I started to answer but just then the scent hit me. Perfume! Yasmina had never told me they used perfume! Slowly my nerveless hand unfolded and the scrap of newsprint fell to the floor. I stooped to pick it up, then handed it over.

He glanced at it. "This is the Rivener Hotel," he said, "*not* the Cooper Building. That's across the street."

"Oh," I said. Maybe that accounted for the carpet in the corridor. "I was never in a hotel before."

"You're looking for a job, I gather." He still spoke impatiently, as if he regretted the necessity for speaking at all.

"Not the kind *you* have in mind," I squeaked, and felt the heat rise into my face.

His face, dark and brooding under the blackest hair I had ever seen except on my mother's head, scarcely altered at all. "You would hardly qualify in any case," he said cuttingly. "All right, girl, sit down."

"No! Give me back the ad and I'll go."

"Oh, sit down, for God's sake. Miss—well, what is your name? I suppose you've got one, haven't you?"

For a white slaver he seemed to have an amazingly unsubtle approach. "Julia Victoria Broadbent," I said, my teeth beginning to chatter.

His eyes never left my face. "If you say so," he finally commented. "My name is Forster Jerome, Miss Broadbent. I have a vacancy in my organization." He began to gnaw reflectively on a knuckle as if he might have forgotten me altogether. "I had expected to fill it with somebody a little—older," he said finally.

My age was the one thing about me that was going to be remedied if I lived long enough, which didn't seem likely unless I found a job pretty soon. "I'm twenty-two," I said.

He retrieved his pen from the floor, sat back down, and

started making notes. "Can you type, take dictation?"

"Yes, "I said.

"What previous experience have you had?"

I forced my eyes to meet his and kept them there. "I worked for three years for the Kendall-Lilly Company," I said. "Then I got what seemed a better offer, only that company started laying off people, so now I'm looking again."

"Perhaps Kendall-Lilly would take you back."

"I wouldn't have the nerve to ask. Anyway, I heard they were laying off too."

That didn't seem to surprise him, since most places were. Still his somber gaze swept over me, searching, weighing. Finally he seemed to arrive at some decision. "Your duties would be varied here, Miss Broadbent. The hours are ten to seven, Monday through Friday, with a lunch break whenever you prefer to take it. Occasionally you may be asked to come in on Saturday morning. The salary would be twenty-five dollars a week to start. Are you interested?"

I was more than interested, I was overcome. I had never made more than eighteen dollars a week, Dorothy was making only twenty. "Yes," I said, before I could get terrified enough to change my mind.

"Very well. Report to me here tomorrow morning at ten o'clock."

As I walked back down that carpeted corridor, my ears were ringing and my heart was still pounding. When the elevator came up from downstairs, a fair-haired stylishly dressed girl stepped out and started confidently down the corridor. I was dying to know whether she would enter the room I had just left but the elevator door closed before she reached it. My whole body was tingling now and I felt a little dizzy. Yasmina, I said, I think I'm going to need you. Kindly stand by.

"He sounds sinister," was Eunice's comment when I reported that evening. "What kind of business is he in anyway?"

He hadn't mentioned that, and I had neglected to ask,

which didn't seem unusual to me under the circumstances but might prove difficult to explain. "Something to do with investments," I said.

I was reluctant to mention that I had suddenly become twenty-two years old, or to admit my earnest conviction that if Mr. Jerome so much as laid a finger on me, I'd freeze to the floor again, unable to move, and he could do whatever he pleased with me.

"If it doesn't pan out, or he gets fresh or anything, you don't have to stay."

I felt myself blushing to the roots of my hair, but if Eunice noticed, she didn't mention it. "Go in there and take off your clothes," he'd said, but not to *me*. He wouldn't ever, to *me*.

"You're dazzled by that twenty-five dollars a week," said Dorothy.

I had been, I knew that. I also knew something much more unsettling: I would have taken the job for less. Much less.

As I was soon to learn, Mr. Jerome both lived and maintained his office at the Rivener Hotel. I would learn much later that he owned the place.

He explained that he didn't maintain offices elsewhere because he liked to travel when the notion struck him and didn't want to be tied down. He didn't appear to operate any specific business either but seemed to have an interest in several.

Besides his personal suite consisting presumably of his living quarters as well as his own office, three rooms along the corridor were occupied by his employees, of which there were two besides myself: a handsome brunette whom Mr. Jerome introduced as Mrs. Wilhoite, his bookkeeper, and a middle-aged man he introduced simply as Mr. Ralston.

The office next to Mr. Jerome's was mine. I was to take his telephone calls when he was out and leave messages on his desk. There was a one-way buzzer which he said he would use to summon me when he wanted me. Two buzzes would mean I was to bring my notepad and pencil and be prepared for dictation.

As it turned out, there was so little to do I soon became restless. Mr. Jerome was away from the office almost as much as he was in it, and during his absences all I had to do was take an occasional phone call and chew on my already abused fingernails. I found myself missing the easy camaraderie of the Freegate Company staff. Even on short-term jobs I'd had, there'd always been someone around to talk to. Mrs. Wilhoite invariably wished me a very pleasant good morning and good night but made it eminently clear she would not welcome further communication. Mr. Ralston seldom spoke except, very occasionally, to Mr. Jerome.

Mr. Jerome remained reserved—and, to me, fascinating. He looked exactly the same every day, as if he might have only that one black suit which was renewed each night while he slept. He dictated clearly and concisely so that I hadn't much trouble taking down what he said, and I soon got the hang of how he liked his letters to look, how many carbons to make, and where to file them.

Several times a week I was dispatched on errands, usually delivering or picking up sealed brown envelopes. After hurrying back to the office in case he should want me to do something else I was likely as not to find him vanished; but there or absent, he filled my thoughts. "He uses perfume," I once reported at home.

"Some kind of shaving stuff," said Dorothy knowledgably.

"Maybe," I said doubtfully. Papa had used scraps of soap in a shaving mug. I wasn't familiar with the shaving habits of other men.

"What else?" said Dorothy.

"Nothing," I said after a moment. I didn't want to talk about how I would watch his hands, long and lean and dark like himself, lighting a cigarette, tipping off the ash, moving among the letters I had placed on his desk, lifting his pen to sign them, handing them back to me. My eyes would wander from his hands to that door which was always kept closed, to the room where he had told—somebody—to go take off her clothes. Somebody, but not I. He hadn't expected me there.

I thought about the girl who had gotten off the elevator that day as I was getting on, and wondered again if she had been that somebody. Probably they didn't hold them captive any more the way they had Julie, or perhaps that was just for girls who fought against being in a place like that. That girl had certainly *looked* as free as anybody, as if she were coming of her own will to undress in that room with the closed door, and then let a man—this man—do *that* to her. For money. I would wonder fleetingly how much money, and then be covered with confusion and hope he would not notice.

The way he called me Victoria—he had started that the second day of my employment—sent little ripples of excitement up and down my spine, although often enough I had heard him call both Mrs. Wilhoite and Mr. Ralston by their Christian names. Sometimes I found myself feeling feverish, other times I sat alone in my little office and shivered as if coming down with a chill. I was likely as not to go tongue-tied or even mute in the middle of delivering a message.

Eunice fretted that I wasn't eating properly. She wondered if it might not be because my routine was being upset by the unusual office hours. I was having breakfast alone at nine, lunch around two, and the girls were keeping my supper warm until I got home around seven-thirty.

I wasn't sleeping well either, even less well than during the period of my unemployment. Since the kitchen also served as our living room, it was understood that the last girl in at night would sleep there. Since I seldom went out, I usually shared the bedroom with one of the others, and I was sure they must both be getting tired of my restless nights.

During those sleepless hours I would think about my mother. "All the things I should have asked," she had said once, "and then it got to be too late." Too late to get answers, she had meant, and now it was too late for me too. In spite of that, or perhaps because of it, it had suddenly become important to me to piece together all her 'lives' into one, and that was when I discovered there must be a segment missing.

If she had been married to Dr. Modesta, whose real name had apparently been Miller, for eight years, then she would have been about twenty-four when she married him. Hating Aunt Hortense's hotel as she had, I did not believe she would have stayed there any longer than she had to, but I had no idea when she had come to Indianapolis, or why, or even whether the woman she had called Aunt Bessie was really her aunt by blood, or just an honorary one as Aunt Tabitha was to me.

It was frustrating not knowing exactly where the Second Life had ended and the Third Life had begun, or whether there might have been yet another life between those two, a life she had not told me about. A life that included the man with whom things had not turned out well. And there was the man of whom she had spoken in delirium, that man or Dr. Modesta or yet another. "You can't possibly know what he was like," she had said, "the glory and wonder of him."

I would turn my thoughts from those fruitless speculations only to have them start gnawing on something else—my job. Was Mr. Jerome satisfied with my work, or was he already regretting that he had hired me? There was no way to tell from his manner, which was consistently brusque and humorless, his eyes penetrating but impersonal. Maybe he was already planning how to tell me I was fired. I had a premonition something dreadful was about to happen. And it did. The very next day.

In midafternoon I carried his finished letters into his office, which I had expected to find empty. Overcome with confusion at seeing him there, I stumbled into the side of his desk, the whole stack of letters sliding from my hands to fan out across the polished surface. I saw his black-clad arm jerk back his brow darken. "For God's sake, Victoria!

What's got into you now!"

I stood there appalled, waiting for the axe to fall. I would be glad when it happened. All he did, however, was push back his chair and sit there looking at me.

I started fumbling with the papers, but he gestured me away. "Let them *go*!" he said, sounding even more wrathful than before. "I'll take care of them. No, Victoria, don't leave. Come back here!"

"I'm so *stupid*," I began, hearing my voice rise out of control. "So *wrong*! Everything about me is wrong. I—I—I don't even *look* right!"

And then the most horrible thing of all happened. I began to cry, right *there*, before *him*.

"I never cry!" I lashed out furiously. "I never do! God damn it to hell, I wish I could die!" And then I fled back to my own office. Blinded by tears, I dragged my coat from the rack, squashed my old felt hat down over my hair, grabbed my purse, and headed for the door. He was standing in it.

He said, "If you're going to cry, Victoria, for God's sake do it right."

I saw him raise his hand, felt the stinging across my cheek, then his hands like vises on my arms propelling me toward the couch. I buried my face in the cushions and cried as I had never cried in my life before, great gulping sobs that seemed to be tearing my whole body apart. There was no use trying to stop them. I could only let the storm take me over and spew me out at the end.

"Here," he said at length, and shoved his handkerchief into my hand. I sat up and began to mop at my face. He said, "My God, Victoria!"

Following his horrified gaze I saw that the handkerchief was splotched with blood. Mine! Even my own stupid nose was conspiring against me! With a long despairing wail I disappeared into the bathroom.

When I came back to the office a few minutes later, he handed me a glass half full of an amber liquid and said, "Drink this."

"No," I said.

"Drink it." His voice was calm now but exceedingly firm.

After one gulp, choking and gasping, I held out the glass.

"Finish it," he said in that same voice, and I did.

"You're trying to get me drunk," I said.

"It would doubtless be an improvement. Sit down, Victoria. Over here, on the couch." He sat down beside me, offered me a cigarette which I refused, then lighted one for himself. He said, "I'm sorry about your nose. I didn't realize I was slapping you that hard."

I explained about my nose. He nodded.

"Kendall-Lilly never heard of you," he remarked, blowing a perfect smoke ring into the air.

I watched it hover for a moment, then start to drift away. I looked back at him then, watched his hands, long and lean and restless, flipping the ash off his cigarette. They say that in the eye of a hurricane it is quiet and peaceful and remote from the rest of the world. I wished I could stay there forever.

"What else have you lied to me about Victoria?"

"Practically everything," I said finally. "Don't expect me to be sorry because I'm not. I'm only sorry I cried. I didn't mean to, and I almost never do."

"Why not?" Another smoke rink took off serenely into the air.

No one had ever asked me why not, not even *then*. The others had only stared at me and whispered behind their hands about what a heartless girl I was. "*She* never did," I said woodenly. "She never would. You could have cut her up in little pieces and she wouldn't have made a sound or shed a tear."

"How long has your mother been dead, Victoria?"

"I didn't tell you—"

"You didn't have to. How long?"

"Over two years."

"That's a hell of a long time to keep it all bottled up inside you. I'm glad I slapped you now."

"You don't understand!" I cried. "It was my fault." And then it began to rush out of me, as the tears had rushed before; all the hitherto mute enduring agony of the barren days and sleepless nights. "I said I wouldn't go to school until she was better, and she was afraid she would never be, so she let herself die so I would go."

He said, "Don't be so presumptuous, Victoria. Your mother died because it was her time to go. You couldn't cry because you were in shock."

I started to get up but he put his hand over mine and held it there. "Stop looking like that. I'm not going to eat you."

He took his hand away to light another cigarette, then turned back to me. "You're an intelligent girl, Victoria, more so than most your age. You're doing a good job here except for your nervousness. You don't have to knock yourself out trying to please people, you know."

Make yourself indispensable, Yasmina had said. I was about as indispensable around here as a toothache. Why didn't he fire me and get it over with?

"I'm not right!" I burst out. "Not for a place like this. I knew that but I—wanted to work here—for you. But I don't *know* anything or do things *right*. I got good grades in school, I always did, and I thought it would be easy, but I don't seem to know *anything* now."

"Suppose we start all over again. How old are you, Victoria?"

"Twenty," I said. "Almost."

"How almost?"

"In four more months."

"You little fool! Didn't you know what chance you were taking, telling a man like me you were older?"

"It wouldn't have mattered," I said. "I would have—done whatever you asked me to do, that very first day."

To my amazement he laughed, a short barking sound as if he wasn't accustomed to laughing. "No, you wouldn't," he said. "You'd have spit and bit and clawed and scratched like a cornered cat." Thoughtfully he snubbed out his cigarette. "You're not a such a bad-looking girl, Victoria, except you're such a frump."

Talk about damning with faint praise! And yet it was the same thing as I had been telling myself. I had brought only four dresses with me from home and I had long been aware of their inadequacy. "I kept thinking I ought to buy some new clothes," I said, "and then I—just didn't. My mother made the ones I have so they're getting kind of worn out."

"Also kind of small," he said, appraising me with a calm critical eye.

"Well, you do grow a little, even after you're seventeen."

"Isn't there someone who could help you with your shopping, some older woman who would know the kind of clothes you should be wearing?"

There were only Eunice and Dorothy, and I doubted they knew any more about the prevailing modes in dress than I "You mean—like Mrs. Wilhoite?" I asked.

Instead of answering he walked over and picked up my battered headgear between thumb and forefinger. "With your leave," he said, and dropped it delicately into the waste basket. Then he came back, sat down, and lighted another cigarette. "Tomorrow," he said, "you and I are going shopping."

"*You*!" I gasped. "Oh no!"

"Why not? Because it wouldn't be proper?"

"I don't know," I said.

"If it's the money you're worried about—"

"It's not that," I broke in hastily. "I've got scads of money."

"Victoria!" I hadn't seen quite that look on a human face since I'd told Miss Waterman I'd read my Primer the night before.

"Well, I have," I said. "There must be quite a bit left in the quilt,"

"I beg your pardon?"

"That's where the money was all the time," I said. "stitched into Mama's best quilt. Justine called it a ratty old thing and said they were going to burn it." I suddenly realized how I was rambling on, freely and easily as I hadn't been able to in a long time. "But you don't know about that," I said.

"Don't stop now. Tell me."

So I started telling him how Mama and Dr. Modesta couldn't bother with banks, traveling around as they did, so they'd started changing their money into twenty-dollar bills which Mama stitched into her quilts.

"Please go on," insisted Mr. Jerome, with more enthusiasm in his voice than I'd heard since I'd been working for him.

I told him everything then, about Aunt Tabitha and the tonic and love potions, and how every now and then another crisp new bill would be folded just so and slipped inside one of the silken blocks and neatly stitched into place. Then I saw his face. "You don't believe me," I said.

"Oddly enough, I do. Even you couldn't make up a tale as wild as that. It's just—my God, with half the banks in the country going under and the rest tottering, here you are, dragging around a couple of thousand dollars stitched up in your mother's quilt. How many people know about this?"

"My roommates," I said, "except not how much. Aunt Tabitha and Dr. Armstrong, of course. And now you."

"And probably a few dozen others if your roommates have the power of speech."

"*They* wouldn't tell anybody," I said. "and you have to trust somebody, don't you? It was the bank Mama didn't trust, because she was sure somebody there would tell Papa."

I thought Mr. Jerome still seemed a little stunned. "It's just that I've lived a long time," he explained, "without ever hearing of such a thing. Or such a woman."

He stood up. "Let's call it a day," he said. "I'll drive you home." Suddenly he almost smiled. "Wouldn't dream of sending you out in this weather without a hat."

I started to get my coat but somehow found myself in his arms. Maybe it was the unaccustomed drink still nestling cozily and treacherously inside me, but I could feel my whole being quicken to his touch. I lifted my face to his; but at the touch of his lips, strangely harsh and dry against my own, I found myself shrinking away. As if enraged with my withdrawal, he crushed my body relentlessly against the hardness of his, kissing me long and passionately before he finally released me, so suddenly that I almost fell. "You see," he said quietly, "you wouldn't like it at all."

"I would," I said, "It's just—"

"Yes?"

"I've done it lots of times," I said.

His fingers were grinding into my arms, crushing the very bones. He said, "If you ever lie to me again, Victoria Broadbent, I'll shake you senseless."

He released me, picked up my coat and held it for me, then went for his own. When he came back he eyed me speculatively for a moment, then said, "If you'd comb your hair and do something to your face, I might even take you to dinner."

"I—can't," I said. I was simply too drained.

"Some other time then," he said. He shrugged into his overcoat, reached for his hat, and then we were walking down the corridor toward the elevator. Truly the prince and pauper, I thought, but I was going to do something about that pauper. I had a feeling that the world had been lifted from my shoulders and put back where it belonged; as if I had been long and critically ill and was now recovered, or at least convalescing.

As we waited for Mr. Jerome's car in front of the hotel, I knew that I had never felt so intensely aware of another human being, or of this one's perfection. I watched some large and perfect snowflakes settle lazily over the black overcoat, and presently the streetlights started coming on like a galaxy of stars. The long black chauffeur-driven car which presently rolled up in front of us was little more than an anticlimax. I wouldn't have been at all surprised to see a golden chariot swoop down out of the sky and carry him away.

XXI

"You surely aren't going to let him take you shopping," said Eunice when I had reported more or less accurately the events of the afternoon.

"Yes, I think I am," I said. "As a simple country girl not far removed from the savage state, I find there are quite a few things I need to learn about clothes if I'm ever going to fit in—well, with the world I'm in now."

Suddenly I felt like giggling. "Somehow or other," I said, "I have to learn how not to look like a frump."

"You seem so different," said Eunice, sounding genuinely disturbed.

I felt different too, exhausted from my emotional afternoon but more at peace with myself than I had been in a long time. "He made me feel—" I hesitated, searching for a word. Certainly not 'beautiful,' he had made that eminently clear! "—as if I mattered," I finished.

She looked at me strangely but said no more. When I started having dinner with him a night or two a week, however, she commented disapprovingly that Mr. Jerome must be fifty if he was a day.

"It's only because it's late when we finish work," I protested. "And it isn't really fair to expect you two to have my supper ready when I'm so seldom here to help with the work."

"We haven't complained," returned Eunice drily. "The thing is, if you keep going out with *him*—"

"Ray Gillian doesn't own me," I said as gently as I could. "I'm sorry he bothers you and Fred about our problems but I can't—just stop. With Mr. Jerome, I mean."

"You don't know a thing about him, Vicki. He may be married and have nine kids for all you know."

I doubted that but, as she said, I didn't really know. What I *could* have told her about him, however, would have shaken her up considerably.

"You know perfectly well what kind of business I'm in," he'd said one afternoon.

That knowledge had come to me gradually, from letters, telephone calls, and all that went on in the office. Surprisingly, he had made not the slightest effort to keep me from learning. "I told my roommates it was something to do with investments," I said.

"How thoughtful of you."

"My mother had a bootlegger," I said.

"For all practical purposes, your mother *was* a bootlegger," he retorted. "And you're a chip off the maternal block or you'd never be caught in public with me. How do your boy friends feel about that?"

"I'm not interested in boy friends."

He gave me a sidelong glance. "You're not still trying to fall in love with me, are you?"

"What would you do if I succeeded?"

His answer came swiftly and brutally as a blow. "I would use you as long as it pleased me and in any way it pleased me, but I would never marry you. Even if I made you pregnant I would not marry you. And when the time came for me to leave, I would go without you, and there would be absolutely nothing you could do about it."

"You don't have to be so beastly."

"No, I do not. I could be dishonest instead, and frequently am. I'm not sure whether it's a father or a lover you're looking for, Victoria, but I have no desire to qualify in either case."

"I've got a father."

"Don't argue with me. Bring your book. I've got some

letters to dictate."

There was no softness in him, no tenderness, no pretense of affection, no warm quality to cling to; and yet I clung, unable to let go.

"I've finished growing up now," I told him once.

"Yes, I believe you have." He came as close to smiling as he ever did. "Some day you will really be twenty-two."

"Blessed be the error that led me to your door."

"You've been a unique experience for me too, Victoria."

"I only wish I could make you happier."

"My state of mind is no concern of yours, but you'll never stop digging, will you, until you reach some kind of pay dirt? I am not a flesh peddler, my dear, nor have I ever introduced a girl to that ancient calling or encouraged one to continue. Any more than I would initiate a girl like you into a way of life that she would have no choice but to continue with somebody else."

"I never would!" I protested.

"That," he said severely, "is the one thing mothers should teach their daughters if they teach them nothing else; that sexual intercourse is not a toy they can experiment with, then put away. Their own desires will drive them to continue. Yes, Victoria, a girl like you. *Especially* a girl like you, so you'd better be damn sure you're married before you start."

"Then I never shall," I said.

"Sometimes you bore me excruciatingly. Will you kindly get back to your own office and try to get a little work done for a change?"

"Yes," I said meekly, and went.

I wondered, though, if this well-insulated character with his hotel suites and his chauffeur-driven limousine had any idea what was happening to marriage these days, that it was in fact becoming almost extinct from lack of funds. Eunice and Fred were always talking about how much they would like to get married if they weren't afraid to risk it. There had already been several layoffs at the mill, so far for not more than a week at at time but it was expected to get worse. With

Eunice sending home money to her father, and Fred helping his folks financially too, marriage just couldn't be managed.

The same specter of unemployment was in fact hanging over most of the people we knew. Even without my association with Mr. Jerome to sully my reputation, I wouldn't have had suitors stumbling over each other to reach my door simply because there were so few young men who could still afford the luxury of taking a girl out for an evening.

Winter became spring, and spring drifted into summer. One day Mr. Jerome came to my door and said, "Come into my office, please. No, you won't need your notebook."

He pushed a small white card across the desk. "You are to report there Monday morning at nine o'clock," he instructed. "There will be a job for you."

I glanced at the card, then mutely back at him.

"You have known that I would be going away," he said. "After today you are not to come here any more, ever, under any circumstances, or make any attempt to see me or the others. Do you understand?"

What I had known had in no way prepared me for the way I was feeling now. "Will you be—safe?" I whispered.

"Quite safe," he assured me.

"You never taught me to say goodbye."

"I don't believe in goodbyes."

I glanced at the card I held in my hand. "You didn't have to do this," I said. "I can find my own jobs from now on."

"I'm sure you could, but you'll find this a pleasant place to work, and I believe you will be happy there. The salary won't be quite what you're making now but the job should be relatively secure, and you've still got a few dollars in the quilt for emergencies."

"I'll get along fine," I said. "Will I—hear from you—or anything?"

"No, Victoria."

"Isn't there—anything at all—I can do for you?"

"Yes. You can remember this, your last lesson from me. When something is finished, don't try to string it out." He stood up and so did I. He said, "Come here, Victoria."

I went to him, put my hands on his shoulders, and kissed his cheek feeling his arms close gently around me. I relaxed slowly against him, my head against his breast. For a long moment we stood like that; then he raised my face to his and gently kissed my forehead, then my eyelids and, still gently, my lips. He said, "Thank you, Victoria," released me and, without another word, walked quickly to the forbidden door, opened it, and passed inside.

XXII

I didn't look at the card until I was on my way home. What Mr. Jerome had written in his distinctive slanting script was: Miss Otilie Zimmerman, Pioneer United Life Insurance Company, with an address a few blocks from our apartment.

When I turned the card over I saw that it was one of his calling cards, engraved simply:

Forster Jerome
Investments

It wasn't until I became aware that my companions on the street car were looking at me a little strangely that I realized I was laughing. You couldn't blame them for feeling curious, it wasn't a year for laughter.

Certainly Miss Otilie Zimmerman, personnel manager for Pioneer United, showed not the slightest inclination toward levity. She was a tall woman, fashionably angular, and wore her hair, of a shade sometimes irreverently spoken of as bottle blonde, in a veritable maze of waves and corkscrews. As we looked each other over critically, I remember feeling surprised that she dared to come to work wearing so much makeup. Her suit, however, looked expensive and very smart. She commented, with a tight little smile which didn't begin to reach her eyes, "Mr. Jerome has recommended you very highly."

I had seen that smile before, and the look that went with it, and would see both many times again whenever Mr. Jerome's name was mentioned. "Mr. Jerome is very kind," I said, modestly lowering my eyes.

Pioneer United's staff was predominantly female, eighty or ninety strong and most of them in their twenties, with about a tenth that number of middle-aged males chanting the cadence and cracking the whip. There was also an agency staff but we didn't see much of them.

I found the work repetitious but not particularly arduous, and the girls were helpful and friendly. There was also the fact that the office was close enough to the apartment for me to save carfare by walking to and from work.

There were also the considerations that jobs were becoming increasingly harder to find, and that the eighteen dollars a week they proposed to pay me, presumably at Mr. Jerome's insistence since it seemed to pain Miss Zimmerman so acutely, was something above their going rate.

In a short time I would begin to become acquainted with a few quaint customs I hadn't encountered before. In common with most offices, Pioneer's policy was to employ only single women and fire them the minute they got married. Miss Zimmerman, however, had added to this procedure certain refinements of her own that would have done credit to the Spanish Inquisitors. In a speech undoubtedly composed at midnight over a bubbling cauldron, she would inform the nervous bride that she was not only an ingrate but also an idiot, and probably not a very nice girl besides, hence the company would no longer be in need of her services. Then, having got the victim suitably softened up, she would magnanimously rehire the poor girl at a lower salary, and with a term of probation attached during which her worth to the company would be re-evaluated.

That was what usually happened but not always. Just often enough to make the game seem not worth the gamble, Miss Zimmerman would fire a girl and *not* rehire her. As a consequence, a number of girls had married secretly and were quaking in their half-soled pumps for fear of being found out; more specifically, horror of horrors, of finding themselves pregnant and thus forced to reveal their dreadful secret.

It occurred to me now and then that Yasmina's anticipated brave new world seemed to be almost as heavily weighted against women as the old one had been, but I could see that men were having their troubles too. Although they were paid more, a man who lost his job had even less chance than a woman of finding another.

As far as Miss Zimmerman was concerned, there were several strikes against me from the beginning. There was Mr. Jerome's recommendation, there was my munificent salary presumably agreed to under duress, and there was the fact that I came from out of town. It had been her practice whenever possible to hire girls living with their parents in proximity to the office, probably, I suspected, so the company could feel less guilty about the meager salaries they were paying. The fact that I was living in an apartment, even with two other girls, seemed to furnish her further grounds for suspicion.

Eunice and Dorothy had been right about that, however; it was costing less for each of us than any other way we could have lived. That was fortunate for, with Eunice not working several days a month and me on a reduced salary, we needed to cut corners wherever we could. Dorothy was still with the Freegate Company but it was barely limping along.

I was determined to live on what I was making, leaving what was left in Mama's quilt for emergencies. The new wardrobe had been a drain but not as costly as I had expected, and—Mr. Jerome having an eye for quality as well as styling—would last a long time. I had only a vague idea how much money was left, having followed Mama's own practice of padding and requilting the places where money had been removed.

Besides the economy involved, there was also a social advantage to having our own apartment. We could come and go as we pleased and entertain our friends whenever we wanted to. Mrs. Walker was the perfect landlady in that respect. Maybe she thought turn about was fair enough; we hand't complained about her impromptu concerts so she wouldn't complain about any annoyance from above.

Not that our gatherings tended to get out of hand, being mostly sandwich and soft drink affairs, or making fudge and popcorn balls, but there was the radio, and an ancient Victrola with several scratchy records we'd picked up at a sale.

Other evenings we cleaned the apartment, did our laundry, and talked; much, I supposed as Mama and The Girls must have talked in that other house all those years before. About how long you should know a boy before you let him kiss you, and how far you should let him go after that; about how far a girl dared let *herself* go before it became too late to change her mind. And if she did happen to get married, what was the surest way to keep from having a baby?

It was taken for granted that a girl wouldn't *want* to have a baby until the Depression was over.

For reference on more intimate matters we had an awesome volume Dorothy had ordered through the mail, and which we referred to as our Sex Book, or simply The Book. Although both text and illustrations sometimes strained credulity to the breaking point, we relied on it all the more because of its highly impersonal approach. There was no attempt at moralizing, no "here's what you must not do" or "here's what will happen to you if you do," but simply "here's the way it is, take it or leave it."

I for one felt much inclined to leave it, especially as the further I read the more horrified I became about the way I'd thrown myself at Mr. Jerome. Suppose, just suppose, he had called my hand!

"Still," I reasoned aloud, "if it were as bad as this makes it seem, no girl would ever get married."

Dorothy giggled. "From the way some of the married girls talk, it isn't bad at all with the right man."

Eunice considered us both quite frivolous. "A girl isn't supposed to *like* it," she said. "It's just something she has to put up with after she has a husband."

But Yasmina had said a woman *could* like it, if it was the way it was meant to be, only how could you tell in advance whether or not it was going to be that way? "The first time a boy kissed me," I said, "I didn't like it at all, but I got used to it."

"An acquired taste," conjectured Dorothy, "like olives."

"Not the tongues, though," I said. "I still can't stand *that*. You needn't look so shocked, Eunice. You know very well they all try that if you let them."

"I don't know anything of the sort," Eunice returned with a strained smile. "There's nothing in The Book about it either."

"They may have left out a lot of things," I said darkly.

"What we need," said Dorothy, "is more boy friends."

And little chance of that, I thought. I seldom had a chance to go out with anybody but Ray Gillian, who had more or less forgiven me for my association with Mr. Jerome, but he was no longer the pleasant easy-mannered man I had known before. Maybe it was because he was worried about his job, but he was drinking too much and, with Prohibition still in effect, goodness only knew what was in it. An evening spent with him was likely as not to end in his near-drunkenness and almost certain unpleasantness. I had on that account broken off with him several times, but in a week or two he would be back, humorously penitent and expecting another chance.

And getting it, because I was used to him and there was no one else. This undoubtedly was all part of the mating game, the jungle for which Yasmina had tried to prepare me. The truth was, however, that I was getting pretty tired of the jungle, as well as in a welter of confusion about my own feelings. Sometimes I was appalled at how close I found myself to giving in, wanting to give in, even to a man I hadn't particularly liked up to then. Other times I wondered if, after rejecting the ultimate intimacy for so long, I would ever be able to lower my defenses even if I did happen to get married.

I hadn't seen Mr. Jerome since the day he'd sent me

away, but I hadn't missed him anything like as much as I expected to, nor at all in the same way. I did, however, keep having the feeling that he was somewhere nearby, ready to pop out and confront me if I ever dared slack off in my grooming. Once when I had hurriedly mended a slip strap with a safety pin, I distinctly heard him say, "What have I told you, Victoria, about going around like a frump?" So vivid was that impression I hastily pulled off the offending garment and mended it properly then and there.

His face, however, was beginning to elude me. There remained only his profile as he sat at his desk, the forbidding brow, the eyes that searched and probed but never warmed, the wide but thin-lipped mouth. And his hands. I would never be able to forget his hands, long and lean and restless as himself, but I knew now that what I felt for him had not been love.

Dr. Armstrong died in October of that year so Aunt Tabitha and I were alone for Christmas. A very old lady and a girl of twenty, but love is thicker than blood and we were bound by other ties as well. Mama had loved and trusted Aunt Tabitha even longer than she had me, may have confided in her more of those things she thought I was too young to understand. She would, when I was older, have answered any questions I asked, but I had not asked them in time. Unless I asked now, I might be making that same mistake again.

"She must have told you more than anyone," I said feeling in spite of myself a slight twinge of envy.

"Only what she wanted to tell me. In my day we were taught to respect a friend's reticence as well as her confidence. What's troubling you, Vicki?"

"Since her name was shown as Miller on her marriage certificate, I suppose that must have been Dr. Modesta's real name."

She nodded. "Victor Miller. She would have told them that at the time if they had asked her nicely."

Victor. Vic-tor. It had not been for me that Yasmina had called during her delirium but a man named Victor Miller, otherwise known as Dr. Modesta.

"Or maybe she wouldn't have," Aunt Tabitha was going on. "She always thought of him as Dr. Modesta."

"I used to hope that some day I would learn he was my father, which was wrong of me, I suppose, trying to shut my own father out.'

"Ollie Broadbent shut himself out. He was never a sharing man, child. He had to have everything his own way, and there was nothing your mother or anybody else could do to change him. The best thing you can do now is put all that unpleasantness out of your mind. Pretty soon you'll be getting married and raising a family of your own."

"Nobody can afford a family any more."

"Fiddlesticks. When you're blessed with a baby, you find a way of taking care of it. God tempers the wind, child, and don't you ever be forgetting it. And that's enough advice for one day from a crazy old lady. Let's go crack that bottle of blackberry cordial."

The Freegate Company drew its final breath that January, but Dorothy was fortunate enough to find another job within a week or two, although at a smaller salary. Eunice sometimes worked only a day or two a week. I had been given additional responsibility but no increase in pay. But, hope springing eternal in the youthful breast, we kept saying that things would soon be better, in a few months, at least by next year, and we could manage somehow until then.

With the increasing scarcity of eligible young men, girls were becoming more than ever restricted to their own society. We dined together, and hurried into downtown theatres before five o'clock to take advantage of matinee prices. For twenty-five cents we could often see a double feature and sometimes a stage show as well. At one theater there was vaudeville, at another name bands held forth every week. At the neighborhood houses there were bank nights and china nights.

While it was a pleasant enough way to pass the time, it wasn't doing a thing toward fulfilling the traditional dream of young Americans for love and marriage. Eunice and Fred were still engaged but the wedding date had been postponed so many times they had ceased to even talk about it. Dorothy was still going with Harold Cornmeier, as she had been when I first met her.

I had received my first proposal, from Ray Gillian, who had flung himself off in a huff when, after due consideration, I refused him. Once again, however, he had, after a few weeks, come wandering back.

One Saturday evening at a party, finding his behavior under the influence of alcohol even more offensive than usual, and all patience spent, I pushed him away from me with such force that he stumbled backward into a fish pond. Leaving him there, I went into the house to call a taxi.

"Aw, no, Vicki," protested our host, a few sheets to the wind himself. "Old Ray'll be o.k. in a little while, or somebody else can drive you home."

Nobody volunteered for this honor, however, until a clear boyish tenor spoke up practically in my ear. "I'll be g-g-glad to drive Vicki home if she will l-l-l-let me."

I'd never learned his name or heard him speak before but he'd been showing up pretty regularly at everybody's parties, usually with three or four girls in tow. He was a wholesome looking boy whose face exuded so much goodwill I had already in my own mind dubbed him the Beaming Cherub. His hair, dark and blonde and wavy and very thick, was brushed neatly back, and his complexion looked delicate as a girl's. Exactly what I needed on a night like this, I reflected, was a stuttering cherub.

"Swell," applauded our host, slipping the old stiletto neatly between my ribs. "You know old Toomey, Vicki. Sure you do."

Old Toomey? He couldn't be a day over sixteen. I fixed this fair-haired boy in the gleam of my jaded eye and said, "Are you sure it won't be out of your way?"

"G-g-g-gosh, no, Vicki," he assured me earnestly. "I g-g-go right past your house."

I supposed he could get me home, and there didn't seem

any use further disrupting a party that had suffered so much already. "Perhaps," I mentioned belatedly, "somebody ought to go pull Ray out of that pond before the fish get sick."

I then turned my attention back to this character called Old Toomey. Old Toomey what? Or did it matter? Whoever he was, he beamed at me and said, "We c-c-can go now if you want to."

"Where are your other girls?" I asked as we started out the door.

"I g-g-got started late. All the b-best ones were already taken," confided the cherub, and beamed some more.

"What in the name of tunket is that!" Probably I shouldn't have been so surprised at the sight of the automobile, but I was already a little shaken from a trying evening. "A fire engine, would you say?"

"Beneath his frivolous exterior b-b-beats a noble P-Packard heart," extolled old Toomey. "The paint job was my idea and s-some of the other things. Pretty snazzy, huh?"

"You bet your boots," I said. "Especially that radiator cap."

"Aphrodite? Isn't she a dream?"

Some dream. At least a foot high and looking to be solid brass. "The poor girl needs a sweater," I said. "Her drapery's slipping."

Old Toomey laughed immoderately and held the door for me.

"Wait till you see how fast he can go," he exulted, vaulting in beside me.

I would have been willing to postpone that experience indefinitely, but the beaming boy evidently misinterpreted my silence as speechless delight. We were off. It not only *looked* like a fire engine, it *sounded* like one too. "Something must be loose," I yelled.

"I k-kind of worked on it this afternoon, maybe I left something off."

Like the lugs on the wheels, maybe. Still, nobody lives forever, and it *was* exhilarating riding in a fire engine, once you got into the spirit of the thing. "Why did you paint a perfectly good Packard red?" I shouted above the glockenspiel.

"What other color is there?" he shouted back, and laughed like a maniac.

After the first few thousand miles, he slowed slightly and shouted, "Where do you live, Vicki?"

I was beginning to notice that sometimes his stammer seemed to disappear altogether; and if he was pulling my leg about that, he could well be up to other tricks too. "If you don't know where I live," I demanded, "why did you say you were going right past my house?"

That sent him into another gale of merriment. "Sometimes I'm an awful l-liar," he acknowledged cheerfully, still shouting to make himself heard.

We drew up in front of Mrs. Walker's house as discreetly as our conveyance would permit, then my cherubic young friend insisted on seeing me up the stairs. Outside the apartment door he settled himself comfortably against the door jamb and said, "If you want me to come in, I can show you some dandy card tricks."

His eyes were a lovely melting caramel with curling lashes an inch long, his mouth as soft and pink as a baby's. "Some other time," I said kindly. "My roommates are probably asleep."

I thanked him for bringing me home, then closed the door firmly against him, although it hurt me to do it. It was like shutting a lovable puppy out of your room when all he wanted to do was sleep on the foot of your bed. Dorothy had not come home yet, so I joined Eunice in the bedroom and was soon fast asleep.

XXIII

"Wake *up*, Vicki!"

Now what? Sundays were for sleeping in, weren't they? certainly for people in their right minds. *Somebody*, however, evidently didn't agree with me. "Go 'way,' I mumbled.

"Wake *up*!" This time the admonition was accompanied by a determined shake.

I opened one eye just a slit. Dorothy. "Toomey's here," she announced. "We're going on a picnic."

Toomey? Picnic? I turned over and closed my eyes but it wasn't any use; sleep was gone. I sat up. "What time is it?"

"Almost ten. Do get a move on, Vicki. He's waiting."

Smack in front of the house, I was sure, having already roused half the neighborhood from its Sunday morning slumbers with his clanking red chariot. Odd I hadn't heard him myself.

Just then Eunice came pirouetting in as if somebody had made her Queen of the May. "We're all going," she announced. "Toomey invited us."

"Good for you," I said. "Now I can go back to sleep."

"Vicki!" I'd have known that voice anywhere. "If you're not out of that bed in fifteen seconds, I'm coming in!"

"Not in the kitchen!" I cried. But of course he was. Where else would a cherub be on a Sunday morning? "Oh, all right," I said resignedly. "What have we got to pack in a lunch?"

"Toomey brought everything," trilled Dorothy. It struck me that both my roommates were speaking pretty familiarly about my beaming boy. "You *know* this character?" I whispered.

"Everybody knows Toomey," Dorothy purred happily. "I put the coffee back on the stove for you, Vicki. Better catch it before it boils over."

"How do you like your toast?" called that same cheerful voice from the kitchen. "No, don't tell me. Just quit muttering and get moving."

"What happened to your stammer?" I demanded, putting my head around the door.

"Comes and goes. Here." He pushed part of a heavily buttered slice of toast between my teeth. "That's all you get for now. Don't want to spoil your lunch, do you?"

"Why," I demanded, "didn't I push you into the fish pond instead of Ray?"

He bit his lower lip and seemed to be trying to quell some disturbance deep within him. Or maybe he was going into a seizure of some kind. That would be the last straw. Soon, however, he seemed to recover. He said, "Here, drink your coffee. We haven't got all day."

"A picnic in a fire engine," I remarked between swallows. "The very thing I've been hankering for and didn't know it."

"I put a new muffler on Peggy," he informed me with dignity. "You can hardly hear him breathe."

"Him?"

"Pegasus," he explained kindly. "My winged steed."

In the light of day Pegasus dazzled the eyes more than ever, but his voice had indeed been muted to a discreet albeit still powerful purr. And Toomey certainly did know where to stage his picnics, even if a girl with practically no breakfast inside her almost starved to death on the way. He'd laid on a splendid lunch, however, of ham and cheese, pickles, bread and butter, and orange soda iced down in a bucket. Then he lifted out a three-layer chocolate cake which he announced somebody named Pinky had baked that very morning.

After stuffing ourselves to repletion we began to help our gracious host repack the picnic basket. "Don't you want the rest of your pop?" Eunice asked him.

He eyed the bottle somewhat disconsolately. "It doesn't fizz any more," he said, and poured the contents out on the ground.

As he finished repacking the basket and stowed it away in the back of the car, I found myself watching his hands, as I had once watched Mr. Jerome's. These were a boy's hands, large and square, with neatly filed nails. His movements were deft and economical. He was as fair-skinned as I had thought last night but neither pallid nor pale, and there was a healthy sprinkling of freckles across the bridge of his nose. It was, I decided, a slight squinting of his unusually expressive eyes, accompanied by the good-humored set of his full lips, which produced the impression of beaming.

"Now we walk," he proclaimed, turning to me and offering one of those large blunt-fingered hands.

"I don't think I can. I'm too stuffed."

"That's why we walk, dear. Come on, Vicki. Am I going to have to drag you?"

We walked along the banks of the shallow stream that wound in and out through the woods. We skipped pebbles, and stopped to watch a school of minnows darting out from behind some rocks. I realized it was the first time I had spent a day in the country since leaving the farm, and that I was enjoying myself. "Do you come here often?" I asked.

"Every now and then."

"We'd better wait for the others, hadn't we?"

He reached for my hand, tucked it through his arm. "They can catch up," he said, "if they want to."

"I don't even know your name," I said, "not anything but Toomey."

The caramel eyes swept over me, then focused on my face. He didn't look quite so young as he had the night before, and his heavy shoulders and rather stocky build made him appear shorter than he was. At least he was taller than I. "Landis," he said. "Toomey Landis."

"The other girls seemed to think I ought to know you."

"Yes," he agreed, "I think so too."

We walked on, the sun hot on our shoulders, my arm still held against his side. After awhile he said, "I promised to have your friends home by six."

"We have dates," I said, then remembered. "*They* have anyway. I probably haven't, after last night."

"You and I could go to a movie then, and later I could show you those card tricks. I'm amazingly versatile."

"I'll bet you are," I said.

"And p-p-perfectly safe," he added, the caramel eyes beginning to melt and glow.

I began to have the glimmering of a suspicion that Peggy might not be the only thing sailing under false colors; there could well be a superdreadnought lurking beneath the friendly puppy facade of my cherub. Still, what harm could there possibly be in seeing a movie with him?

None at all, it seemed. He brought me home and left me at my door with no more mention of card tricks, or even a goodnight kiss. He was a nice boy, and it had been sweet of him to spend his day—and evening—entertaining three older girls who probably didn't interest him much. But I fell asleep wondering how it would feel to be kissed by a man with lips as full and soft as that, and wondering why he hadn't tried.

"So give," I said next morning at breakfast. "Exactly who, and what, is Toomey Landis?"

"But *everybody*—" began Eunice.

"—knows Toomey," I obligingly finished for her. "Everybody but me, that is."

"But you've seen him dozens of times. He's always circulating around somewhere, parties and places. You can't possibly have missed him."

"I thought he was somebody's kid brother," I said.

"Toomey's not exactly a kid He must be at least twenty-three or four."

He also worked at PureSilk, she told me, inspecting and

servicing the knitting machines, in addition to which he had patents on a thing or two he'd whomped up in his home workshop. "The men think he's some kind of genius," she said.

"He doesn't smoke," said Dorothy, "seldom takes a drink, and must be well off. At least he always has money to spend, and the girls are crazy about him."

If he were only a little taller," I said.

"You and your tall, dark, and handsome," said Eunice. "As if you hadn't had one experience with that."

Not altogether a painful experience, I might have pointed out, but I only conceded equably that Mr. Jerome had been too old for me. "But," I said, "get on with your story about the boy wonder. If he's such a prize, how come some girl hasn't copped him?"

Partly his method of courting, Eunice conjectured, if you could call it that, three or four or more certainly constituting a crowd where intimate moments were concerned. "Then," she said rather ominously, "there's his mother."

I remembered that Fred Currier's mother was dead set against her darling boy taking a wife and seemed determined to prevent it at all costs. "Oh," I said, and then, "Where's his father?"

There had been, she told me, quite a scandal about that, which was still being talked about. Mrs. Landis had inherited a small furniture factory from her father and her husband was running it. He had, without her knowledge, milked the business of all the cash he could get together, then gone away with another woman. Both had been killed when their automobile collided with another during a rainstorm.

"So mother hangs on to son for dear life, is that it?"

That seemed to be the consensus, at least among Toomey's girl friends. "I've never met her myself," admitted Eunice, "and I don't really know anybody who has, but everybody talks as if she was—well, kind of balmy."

"Were you ever one of his girls?"

She shook her head. "I was already going with Fred.

Dorothy's been out with him a time or two."

"But only as part of the mob," said Dorothy, and added, "Worse luck."

I doubted that I would enjoy his form of group dating either, and anyway would probably never see him again. A few evenings later, however, I found him and Peggy waiting outside when I got off work. "Get in, Vicki. We're going swimming."

He plucked up three more girls from the sidewalk before we'd gone as far as the next corner and tucked them into the back seat, chirping away like sparrows. "I don't even have a bathing suit," I said.

"Borrow one then. Hester, Alice, Rita, who's got a spare suit Vicki can use?"

So we gathered up suits from the girls' houses and went swimming. Afterward he took us all to a restaurant to eat.

"Isn't that Toomey a card?" Alice said to me next day.

"A healthy growing boy," I said.

"Oh, Toomey can be a tiger when he wants to be," she said, and giggled.

It seemed that everybody *did* know Toomey but me, and some of them rather well, but I was getting better acquainted all the time.

"You don't learn to roller skate on a gravel road," I explained to him.

"So I'll teach you. Come *on*, Vicki."

"I don't dance very well," I apologized, "and it would be better if you were a little taller."

That seemed to induce another temblor similar to the one that had threatened in our kitchen that Sunday morning, but he got it under control. "I'm tall enough, baby—for just about anything you might have in mind."

I felt myself blushing to the roots of my hair. "You're pretty too," I said, hoping to squelch the bumptious boy just a little.

"My teeth are like pearls," he confided solemnly, and whirled me onto the dance floor.

So we swam and skated and danced and picnicked the

summer away; but for all Toomey's ingenuity and enthusiasm, it was not nearly as frenetic as it sounds. There were quiet moments too; and even with a few spare girls in his entourage, Toomey didn't exactly exert himself. It was just that way he had of catapulting people right along with him into the center of things without them more than half realizing how they'd got there. I was beginning to realize just how little such play there had theretofore been in my life; and with a harem along, there wasn't even any attempt at heavy wooing to worry about.

Then the harem disappeared without a trace. Whatever had happened to Rosalie, Betty, Helen, Mary, Katie, Nicole, and Catherine? And a few dozen others? "Don't you like girls any more?" I quizzd.

He looked at me with that slow smile that seemed to kindle from his eyes and keep on going. "Girl," he said, "not girls."

Don't spoil things, Toomey; leave them the way they are. That's what I thought I was going to say but then I changed my mind because I wasn't sure.

He said, "Let's go on a picnic tomorrow." And that was different too, suggesting something instead of just whirling me along.

"All right," I said. "We'll pack the lunch this time."

"Just us," he said, "you and me. I'm tired of crowds, aren't you?"

I hadn't thought he would ever be tired of crowds. I wondered if I really wanted him to be.

We drove to the same place we'd gone for the first picnic, walked after lunch beside that same stream, hand in hand; then suddenly we were in each other's arms.

The flesh of my beloved was warm and sweet, his lips full and soft against my own. "You've been leading me down the garden path," I whispered.

"But aren't the flowers lovely?"

I didn't know. I couldn't see anything but stars. We kissed again, our bodies melting together. "Toomey," I whispered. "Toomey."

"I love you, Vicki." He wasn't smiling now, and the caramel eyes were steady and true; but when I drew away, he let me go.

"If you'd climb yonder hill with me," he said, "I would show you the world."

"You would show me another house and barn and fields, and maybe a horse and cow." My voice did not sound as steady as I wanted it to be.

"Let's go and see."

We dropped onto the warm grass at the top of the hill, gasping for breath. "You were right," I conceded, "it *is* the world."

"You see how dependable I am?"

I saw—and felt—a lot of things I wasn't sure I was ready for yet. "I've never doubted your dependability," I said.

"Besides being terribly pretty."

Suddenly he was shaking again. The man was getting more convulsive than Vesuvius. And this time he erupted.

"You're laughing!" I accused him hotly. "At *me*! All those other times you were laughing, when I thought—"

"I'm s-s-s-sorry, Vicki."

I regarded him with disfavor, remembering all those times Yasmina had seemed to be stricken speechless, remembering Mr. Jerome's caustic reaction to some of my more gauche comments. "Everybody laughs at me," I said.

"It's just that you're such a serious little thing, so f-f-funny and sweet."

"Maybe I can get on the stage at the Lyric," I said. I thwacked him resoundingly between the shoulder blades. "All right, buster, get it out of your system before you choke to death. Have you always been so all-fired happy?"

I saw his face change, the light die out of his eyes. It was like a cloud coming over the sun. "Only since my father died," he said.

"Toomey!"

"You asked me, I told you. Are you shocked?"

I thought about that. "No," I said.

"My father was going to make a gung-ho sporting chap

of his boy even if it killed me."

Obviously it hadn't but I wasn't quite sure what he meant by 'sporting chap.'

"Boxing," he explained, as if reading my mind. "Football, baseball, hunting, fishing. The works."

His eyes stayed glued to my face as if in some Herculean effort to explain more to me than his words conveyed. "I shot a squirrel," he said. The muscles of his jaw tightened and a vein started throbbing in his temple. "I was very young at the time, and I'd only aimed at targets before. Stupid as it may seem, it had never occurred to me that the squirrel would really be dead. Until I saw the blood."

I reached for him, gently pulled him to me, pillowed his head against my breast, and felt some of the tension leave his body. "I haven't had a gun in my hands since," he said, in a voice carefully stripped of all expression. "I never shall."

I remembered my father and my half-brothers coming home from the hunt with limp furry bodies dangling from their hands, remembered the revulsion—and the pity.

"In the world of he-men I am a sissy," Toomey said. "I thought you'd better know."

My arms tightened, my hands caressed. Presently he drew away from me and sat up, looking a little drained but otherwise very much himself. "Let's go back to my house," he said. "I'll show you my dungeon."

So that had been his game. He'd only been softening me up for this dungeon he mentioned. I tried to glare at him.

"No etchings, baby. Honor bright, not a single etching. Haven't you heard about my dungeon?"

Maybe that was where his workshop was. Maybe not. "Don't mind me," I said. "I'm always the last to know."

"Well, here we are," he said an hour or so later, as he pulled Peggy to the curb and stopped.

It was pretty dark by then, and there were lots of trees, but I had an impression of rather a large white house set rather far back from the street. We were hardly inside the door when a woman's voice called out, "Is that you,

Toomey?"

"Yes, Mother." He took my hand and led me into a large room dominated by a grand piano—and by Mrs. Landis. She was about my height but with the kind of bone structure that made her look almost ethereal. She was beautifully dressed in grey voile, her ashe blonde hair drawn simply back into a bun, but there was a faraway look in the washed gentian eyes. She said, "How nice to meet you, dear," in a voice which confirmed my impression of detachment, then added graciously, "Won't you sit down? Can Pinky get you something?"

"No, Mother. I'm going to show Vicki the dungeon."

At that moment a short plump woman came into the room carrying what looked like a piece of embroidery, stopped when she saw us, and then her whole face crinkled into a smile. Toomey said, "this is Mrs. Pincus, Vicki."

The smile was so contagious I couldn't help giving it back. "The chocolate cake baker," I remembered, and Mrs. Pincus said she was pleased to meet me.

"We're on our way to the dungeon," Toomey told her, and winked.

"You naughty boy," she said, and then to me, "If I hear any screams, dear, I'll ride straight to the rescue."

"Restrain yourself," advised Toomey, "if those screams happen to be *mine*. Come along, Vicki."

I started to tell the ladies it had been nice meeting them but was whisked away before I could finish. I wondered if they were accustomed to meeting Toomey's girls only in transit and decided they probably were.

Toomey's dungeon was simply the biggest basement I'd ever seen, not even excepting the one at Aunt Tabitha's. It was, in fact, not a dungeon at all but a brilliantly lighted area with work tables, benches, tools and machines, the likes of which I had never seen before. "You invent things," I remembered, "only I don't remember what."

His interests as well as his talents were varied, it seemed. One of his brain children had been a knitting process for producing ladies' silk stockings that wouldn't run. He said he'd got the idea from studying some of his mother's knitting patterns.

With practically every woman in the country suffering a small death when she discovered a run in her last pair of silk stockings, you'd think they would be beating a path to Toomey's door. Might have come to that, conceded the boy with the caramel eyes, if the whole lovely process hadn't been stopped cold by people who liked to sell lots and lots of silk stockings.

"If PureSilk won't buy it, somebody else will," I said warmly.

PureSilk *had* bought it, he said, but there'd been no royalties because they'd also buried it. "That was before I started having a lawyer go over my royalty contracts," explained Toomey, a little grimly.

"Didn't they pay you anything at all?"

His face brightened. They had paid him a lump sum, he said. "That's where I got the money for Peggy and for Mother's piano."

One of the other patents, also acquired for a lump sum and forthwith interred, had been some kind of gadget for automobiles to cut gasoline consumption. He'd used that money to finish paying off the mortgage on the house. "Built on a utility room too," he said, "and finished off another bedroom upstairs for Pinkey."

Mrs. Pincus had worked for them by the day for several years, until her son and daughter were grown up and married, at which time she had agreed to live in. As far as I could figure out, she now functioned somewhere between cook and companion, doubling in brass as a kind of benevolent aunt.

"Couldn't you invent something people would use instead of burying?" I couldn't quite resist asking.

He didn't exactly invent things, Toomey explained, the caramel eyes dancing now. He just kind of fiddled around and occasionally something interesting happened. Gadgets, he called these unexpected offspring. He was getting a little royalty now from some of those. "Not much," he said.

"About enough to support me and Peggy in our pleasures and pastimes."

"You've done all that since you finished college?"

"Didn't go to college," said Toomey. "I c-c-couldn't seem to find the time."

That certainly seemed reasonable. With a job and gadgets and girls, he must have been stretched pretty thin as it was. "How come you came alone to the Johnsons' party?" I asked suddenly.

The question seemed to take him by surprise. "W-w-why do you think?" he asked.

"What I thought then was that you were somebody's kid brother."

His arms came around me from behind, his hands lightly cupping my breasts. "And now?" he asked.

"I'll scream," I warned him.

He grinned delightedly. "Pinky was only kidding. She gets a terrific kick out of hearing my girls scream."

She didn't hear *me* because I hadn't any breath left to scream with. Toomey seemed to undergo certain Protean changes when an amorous mood came over him. Not only did he seem older and taller and stronger but also more determined. I must have been out of my mind to imagine only tall dark men were masterful.

When I could speak again, I said, "You didn't answer my question."

"I was stalking you, naturally."

"Wouldn't it have been simpler to just ask me for a date?"

"You might have said no. Anyway, I knew you'd fall into my clutches sooner or later."

"I suppose you even knew I was going to push Ray into that fish pond."

His face suddenly darkened. "If you hadn't," he almost growled, "I'd have done it myself."

This was a mood I wasn't familiar with, and I was finding it disturbing. "Just to hurry your luck along?" I asked.

Almost reluctantly he said, "To shut his mouth for a

change."

So he must have heard Ray sounding off publicly on his favorite theme. "I should have pushed his head under," I said.

I had never been particularly bothered by what people said abut me, but suddenly I wanted Toomey Landis to know, and believe, the truth. "I worked for Forster Jerome," I said, "when nobody else would hire me."

His steady gaze never wavered.

"I was infatuated," I said, "but Mr. Jerome was a gentleman. Which was fortunate, because—I didn't care about him the way I imagined I did."

He smiled a little but his eyes remained still and watchful. "I know about father hunts," he said.

Surely not from personal experience, I thought. *He* seemed to have had more father than he was prepared to handle.

But then, so had I; and despite the fact that *my* father was still living, I had nevertheless searched for one, first in Dr. Armstrong and next—although I had refused to recognize that at the time—in Forster Jerome. And the reasons for both Toomey and me were the same—our fathers had rejected us. But not our mothers.

"My mother had a dungeon too," I said.

"Yes?"

I watched his face quicken and come alive, and determined to keep it that way. "That's where she and my Aunt Tabitha brewed up the famous elixir."

"Tell me," he demanded, leading me over to a couch and pushing aside a spill of cushions so we could sit down. "Tell me all about it."

XXIV

Trying to sort out my feelings about Toomey made untying the Gordian Knot look easy. When I was with him there was seldom time to think about how I felt. Not to coin a phrase, of which there seemed far too many in the world already, he knew how to treat a girl. The entertainment varied but his attentiveness did not. He had a way of fixing his eyes on your face when you were talking, his lips slightly parted as if he were drinking in every word. Even when you *knew* he was only calculating how long it would take to soften you up for a petting session, you couldn't help being impressed. And he wasn't exactly objectionable when it came to that either.

On the other hand, he had never mentioned marriage, probably because marriage was not part of his plans. Maybe that was just as well. Wasn't it doubtful that a man who enjoyed life as exuberantly as he did could ever settle down to the serious business of marrying and raising a family? How would he react when things went wrong?

And yet he *could* be serious—very serious indeed. And he wasn't ever, even at his worst, malicious or intolerant or careless of other people's feelings.

May she always know the value of what she has while she still has it. All right, Yasmina, I've never had a playmate before and may never have another. After all, I'm in no real rush about getting married myself.

I had been attending cooking classes sponsored by the gas

company on Wednesday nights, and Toomey had been picking me up afterward. There was one thing about an automobile that looked like a fire engine with a half-naked woman on the hood, it was easy to spot in a crowd, but one night it simply wasn't there. Sometimes he was called back to the mill in the evening, or something else could have detained him. No matter, I'd take the street car home. I set off walking toward the corner.

"Hi, cutie. How about a lift?"

I swung around ready to give some would-be masher the benefit of my opinion; but there, in a long dark blue car polished within an inch of its beautiful life, sat Toomey Landis, laughing fit to split. Had he sold another gadget and blown himself to a new car? But wait. "No!" I cried. "Oh no! What have you done to Peggy?"

"I blew him to a new paint job. Pretty snazzy, don't you think?"

I didn't know whether to laugh or cry. Still, you shouldn't expect a fire engine to be forever, should you?

"Hop in, girlie." He pasted something over his face that was probably intended to be a leer, reached over and opened the door.

"Watch that girlie stuff," I said, and started to get in.

At least he'd left the inside the same, I thought, reassured by the sight of the familiar red and white upholstery. "Aphrodite's gone!" I wailed then. In her place was a lion's head, not more than six inches high.

"More appropriate, I thought, for a married man."

The headlights of oncoming cars began to shimmer the way they do in the rain, only it wasn't raining. In fact, my mind was beginning to feel a little shimmery too. Never careless of other people's feelings, I thought. Oh, Toomey!

"Oh damn," said Toomey, pulled Peggy over to the curb, and stopped. "I was going to be so romantic about it. I had it all planned, exactly what I was going to say, and where, and how. Oh, well. Will you marry me, Vicki? Please."

I knew exactly how a bullet must feel when it is blasted out of a gun. I buried my face against Toomey's shoulder, and this time I was the one shaking inside, and not from laughter. He could at least have warned a girl, couldn't he? How could I ever get married anyway, and quit work, and have to ask him for every cent I needed? And—

"Please marry me, Vicki."

"I—I—I can't *not* marry you, can I?" I finally managed.

"Oh, Vicki."

Stars fell, cymbals crashed, somewhere a trumpet blew and blew and blew.

"All *right* buddy, lay off that horn, will you!"

A very large policeman with a very belligerent face came over and poked his head through the window. "Everybody knows you're here now," he said with exaggerated politeness, "so if you would be so kind as to lay off the bugle?

"Not that I blame you, buddy," he conceded, in what turned out to be the very last of that unnaturally dulcet tone, "but could you just kindly MOVE IT SOMEWHERE ELSE!"

"Doesn't anybody believe in love any more?" Toomey protested soulfully—and moved it.

"We shall repair to a quiet bower," he told me presently, "and I shall propose all over again."

"Must you? I'm not sure I could stand two proposals in the same evening."

"Well, if you're sure the first one took. You did say yes, didn't you?"

"Sort of, but—"

He hugged me to him, effectively forestalling any further protests, but it didn't stop what was going on inside my head. Now that it had happened, I was scared to death. What had I ever seen of marriage to recommend it? Certainly not my parents' marriage, or my sisters' marriages, or the marriages of anyone else I could think of. And it would be so final. If it didn't work out, what else could there be, ever?

"Toomey, what did your mother say?"

"My dear girl, one announces one's engagement only after it becomes one, even to one's own mother. After all, you might have turned me down."

"And if I had?"

"I'd have kept on asking, of course, but I'm glad you didn't waste time because now we can get on to more enchanting pursuits."

"Toomey!"

"You don't think I'd compromise you, do you?"

"Why not? The girls at the office refer to you as Tiger Toomey."

"That was when I was young and foolish."

"I'll probably lose my job if I get married."

"You'll have a job, baby."

"Suppose you're laid off work, like some of the others?"

"Impossible. Nobody else understands about the machines the way I've got them rigged. There," he added with satisfaction as he brought Peggy to a stop and reached for the ignition key. "A nice quiet nook at last."

But he did not immediately get on with what he had called 'enchanting pursuits.' "I muffed it," he confessed, "Because I was scared. You want me to try again?"

"Not unless you want to take it back."

He gathered me into his arms and held me so close I could scarcely breathe. "I'm such a mess," he whispered, "but I love you so much. I'll take care of you, darling, and I'll never let you down."

The voice on the telephone next day was perfectly modulated, cool as mint, and quite as impersonal. It said, "This is Mrs. Landis, Vicki. I wonder if you would have dinner with us tomorrow evening."

I knew then that the rumors regarding Toomey's mother had been all too accurate, and that the showdown was at hand. This was going to be one of the shortest engagements on record. "I'd like to," I said.

"I'm so glad, dear. We usually have dinner at six. Toomey will pick you up sometime before that."

I thanked her and hung up. Miss Zimmerman was glaring at me, personal telephone calls being *verboten* for Pioneer wage slaves. Fifteen minutes earlier I might have glared back but, since it looked now as if I was going to need a job for the rest of my life, that was a luxury I could no longer afford.

If I seemed to be running up the white flag too easily, it was because I'd spent a large part of the previous night thinking about it; and I had already decided that, even if Toomey was willing to override his mother's objections to our marriage, I was not. I had spent enough of my life being a bone of contention between two people who might otherwise have rubbed along fairly amiably. Besides which, wouldn't it be hard enough to get used to living with Toomey without taking on a load of mother-in-law problems to boot?

"You don't really *know* she's going to object," Eunice had argued at breakfast that morning.

"Everybody says she doesn't want Toomey to get married. You said so yourself."

"I've never met her, though. You have. How did she seem to you?"

Airy as a cloud, I was tempted to say; but after all I had only met her two or three times enroute to the dungeon. "I wasn't engaged to Toomey then," I said.

Not at all unexpectedly, Mrs. Landis turned out to be a competent and gracious hostess, presiding over her table and guiding the conversation with never an awkward pause. Toomey beamed, Mrs. Pincus beamed, I made a noble effort to beam back. So far, so good. Then, still beaming, Toomey dropped his little bombshell, right in the middle of our strawberry mousse. He had to go back to the mill for an hour or two to fix something that had gone wrong.

To be abandoned at a time like this! Toomey, darling, take one last fond look at your fiancée who, within the hour, will be so no more.

"Of course, dear," Mrs. Landis told him kindly. "That will give Vicki and us a chance to become better acquainted with one another."

"You don't have to tell her everything, you know. Bear

in mind I'm going to marry the girl."

"Yes, dear," returned Mrs. Landis fondly, and watched him out the door. Then she said, "Why don't we have our coffee in the living room, Vicki? It's so pleasant in there with the fire."

Will you walk into my parlor, said the Spider to the Fly. And what chance had the Fly ever had? That parlor was only additional evidence, if I needed any, of the chasm between my background and that of Toomey Landis.

I had by then made up my mind to surrender my love, if not gracefully, at least without an unbecoming struggle; so when Mrs Landis began, "This is the first time we've had a chance to—" I plunged right in before she could finish.

"I'm not right for Toomey," I said. "I know that, and—"

She seemed to have frozen with her coffee cup held in her hand. Her face, however, looked perfectly composed, although I thought I detected a slight quickening of interest in her eyes.

"My mother was a witch!" I burst out.

"How lovely, dear. I don't believe we've ever had a witch in the family before."

I felt my jaw slacken and pulled it quickly back into place.

"My grandfather may have had negro blood," I said, aghast at my own words. I had only the glimmer of a suspicion regarding that, bolstered somewhat precariously by a certain amount of research at the public library.

"I shouldn't think it matters after all this time, should you, dear?"

Didn't she even *hear* the things that were said to her? If she did, and if all that didn't shake her, what had she heard about me? And then the awful truth finally struck home. "You *want* Toomey to marry me," I cried. "You actually do!"

"Well, of course," she said. Suddenly, however, she set her coffee on the table and leaned forward in her chair. "You *do* love him, don't you?" she asked, with a kind of terrifying intensity.

"Too much," I said, "to fight over him, and everybody said you wouldn't want him to marry me."

"People say such ridiculous things, don't they? I knew the first time Toomey brought you here that he would ask you to marry him, and I hoped you would accept."

"But you couldn't have known. We hardly saw each other."

She smiled and reached for her coffee. "Toomey had never taken a girl into the dungeon before."

"But he said—" And then I bit my lip and started to laugh. "He said Pinky, Mrs. Pincus, liked to hear his girls scream from down there."

The look on her face was a mixture of love, pride, and resignation.

"That—things like that—I didn't know for a long time whether I loved Toomey or not because he was so different from the kind of man I'd always thought I would fall in love with."

"Tall, dark and handsome," she said. "A stranger, of course, and mysterious." She made it sound like a formula.

"I suppose all girls have silly dreams like that."

"Unfortunately some of us marry our dreams." A tartness had come into her voice, and I glanced quickly at her face, but there was nothing to be read there.

"About the dungeon," I said quickly. "I don't understand. How you knew, I mean."

"Because the dungeon is Toomey's sanctuary. That is where he picked up his life again after his father had driven him to abandon it. He would never risk filling it with memories he didn't hope to keep.

"Has Toomey told you about his father?"

"Only about the squirrel," I said.

Her face suddenly twisted with remembered pain. "He was only eight years old at that time," she said, "and he loved animals. The squirrels in our yard were so tame they would eat from his hand."

"Didn't his father realize how it would hurt him?"

"Toomey's father had no regard for anyone's feelings but his own. He was determined to make his son in every way an extension of himself—or destroy him. Ridicule is always a cruel weapon. Used against a sensitive child, by a beloved parent, it can be deadly. Toomey had started to stammer before he was six. After the squirrel incident he stopped speaking altogether.

"After his father's death I went to the special school where he had been for almost two years. I explained to him as well as I could, and in a way I hoped would prevent him blaming himself, what had happened, and then I told him I needed him at home with me. Only his eyes answered me; he did not try to speak.

"I had kept my father's tools—he had done fine woodworking in his spare time. We moved to this house and I had a young teacher from the manual training department of the high school come in and teach Toomey to use them. For months he sawed and pounded and sanded and polished out the storm inside him, while I sat nearby, knitting or reading his lesson to him, or sometimes just talking in a way that required no answer.

"It was almost a year before he began to speak again, with only an occasional stammer. The natural ebullience he'd had as a small child began to return, and it has been there ever since."

"And to think I wondered how he might react if the going ever got rough."

She smiled, and started to speak again, then glanced up as Mrs. Pincus entered the room with the coffee pot.

"And now," she said, after Pinky had seated herself and brought out her bit of embroidery, "do tell us more about your mother. Was she really a witch?"

"Women!" ejaculated Toomey when he came home an hour later and found the three of us chattering away as companionably as if we'd known each other forever. "Always ganging up on a guy. I must be out of my mind to take on another one."

I was, temporarily at least, unable to supply a fitting retort. All I could see was a little boy badgered into silence, fighting his way back, beaming. "Too late to wriggle out now," was the best I could finally manage. "You've already painted Peggy."

"Goodbye to careless youth," he said. "Let's get you out of here before Mother corrupts you completely."

He became satisfactorily loverlike, though, a short time later when he slipped his ring on my finger. 'It isn't much," he deprecated. "Just a ring."

It looked like rather a great deal to me. I told him so.

"Some day," he promised, "I'll buy you a diamond as big as a hickory nut, and an automobile so long it will have to be hinged to get around corners. In the meantime, of course, you'll have me."

"Beautiful life," I managed to murmur, before his lips came down on mine.

XXV

So Toomey and I stayed engaged, with his mother's blessing and with the wedding date tentatively set for mid-January, and I wore my engagement ring on my finger instead of on a chain inside my dress as some of the girls were doing. Miss Zimmerman kept glaring at it as if she more than half expected it to come sailing through the air and sting her to death. She said, "What do you hear from Mr. Jerome these days?"

"Hardly a thing," I returned cheerfully. "What about you?"

With autumn in full swing and winter coming on, Toomey's interests and mine switched more and more from city to country. We drove south toward the hill country to see the autumn-colored leaves and took long hikes through the woods looking for walnuts and hickory nuts for Pinky to use in her baking. One Sunday we drove north to the apple orchards, bought several baskets to store for winter use, and drank fresh cider as it poured from the presses. "Worms and all," remarked Toomey with cheerful relish, holding his empty glass for a refill.

With the first heavy snowfall he showed up at our own apartment in his unique version of outdoor winterwear, topped by a bright red stocking cap, and announced we were going bobsledding on Monument Hill. "In the dark!" I expostulated.

The hill was lighted, he explained. "Get a move on,

Vicki. Do you want the snow to melt before we get there? No, not that hat, this one." He pulled from one of his pockets a long-tasselled woollen cape like his own except that it was bright yellow. "Mother's compliments," he said.

'Mother's compliments' had been showing up frequently of late. Although I had little hope of ever understanding Mrs. Landis' mental processes, I was fast coming around to the point of view that if she was unbalanced, she was at least leaning in the right direction.

"Nothing seems to turn out right with you people," I commented. "Doesn't your mother know she's supposed to resent me?"

"Whatever for?" He seemed honestly astonished. "Who else would be crazy enough to take me off her hands?"

"Crazy me," I agreed. "With your mother to knit and Pinky to cook and you to bring home the bacon, I can look forward to a life of ease."

"Oh, didn't I tell you? Mother and Pinky are moving out the first of January."

"Toomey!" You did *not* tell me, and we are not driving your mother out of her own home. If anybody lives somewhere else, it should be us."

"Bravo! So just where—and how—do you propose transporting my dungeon?"

"I don't know, but I just naturally supposed we would all live together." I had accepted that concept, I realized now, with surprisingly little pain.

"And have Mother sobbing into her apron every time I take a strap to you! Don't be crazy."

"*You* be *serious*, just this once."

He was, more or less. It seemed the house they were moving to was one Mrs. Landis owned and had been renting out.

"But Toomey, she was unhappy there."

"Not *that* house," he said with ready understanding. "This used to be my grandfather's home."

He was your grandfather, Nubbin. Was Dr. Modesta a

grandfather too? Grandfather was a magic word that had never in my experience been implemented with reality. "Do you remember him, Toomey?"

The slow smile came on and moved into his eyes. "He was a quiet man, big and slow-moving like a friendly bear, and infinitely patient. That's what I remember most about him, his absolutely phenomenal patience. He had a dungeon too. He set up a child-size table and bench for me right beside his own. He'd show me how to do the same thing over and over and over, without a sign of impatience. We'd spend hours together, hardly speaking a word except for his instructions."

"I suppose it's all right then, for *them*. *You're* the one who's going to suffer. I'll never learn to cook as well as Pinky."

He shrugged elaborately. "After the first few lashes, you may knuckle down to it real well."

"Fudge," I said, and then explained to Toomey's cocked eyebrow, "Something I caught from Yasmina."

"Ah, that one," he said with an air of familiarity, for by that time he had heard enough about Yasmina to feel he knew her rather well. The process of revealing her to Toomey and Mrs. Landis had finally finished what Forster Jerome had started, the restoration of Yasmina to myself, not as the confused and driven woman of those final weeks of her life but in all the strength and beauty and pure hell-raising magnificence of what she had been before.

"Have you written your father about our engagement, Vicki?"

"He wouldn't be interested," I said.

"Are you sure?"

"Toomey, you don't understand. He never really approved of her, or of me, and he can't tolerate anybody going against him, in anything. He never forgives anybody for anything either. If you knew him, how he is, you wouldn't even worry about him."

"I'm not, believe me. It's you I'm thinking about. Hating isn't any good, Vicki."

"Don't you hate *your* father?"

"I've never been much good at hating, not over the long stretch anyway. To go on hating people no longer able to hurt you seems like wasting water on a fire that's already out."

That sounded suspiciously like Mrs. Landis to me, and probably was, but it was worth thinking about all the same. "I shouldn't have brought up your father," I said. "Darling, I'm sorry."

"I'm not. This is the first time you've called me darling."

He was right, and it had been bothering me that, while he spoke the language of love as naturally as he breathed, I found it difficult to respond in kind. "I *think* it," I whispered. "I think it all the time. I just don't seem to be able to say—such things."

He turned my face to his and kissed me gently on the lips. Then again, not so gently.

"Oh, Toomey!"

"Say it."

"I love you. I do love you, Toomey. You know I do."

I felt a weight move away from my heart. If this wasn't love, then I would never know love at all.

And if I still had reservations about our marriage, they were only vestiges of dreams left over from an overly sentimental girlhood. Not the 'tall, dark and handsome' nonsense, that had long since been driven quite out of my mind. Maybe it was that wonder and glory Yasmina had spoken of. Toomey seemed to operate on a much more earthy level, but maybe that was all right too. You couldn't expect a perfect playmate to be everything else as well.

"Will we still do things together after we're married?" I asked, suddeny wistful about the dancing and skating and picnics and all the rest.

Not until I felt his body begin to quiver, heralding another of those eruptions that shook him from time to time, did I realize what I had said. "If you dare laugh," I said, pounding his shoulders with my fists, "I'll murder you."

"Yes, sweetheart." he said. And then he did laugh, until the tears came. Mopping his eyes with his handkerchief and trying to pull a long solemn face, he said, "Vicki, baby, I swear to you we will keep right on doing things together even after we're married."

"Oh, hush," I said, feeling the heat rush into my face. *That* was the one thing in the world I didn't want to talk about, especially with him. I had pored over the pages of The Book until I was bleary-eyed, practically inscribing those provocative drawings upon my fevered brain, but I couldn't quite overcome the feeling I was overlooking something important, the way I had when Mama had explained about menstruation. As a clinical procedure, intercourse was probably possible to endure, and men certainly seemed to set great store by it, but there couldn't be much in it for a woman. Still, Yasmina had said in so many words that a woman *could* enjoy it. I lifted my head to meet Toomey's quizzical gaze. "Don't you dare start reading my mind," I warned, and then laughed with him.

Aunt Tabitha died the week after Thanksgiving, quietly and painlessly in her sleep. As soon as I was notified, I packed a few clothes and started downtown to catch a bus to Springhill, asking Eunice to let Toomey know.

"Why don't you?" she asked.

I had to admit that my thinking on that was a little confused. Toomey and I had planned to drive to Springhill some weekend soon so he and Aunt Tabitha could meet each other. I had thought we might see Margaret and Bob then too. I had no desire to re-establish contact with anyone else in the family, but I would no doubt have to see most of them, including my father, at Aunt Tabitha's funeral.

Knowing that Toomey was deeply concerned about my feeling for my father, I had said no more about it, and I told myself the reason I wanted to leave without telling him was that I wanted to spare him any further involvement with my family. The truth was, I felt ashamed for him to see that my own father would not speak to me; and I had no doubt at all that Justine would delight in involving both Toomey and me in a disgraceful scene if she found the slightest opportunity for doing so.

Eunice listened to my explanation, said Toomey wouldn't like it, but agreed to call him.

My idealistic if slightly scrambled notions carried me downtown, onto the bus, and about a third of the way to Springhill, whereupon they abruptly dissipated and left me feeling lonelier than I ever had in my life. From there on it only got worse.

The only friends I'd had in Springhill had been schoolmates, many of whom were no longer there, and the others had become little more than strangers. Exclusive of my own family, most of Aunt Tabitha's relatives were total strangers. I longed for Toomey with all my being; but having committed myself to seeing it through alone, I could only continue to do so.

Aunt Tabitha's lawyer called upon me the day before the funeral to assure me there were ample funds in the bank to cover the funeral expenses. He also told me that Aunt Tabitha had changed her will after my mother died and left the house to me.

I thanked him but without much interest. It wasn't a house I wanted, it was Toomey. He was a merry bouncing boy who was sure to drive me out of my mind sooner or later; but his arms were strong and his lips were sweet—and I wanted him.

I had in fact been wanting him so steadily and intensely that when he arrived, early next morning, I almost felt that I had wished him into being. If so, I'd made an inferior job of it because for once Toomey was looking as serious as I'd once thought I wanted him to be. "Why didn't you let me know?" he demanded, and I knew that he was angry.

"Oh, Toomey!" I whispered, and reached for him, right there in the middle of Aunt Tabitha's living room. "Toomey," I whispered into his coat collar. "Toomey, darling."

He didn't push me away but he made no move toward

receiving me either. "I'm afraid Mr. Wilson doesn't approve," he said, after a moment.

I took my arms away. "Mr. Wilson isn't the only one, is he?" I said. "Let me take your coat, and come on back to the kitchen. Have you had breakfast? I've just made a fresh pot of coffee."

"Vicki. Why?"

I looked at him and wanted to lie, but could not. "I was ashamed," I said, "for you to see the kind of family I came from."

"Yes," he said after a moment. "I would have been ashamed to have you meet my father."

"It was them I was trying to close the door on but it caught you instead. I'm sorry."

"Well, in that case." He smiled and patted my hand, and my world flipped right back into orbit.

My father did not come to the house but arrived with Justine and some of the others at the church, sitting just across the aisle from me without once meeting my eyes. Maybe it wasn't deliberate, I had no way of knowing. What I did realize was that I didn't hate him any more if I ever had, but that the paternal cord had been permanently severed. I saw him now simply as a tired, futile old man whose power to hurt me had been forever diminished.

After the graveside services were concluded, I went over to him and held out my hand. "Papa," I said, and he turned toward me. I thought he was going to speak, but presently his eyes slid away from me, he pressed his lips tightly together, and started to walk away.

"Papa—"

Justine darted a look of triumph in my direction before taking off after him. I took another couple of steps before I felt a detaining hand on my arm. "Let him go," said Toomey quietly.

"I had to try," I said.

"So now you have. Is your mother buried here, Vicki?"

I shook my head. "She and Dr. Modesta are in what they call the New Cemetery on the other side of town."

He led me to his car and opened the door. The starter ground and the engine caught. "Do you want to go back to the house?"

What I wanted was to curl up against him and be driven far away from this place and never come back. "I suppose I ought to," I said, "just to see that the house is straightened up a little, and be sure it's locked up. Since it's mine now," I added, and told him about that.

"You mean I'm marrying a property owner? How nice."

"Nice of Aunt Tabitha," I said, "but I won't be living in it and her lawyer says there isn't a prayer of selling it right now."

"Never mind, you can live in my house." He patted my arm.

I wanted to take Mama's dress back with me. It had been packed away in Aunt Tabitha's trunk in layers and layers of tissue paper; and when I lifted it out and held it up in front of me, it looked beautiful as ever except for a light tarnishing of the the metallic embroidery.

Toomey whistled appreciatively. "She was taller than you," he commented.

"She was a lot of things more than me," I said.

"Maybe, but not more a rebel. You are, you know."

"I'm not really, It's just that I seem to have a natural affinity for rebels."

"In case you're referring to me, I certainly do my rebelling much less flamboyantly than Yasmina ever did."

"You bet," I jeered. "Tearing around town in a fire engine with a naked woman on the hood, and cornering the market on girls. Very unobtrusive indeed."

I sobered then, remembering where we were—but then remembered something else. "Aunt Tabitha was as much a rebel as Mama. Who else would have dared display Mr. Wilson's picture all these years in the dead center of a Republican stronghold?"

I finished packing the dress in a box, then decided we ought to check the furnace to make sure it wouldn't burn the house down after we'd gone.

"Hey," said Toomey, "this must be where they bottled the famous elixir."

All the bottling equipment had long since been cleared away but the oil stove was still down there, along with the washing machine, ironing board, and a couple of ancient wicker rockers, in one of which Toomey promptly deposited himself. "Come here," he said, pulling me onto his lap and causing the old chair to groan alarmingly beneath the double weight.

"Toomey," I protested, "not now!"

His kiss effectively stopped further dissent. "Tiger Toomey!" I gasped with the first breath I was able to draw.

He grinned. "Gets better as we go along," he promised, and kissed me again.

"I'm hungry," I said, "aren't you?"

"You're always hungry. Maybe you've got a tapeworm."

"I didn't have much lunch," I protested, "and neither did you."

"Anything in the house to eat?"

The Ladies Aid from Aunt Tabitha's church had brought in a lunch but from the looks of things had carried any remains away with them. "Ought to be something in the refrigerator," I said. "Let me up, Toomey. I've just thought of something."

"So have I," he said, but let me go. "Ah, lovely," he said appreciatively, when I came back with my find. "What is it?"

"Blackberry wine. Last two bottles. Aunt Tabitha would be delighted for us to have it."

"Intoxicating?"

"Not really, but maybe we ought to eat first."

"We could just sample it."

So I obligingly got glasses and we repaired to the living room couch to do the sampling in style.

"Not bad," was Toomey's guarded verdict.

"Not much kick," I said. "Didn't figure there would be. Pour me another drop or two."

"Kind of sneaks up on you," I mentioned a few drops

later.

"Smooth," said Toomey, "and not a bit intoxshicting."

"Of course not."

"Mr. Wilson seems to be offended by us, though."

"He's lonesome. Aunt Tabitha's husband used to hang beside him before she moved him into her bedroom."

"I should think sho. Proper place for a husband." He stood up, walked carefully over and turned Aunt Tabitha's favorite president's face to the wall. "No offensh meant," he said, patting the back of the picture reassuringly, "but some things are private."

He came back and sat down, carefully, like a hen easing cautiously onto a setting of eggs. "Vicki," he said solemnly, "you deceived me. Your Aunt Tabitha's blackberry wine ish very very potent."

"Toomey, baby, you're getting drunk."

"Nonshense. You know very well I'm not a drinking man."

He regarded me reproachfully. "What're you going to do about it, push *me* into a fish pond?"

"Frozen over," I returned absently. "Aunt Tabitha's wine never made anybody drunk before." Hardly a fair comparison, I realized, since I'd never had more at one time than a small glass following a substantial meal.

"Bottle'sh empty," Toomey announced presently. "Mus' have had a leak."

"Mus'," I agreed, and stood up. When I returned with the second bottle, Toomey was carefully pulling down the window blinds. "Cozier this way," he explained with a dazzling smile.

Warning signals came on deep inside my brain and started buzzing like a swarm of bees as Toomey worked the cork out of the second bottle and refilled our glasses. "Here's to us," he said thickly. *"Skoal."*

Presently he took my glass out of my hand and set it down carefully on the table alongside his. Then he was holding me close, covering my face with quick warm kisses, his hand fumbling at the front of my dress.

"No," I said, but it was only a token protest. My arms gathered him closer.

Suddenly he released me and got to his feet. "Get up!" he said harshly, reaching for my hand. "Where's your coat?"

"Toomey!"

"Here it is. Put it on!"

My arms were pushed into the coatsleeves, my hat shoved down over my hair, and I was halfway dragged to the door and outside "Toomey, please," I protested.

"Come *on*, Vicki! Get a move on."

"You are a mean domineering brute," I pronounced with all the dignity I had left. And then we walked.

The freezing air soon did its work. My head began to clear and then I began to shiver, but still we walked. Presently I sneezed, and then again. "Don't mind me," I said crossly. "I enjoy having pneumonia."

We stopped. Toomey put his arms around me, pressed his cold cheek to mine. He said, "I'm sorry, baby."

"You could have," I said.

"Hush. I'm saving you for better things."

"Then you'd better be thinking about feeding me. You never did let me cook anything to eat."

We had ham and eggs with the last of a home-baked loaf, butter and honey, and lots of strong black coffee, then washed up the dishes together.

"Anything else will keep," Toomey said firmly. "We can drive out over the weekend if we think of anything to be done."

He recorked the bottle of wine. "We'll take this with us," he said. "I might be able to take out a patent on it. Ah yes, wait till I restore Mr. Wilson to his proper place in the world."

He straightened the picture and patted it gently. He said, "You take care of things here, Mr. Wilson, until we get back."

We turned out the lights and left, locking the front door behind us.

"Darling," I said, taking his arm, "you simply have to be the sweetest man in the world."

"Oh, well," said Toomey.

It occurred to me that of all the considerable effort that had so far been expended to bring me to my marriage bed a virgin, hardly any of it had been mine.

XXVI

I felt certain I loved Toomey, I even liked him most of the time, and a session of heavy petting on Peggy's front seat left me dazed, drifting and, let's face it, willing. Still, something was missing. Maybe the glory and wonder Mama had mentioned would come later, or probably it never came to most people at all.

Then it happened. As we came out of the church after Christmas Eve services, we stopped before the crêche which had been set up on the front steps. Father, mother, child. The eternal trinity, the very core and meaning of existence. As it was in the beginning, is now, and ever shall be.

I looked at Toomey. His head was bare and a few big snowflakes had caught in his hair. There was a radiance in his face, and strength and goodness. Father, mother, child. Our eyes met, our hands went out to each other, and I could say from a full heart what I had not been able to say at all before. "I do truly love you."

Once inside the car, we were in each other's arms. "We must come to church more often," he whispered, between kisses.

"It—just kind of came over me," I said.

The day after New Year's I proffered Miss Zimmerman my resignation, deliberately forestalling her jolly little ritual of firing me, then grudgingly allowing me to stay on. It was naturally frustrating for her. "You may be sorry," she prophesied, "this time next year."

"This time next year," I declared rashly, "I expect to be rocking a cradle," and was rewarded with a horrified stare.

Hoist by my own petard, in a manner of speaking, since my prediction was more unsettling to me than hers had been. With my wedding little more than two weeks away, I had a number of problems that were nowhere near being resolved.

The Book, a comfort in times past, had simply nothing to say about birth control. Dorothy asked me if I still remembered how to make The Stuff, but the truth was that I had never known. Mama would undoubtedly have told me if I had asked, but I had not.

I had heard about preparations you could buy but I would never in the world find courage to ask for such a thing, even if I knew what to ask for. I nearly died of embarrassment when I had to buy Kotex, even from a woman. I'd also heard of something called a diaphragm, but apparently one had to go to a doctor for that. As if I ever would!

While I was still sweltering in this dilemma, Toomey not only brought up the subject himself but volunteered to place himself in charge of all necessary purchases. He even had a suggestion or two on the subject. Tiger Toomey indeed!

"Would you rather I used something?"

"Please! I don't want to talk about it."

"You don't want to get pregnant either, do you? At least not right away."

Why should the man imagine a mere pregnancy would loom large in the mind of a girl who had no real expectation of surviving the wedding night! "Would *you* mind?" I countered.

"Oh no. I'd like a baby fine, the sooner the better; but owing to a light quirk of nature, you'd be the one to do the heavy work."

All I needed at a time like this was a physiological discussion of male vs. female. "Toomey, I—just don't want to bother with anything like that. Not with you."

"Sweet girl!"

"What did you do with Aunt Tabitha's blackberry wine? Let's finish it off."

"Sure we ought to risk it?"

"I *need* it, Toomey."

It may have been my ragged emotional state, or the fact that I'd recently finished a hearty lunch, but the wine had practically no effcct at all. Maybe that was just as well, I thought, considering what had happened—almost happened—on a previous occasion.

Toomey had, by some miracle of persuasion, wangled a week's extra vacation form PureSilk; but having no particular destination in mind, we planned to just get into Peggy after the ceremony and start out.

Toomey had looked pale even before the wedding, and his voice as he repeated his marriage vows sounded strange, although he didn't stammer even once. Even his kiss was restrained. I wondered if he too was having second thoughts about matrimony or if, heaven forbid, he was coming down with something catching.

We stopped a few miles out of town to remove the old shoes and wipe off the 'Just Married' soap scrawls from the car. When we got back in, Toomey loosened his tie, released the top button of his stiff-collared shirt, and heaved a vast sigh of relief.

"Your color's coming back," I observed kindly. "For awhile there I was afraid you were a goner."

"What a man has to go through in this world." He mopped his noble brow with his handkerchief. "At least it's over now and I can get down to some serious courting."

"It's a little late for that, isn't it?"

"Goodness, no. We've hardly scratched the surface!"

It was then that the fine philosophical approach to marriage I'd been so carefully nurturing for the past few days began to fall apart, and I spent the next couple of hours mulling over my apparently hopeless predicament.

I was an independent type, marriage was not for me. I didn't enjoy keeping house, my cooking came out with variable results. After making my own way for the better part of the four years, how could I stoop to asking a man for money, even to run the house? I must be out of my mind to go tearing around the country like this at the mercy of a half-crazy cherub who was, after all, little more than a chance acquaintance. How could I go to bed with him! Maybe I wouldn't be able to give in to him after all those years of protecting myself.

As soon as I got the chance, I'd slip away from this character, take the next bus back to Indianapolis, beg Miss Zimmerman for my job back, and live happily ever after listening to Mrs. Walker murder "Home on the Range."

"This looks like a nice hotel," said Toomey in my ear.

It didn't look like a very big hotel, but then it wasn't a very big town either. And what was I doing at a hotel anyway? It was snowing. Why had we ever come out in such a snowstorm?

"Happy, baby?"

"Of course I'm happy," I snapped. "Oh, darling, I really am happy, only—I'm so hungry. When are we going to eat?"

Eat, that was the ticket. Drink and be merry. Carouse the night away. Anything to delay the fatal moment.

"Poor sweet," sympathized Toomey. "We'll register and have our luggage sent up, then we'll eat. O.K.?"

I sat across the table from him and forced food bravely past the lump in my throat, felt it go down down down to form an even larger lump in my stomach. I would undoubtedly have indigestion. Maybe even a heart attack. I might even be going to cry.

"Feel better now?"

Toomey asked solicitously. He looked so *good,* damn him; so handsome and sweet and kind and considerate. Not exactly cherubic anymore, but *good*. "Fine," I said, "and you?"

He grinned at me, then reached across the table and patted my hand. "Let's go," he said.

He unlocked the door to our room, then stepped back for

me to go in ahead of him. When I turned he was leaning against the door jamb eyeing me speculatively. "I know a lot of dandy card tricks," he said.

"You're a liar," I said. "You haven't even got a deck of cards."

"So who needs cards for card tricks?"

He came inside and closed the door. Then I was in his arms, cradled lovingly and gently. "I love you Vicki," he whispered huskily. "I always will."

I felt the tension leave my body, along with all my doubts and fears, and then we began to kiss.

"Ah no, sweetheart, don't cry."

"I'm not crying,' I whispered. "it's just—oh darn it, it's running in my ears."

He lifted a corner of the sheet, tenderly attended to the tears I wasn't shedding, kissed my eyelids, then gathered me gently back into his arms, petting and crooning and kissing. I had never felt so cossetted in my life, so thoroughly content. Then other things started to happen. "Are you going to—do that again?" I whispered.

"Ummmmm. You don't mind, do you?"

What a question! "No," I heard myself say. "It isn't anywhere near as unpleasant as I thought it would be."

If he laughs now, I thought I will kill him. I will really and truly kill him. He didn't laugh.

Later, curled in his arms, my head on his shoulder, I heard him whisper, "Still love me?"

"Ummmmm," I murmured drowsily. "You're so nice and warm."

"That's the advantage of getting married in the winter," he chuckled. "Isn't it wonderful?"

"Better then The Book," I murmured, and heard him chuckle again.

"Where are we going tomorrow?" I asked, rousing a little.

"Baby, there is no tomorrow."

Next morning I came awake slowly, unaware for a moment where I was, then memory came flooding in. I moved carefully away from Toomey, then turned over on my stomach and propped myself on my elbows to look him over. He slept sprawled as a child sleeps, his lashes fanning his cheeks, and there was a sprinkling of fair-sized freckles across the bridge of his nose. I smoothed his eyebrows, then kissed his lips, feeling the roughness of his morning beard, watched his eyes slowly open and awareness come into them. He said, "Who's this sleeping in my bed?"

"Not Goldilocks exactly," I said, "but I had to sleep somewhere."

"Ummmmm. Now that you're here, you might as well kiss me again. Not like that, like this." He pulled me roughly down to him.

"Tiger Toomey!" I gasped.

"Now you know."

"What I wonder is, how did *they* know?"

"Hush! Still love me?"

"Oh Toomey," I said, burying my face against his shoulder. "I'm so glad you-re—you."

"It's very nice," he agreed, "especially now."

"I suppose we ought to get up."

"Not yet."

"Toomey—you're not—you wouldn't! Not in daylight!"

His face was flushed, a lock of hair had fallen over his forehead, his lips looked swollen, his eyes hot and unfocused. Then as I watched, his ears grew long and pointed, his eyebrows darkened and triangulated, tiny golden horns emerged from either side of his forehead. I clutched him fiercely to me.

After a while he sat up on the edge of the bed and stretched luxuriously, allowing me to admire his splendid physique.

"Toomey," I cried, "what happened to your back!"

He turned his head and gave me a long calculating look. "Don't you really know?"

"How should I—oh no!"

Oh yes, said the look on Toomey's face.

"Darling," I said, reaching out to touch those savage weals. "Darling, I'm sorry."

"Kindly watch your tongue, Mrs. Landis. Those are my stripes of honor. Only happens when a man is—if you'll pardon my saying so—a truly stupendous lover."

I gave him a look that should have disintegrated him on the spot but it didn't even singe his eyebrows. "I'll have to wear gloves," I said.

He stood up and continued flexing his muscles. "Something wrong?" he inquired after a moment.

"Hard to be sure," I said, "with so little to compare you with. No, Toomey! We've got to get up!"

"Explain that 'so little,' please."

"My nephew Robert, if you must know. Of course, he was only three years old at the time."

Temporarily stunned into silence, he shrugged into a dressing gown and walked over to the window, pulled aside the drapery. "Haven't glanced outside lately, I suppose," he mentioned presently.

"Haven't found the time," I returned.

"Come," he said. "Look."

"Snow," I said, quite unnecessarily. During the night of my deflowering the entire town had been practically submerged in the pretty fleecy stuff, and it was still coming down. Across the street it had drifted halfway up the doors of the shops, and the street itself seemed completely deserted.

"Well," said Toomey, "we won't be doing any traveling today. Might as well go back to bed."

"Nothing doing. I want my breakfast."

"Why should you always be the one who gets hungry when I do all the work? Oh well, if you want to eat, we'll eat. We can go back to bed later."

"Later we are going for a walk," I said firmly. "Snow or no snow, we are going for a nice long cold walk."

I was beginning to sense, however dimly, that there had been more than one reason for all the physical activity of our early courting days.

"Yes, sweetheart," he said, with a meekness that didn't deceive me for a minute, and trotted off whistling to shower and shave.

Heaviest snowfall in thirty years, they were saying in the coffee shop. Planes had been grounded, trains were running hours late, and all roads were impassable until further notice.

"Marooned," I said. "Wouldn't you know?"

"Do we mind?"

"Of course not. You know some dandy card tricks."

He beamed at me approvingly, snapped his fingers, and waltzed right off to buy a deck of cards. He actually had mastered some rather cunning card tricks and soon had attracted a small audience in the hotel lobby. A walk, however, proved to be out of the question. We read day-old newspapers, and Toomey swapped tall stories with some of the other men in the lobby, which at least kept his mind off going to bed until after lunch.

By the second day the sidewalks had been partially cleared so we could walk and window shop, and that evening a movie house opened its doors just down the street. "Sort of gives me a new slant on things," I observed when we were back in our hotel room, "now that I know what happens after the fadeout."

"Stick with me, baby, and you'll never stop learning."

"I'm sure."

"Vicki, are you still sure you don't want—one of us to use something?"

"Why?" I asked.

"Because, if we don't, the way we're going at it, you're sure as hell going to get pregnant."

"Not a chance," I said. "It's the wrong time of the month."

"Oh," said Toomey, sounding impressed, and for once not inclined to pursue the subject. Which was fortunate because I didn't know whether it was the right or wrong time of month, or even what that had to do with it. I only halfway remembered Mama mentioning something along those lines a long time ago.

"Vicki, I'm not—being too much for you, am I?"

Those waves of tenderness which kept sweeping over me were going to swamp me yet. "No," I said. "After all, it's like you said, you do most of the work."

"Call it labor of love. Darling, I have never been so happy."

"Neither have I," I said. "And Toomey—I like for you to love me."

"Baby! Don't say things like that when I don't even have my shoes off. But I'll hurry."

XXVII

Home from the honeymoon, it took me less than a week to figure out exactly why Mrs. Landis and Pinky had been so cooperative about moving out and leaving the house to us; more specifically, leaving their darling boy to me. "Mrs. McSwain," I reminded him, "comes on Monday, Wednesday, and Friday. On Monday she does the washing."

Not a smidgen of embarrassment on that cherubic face, only a polite questioning look.

"Unless, of course, something prevents it, in which case she will make an effort to get it done on Wednesday, which is tomorrow."

So now something does move into his face. Possibly a remembrance of our disemboweled washing machine, its vital organs scattered over the laundry room floor? "I need some special washers that had to be ordered. They may be in by now, though; I'll drop by tomorrow and see. When I get that old machine going again, it's really going to whiz."

A quick glance at my face dampened his enthusiasm, but only a little. "Maybe she could do something else tomorrow."

"The thing is, that's what she did on Monday. Actually tomorrow's her ironing day, except there's nothing to iron until something get's washed—and dried. She could clean a little, I suppose, but only with the broom. Something seems to have happened to the vacuum cleaner."

"Oh, did I forget to tell you? I took it down to the

dungeon. I'm figuring out a new way to set the brushes, then it'll really . . ."

"—whiz," I finished helpfully. "And while I think of it, in case you should happen to be looking for my wrist watch, I've hidden it."

"Gosh, honey, I'm sorry." He actually *looked* sorry, although I more than half suspected it was mostly for the unavailability of my wrist watch. His next words bore that out. "I'm a wizard with a balance wheel," he said.

Mrs. Landis had the grace to appear somewhat embarrassed when I tackled her on the subject. "Oh dear," she said, "it would have sounded so discouraging to have told you *everything*." She was biting her lip but I wasn't sure whether it was to keep from laughing or crying.

"It wouldn't have made any difference," I admitted. "I'd have married the scrounge anyway. At least it can't get any worse."

She and Pinky exchanged somewhat startled glances, then pressed me to have another slice of orange pound cake and more tea. I accepted. I had a feeling I needed to build up as much strength as I could, it being clear to me now that Toomey simply couldn't resist unrigging anything that had moving parts and shifting them around a little. "I'm surprised you haven't started on me," I'd muttered only that morning.

"You sort of have to get the feel of things before you start taking them apart," he'd explained. "It won't be much longer now."

"Mrs. Mullery says *she* wouldn't put up with such goings-on for a minute," I reported now to Mrs. Landis and Pinky.

"How fortunate that she will never have to," replied Mrs. Landis, quite serene again.

The thought of sour-faced Walter Mullery sitting in the middle of the floor surrounded by the ruins of a washing machine was too much for me. I laughed. Even if the Mullerys *were* another of the problems she had abandoned to me.

I had first made their acquaintance on a Sunday afternoon shortly before our marriage when they had appeared, unyearned for and unbidden, on the Landis doorstep. I heard Toomey say, "Quick, Mother, let's hide. Here come the Mullerys."

Mr. Mullery was a tall man, broad-shouldered but skinny, with cold gray eyes and a mouth like an inverted U. Mrs. Mullery's eyes were a watery blue but sharp and inquisitive. Her reddish brown hair was in tight little sausage curls that never looked combed between one setting and the next, but it was her figure that fascinated me the most. Her bosom appeared to have melted downward and settled around her hips, both being draped on that memorable occasion in bright green chiffon. I had not yet dared to look at her feet, so even now I wasn't sure whether they had become the final depository for the melting process, or if that had reversed at her thighs, leaving her lower limbs as skinny as her bosom.

Mr. Mullery had done most of the talking on that occasion, and would continue to do so. They had just heard, don't you know, of Toomey's engagement, and the just *ha-a-a-d* to meet his lovely *fee-ancy*.

Judging from their faces, they weren't in the least favorably impressed with what they saw, but they were *so-o-o-o* glad to meet me. Did my parents live in the city? What did my father do for a living ? How long had I known Toomey? What a lovely ring! A stone that large—don't you know—you couldn't help wondering if it was *real*.

When the questions stopped—if they ever did—answers were going to be expected, and that was when Julia Victoria Broadbent was going to blow a gasket.

But no. My shining knight was already on his feet, dragging me to mine. "Sorry to rush off, folks, but we're late now. You know how it is, can't keep the party waiting." And we made our escape—that time.

Mr. Mullery, I learned, had been district manager for a farm machinery corporation. It was a traveling job so he hadn't been around home much until he'd been laid off a year or two earlier. They were reported to "have enough money to live on," whatever that was supposed to mean. In an effort to augment that income, however, Mr. Mullery was prone to institute lawsuits against people, including a man whose car he'd collided with, a woman across the alley suspected of slipping her potato parings into the Mullery garbage pails, and a woman who had allegedly slapped Mrs. Mullery's face during an altercation over a bridge score.

"And they live right next door to you!" I'd cried after that first meeting. How on earth do you put up with them?"

"It isn't so bad," Mrs. Landis had returned in her usual lightsome manner. "We hardly ever see Mr. Mullery and she's such a wonderful example."

"Example!"

"Yes, dear. Nobody in the world sets quite as good an example as a bad example, do you think?"

What I thought was, if Toomey Landis didn't finish me off, his mother was sure to. And failing that, there was always Mrs. Mullery, who now lived next door to *me*. "I certainly hope Toomey doesn't turn out like his father, dear. There was quite a scandal about that, I can tell you."

"I can guess who started it," I shot back.

Mrs. Mullery and I were *not* going to be friends. The battle lines were drawn but I was already faced with the necessity of building up a more effective arsenal, simple irony being wasted. She nearly went into convulsions, though, the morning the fire engines pulled up in front of our house.

After the worst of the commotion was over, I called Mrs. Landis. "I'm sorry," I said into the telephone, "but we won't be able to have you and Pinky to dinner this evening after all."

"That's quite all right, dear. I do hope there's nothing wrong though."

"Not really. It's just that the kitchen is a little waterlogged."

"Oh, dear. What's Toomey been up to now?"

That started a giggle, which ended abruptly in a hiccup. "Toomey isn't *altogether* responsible *this* time," I said, and hiccupped again.

"Vicki, dear, are you all right?" This time my mother-in-law's voice sounded satisfyingly anxious.

"I think so. Look, I'd better tell it from the beginning. I was just starting breakfast, and when the bacon started sizzling, I—well, I ran for the bathroom, and Toomey came after me. And you know how he is, I couldn't get it through his head it was nothing to worry about, so—well, we both forgot about the bacon, and it caught fire. And then the curtains caught."

"Oh, dear!"

"It wouldn't have been so bad, only the fire department sort of messed things up more than they were already."

"You poor darling. Pinky and I will come right over and—" She stopped short. After a moment she said, "Vicki, it isn't—you're not—"

"I wouldn't be at all surprised," I said, "although it's disgracefully soon."

"It's nothing of the sort. It's perfectly lovely. Did Toomey go back to work?"

"He had to," I said, "although in his present state, he'll likely as not knit himself up into a stocking. And we aren't actually sure yet. I haven't seen a doctor."

"Then you must, dear. And don't do a thing to the house until we get there. Vicki, I'm so excited!"

"So am I," I said, "I think."

All right, Yasmina, chalk up another blooper for your darling daughter, this tone-deaf creature you raised from a nubbin knowing all about The Stuff. And there are other things now, Yasmina, just as you predicted there would be. Don't imagine, either, that I'm in all that hurry for a baby, nor do I labor under any delusion that I am at all well qualified for motherhood; in fact, the very idea scares me half out of my enfeebled mind. So exactly how do I account for my present predicament? I'll tell you, Yasmina. I'm nuts about the guy.

"I am the kind of girl other girls talk about," I had mentioned to Toomey a few nights earlier.

"Oh?" he had returned equably.

"Brazen, sort of."

"Naturally."

"Not naturally at all. A nice girl isn't supposed to enjoy it, at least not very much."

"Who says?"

"Scads of people."

"Even The Book?"

"Oh that thing. It led to so many misconceptions in my poor twisted mind, somebody ought to burn it."

"Tell me more."

"Well, for one thing, it made it seem that *it* wasn't—well, much of anything, really. It did mention that it—you know—swelled a little and got maybe seven inches long, but then so is a pencil."

"Don't stop now, for heaven's sake!"

"Well, from what it said—I mean it just seemed to—sort of—go in and then—out again—sort of like swabbing out an ear or something—and I never dreamed it would be so much work. For you, I mean, although I do try to help. There, you see how depraved I'm getting?"

"Poor little mixed-up baby," he crooned. "A man and a woman in love are supposed to enjoy each other's bodies." He began to wax eloquent about the Etruscans and the early Romans, the mating habits of the South Sea islanders, and about it being modern laws and religious restrictions that had messed up people's natural impulses and given them complexes, which was a shame, because—

His voice began to exert a hypnotic effect. I found myself nodding even when I didn't in the least agree with him. "There now," he finished. "See what a fortunate girl you are to have a husband who can explain these things to you?"

"You're probably the devil," I said.

He looked momentarily nonplused but almost immediately recovered. "Tell you what we'll do," he said. "We'll write a book ourselves giving the straight dope."

"Good for us. You can do the drawings."

"We'll probably have to do a good bit of research. Which reminds me, don't you have periods like other girls?"

"Not exactly. Mine are variable. I should be starting any day now though."

I should have started a couple of weeks earlier, I knew full well, but no point in giving everything away in advance. Much more exciting to set the house on fire.

After another week or two the nausea eased off, which was about the same time the workmen completed the repairs to the kitchen and we could start eating at home again. Mrs. Landis ordered several skeins of soft wool in baby shades, Pinky laid a supply of flannel for gowns and diapers, and Toomey traded in his beaming look for one more appropriate to a prospective father, that of a cock who hasn't the slightest doubt he is crowing the sun up.

"Dr. Roberts says around the first of November," I said in answer to Eunice's query, and received the response that was going to become routine. "So soon?"

"What would Yasmina say?" Toomey wondered.

"Well, she forgave me a tin ear, so maybe she'll overlook this too. As a matter of fact, she's probably pleased, and *your* mother's certainly happy about it. And Toomey, I'm quite durable, and the baby is firmly lodged now, and not more than a couple of inches long, so we can perfectly well do skating some night."

He looked horrified. "You m-m-m-m-mustn't risk it, sweetheart. L-l-let's go to a movie instead and hold hands."

I had written Margaret about my marriage, and now I wrote to tell her about my pregnancy. I thought of writing Papa too, and then I was sure it would be no use. Left to himself, he might have relented, but with Justine to keep prodding his prejudices, he would never have a chance. I added a note to Margaret's letter asking her to tell him about it when she had an opportunity and thought he might be interested, and left it at that.

This baby would simply have to go short on grandfathers, but he would have a father who was a dynamo, besides being gentle, sensitive and understanding.

The first two weeks in June PureSilk closed down to give all employees simultaneous annual vacations. Toomey came home from his first day back at work and reported, "Fred Currier got married on his vacation."

"Oh?" I looked at his face. "Not to Eunice?"

"No. Some girl he met when he was at home visiting his parents."

"I wonder what happened."

I felt a little guilty for not *knowing* what happened, but I hadn't seen either Eunice or Dorothy in several weeks.

"Fred doesn't say much, just goes around acting like a spanked puppy. He did mention something about a party he had attended where everybody got pretty drunk."

"They've been engaged forever," I said.

"We can drive over after supper if you like."

"Yes," I said. It would be hard to know what to say to Eunice but she had always been good to me. If I could help her now, I would.

After saying hello to the girls, Toomey with exquisite tact left us alone to discuss the situation, but Eunice didn't have much to say. She was annoyed that Fred hadn't told her himself instead of letting her find out by the plant grapevine, but she said she wasn't really surprised. "It wasn't his mother's fault," she said. "At least, we could have got married if we'd wanted to badly enough. Other people do and manage to get along but we—just didn't."

It was on the whole a stilted uncomfortable visit, and I was relieved when Toomey came back and swept us all along to go have a root beer.

"Toomey," I said later that evening, "thank you."

"For what?" he asked, a certain wariness in his manner.

"For sweeping me off my feet before I'd wasted years of my life on you."

"Pah, I didn't have a chance. You were already laying for me before you shoved old Ray into that fish pond."

"So you finally caught on," I said.

"You really are a hussy," he said, seizing me.

"I'm getting big enough to be *two* hussies."

"Reminds me of what the midget said when he married the fat lady. 'Acres and acres of woman, and she's all mine.' "

"Toomey Landis!"

"Hush. I love every acre of you, baby."

XXVIII

As if in retribution for my secret worries about asking Toomey for money, the first thing he had done after our return from the honeymoon was to dump the handling of our financial affairs squarely into my lap. I was sure if Mrs. Weaver of Sylvester's Fine Shoes ever got wind of it, she would fall into a trembling fit. "I don't know a thing about bookkeeping," I protested.

"Nothing much to it," said Toomey. "Here, I'll show you."

Temptation was strong to mention that anybody who knew enough about anything to show somebody else might as well go on handling it himself. I resisted only because, with Mrs. McSwain doing most of the housework, I felt I ought to be making myself useful in some way.

Actually it was fairly simple from a bookkeeping standpoint. Income came from Toomey's salary, which varied from week to week, depending on the time spent on emergency call-ins, and from five sources in the form of royalty checks arriving at intervals throughout the year. There might also be an occasional windfall from one or another of the various projects Toomey undertook from time to time, such as once he'd ordered a carload of citrus fruit from Florida and sold it in small lots to fellow employees. On another occasion he'd done the same with a carload of coal. Occasionally he might accept a commission for a table or a cabinet. Nothing but versatile was Toomey.

Our outgo was pretty versatile too, and there seemed to be considerably more of it than there ought to be, but I acknowledged my lack of experience in such matters, especially as related to an urban household in, as Springhill would have put it, "comfortable circumstances." Most of Toomey's personal expenditures were for tools and material for use in the dungeon, and I could scarcely hope to understand all that was going on down there.

Toomey was addicted to giving presents too—small, medium and large presents for me, his mother, Pinky. Shortly after our marriage he had presented me with a new Chevrolet coupe like the one his mother drove. He had insisted we needed a piano to replace the one which Mrs. Landis, being the only serious musician in the family, had taken with her when she moved; said he liked to "sort of fiddle around on a piano" now and then, such fiddling usually consisting of playing popular tunes by ear, although he'd had lessons when he was younger. One needed a piano anyway, for parties and things, and I rather enjoyed "fiddling around" on it myself, even with my defective musical ear. We'd bought an upright, however, to take up less space.

I silenced any misgivings I might have had about all this cheerful spending by reminding myself that it was and had been Toomey's and his mother's way of living, so they could evidently afford it. Personally I expected to not have the slightest difficulty getting accustomed to it, having thoroughly enjoyed the glimpse I'd got of gracious living during my association with Mr. Jerome. If this was another of the attractions of Yasmina's brave new world, I could bear it well.

Nevertheless, when the Mattson royalty check arrived in August, I did feel impelled to mention to Toomey that it was much smaller than previous ones had been.

"Yes," he said, "it would be. They were closed down for several weeks." Royalty, he explained was paid only on units actually manufactured. "Some of the others may come up a little short too."

"We could cut back some on expenses," I suggested.

"Certainly not," he returned, seeming displeased at the thought. "There's no necessity for cutting back."

Ah well, he probably had irons in the fire I knew not of. Probably he would get around to telling me about them sometime. In any case we were living within his salary except for the piano and Chevrolet, which were once-in-a-long-time items.

It was a comfortable feeling knowing Mrs. Landis had her own income, besides which I was coming to believe as much as Toomey did in his indispensability at the mill, because so far he'd not been laid off for a single day, even when they were running at less than half strength. So why worry, especially when my own little manufacturing project was requiring my best efforts just now? Lately he was becoming very restless indeed.

"Like his pa," said Toomey, the now familiar lord-of-all-creation look taking over his face.

"Suppose he's a girl?"

The beaming was in no wise dulled. "I always liked girls," he said.

"Going to be a big one anyway, judging by the bulge."

"Oh, Vicki!" Suddenly burrowing his face into my shoulder, he held onto me as if he would never let me go. "If anything should happen to you—"

"Nothing's going to happen except I'm going to have a baby."

"Doesn't it bother you at all? You never complain."

"I'd be scared silly if I thought about it. So I don't. They say you don't even remember it afterward."

"I should have *made* you use something," he said savagely.

"You were too busy making *me*," I reminded him. "It's going to be all right, Toomey. Just go on being happy about it."

"Oh, I'm happy, but I'm scared too." He kissed me hard, then walked over to the piano and started picking out a melody with his right hand, gradually moving in chords with his left.

". . . Vicki and me . . . And baby makes three . . .
. . . We're happy in my . . . blue . . . heav . . . en."

He warbled joyously with his head thrown back, his eyes half closed. *May she always know the value of what she has*. Yes, Yasmina, I do know. Father, mother, child. Toomey, me, the bulge. In that moment even the bulge was doubly precious to me.

Since I had outdistanced even the dresses Mrs. Landis and Pinky had made for me, Toomey and I decided to celebrate our nine-months wedding anniversary at home, just the two of us.

"More wine?" inquired Toomey solicitously, after we had finished our dessert.

"It isn't fun any more now that it's gone legal."

"That's a fine law-abiding viewpoint. Just because the porch fell in when you were trying to vote for Mr. Hoover."

"It would fall faster and harder if I stepped up on it now. Oops!"

"What's the matter, Vicki? What is it?"

I wished I could be more certain. "This kid turns over like a rhinocerous," I complained. "I'll bet he weighs sixteen pounds."

"Maybe he's more than one."

"Why not? Why should the Dionnes have all the glory anyway? Maybe I can have six and bring the title back to the United States."

"Heaven forbid! Vicki, you're—"

"That wasn't a kick," I said, "unless he's wearing cleats."

He blanched a little but his manner immediately became brisk and businesslike. "Better time it," he said.

'Better write it on the calendar. There may not be another for two weeks."

"I'd better call Dr. Roberts."

"For a false alarm? Leave us continue this celebration."

"I'll sing to you then."

"Do so. That should make up his mind for him in a hurry."

Toomey obliged by a spirited if not entirely accurate rendition of a couple of popular favorites, which I attempted to join him in singing with somewhat disastrous results. The effort left us both breathless with laughter, and brought on another pain.

"Twenty-five minutes," said Toomey.

"If this kid values his mother's reputation at all, he will see his shadow and retreat for another couple of weeks. We have been married exactly nine months today. Anyway, it's raining."

"Sleeting, as a matter of fact," Toomey announced somewhat gloomily, then launched determinedly into "Sonny Boy," but stopped almost at once, explaining that if it did happen to be a girl, and waiting on the threshold so to speak, he didn't want to hurt her feelings. He slipped into "Blue Room" instead, but his heart wasn't in it any more; and when the next pain arrived in just under twenty minutes, he insisted on calling Dr. Roberts, who after hemhawing a bit decided that, since it was such a stormy night, maybe we should start for the hospital.

Toomey brought our wraps from the hall closet and dropped them down in a pile on the sofa, then fell upon them and began digging frantically. "I thought somebody was supposed to keep calm," I remarked.

"I'm p-p-p-p-perfectly calm. I just want to get started. Here. I'll help you with that."

"I can put on my own hat," I said. "You get the suitcase."

He tore off, tore back with the suitcase in his hand, started out the door, came back and turned off the lights, then went rushing, hatless and coatless, into the night. In something like thirty seconds he was back, moisture dripping from his hair.

"It's all right," I said comfortingly. "I need all the delaying action I can get."

"Oh, Vicki, sweetheart!" He threw himself down beside me and placed his arms around where once my waist had been.

My tower of strength, my ever-present help in time of trouble, my bulwark against all disaster. I wasn't sure I wanted to go tearing off to the hospital with this mercurial creature even if I did decide to have a baby. "Unless you plan to add midwifery to your accomplishments," I advised, "best you pull yourself together."

"I know, honey. It's just that—oh God, Vicki, I love you so much!"

"I love you too, darling. That's the way it all started, remember?"

We finally made it outside and into the car, but it was indeed a horror of a night; windy, well below freezing, and a sleeting rain pelting down and freezing in sheets on everything it touched, including the streets and, of course, the windshield. Toomey drove most of the way to the hospital with his head out the window, but Peggy's faithful Packard heart never missed a beat.

John Toomey Landis was born at five o'clock the following morning, exactly nine months and one day after our wedding. By the time Toomey was allowed to see what was left of me, I was already drifting off into a drug-induced haze, but there was one more thing I had to take care of before I let go. "You look him over," I instructed Toomey, grabbing him by the lapels. "You look him over good and be sure he's exactly what we ordered. No telling what these people may try to palm off on us."

"I already have, baby; counted everything three times and it's all there. He's beautiful, honey; absolutely beautiful."

I knew better than that. He was wrinkled, red-faced, and probably squalling his head off.

"What about you, baby?" Toomey's voice was still coming to me through the haze.

"I am absolutely pluperfectly dandy," I said, and went out like a snuffed candle.

XXIX

"One would think," I said, fixing my most baleful eye on my lawful wedded husband, "you'd had the baby yourself."

"My contribution may have seemed comparatively negligible," he conceded, "but—or at least so am I assured—necessary. And I assure you it was most willingly given."

"How well I remember!"

"Oh, by the way, this is for you." "This" turned out to be a small white box which contained a ceramic bowl full of purple violets with a pearl choker coiled in the center like the stamen of some exotic flower. "But Toomey," I protested, "these look like real pearls!"

"Real pearls for a real girl," he said, fastening them about my throat. "And that's a real baby too, honey. He's absolutely beautiful. Intelligent too. Lies there with his eyes wide open, just looking around."

I had seen this infant myself, briefly it was true, but long enough to be absolutely certain that he was red-faced, wrinkled, his eyes were completely unfocused, and his head was covered with some long spiky-looking stuff with only the slightest resemblance to human hair. He was mine, and when I got him home, I'd do the best I could with him, but he was certainly no beauty.

"Was it—so very bad?" Both Toomey's face and voice had suddenly gone very serious.

"I don't remember much about it," I told him, more or

less truthfully. "You didn't forget to call your mother, did you?"

"She and Pinky are both spinning cartwheels. I just wish I could touch him, Vicki, maybe hold him for a minute. I asked the General but she sniffed at me as if I was breaking out with smallpox."

The General had already become his name for Miss Tower, Supervisor of Nurses, a harsh-voiced strapping sort of individual who ran the maternity ward as if it were a boot camp. "So I heard," I said. "She's afraid you'll fall asleep outside the nursery window and crash through the glass."

"Bah! He's my baby, isn't he? Why can't I hold him a little?"

I caressed his face gently with my fingers. "You really did want a baby, didn't you?"

"I've always wanted a baby. I used to ask Mother for one every Christmas until I found out what caused them."

There was nobody like him, absolutely nobody, and he was mine. It was a sobering thought.

Mrs. Landis and Pinky arrived that afternoon with "Just a few little things now, dear. We'll bring the rest over after you get home from the hospital."

Fortunately, I reflected, we hadn't furnished the upstairs bedrooms since they'd moved out; now they could accommodate the overflow. I also reflected that this was undoubtedly going to be the most thoroughly spoiled brat in the universe. Pinky, having no grandchildren of her own, was as bad as Mrs. Landis.

"You can try nursing the baby in the morning," the floor nurse told me that evening.

"Good," I said, but the truth was I had no enthusiasm whatever for the undertaking. Maybe I was an unnatural mother, but that was the way it was.

Next morning another nurse carried him in, swaddled in a blue blanket. "Now then," she crooned in that ridiculous way some nurses have, "both mama and baby have to get the hang of this so we just have to be patient."

Mama could be patient all she wanted to, but not baby.

After a couple of exploratory nuzzlings, he attached himself like a limpet and began to suck. "Well, I never," said the nurse. "Not very often that happens."

"He's a smart baby," I said. And he was really rather a pretty baby, now that I took another look at him, hair and all. "Mama's little love," I said tenderly. "Mama's poor hungry baby."

Good heavens, who was that maudlin creature rambling on and on? But he *was* pretty, and so good and trusting. "Little John," I said experimentally, then, "John Toomey Landis."

"Better try to burp him now, Mrs. Landis. We don't want our boy getting a tummy ache, do we? Here, I'll help you."

Nothing simpler. I'd read all about it. But once more I was being betrayed by the printed word, which hadn't mentioned a thing about baby's capacity to become spherical. How do you burp a ball anyway? Well, first you unfold it, straighten out the little legs, pat the tiny back. There it comes. Good baby. You and mama are going to be great friends.

"Your husband was up here looking at that baby around midnight," the nurse said, and giggled. "Miss Tower was fit to be tied when she found out about it."

"Miss Tower can go roll her hoop," I said.

Toomey arrived late that afternoon, as usual bearing gifts: a teddy bear, a large red rubber ball, and a woolly lamb on a platform with wheels. I said, "Really, darling, he's only two days old."

"He doesn't like it here. Let's bust out and go home where I can play with him."

"He doesn't want to play, he wants to eat and sleep. You could do with a little more sleep yourself. Such as around midnight."

He looked aggrieved. "The General ratted on me," he said.

"But you do need your sleep. You're looking tired."

"I went in a little late this morning. Nobody minds as long as nothing goes wrong with the machines."

"There's nothing wrong with the baby, is there, that you keep watching him so much?"

"No, sweetheart, of course not. I just like to look at him."

"Well," I said, "he is not, on the whole, a bad-looking baby."

"Not bad-looking!' And then we both dissolved into gales of laughter.

A day or two later I heard a couple of nurses gossiping together in the corridor outside my door. ". . . a wife and three kids," I heard one of them say. "Heaven only knows when he'll be able to find another job."

It didn't indicate an unusual situation for those days but it did have its usual dampening effect. I would never quite be able to forget the anxiety and hurts of my own period of unemployment, and it must be a million times worse for a man with a family to support.

"Closed down for good," I heard another nurse say. "And where are all those people going to find jobs, I ask you?"

"What's closed down for good?" I asked when one of the nurses came into my room a few minutes later.

"PureSilk." She turned to me, frowning. "But you must know that. Your husband worked there, didn't he?"

"Worked," she had said. Not "works" but "worked."

"You're not feeling sick, are you, Mrs. Landis?" The voice seemed to be coming to me through a fog, but fortunately helped to clear it as well. "No," I said. Because Toomey was indispensable. Everybody said that. Nobody else knew about the machines. And the mill wouldn't close for good. Women had to have silk stockings, didn't they?

On another day, while we had waited for Dr. Armstrong, I had prayed, desperately but silently, that my mother was not really dead. I had much that same feeling now, but I tried to push it away. I couldn't afford to worry about it. I was a nursing mother. Having brought the helpless mite into the world, the least I could do was protect his food supply.

Besides, I was being selfish to think only of us. What

about Eunice? And Ray Gillian and Fred Currier and a lot of others? To say nothing of a few million other people I'd never so much as heard of?

While I was still tossing that around in my mind, a nurse came in carrying a long white florist's box which she'd just picked up from the desk.

"Oh!" I breathed, the way any woman would at the sight of two dozen American Beauty roses barely into bloom, and in my case there was another reason for elation. If Toomey had lost his job, or was in the slightest danger of losing it, he wouldn't be blowing his money on pearls and roses, would he?

"I'll get a vase," said the nurse, and left.

I reached for the small white envelope, pulled out the card. The angular black script struck at me like the crashing of cymbals. "Now you understand," it said, and was signed "Forster Jerome."

There was no doubt in my mind about what I was meant to understand. It was his reason for refusing to take advantage of a troubled girl's infatuation for him.

The nurse came back carrying a vase. "If I put it here on your bed table, Mrs. Landis, perhaps you'd like to arrange them yourself."

I would like a great many things, I thought, such as not having to explain to Toomey why Forster Jerome should be sending me roses upon the birth of my child. "Yes," I said to the nurse, "I would."

It would, I decided, furnish an opportunity to reflect upon my own behavior during those days. I must have been a dreadful trial to Mr. Jerome, with all my girlish neuroses, and in return he had given me another chance. A chance that had led me ultimately to Toomey and little John. Dear God, I ought to be sending roses to *him*!

Toomey's reaction was a long low whistle, then, "You've been holding out on me, baby."

I handed him the card, watched his face become puzzled, then something more than that. "I told you about Mr. Jerome," I said.

His face was a study of emotions, none of which I felt inclined to try to interpret. "Mr. Jerome," he said reflectively. "Come to think of it, that's all I ever heard you call him."

"I'd have been scared to death to call him anything else."

Then we were both laughing like fools. That was when the General came striding in, sniffed the air suspiciously like a bloodhound entering unfamiliar territory, said, "Good afternoon, Mr. Landis. Nice to see you here during visiting hours for a change."

"Thank you, ma'am," beamed Toomey at her disappearing back.

"Which reminds me," I said. "Don't you ever go to work these days?"

His face stilled but his eyes remained watchful. "Why didn't you tell me?" I asked.

"You'd have worried," he said lightly, "and there's no need to."

"Is the mill really closed for good?"

"For better or for worse," he said, more or less solemnly. "The company's bankrupt."

"I see." It was the one thing we had never considered, that the mill might go broke.

"Look, honey, just don't worry about it, will you? When you get home, we'll talk it all over, finances and everything. Until then, just forget about it. Please."

"All right," I said.

"No matter what happens, I will always take care of you and little John. Trust me, darling."

"Of course I trust you. And so does he. He's such a darling, Toomey. I can't wait to get him home."

"*You* can't wait!" he exploded. "*You* get your hands on him now and then. *I* never do."

"Only a few more days," I said, but he scowled darkly.

He came in again that evening but left promptly when visiting hours were over at nine. The General should have pinned a medal on him.

I must have been asleep for an hour or more when a nurse brought the baby in for his eleven o'clock feeding. "It's a good baby," I crooned over him. "Such a good boy."

He sucked steadily, his eyes squinched so tightly shut they looked swollen. I heard the nurse come in but didn't look up. I reached for the tiny foot that had kicked itself out of the blanket. "This little piggy went to market. This—"

"May I play too?"

I looked up, startled, to see Toomey standing by the side of the bed taking off his shoes. "What are you doing?" I gasped.

"Sssssh," he whispered. "I overpowered the General."

He lifted himself onto the bed, leaned across it, and placed his hand under mine that was holding the baby. "Time for burping," I whispered, hoisting the warm little bundle to my shoulder, but it was Toomey who straightened out the little legs, gently patted up the bubbles.

"I just had to *touch* him," he murmured, caressing the tiny feet as the baby finished feeding. "It isn't civilized, keeping a father away from his own baby."

I pulled his head down and kissed him.

"*Mis*-ter *Lan*-dis!" But for once the scandalized voice was muted to a whisper so as not to wake the baby.

Toomey kissed his son, kissed me, leisurely disentangled himself, and started putting on his shoes while the General stood there marking time, her lips tight with disapproval. On the verge of going out the door, Toomey suddenly swerved, grasped her by the shoulders, and kissed her resoundingly on the cheek.

"That husband of yours!" she said, shaking her head despairingly in his wake.

"He fizzes," I said.

To my surprise I saw the stern mouth relax a little. She walked over to the bed and looked down at the baby. "I'll take him back to the nursery now if he's finished."

She lifted the baby, rewrapped the blanket expertly around him, and looked down into his sleeping face. "They try to tell you they don't know whether they're loved or not at this age," she said in a curiously gentle voice, then added on a rising note of triumph, "but they do!"

With that she went striding off before anybody could possibly get the idea she might be going soft.

XXX

Our financial situation, duly assessed, as Toomey had promised, after I came home from the hospital, was anything but reassuring. Future income from salary, none. Royalties from patents, negligible and still dwindling. Special projects, ditto.

"What about the patent PureSilk bought and shelved?" I asked.

Toomey wasn't sure. There had been a ten-year reversion clause which still had six years to run, at the end of which time control would revert to him if the process wasn't being used. If somebody bought the mill, they would probably get control of the patent too, for the unexpired period.

"If they'd used it," I said, "they might not have gone broke."

"That's my girl," he said.

In what Toomey referred to as our 'exchequer' there was enough to last for only three or four months at our present rate of spending. "Only," I said, "we won't be using that any more. No more pearls or flowers—or anything at all we don't really need."

He made a wry face. "Anyway, it won't be for long. I'll find a job soon, of some kind."

"There's a little left in the quilt too; I'm not sure how much."

"Leave it there and we'll never be broke."

"Pioneer takes on extra typists for a few weeks after the

first of the year. Something to do with proxies."

"I'm the breadwinner in this family."

"But it would only—"

"No, Vicki."

"With no rent to pay, and cutting back to utilities and groceries, we might hold out for as long as a year, but we've got to keep our feet on the ground."

At that he managed at least a semblance of his former derring-do. "If we keep our feet on the ground, how're we ever going to soar?"

I was pretty sure he was as scared as I was but no one else would ever guess it. It takes a brave man to talk about soaring when the ground's just been cut out from under him. Someday somebody might wipe that look off his face but I made up my mind then and there it wouldn't be me. I'd bite my tongue off first.

"Does John have to sleep *all* the time?" my brave man demanded plaintively.

The baby had become the hub upon which our altered universe revolved. Little doddle-head himself, a good baby, patient with his elders. Toomey adored his son, even to the extent of taking on bathing and changing chores. He'd made most of the nursery furniture with this own hands, including the cradle over which he now hung, willing his son to open his eyes.

"Hardly ever see a man that handy with a baby," was Mrs. Mullery's comment, uttered in that rasping voice of hers that made even her most innocuous remark seem tinged with malice. "Too bad he lost his job. Not that it seems to bother him any."

"Hardly an occasion for crape-hanging these days," I returned.

"Him and the old lady always had plenty of money, spent it like they did anyway."

The dreadful woman might have a point but I didn't in the least approve of her referring to my mother-in-law as "the old lady." "Easy come, easy go," I said.

But not now, I reminded myself, reflecting that one of the

more dismal aspects of being unemployed was all the extra time you had to spend money if you had any to spend.

Despite Toomey's determined optimism, looking for work was turning out to be both discouraging and futile. For two weeks he worked in a garage and, just before Christmas, for several days at one of the department stores. He also made and sold a few jewelry and handkerchief boxes. After that the clouds closed in more darkly than before.

"If I'd ever really trained for something," Toomey fretted, "instead of just sort of falling into a job."

It was true that seldom had a man been so molded and conditioned to the job he'd had. He'd worked at PureSilk summers while he was still in high school, got interested in the machines and started a fulltime job as soon as he graduated.

"People who trained are out of work too," I pointed out.

"Jack-of-all-trades, that's me. Only I do have one specialty."

That he did, and there was no diminishing of our desire for each other, even with the necessity for being careful. We simply couldn't afford another baby now. Maybe it would have been better, I mentioned to Mrs. Landis, if we'd waited awhile for the one we had. "Nonsense!" she'd retorted, more sharply than I'd ever heard her speak. "The worse times are, the more we *need* a baby."

Apparently not too many people shared this philosophy, babies having become a rarity among our circle of friends; a circle which seemed to steadily widen as we began to rediscover old ways to socialize without spending much money. Popcorn, fudge, and parlor games came into their own. Chinese checkers and elaborate jigsaw puzzles helped pass long evenings. Conversation again came into popularity. We would gather around somebody's piano and sing "Happy Days Are Here Again" as if we really believed it.

But during the night Toomey often left his bed to wander around the house, as *she* had wandered. "Go back to bed," he would tell me when I went to find him. "No use you losing sleep too."

If sleep was all I lost I would go my way rejoicing. What hurt was that, though Toomey remained the gentlest and most considerate of husbands, and sometimes even fizzed a little, I was having to watch the light slowly die from his eyes. I saw no way of restoring the light but, if he wandered, I would wander too.

He would stir up the fire in the grate and pull up a chair in front of it. There we would sit in each other's arms, often for hours, sometimes not speaking a word, but together. We could always catch up on our sleep in the morning. If, that is, young John saw fit to allow it. Usually, however, he had no use for dullards. The morning was the time to be up and doing. Fed and bathed, he would lie in his cradle in front of a sunny window, making contented noises and flailing the air with hands and feet.

"Poor little tyke," I heard Toomey say one morning, and turned quickly, relieved to see him laughing. "Has to catch his own sunbeams," he explained, still laughing gently.

This child was quicksilver, with all his father's easy charm and effervescence. Toomey had put up a playpen in the dungeon so he could have the baby near him when he was working down there. Sometimes I would sit there too with some mending or sewing in my hands.

John was a loquacious baby, babbling away in his infant jargon punctuated at intervals with "Dah," which seemed to be an expression of satisfaction, interrogation, displeasure, or simply a bid for attention. "Dah," he would say and then—yes, beam. I nearly fell out of my chair the first time I saw it, but there it was, unmistakably a beam. Now I had two beaming cherubs, and in each I beheld the other, the father in the child, the child in the father.

I had deliberately set myself to ignore our dwindling resources but, of course, could not quite do so. Fortunately we had all so far stayed well but there had been a larger than usual fuel bill, and we'd been unable to let Christmas go by without a few presents. If Toomey was to survive without losing his mind, he needed to work off some of his frustrations on dungeon projects, which meant outlays for material and tools.

I'd considered letting Mrs. McSwain go but my conscience wouldn't let me. A widow with two children to support, she was barely keeping her head above water anyway. Besides, that would have been one more blow to Toomey's self-confidence, which was already wearing dangerously thin.

I dared not mention again that I should look for a job. He had been the man of his household for so long that the responsibilities that position entailed had become part and fiber of his being. Better to eat backbone than destroy it.

We had luckily been able to rent Aunt Tabitha's house, furnished, to the new Methodist minister in Springhill, for almost enough to offset Mrs. McSwain's wages; but without Toomey's knowledge I was also dipping into the quilt. Finally the day came when I could no longer put off telling him how near we were to the wall.

It was always pleasant in the dungeon, warm in winter and cool in summer. Mrs. Landis had made braided rugs for the floor, and there were a few old but still comfortable chairs and a chintz-covered couch. "I can't get over how much roomier it seems down here than upstairs," I remarked, "even with all your junk, if you will pardon the expression."

Toomey's quirked eyebrow reminded me that there was a certain amount of 'junk' upstairs too, including another playpen, a rocking horse that could in size have doubled for a Shetland pony, and various other appurtenances of young John. Toomey was now working on a tiny rocking chair, which would soon be added to the collection.

I saw with a pang that he was looking older, his features more finely honed, and there were tired lines under his eyes. It simply wasn't fair! I put down my sewing, walked over and put my arms around him. "I don't know what caused this," he said, "but I like it."

"Remember the first time you brought me down here?"

"You should have screamed," he said; but he turned to

me, put his arms around me, and presently began to kiss me.

At least that part of our lives had remained sweet and good. John, however, didn't approve. "Dah, dah, dah," he scolded from his playpen; but when we turned to him, he favored us with a million candlepower smile, then started chewing on his teddy bear's ear.

"How's the exchequer holding out, baby?" Toomey asked, not quite able to conceal his anxiety.

"As well as can be expected," I said, although I had come down expressly to tell him that it was all but exhausted. Then I went upstairs, got the quilt down, and did some more ripping. With luck it would be enough to see us through another two or three weeks; and if Toomey hadn't found a job by then, we'd simply have to mortgage the house, sell the cars, and take it from there.

Even Judgment Day deferred rolls around sooner than you're ready. Ours arrived shortly before John's first birthday, by which time we were flat, cold and stony broke. I *had* to tell Toomey then, there was nothing else to do.

"Looks like we'll have to draw on the quilt after all." He was keeping his voice calm but the familiar strained look was moving over his face.

"We already have," I said.

He nodded and turned away, but then his control broke. "Why did you have to marry such a stupid failure!" he shouted at me.

"You stop that!" I shouted back. "You stop it right now!"

God in heaven, what were we doing? Toomey and I *shouting* at each other! What could I say to comfort him? What could I do?

John took the decision out of my hands; he burst into loud and frightened wailing. "Now see what you've done!" I yelled at Toomey, however unjustly. "Pick him up. Tell *him* what a failure you are. See what he says."

I turned and ran up the stairs as fast as I could go. Clutching the edge of the kitchen sink with both hands, I stood there staring out the window, across the Mullerys' back yard. It was just starting to rain again, a cold dreary October rain striking obliquely against the window pane, and into my heart. My despair was for John, for me, but most of all for Toomey. He had never been like this before. *Somebody* had to do something.

He's not a failure, you know that as well as I do. He's good and true and loving, and his courage never falters, not for long. Is that why you're trying him so, because of all the laughing he's done? Surely you know how much the world needs to be laughed at sometimes, especially now.

I wasn't sure whether my entreaty was addressed to God or Yasmina but it probably didn't matter; I was sure they kept in touch.

Help him find a job, soon, so he can laugh again. That isn't asking too much, is it? It doesn't have to be the best job in the world, just a job. He'll do the rest, the way he always has. And please don't think I'm asking you to do it all because I'm not. I'll do anything in the world for Toomey if you'll only let me know what it is.

I felt his arm go around me, turning me to him, John in his other arm between us. "There's so much moisture outside," he said. "Must we have more in here?"

I hadn't realized until then that I was crying, but my cheeks were wet with tears.

"Dah," said John disapprovingly. Mothers are not supposed to cry. *He* had stopped and now, all grief forgotten, was squirming to be put down. Toomey let him go.

"Let's go into the living room," he said to me. "We'll talk about it."

I wondered if my prayers had been as silent as I had thought. If some of them had been spoken aloud, how much had Toomey heard? "We can sell things," I said, "one of the cars anyway, and we can put a mortgage on the house."

"Banks are being pretty cagey about that sort of thing right now."

"But they would get the house if we didn't pay."

"They've got houses, honey, too many of them already. That's the trouble. I've been trying."

"Sell my car then. After that we'll just have to ask your mother for help. I don't like to, but she would expect us to if she knew."

"Mother's sort of reached the end of the trail too."

"But I thought she had plenty of money."

He managed to smile a little. "Never did, really. Most of what she inherited from my grandfather was in the factory, and Dad gutted that before he set forth with his lady friend. Had it on him, in fact, at the time of the accident, so it burned when the car caught fire."

"The dirty skunk!" I said feelingly.

"I do agree, but nothing to be done about it. Mother invested part of what she had left in securities. You can guess what happened to those. She used the rest to buy this house, and supported me until I was old enough to help. Most of her current income has been from three small rent houses, also inherited from her father, but two of her tenants are out of work now and can't pay, and she hasn't the heart to evict them."

So he hadn't been ignoring those possible opportunities for our survival, he'd explored them and found out they didn't exist any more. "You should have told me," I said.

"I didn't see any need to worry you. I hoped there never would be, and so did Mother, naturally."

Naturally. There was considerably more to both mother and son than I had given them credit for, even after being in the family for close to two years. "Your mother will just have to move in with us," I said, "but we can't possibly afford to pay Pinky."

He looked mildly surprised. "*Nobody's* been paying Pinky since they left here. In fact, she's been paying a share of the expenses over there."

She'd sold her own house when she moved in with them, Toomey said, and still had some of the money from that.

"She must come here too, then," I said.

She was dragging her heels, Toomey said, because she

thought it wasn't fair to impose on us when she had children of her own.

I knew about those children of hers. The son lived in Oregon. The daughter's husband, who worked in a bank and was sensitive about the fact that his mother-in-law did housework for a living, didn't encourage her to visit them. "She says she'll find a room somewhere," Toomey said, "maybe some place she can cook a little."

"She can do her cooking here. Toomey, we can't have her going off alone like that."

"What I told her," said Toomey, seeming almost cheerful again. "They're coming for dinner this evening, aren't they? We can talk it over then." He kissed me, then again. It wasn't the first time I'd noticed that one highly emotional episode frequently led to another.

"We don't even have any blackberry wine," I said presently.

But we had John. "Dah!" he said disgustedly, and came crawling over to break up this disgraceful affair.

Mrs. Landis and Pinky arrived around midafternoon for what Toomey insisted on calling our "regrouping conference." You'd have thought they'd show *some* sign of their present beleaguerment but, unless you counted a trace of tiredness around the eyes, they might have just been dropping in for a pleasant visit over the teacups.

"You'll move back here, of course," I said at once. "It isn't as quiet as it used to be but ear plugs are available on request."

"You really don't mind, Vicki?" asked Mrs. Landis.

"I minded more when you left," I said, and realized it was true. She had never taken my own mother's place, nor had she tried to, in fact she was probably the least assertive mother-in-law in the world, but I knew I would welcome her presence in the present emergency.

"This house is larger," she commented, "and newer. I don't suppose there would be any chance of selling it but it might be easier to rent than mine."

Toomey started to answer her, then inexplicably began to

laugh. "All right," he said finally, "my guilty secret may as well come out. Vicki has commented a few times that the dungeon seems large compared to a similar area upstairs, and she's right. The dungeon *is* bigger."

"How can it be, dear?" asked Mrs. Landis. "I thought they used the walls of the basement for the foundation of the house."

"I'm sure they did, but unfortunately that didn't occur to your fifteen-year-old son who was *adding onto* it. Finishing some rooms upstairs and, now and then, pushing out the walls below to make more room for my equipment."

"But you had a man to help you, Toomey. Didn't *he* know?"

"Mr. Wynmore was seventy if he was a day. Maybe he, like your son, was missing a few marbles, or maybe he simply didn't care; but the sad truth is that the dungeon at this moment extends something like eight feet beyond the kitchen wall."

"Under Mr. Mullery's driveway," I said, awed. "It won't cave in or anything, will it?"

"It never has, and you're the only one who's noticed the discrepancy, Vicki, or at least the only one who's mentioned it."

"When did *you* know?" I asked.

"Five or six years ago. One day when I'd gone down there from the kitchen, it suddenly struck me, as it did you later, that something seemed out of plumb. I took some measurements then but couldn't do anything about it because Mullery had just finished his new garage and was having the concrete poured on his driveway."

"*New* garage?"

"Yes. They had one on the other side of the house but it was too short for their new car, so they tore it down and put that pagoda thing over there. Then they built a garage on this side and put in the driveway. I have never," he added, "invited Mr. Mullery into the dungeon."

"I should hope not," I said fervently. "He'd be suing us forever. That answers one question anyway. We all live here."

"*I* shouldn't," said Pinky. "I told Toomey—"

"That you were trying to get away from us," I interposed, "but you're just not going to get by with it. So now we've all got a roof over our heads, but the grocer, the milkman, and the butcher rather like cash. What do we do about that?"

"Well, goodness," said Pinky, "if I'm going to stay here, I'll certainly put in my share."

"And there's my rent money," said Mrs. Landis. "That's thirty a month, and we'll try to rent the house we're living in now."

"And twenty from Aunt Tabitha's house if I can find another job for Mrs. McSwain, which I've just got to because we can't afford her any more. We won't need her anyway with three women in the house. And what Pinky puts in, and there's still a little coming in from the patents. And Toomey, you've simply got to let me do some work if I can find it."

"No," said Toomey.

"But with your mother here to take care of John . . ."

"It's *your* mother I'm thinking about. She wouldn't like it any more than I would. And speaking of *her*, didn't she ever have any bright ideas that might apply to the present situation?"

I could have told him she had never anticipated a situation where people had so many *things* that couldn't be converted into cash, that I was, in fact, having a little trouble believing it myself, but it would only have made him feel bad. "She kind of improvised as she went along," I said. "The tonic, of course. And The Stuff, only that was free. And the aphrodisiac, which—"

"The *what*?"

"I told you about that, Toomey, I know I did. The love potions, which was just the tonic in little tiny bottles."

"I remember now. And what was it the medicine man said? That nothing in the world could cure a man who didn't believe it was going to? So all we'd have to do is make him believe."

To my astonishment the caramel eyes were beginning to melt and bubble. I said, "Nobody believes in things like that any more, except possibly in places like Springhill."

"People are people," he said, "in Springhill or anywhere else. I don't know what you and your girl chums chatter about when no men are present, but I do know what the fellows talk about—almost as much as they do about unemployment. It's the fact that since they've lost their jobs, their sex lives are going to pot too. If you and Pinky don't want to listen, Mother, you can stop up your ears."

"I wouldn't miss it for anything," said Mrs. Landis. "Please go on."

"Very well. That hasn't happened to us, I'm happy to say, because Vicki won't let me use a naughty word like failure; but if our sexual relationship *were* suffering, and somebody offered me something in a cute little bottle and said it would help, I'd drink it down in one gulp and pay for the privilege."

"But Toomey," gasped Pinky, "you wouldn't dare try to sell anything like that now. The police would run you off the street."

"So we call it something else. In fact we could incorporate the whole idea into a tonic that's good for a multitude of ills, including hangnails, muddy complexion, ingrown hair follicles, and cavities in the molars. Then we give it a suggestive name—we'll have to think of one—and somehow or other get the word around that it's an aphrodisiac too."

Talk about pie in the sky. He was steadily building up more zeal than a hot-eyed Old Testament prophet. "And," I said, "you will fill your little basket and go peddling from door to door. Somehow I don't see it."

I was immediately ashamed of myself. It is not in the least enjoyable to go around pricking other people's balloons just because you have a sudden attack of Broadbent conscience—and prejudice. Besides, I had promised. God or Yasmina or both, I had promised. "Because," I appended in a veritable brainstorm of inspiration, "if you keep your feet on the ground, how're you ever going to soar?"

Toomey snapped his fingers and began beaming more brightly than he had in weeks. "So," he said happily, "we'll get our feet *off* the ground. We'll aim higher, marketing through drug stores maybe. And we could advertise, might even take radio time."

"Mr. Freegate was still going strong," I remembered aloud, "quite awhile after other businesses were floundering, but eventually he failed too."

Toomey looked thoughtful. "He was selling directly by mail, and his overhead must have been ruinous, with all those personally typed letters, but there may have been other reasons for his downfall. And it would be interesting to know what restrictions there are on selling a patent medicine these days. I think we ought to look the old boy up."

"You're serious about this, aren't you?"

"I believe I am. At least it bears looking into."

"I don't see why not," Mrs. Landis chimed in, "if Vicki can remember the formula."

God protect the innocents! These people would thank a shyster for selling them the Brooklyn bridge in exchange for their life savings, then insist on him staying to dinner to celebrate the deal. Promise or no promise, *somebody* had to exercise some judgment around here.

Before I could voice this heresy, however, my thoughts swung back to those other innocents in their pink-checked aprons in Aunt Tabitha's basement. *Everybody in this world is crazy, God, but Thee and me; and somehow I have a feeling that from now on You might as well count me out*. In that moment I cast my lot irrevocably and forever on the side of the fakers. "Corn whiskey well watered down," I said. "We won't even have to find a bootlegger, now that Prohibition's ended. And something added to make it taste absolutely revolting."

This was received in exactly the spirit in which it was offered. "We can mix it in the wash tub to start with," said Pinky.

"All we need is money," stated Toomey, "considerably more than we've got, just to get started."

"Well, goodness," said Pinky, "there's my little bit. You're more than welcome to that."

"Thanks, Pinky." Toomey walked over and kissed her on the cheek, leaving her rosy with pleasure. "We need even more than that, however, if we're to start off in a big enough way to do any good. I'll see what I can do."

John seconded that with a resounding crash from the kitchen, announcing he was at the pots and pans again. As usual, Mama had stacked them in the cupboard Fibber McGee-wise so they came cascading out very satisfyingly the minute he managed to open the door. Good boy, now he's found his wooden spoon. "Dah, dah, dah." Bang crash, clang, bang, bang, bang.

Toomey went to investigate and came back carrying our dimpled drummer in his arms.

"Watch him," I warned, but he was already extracting Toomey's pen and pencil from his breast pocket, jabbering ingratiatingly all the while.

"The darling," said Mrs. Landis fondly.

The darling, I found appropriate to mention, had begun pulling that act on every man he met, and it was not always well received.

"But he's only a baby," said Pinky.

"Baby con man," I said. "See the pretty pencil, mister? Fell right out of your pocket the minute I touched it. Like me to look after the bothersome thing for you? No? Come now, sir, a busy man like yourself can't be expected to bother with a little tiny pencil. Still no? Wonder what it tastes like? Not bad. Not so good either. So maybe you're supposed to peel it. Oh well, take the thing if you must."

Pinky was laughing helplessly, Mrs. Landis was fondly shaking her head, and John had dived a plump hand back into the pocket in search of other treasures.

"I want to give him the sun, moon and stars," said Toomey softly, and began rubbing noses with his son.

"Why start putting ideas into his head," I said, "when all

he wants is pans?"

XXXI

Mrs. Landis and Pinky had soon settled in upstairs as if they had never been away. The grand piano once more reigned over the living room, the upright having been evacuated to the dining room until we could find a buyer for it. The middle upstairs bedroom had been converted into a sitting room, and Toomey was setting up a kitchenette in an alcove with facilities for making coffee and tea, and even cooking small meals when they chose.

Can five rather oddly-assorted people in one household tottering on the brink of financial ruin achieve happiness? Yes, if they are people of goodwill who value their own privacy and respect that of others. And if one of them is a mischievous toddler with love enough for everybody. In no time at all we had settled into a routine that was to continue, as the expression went, "for the duration."

I prepared breakfast for all of us except when Pinky and Mrs. Landis preferred to fix their own upstairs. The three of us shared the rest of the cooking and the household chores. We took turns grocery shopping. Now that we were five, we found that we could save money by buying whole bushels of apples, potatoes and onions at the city market. Cabbage and carrots were also cheaper in large lots. We bought a pig from a farmer, who for only a little extra agreed to butcher it for us. We cured the meat ourselves. With two other families we bought a calf from the same farmer and shared out the meat. There was a feeling of security about having food in the larder for several weeks ahead.

Toomey began to absent himself from home for several hours each day in search of an angel to back our tonic venture. "Has anybody got any money these days?" I wondered.

"More than you might think," he returned, "but they can't see their way clear to risk it on what they consider a hare-brained scheme."

Possibly they were right. Dr. Modesta's income, while sufficient for their needs, must have been relatively small, as had Yasmina's. On the other hand Mr. Freegate had at one time been supporting a sizable office force in addition to his own family, and Lydia Pinkham hadn't done that badly either. "Keep on trying," I encouraged, "if you're sure that's what you want to do."

"What I want to do," he said, the sharply honed look taking over his face again, "is support my family. Anyway, it might turn out to be fun."

Mr. Freegate, we soon learned, had been dead for almost two years. Mrs. Freegate, a friendly little woman now in her sixties, professed herself delighted to talk to Toomey. She said her husband hadn't exactly failed in the business but profits were down and he decided it was time for him to retire. "Not that he ever exactly coined money at any time," she admitted, "but we did manage to send the children to college and save a little bit for retirement." No one else, she said, had been sufficiently interested to continue the operation.

"So that's that," said Toomey.

"Maybe we could start small and make a little money," I said.

"We may have to. How much longer can we hold out?"

"Indefinitely if our tenants keep paying, and we can limit our expenditures to groceries and utility bills. And if we continue to enjoy eating beans and cabbage."

Mrs. Landis had succeeded in renting the house she had moved from, and she had also found another job for Mrs. McSwain so we had her off our conscience. We had also found a buyer for the upright piano. Toomey wanted to hang onto the cars if we possibly could; he said we'd be needing them when things started looking up. In the meantime the upkeep wasn't excessive since he did all the mechanical work himself.

"We can't sell Peggy in any case," I said, "or the grand piano."

Musical barbarians that the rest of us were, we all enjoyed hearing Mrs. Landis play. Even John, whose musical ear was, I suspected, inherited from his mother, since he was all too frequently inspired to run to his pots and pans to provide accompaniment.

So our lives weren't unpleasant at all, as long as we could avoid thinking ahead. But the Depression *had* to be over sometime, didn't it? Times *had* to get better.

Toomey came home one evening literally vibrating with excitement. "I've captured an angel," he announced jubilantly. "Guess who?"

"I can't imagine."

"An old friend of yours."

"Impossible. I never had a friend with money."

"Forster Jerome, your gentleman bootlegger."

"Oh No!" I said, and saw the light dim, just a little, in Toomey's eyes.

"He sent for me when he heard I was looking for some backing. It's all right, isn't it?"

One does not enjoy having one's earlier indiscretions disinterred. On the other hand, no thanks to me, that particular indiscretion had been nipped in the bud. Besides, there was my promise to Yasmina. "Of course it's all right," I said. "How much is he willing to invest in this venture?"

"As much as necessary, he says, to get it going. He's enthusiastic, Vicki, he really is. Say's he can't imagine why he hadn't thought of it himself. We'll share fifty-fifty, repaying our half of the investment from our part of the profits. I'll handle production, and Jerome will take charge of advertising and distribution."

"Shall I alert Pinky to scour out her washtubs?"

"Thanks to Jerome, we won't need them. He owns a vacant building over on Thirty-third Street which ought to be about right for us, after a few interior alterations. We're going to need some help too, somebody dependable and not afraid of work. I wondered if Eunice might be willing to come back,not that we can guarantee how long the job will last."

"We can't fail, Toomey, not now. I'll write her right away."

She had been staying with her father ever since PureSilk had closed its doors. I was sure it couldn't have been very pleasant for her and that she would be delighted to have a job again.

Toomey plunked himself down at the piano and started pounding out "Blue Skies" loud enough to raise the dead. John, frypan in one hand and teddy bear in the other, wandered in to investigate and stood in the doorway, round-eyed and open-mouthed. "Dah," he commented sagely when the concert was finished.

So happy days were with us again or hopefully in sight. Toomey was regaining his bounce, and Mrs. Landis and Pinky were going around giggling like schoolgirls. Mrs. Mullery couldn't have helped noticing even if she'd tried, which she never did. "What's going on with you people?" she demanded. "You'd think somebody had left you a million dollars."

"We hit it rich on the bank at the Zaring," I said.

"Such a dreadful lie," I mentioned when our gloom-dispensing neighbor had departed, "but she wouldn't have believed the truth anyway. Sometimes I hardly believe it myself."

"I know, dear," said Mrs. Landis, "but then nothing Toomey has ever done has been exactly conventional. Except marry you, of course."

"I'm not very conventional either."

"I'm so glad, dear. I was *such* a conventional girl, and such a crashing bore. I sometimes wonder what would ever have happened to me if Norton hadn't come along."

I could hardly believe my ears!

"I know he behaved badly," she went on, "and it hurt me terribly the way he treated Toomey, but without him I'd have never even had Toomey, and there wouldn't have been you or little John, or anybody, really. And now we are all so happy."

"We are all so broke," I said.

"Not really, dear. We just don't have any money." She bit her lip a little shyly, winked at me, and started up the stairs.

A few afternoons later I left John in the kitchen and went to answer the doorbell. There was Toomey's new partner in the flesh. "Mr. Jerome," I said, and stared at him for several seconds before I recovered myself enough to invite him in.

"Victoria," he said, with the half smile I remembered. "Am I still allowed to call you Victoria?"

"Of course," I said, surprised at how glad I was to see him again.

"I was just passing this way and thought I might catch Toomey at home."

"I'm not sure where he went but he ought to be back before long." I showed him into our cluttered living room, where we stood for a long moment frankly scrutinizing each other. He appeared to have taken on weight since I'd last seen him, although it wasn't apparent in his face, which was as lean and dark and brooding as ever. "I wanted to thank you for the flowers," I said, "but I didn't know where to write."

Again the almost-smile came into play. "Your husband appears to be a man of wisdom," he said.

"You can't think us completely crazy," I countered, "or you wouldn't have agreed to join us."

"Certainly you're crazy. So am I. It's the only state of mind that's tolerable these days. I've been looking forward to seeing your son."

"You can hear him too," I said, as right on cue John began beating out his clangorous concert. I started toward the kitchen with Mr. Jerome hot on my heels.

John sat in the middle of the kitchen floor surrounded by his pots and pans, one of which he was beating the bee-jeebers out of with a wooden spoon. Eyes squinched against the glockenspiel, wincing at the force of every blow, he hunched over his instrument like a professional drummer in the throes of a wicked downbeat.

"Hey, John!" I shouted. The spoon stopped in midair. John's head turned and his eyes fixed themselves on the stranger's shoes, then moved slowly upward. "Hi!" he said, beaming his million candlepower grin in what seemed to be the direction of Mr. Jerome's face but I suspected was actually his breast pocket, from which peeked the fastidiously arranged corners of a white linen handkerchief. Then he clambered to his feet and lifted his arms to be picked up.

This time, child of mine, you may be in for a bit of a freeze. But no. Mr. Jerome stooped and lifted him with the ease one usually associates with experience. "Watch your handkerchief," I warned, but not in time. Already chubby fingers were extracting the handkerchief and floating it to the floor.

But what's this? Surely not *another* handkerchief! What's this chap up to, anyway? And a *red* one this time!

"Dah," says John, and reaches, then pauses for a searching look at the gentleman's face before, slowly, between thumb and finger, easing out the red square, which proves to be of thin silk—and is promptly replaced by a green one!

"Well, I never," said Pinky, walking into the kitchen a few minutes later to find the floor littered with brilliantly colored silk squares and John stunned into speechlessness for the first time in his life.

Finally the pocket was really empty. "Dah," said John, managing to register in that one word both relief and displeasure.

Mr. Jerome put John down and picked up the squares, rolled them willynilly into a ball which—whist—disappeared.

"Watch," he commanded then, and, reaching into his

sleeve, withdrew a purple pennant which he handed to John. Before you could say abracadabra, there was a whole string of pennants across the kitchen with an entranced toddler on one end and Mr. Jerome on the other.

"Here," says the magic man; and while John examines the latest wonder which has just been popped into his hand, the pennants too disappear, and John now clutches in his fist an enormous yellow blossom.

"That's yours," said Mr. Jerome, "For helping me. Show it to your mama."

"You haven't gained weight after all," I said.

This time the smile came all the way through. "My special coat. I go to the children's hospital every Monday."

I remembered then to introduce Pinky, who was looking as entranced as the baby.

I noticed that Mr. Jerome was looking interested too. "The most delightful smell seems to be coming from that kettle," he commented.

"Ham hocks and beans," twinkled Pinky. "I'm just fixing to mix up a batch of cornbread."

That was when Toomey arrived, greeted our guest fondly, and carried him off to the living room, trailed at a respectful distance by a still-mesmerized John.

"You never told us he was such a nice man," said Pinky.

"I don't seem to have known as much about him as I imagined I did," I admitted. "We've got plenty of food, haven't we, for one more?"

"Oh, yes," Pinky assured me. "And plenty of the orange pound cake left for dessert. He does seem such a fine gentleman."

A fine gentleman who lived in my mind as a gourmet of some distinction, but if he didn't like beans he could always refuse our invitation. He didn't refuse, however. He said, "I wondered if you were ever going to ask me," and presently tucked into our simple meal with a gusto equal to our own.

We began to see a good deal of him after that. "I had no idea Mr. Jerome was such a nice man," Mrs. Landis would say.

"You and Pinky! You're as bad as John."

But they weren't quite. John had been prompt to appropriate this dark unsmiling man as his own, claiming first dibs at the breast pocket which only now and then triggered a magic show—lest custom stale the child's delight, he said—but always contained something. A balloon, or a small toy, or a piece of foil-wrapped candy.

"When it's so easy to make children happy," he remarked one day, "you'd think more people would try it."

Had he been delighting children four years ago too? Then I had been able to view him in only one dimension, through the eyes of an infatuated, immature, and deeply troubled girl, and even now he seemed much too forbidding to tolerate impertinent questions. Had he once had children of his own? And what about a wife?

"*You* like him," I said to Toomey.

"Yes, I do, and gosh, Vicki, we'd have foundered in short order if we'd tried to go it alone, even if we'd had the money to start. He knows all the legal angles, and about a trillion other things too."

And if I'd suspected in the beginning that his reason for going into this venture had been just to help us, I soon learned how wrong I'd been. As much as anything else he was doing it for kicks. He was quite obviously having the time of his life. As was Toomey; and, enthusiasm being highly contagious, as were we all. If now and then my cautious Broadbent blood cried out for prudence, I told it to go away and hide its silly head. What did your prudence ever get you? I asked. And look what it did to me.

Mr. Jerome had insisted that our product be named for Toomey and me; and after much wracking of brains and experimental scribbling on scraps of paper, we finally came up with Vituminol, as also being reminiscent of vitamins, which were getting considerable play in the medical news right then. The label would feature a Charles Atlas type showing off his biceps to an admiring blonde in a beach chair.

When alterations to the inside of the building had been completed, Mr. Jerome brought in a bookkeeper to set up the office records. Eunice would come the first of the year, and we hoped to start production shortly after that.

The sooner the better, insofar as the Landis resources were concerned. Mr. Jerome had offered us a personal loan which Toomey, quite rightly, had refused, hoping to hold out on our own until such time as the business started turning a profit. With Christmas coming on, we decided to subject Yasmina's quilt to one final rigorous examination for any stray bills that might have been overlooked. A futile hope, as we had expected, until Toomey's exploring fingers located something. "It doesn't feel like the other money," he said, "but it's something."

"So let's find out," I said, reaching for the scissors.

"Not money," I said, as I finished unfolding the crisp yellowing paper. "It doesn't look—it's a marriage certificate Toomey! 'Julia Mary Smith and Victor Howard Miller,' " I read, ' "were by me united in marriage this twelfth day—' "

Something was wrong. Victor Howard Miller had been Dr. Modesta, and it had been my mother he married. Yasmina Smith, my mother, not Julia Mary Smith. I glanced again at the date. That was right too, at least the year was right, for his marriage to my mother, who had named me for him and for her dearest friend. Julie had married someone else; it was Yasmina Dr. Modesta had married, Yasmina the princess he'd made up out of his own head. "As he made up her name," I said aloud. "I asked Aunt Tabitha the wrong question.

"*Yasmina's* real name," I said to Toomey's questioning face. *That's* what I should have asked for, not Dr. Modesta's real name but hers."

"Does it matter?'

"Does it matter! It matters more than anything else in the world! It means Julie—I told you about Julie—my God, Toomey, Julie wasn't my mother's friend, she was my mother!"

It was all whirling around in my mind now like scenes from a tragic movie. Aunt Bessie and the big house with the crystal chandelier in the parlor, The Girls scattered like broken blossoms among the red carpets and canopied beds.

"You're jumping to conclusions," said Toomey.

"Isn't she always?" asked Mr. Jerome from the doorway. "The ladies admitted me as they were leaving but obviously I'm intruding."

"No," said Toomey. "Of c-c-course not. Let me t-t-take your c-c-c-coat."

Mr. Jerome stared at him for a long moment, then shifted his gaze to me. "Yasmina's quilt," he said, seeing it still across my lap. "I told Toomey if you needed money—"

His voice trailed off as he continued to study our faces. "That isn't it, is it?" he said. "Tell me, Victoria."

I couldn't possibly tell him. I would rather die.

"Victoria," he said.

I did not have to look at him to know he was no longer the pleasant caller of only minutes before, nor was he the affable magician who had charmed my son, but the Mr. Jerome I had first known, the dark-browed Mr. Jerome of the stern voice and compelling eyes.

"I—can't," I choked out, and then I *was* telling him, the words pouring out of me as they had on that earlier occasion. Different words this time, words so shattering that even to speak them was to threaten my reason. Aunt Bessie, the house, The Girls, the killing of Julie's betrayer.

XXXII

Exhausted from my emotional catharsis, I found myself sitting on the sofa with Toomey's arm around me. Mr. Jerome had remained silent and unmoving during my recital but now he stirred, looked at me, and said quite matter-of-factly, "Toomey was right, of course. You were jumping to conclusions."

I felt too tired to rise to that challenge, but then I did. "Not exactly jumping," I said. "That marriage certificate is real enough."

"Canopied beds," he said. "Crystal chandeliers, red carpets." He actually smiled. "I, my dear, am an expert in the matter of—houses, and I assure you there was never one like that except in romantic fiction and melodramas. Don't try to argue with me, Victoria. I know. When I was a boy I earned my spending money running errands for the girls in those houses.

"It was a boarding house your mother was telling you about, and I very much suspect embroidering a bit in the telling, for boarding houses as a rule weren't anywhere near that fancy."

"But before that, if she was Julie—"

"*If* she was, and you don't know that. Even if you did, after all this time, it shouldn't make a great deal of difference."

"Not to *you*, maybe. Why should it, when the very first time I met you, you were waiting for a girl like that?"

"Not exactly, as it happened, but I will concede you the difference except on one point. That girl was coming to me of her own free will. And I had summoned her—"

Then transfixing me with that somber gaze, he dropped six words between us as carelessly as a child drops pebbles into a brook: "—not from necessity but by choice."

I had not the slightest doubt what he meant. He could have had other women without paying for them. He could have had—me.

"Free choice was one of the things Julie didn't have, along with parents or a husband or a home. All she had was her own courage and she used it. To kill a man who deserved killing."

"It isn't that so much as—the other. It's just so awful not knowing."

"Whether or not your mother was a prostitute?" His voice lashed and tore at me. "I'm afraid I can't help you there because there was never the smallest doubt about *my* mother."

Before his meaning could more than begin to reach me, he was speaking again.

"I knew from the time I was old enough to know anything at all that my mother put food in our stomachs and clothes on our backs by selling her body—and I loved her beyond all reason."

"I don't believe you."

"Why not? Do you imagine love is limited to the virtuous and the pious? If it were, there would be even less of it in the world than there is now, and a chilly kind of love at that.

"Love is too precious to waste, Victoria," he said in a gentler voice. "You loved your mother and she loved you. Once you almost lost that love because you were too full of yourself. If you lose her again, you may never get her back."

I remembered an afternoon long ago when a tall proud woman had knelt to comfort a child. "I'll always love my Nubbin," she had said, "no matter what I call her."

"I suppose a name doesn't really matter so much," I

said.

"Hardly at all, in the grand scheme of things. And there could well have been another Julie, or the one your mother told you about may have never actually existed."

"You said yourself," Toomey put in, "you weren't always sure which of your mother's stories were true and which she was making up."

"Exactly," said Mr. Jerome, "so all you can be reasonably sure of is that a woman named Julia Mary Smith married Dr. Modesta, who changed her name to Yasmina—in love."

"Is *your* mother still living?" I asked after a moment.

"She died when I was nine."

I knew if I did not ask now, I never would, but even so the question trembled for a moment on my lips before I could release it. "Do you—have any other family?"

"My wife divorced me for excellent reason. My son died when he was twelve. I have never been inclined to accept a substitute for either."

I could feel his pain mingling with my own but I could almost see him putting up his defenses against any expression of sympathy I might dare to offer. "Then you are free," I said instead, "to come to us for Christmas."

"Yes," he said, and presently added, "thank you."

I had emerged from the storm bruised and abraded but I was already beginning to heal.

XXXIII

Despite considerable effort and my sincere resolve to do so, I was not entirely able to put questions concerning Yasmina's past out of my mind. I wondered if she had not planned to some day bring all her stories together into one coherent whole, but I would make no further effort to do that for myself. The spectre of what might have been would rise now and again to haunt me, squirming around in my consciousness as a worm had once wriggled across my childish palm, and I would make myself look at it long enough to be sure I was no longer afraid before tipping it back into my subconscious.

Eunice arrived the day after New Year's, Toomey hired two men to help with the bottling, and Mr. Jerome secured trial orders from two local drug store chains. The first production would be released the last week in January, preceded by ads in all three daily newspapers. Beneath the tall black headline TRY VITUMINOL were listed a dozen or so common ailments which, it was suggested, might be remedied thereby.

With our campaign launched, outlets stocked, and a sufficient backlog of tonic for anticipated reorders, we sat back and waited. And waited. And waited. The world was positively *not* beating a path to our door.

"People simply don't have the money to spend," I said.

"Not for necessities," said Mr. Jerome, "but they can usually scrape up a buck or two for something they especially want. What we have to do is figure out a way to make them want it."

The following week the drug chains were persuaded to include Vituminol, at a discount, in their store ads, but the world still could not have been less interested. By the end of six weeks we had received a small reorder but sales remained sluggish. "We're a bust," I said.

"Wailing Cassandra," said Mr. Jerome disgustedly. "Sometimes I despair of you, Victoria. Just for that you're going to help me. You own a long black dress, I presume?"

"I wouldn't wear black to my own funeral. You had something in mind?"

"A magic show, my dear. I have even learned to pull a rabbit out of a hat. And you shall be my assistant. We'll put it on at the plant, and we'll advertise and pass out free samples. I might even be able to persuade one of the newspapers to give us some coverage."

"What about your mother's dress, Vicki?" Toomey seemed to be catching Mr. Jerome's enthusiasm.

"The very thing," said Mr. Jerome. "We'll even bill ourselves in proper fashion—Dr. Jerome and the Princess Victoria." He was watching me closely as he spoke, almost daring me to refuse.

It had once been the dream of my life to wear that dress but there had never been an occasion when it wouldn't have looked ridiculous. Until, possibly, now. "All right," I said, "but it will have to be altered."

"Too big," agreed Mrs. Landis, "and too long. I'll start working on it right away."

The magic show, purposely scheduled for a Saturday when children would be out of school, drew a satisfactory crowd and played to an appreciative audience. Sales took a slight surge forward the following week but slumped the next. We continued the shows for three more Saturdays, until in fact we lost the services of a critical member of the cast. John caught the white rabbit and refused to give it back.

Over the next few weeks sales picked up a little but not

enough for us to show a profit. The one thing we felt might help was to get our original idea across, that the tonic was also an aphrodisiac. But how, when we dared not come right out and say so, at least not in print?

"Lydia Pinkham managed to get the 'baby in every bottle' idea across somehow," remarked Mrs. Landis, "although it may have been by accident. If so, it would be nice if we could have one."

"Elucidate, Mother," Toomey chortled. "A baby or an accident?"

Mr. Jerome glared at him. "We've gone about as far as we can with the label," he said.

I thought about that label: "Recommended for . . . improving digestion, liver function . . . stimulation of certain essential glands . . . "

"It doesn't say an awful lot," I commented, "and what it does say sounds kind of depressing. But," I added, risking another of Mr. Jerome's lightning bolts, "maybe nobody reads it anyway."

"I didn't understand it very well myself," said Pinky. "About those glands, I mean. Until Mrs. Landis explained it to me."

"I don't suppose you're alone," I reassured her, with a warning glance at Toomey, who was already showing signs of going into a laughing fit. "Anyway, people just naturally associate a patent medicine with stomach trouble and irregularity and nervousness, that sort of thing. Which may not be bad. I mean, if we could find some way to put over the idea that what's good for the rest of the system is also good for love."

"Keep talking," said Mr. Jerome.

"That's all, about that. Only I did have another idea. When we went to the farm last week to pick up eggs and butter, the farmer's wife and little girls were wearing quite attractive dresses that had been made from feed sacks."

"I hope all this comes together somewhere."

"Wait and see. It seems the people who manufacture the feed, or whatever they do to feed, put it up in cotton print sacks for that very purpose, as a sales gimmick. And I was wondering if we could have some kind of fancy bottle people could use for something else after the tonic was gone."

"Not bad, but what does one use a bottle for except a bottle?"

"If it were the right shape it could be used for a vase, for flowers, or something like that."

"The cost of specially shaped bottles would probably be prohibitive, and there'd also be the problem of packing and shipping. However, think some more, Victoria."

"The little bottles, the ones they used for the love potions, had flowers painted on them. Aunt Tabitha had painted them herself, and sometimes she'd tie a scrap of ribbon around the neck. They used the same bottles over and over, of course, but maybe we could paint just a few for the tonic and see how it works."

"I used to do china painting when I was a girl," volunteered Mrs. Landis. "I'll bet Pinky did too."

"You're not talking about a couple of dozen tiny bottles," Mr. Jerome warned her. "You're talking about hundreds, hopefully thousands, of fair-sized bottles each week. We couldn't paste the present label over the flowers but that shouldn't matter, since the same information is on the box. How many bottles could one person do in an hour, painting a simple design on one side of each bottle? Just a rough estimate."

"A dozen," she ventured, "probably more once we got into the swing of it. It doesn't have to be anything fancy, just a few simple brush strokes."

"It might cost too much over the long term, doing it by hand like that, but if it works, we can think about that later."

"For a limited time only," enthused Toomey. "Put that in the ads. 'Get your Vituminol in a hand-painted bottle which can be used later as a flower vase or simply a decoration. This offer good only as long as present supplies last.' "

"Whoever's been pasting on labels could spend his time painting," said Mrs. Landis, remembering that the labels were still being applied by hand.

"Henrietta, you're a girl after my own heart."

I nearly swallowed my tongue. He had never called her Henrietta before, and he had certainly never smiled like that, at anybody. She didn't seem to mind at all.

So the Landis household took up bottle painting, along with the plant staff, and two more girls were hired to help out in the afternoons. Even John, who insisted on his own brush and paint jar but found it quite impossible to confine his burgeoning talent to bottles with so many nice walls handy. No matter, all that could be taken care of later, and John had never enjoyed himself more, even among his pots and pans.

And it worked. People liked our fancy bottles. Sales increased and held steady even after we returned to the plain bottles with regular labels. By that time Mr. Jerome was turning another idea over in his mind—movie advertising. There were always a few commercial ads flashed on the screens of neighborhood theatres between double features, or between features and news.

"Nobody pays much attention to them," I pointed out. Nobody did. That was when people left the theater or went to the restroom or out into the lobby for a cigarette.

"Croaked the raven," retorted Mr. Jerome. "Of course they don't watch them because they're boring. But they *do* watch the animated cartoons. And in something like that we might be able to put over the idea of the aphrodisiac qualities without risking legal repercussions."

He said he knew a young commercial artist who'd be glad to pick up a little extra change. He'd see what they could work out.

It was about that time that, after a three-week slump, a sudden avalanche of orders came in and had us working night and day and still unable to keep up. Some of our retail outlets even reported turning customers away. "When John is denied anything," I commented, "it only makes him all the more determined to get it. I hope it works that way with our customers."

"You may turn out to be a credit to me yet," said Mr. Jerome, patting me enthusiastically on the head.

The next day quarter-page ads appeared in all the newspapers announcing:

Due to an unexpected avalanche of orders, our supply of one critical ingredient of VITUMINOL, the tonic that puts pep in your step has become completely exhausted. As soon as additional shipments are received from our Far Eastern suppliers, we will immediately resume production. Thank you for your patience.

"Far eastern Indianapolis," I said, and made a face at Mr. Jerome, but Mrs. Landis regarded him fondly. "Don't you ever run down?" she asked.

"Never before I reach the top of the hill," he replied. "That's when boredom sets in, when you start coasting."

"Even in bootlegging?" I inquired.

"You do persist in being the burr under my saddle, don't you? The tragedy of my whole life has been that nothing remained exciting after a time, not even bootlegging. Maybe it will be different now that I am growing old."

"Are you?" I asked, not expecting, or getting, an answer.

Next afternoon I found him down in the middle of the living room floor playing ball with John and trying to teach him to say Grandpapa. It seemed to me rather a mouthful for a child who until quite recently had been getting along splendidly on his two-word vocabulary, *dah* and *hi*. Besides, I wondered if it was going to be worthwhile. I had a feeling that when the excitement began to wane and the coasting started, Forster Jerome would disappear from John's life as swiftly and silently as he had once disappeared from mine.

XXXIV

That was the year people began to say times were getting better. They claimed the depression had bottomed and there was no way to go but up. Certainly at our house the clouds were rifted and light was shining through, for Vituminol was finally catching on in a big way. A large share of the credit was due Abner Wagon, the young cartoonist Mr. Jerome had found to do the ads for the movie screens. What Mr. Wagon had come up with was a series of animated cartoons featuring Dan Cupid and his cousin Stan Stupid with Stan's girl friend Ruby Shy. In one of the early episodes Dan Cupid, answering Stan Stupid's desperate appeal for help in winning his girl, shoots both Stan and Ruby with his love arrows, and keeps right on shooting while Stan pursues the still unsmitten Ruby through fire, flood, and hurricane. Faced with a choice between Stan and a slavering grizzly bear, Ruby unhesitatingly opts in favor of the grizzly and is about to be carried off.

But wait. Dan Cupid pulls from his quiver—another arrow? No. A bottle of Vituminol, into which he dips an arrow pours the rest of the bottle down his throat, fits arrow to bow, and lets fly. Behold! Ruby's eyes start flaring like searchlights. Stan isn't stupid any more, he's all lit up to take off like a rocket. They run into each other's arms. They clinch. And the bear? Still slavering, he goes lumbering off to the top of the hill where waits a lady grizzly guzzling down a bottle of Vituminol. He grabs the bottle, guzzles down what's left, and he and the lady bear go into a clinch. At fadeout even the arrows are embracing each other.

The kids in the balcony were soon greeting the cartoon's appearance with hoots and catcalls to show their appreciation, and it was they who finally put the word around. Stan Stupid and Ruby Shy as well as "Try Vituminol" became part of their youthful slanguage. Not that anybody really believed in that sort of thing, of course, but sales rocketed all the same, then settled down to a steady growth.

Once more we were in a position to support ourselves and our accumulation of cars and houses, upgrade our diet, and even splurge a little, except for one thing. We'd got too rich too quickly to feel entirely comfortable about it, especially with so many of our friends still out of jobs and living on their uppers. Not that we hadn't done our bit by providing jobs for a dozen or so people; but for some reason probably only Stan Stupid would have understood, we were plagued with a slight feeling of embarrassment.

On second thought, except Mr. Jerome from that embarrassment. *He* was taking it perfectly in stride. Irascible as ever, seldom betraying the slightest tender emotion, he went his way as usual. Or almost as usual. Eunice came to see me one day, flushing becomingly and stammering worse than Toomey had in years, and announced that Mr. Jerome had invited her to dinner that evening.

"Fine," I said. "You accepted, I hope."

"Yes, I did, but I—well, you know I said such awful things about him when you were going out with him."

"Nothing that wasn't true," I said, and laughed. "We still don't know much about him, and he can certainly be hell on wheels at times, but he'll take you to a nice place, and he'll treat you nicely too. No reason you shouldn't enjoy yourself for a change."

"Hi," said John, strolling in with a wagonload of blocks and submitting gracefully to Eunice's hug and kiss. Submitting, did I say? Perish the thought. He enjoyed every minute of it. The more people he had paying court to his infant charms, the better he liked it.

"The scrounge," I said. "Spoiled rotten, of course. But he *is* toilet trained, even if it was through a fluke."

It wasn't that John had objected to sitting on his nursery chair at intervals through the day, he just couldn't seem to get it through his downy head what he was there for, nor did he mind in the least going around soaking wet, a combination of circumstances which served to frustrate all my efforts at training.

Mrs. Mullery told me a few hearty smacks on the bottom were what he needed to set him straight; but besides feeling diametrically opposed to any and all of Mrs. Mullery's pronouncements, it hardly seemed cricket to start thwacking away on somebody about a fourth my size. John would have cried and I would have felt like a brute, neither prospect filling me with joy. Besides that, I'd once slapped his hand to keep him from grabbing a hot pan on the stove, and he'd kept running to me the rest of the afternoon to kiss it and make it well.

Just to feel I wasn't neglecting my maternal duty, however, I did keep up the routine of the potty chair, accompanying those sessions with some choice bits of moral suasion which I had some faint hope might result in John getting the idea sometime before he had to start to school.

Then one bright spring morning he declined to sit, became in fact quite verbose about it, stiffened his back as if somebody had driven a steel rod through his spine. His vocabulary had grown by leaps and bounds in recent months but interpretation was still a problem, especially with him flinging his arms about and becoming more indignant by the second. What I finally made out of part of it was: "Me do like daddy inna bafroom."

With him still yammering away like crazy, and Mrs. Landis and Pinky hovering discreetly in the background, I telephoned Toomey at the plant. "Oh, that," he said nonchalantly. "Well, he saw me, you know."

"So?" I said impatiently. He trailed Toomey more faithfully than his shadow, snooping uninhibitedly into everything Daddy was doing.

"Oh, well, you know how it is. Sometimes you just start noticing something that's been right under your nose for a long time. Anyway, he was hooked, so I stacked some books for him to stand on and—well, that's it. Evidently he remembered."

So that was what all the catalogs were doing in the bathroom. "Goodbye," I said. "He's in a hurry."

"Men," I muttered scathingly, as I rushed off to start pyramiding catalogs, and not a second too soon.

Immensely gratified with his performance, John hurried off to tell Grandmama all about it.

So maybe I was as lousy an excuse for a mother as Mrs. Mullery implied but there must have been a few bugs in her system too because she was constantly bemoaning the fact that their married sons, all living within spitting distance, visited them so infrequently she hardly recognized her own grandchildren.

"Why don't they sell out and move away?" I would bemoan after each encounter. Even accepting Mrs. Landis's theory that Mrs. Mullery was the world's prize bad example, I'd absorbed the lesson now and could well get along without reminders.

With all her spying, however, and all her unscheduled visits to our otherwise pleasant household, it was a long time before she tumbled to the fact that Toomey must be, in a manner of speaking, employed. She did not, in fact, bring up the subject until the early trials had been overcome and Toomey had begun to observe more or less regular working hours.

"PureSilk starting up again?" she demanded one day in that you-may-as-well-tell-me-for-I'll-find-out-anyway manner of hers.

There wasn't a reason in the world not to confess all except my own mental block against satisfying her curiosity in any way whatsoever. "Not that I've heard," I replied.

"Oh?" Her look was hard and suspicious. "Your husband's been going back and forth to work. Somewhere."

Well, let me see now. I could tell her he couldn't stand

staying around the house any more and was spending his days in the bus station, or that he was dividing his time between us and his other wife and children in Kokomo, or—oh, the heck with it anyway. "That's true," I said.

"He's got a job then. Where?"

I took my time about answering. Finally I said, "A new place just starting up. Sort of a bottling plant."

"Well, you have to take what you can get these days, even if it doesn't pay much."

"As you say," I returned, trying to look depressed instead of disgusted.

"Why doesn't *she* crash through the driveway?" I demanded after the miserable creature had taken her leave.

"We could just wall her up in the dungeon then, and no one would ever know."

"Mother Landis," I reproved. "Sometimes you rather shock me."

"Oh, I become quite devilish every now and then, at least on the inside."

I didn't doubt it. Toomey had to get it from somewhere, and I doubted very much that it had been from his muscle-headed father. His latest approach to devilment, now that Vituminol had passed the crisis, was to launch another whirlwind courtship.

"Remember what hapened during the last one," I warned him.

"Actually I was thinking more in terms of the educational aspects. We who grew up under the Volstead Act are a deprived generation."

"Having missed out on the cultural influence of the corner saloon, I suppose you mean."

"Cocktail lounge, if you don't mind. Get hep, baby. There's a new one opening up on Thirty-fourth near the Ritz Theater. The Rocking Blue Note."

"You're not a drinking man," I reminded him.

He shrugged. "I can take it or leave it alone. It's the atmosphere that matters. Dim lights, seductive music, and the booths have high backs, very private for necking."

"So's the living room sofa," I pointed out. "So's a bed. And just where's the percentage in trying to seduce a girl who's already been?"

He regarded me somberly. "A careful man keeps reinforcing his fences," he said.

So we went to the Rocking Blue Note, which was dark enough to discourage sampling anything that didn't have enough alcohol in it to kill the germs. We went to a lot of other places too: Hideaway, Bide-a-Bit, Linger Withus, Rose Room, Sammy's Snappy Subway, Zeke's Famous Bar and Grill, and a few dozen others. There seemed to be a new one springing up every other week. All had the same murky atmosphere and the same tubercular-looking piano player pounding out with consummate boredom a succession of popular tunes.

The experience was, as Toomey claimed, educational in a way but eventually it began to pall and I could see my gallant courter becoming restless again. Then one night when the Rocking Blue Note was more crowded than usual, we agreed to share our booth with a pair of late comers, a man whose face looked to have been shaved with a rasp twice that day, and a tall pale blonde with hyperthyroid eyes and slightly protruding teeth. Noting that she was wearing a tiny diamond but no wedding ring, Toomey snatched my left hand off the table and imprisoned it on his knee before observing gloomily, "You're not married either, I see. God, ain't it hell?"

"Yeah," returned the redfaced man with a sickly smile. "No use thinking about it though, with both of us having to help out at home."

Toomey's answer to this was a despondent rise and fall of the shoulders and a mouth almost as inverted as Walter Mullery's.

"Stella's dad lost his job three years ago," the other man volunteered in an aggrieved tone of voice. "My mother's a widow."

"Same here," gloomed Toomey. "Ma could manage maybe if it wasn't for the kids. Seven of them," he deplored, raising his eyes despairingly to somewhere in the general direction of where he evidently assumed heaven to be.

"Three husbands," he continued unhappily. "That's what we call them anyway."

Then, almost as an afterthought, "Little Billy's four now but Ma's only thirty-six herself so there may be a few more."

"It's your duty to help your parents," Stella chimed in, speaking earnestly in a voice like chalk squeaking down a blackboard. "That's what I say to Ernie here, I know my duty."

"And you *do* your duty," returned Toomey with equal fervor. "I can tell that just looking at you." And then I saw to my horror that he was quaking inside again, although he had seemed to recover from that after our marriage. "What I say is, what's a *guy* supposed to do? Blow up? I mean, all the other fellows are doing it, ain't they?"

"Well," equivocated Ernie with a desperate glance at Stella.

"Exactly. So where does that leave us? Feeling exactly like Stan Stupid. Worse than Stan. After all he could try Vituminol. If I did that, I'd really blow a gasket." He slumped disconsolately beside me.

"But it's for a good cause," exhorted Stella. "That's the way you have to think about it. Like with Ernie here. 'I respeck you, Stella,' Ernie says. And that means something. Just ask your girl friend here if it doesn't mean something."

"Theodosia, darling, does it mean something to you?" He looked at me soulfully, practically strangling in his own cussedness. "Tell me it means something," he implored. "Please do."

"Sure it does, lover," I replied in a nasal whine. "If there's one thing in this world I respeck it's respeck. It's the kid I worry about, though." I turned to Stella. "Always pestering me," I explained, "about why don't his daddy live with us all the time like the other kids' daddies. What am I supposed to tell him?"

The silence was thick enough to slice. I saw that Stella's face was almost the same brickish shade Ernie's had been before he started turning pale. "You have a child—I mean by a previous marriage—or something?" she managed to choke out.

"Well, not exact—" I started to say, but Ernie drowned me out. "What's the matter with *him*?" he gasped. "My God, he's choking to death!"

Toomey was partially slumped over the table and I saw that his face had indeed gone an alarming shade of purplish red. I thumped him vigorously between the shoulder blades until he began to breathe again. "Fits," I explained succinctly. "He has them all the time. Come along outside, tiger, let's cool you down."

Eyes streaming, Toomey struggled gamely to his feet and slapped a ten-dollar bill down on the table. "There," I said soothingly to Ernie and Stella. "Take care of the waiter, will you? And order another round for yourselves."

Toomey gave them a sad watery smile. "Try Vituminol," he advised bleakly. "See you around."

"You're ashamed of me," he accused, once we were safely back in Peggy and on our way home.

"Put it like this, buster; from this point on there's no way to go but up. Watch your driving, for Pete's sake!"

"Yes, baby. Want to know what I've just decided?"

"Can't it wait until morning when I'm stronger?"

"Might forget by then. The bars don't fizz any more, sweetheart. We'll just have to do the rest of our courting in bed."

"Amen," I said fervently.

XXXV

A few days before Christmas Mr. Jerome took John downtown and brought him home carrying a doll almost as tall as he was; a glamorous creature too, with long blonde curls, moving eyes, and wearing a gorgeous lace-trimmed velvet dress. "He wanted it," was Mr. Jerome's simple explanation.

"Honestly!"

"A doll won't hurt him, honey," Toomey interposed.

"Whoever said it would? It's grandpapa's mentality I'm concerned about, giving an expensive doll like that to a two-year-old."

Then I saw John's face. There he stood, poor tyke, clutching his imperiled darling to his bosom like Eliza preparing to take to the ice. I picked him up and kissed him. "She's a pretty baby," I said. "Show Mama how she goes to sleep."

He tilted the doll's head until its eyes swung down, real hair lashes fanning out over the pink bisque cheek. "Pretty baby," he echoed softly, his little face luminous. "Sleep in my bed."

"Gets more like his father every day," I remarked, as John started wriggling to be put down.

"Now that we have that settled," said Mr. Jerome, "I have an announcement to make. Eunice and I are going to get married."

Maybe I shouldn't have been so surprised. He and Eunice

had been going out together for several weeks but I had never thought about them getting married. "I'm truly happy for both of you," I finally managed to say. "When is the wedding?"

"In January. Just a small affair but you're all invited."

"We'll be there," I said, and Toomey agreed.

Somehow, though, it still bothered me. Eunice must be around thirty by now, and Mr. Jerome somewhere past fifty, so they ought to know what they were doing, but—then I deliberately put the matter out of mind. It was, after all, their affair, and I was simply being silly.

The next morning Toomey popped out of bed when the alarm went off, closed the window, and tossed me my bathrobe. It was still lying there when he came back from the bathroom, and so was I.

He said, "Shake a leg, woman. Aren't you going to get my breakfast?"

"I doubt it," I said.

He did a double take. "You're not coming down with the flu or something, are you?"

"What a weird idea. It's just—I mean, there seems no real point to setting the kitchen on fire this time."

He staggered over and dropped heavily down on the edge of the bed. "You mean—maybe—again?"

I nodded.

"During the last courtship, you think?"

"Perhaps, but I was being careless before that. It just comes over me sometimes. Like if you keep your feet on the ground, how're you going to soar?"

"Yeah." He was trying terribly hard to appear blasé but the grin was coming on in spite of his efforts to control it. "I wonder what the General will say?" he asked in delighted anticipation which seemed a little premature to me. "I'll fix breakfast. What do you want?"

"Not a thing, not even a smell. *Especially* not a smell," I amended after a hasty consultation with my stomach.

But even this would pass away, as it had done before. Until it did I would just lie here quietly and think about

Eunice and Mr. Jerome, and the General, and how nice it would be to have another baby to cuddle, and wonder what John would think about it.

"You want anything before I go?" Toomey poked his head around the door, then followed it into the room.

"You're already getting that cock-who-crowed-the-sun-up look," I accused him.

"Think of that, and I didn't even need Vituminol. Can I start telling people?"

"Why bother? All they have to do is look at your face. And please, if you don't mind, put a sack over that when you go out to the car so Mrs.Mullery won't see it. Anyway, we're not sure yet."

"Want to bet?"

"Not with you, thanks. Don't forget to wish Eunice happiness. And tell her we're expecting both of them for Christmas dinner."

"How about that?" He looked suddenly thoughtful, then shrugged, kissed me again, and went out.

Pinky and Mrs. Landis came to the door, both of them looking pleased as Punch, looked me over, then smiled knowingly at each other. "How did *you* find out already?" I demanded.

"Toomey was talking to himself as he went out the door," explained Mrs. Landis.

"And what was Toomey saying?" I asked suspiciously.

" 'Remember you are only a man.' "

John arrived, barefoot, in his pajamas, and lugging his oversize doll, to investigate the situation. He laid the doll on my pillow, then climbed up beside me, twisting this way and that until he'd got his nest made, then settled down for a long serious discussion of Pretty Baby's 'turls,' eyes, shoes, socks, and the lace on her underwear. This boy was really hooked. For the nonce at least Pretty Baby had displaced even Teddy in his affections. And that reminded me of something else.

"Did Toomey have a doll when he was little?" I asked when Pinky came in bearing tea and some soda crackers. "I suppose not, though; his father wouldn't have allowed it."

"He took it away from him once," she said, "but I got it out of the trash and cleaned it up. After that we kept it hidden during the day but Mrs. Landis slipped it to him every night when he went to bed."

"Bless you," I said warmly.

"It's a wicked thing to hurt a child, especially when there's no call to." She leaned conspiratorially close. "You really do think?"

"I really do, and I'm glad. Or will be when my stomach gets anchored again."

"It won't be long if it's like the other time. And it's such a good thing to have children around. So many women don't seem to want them these days."

I wondered if she was thinking of her daughter and her daughter-in-law, neither of whom had yet seen fit to provide her with a grandchild. "Maybe they're just trying to prove how clever and up-to-date they are," I suggested, "by using the latest things available to avoid getting pregnant."

She chuckled appreciatively. "Just like my dear mother said about dresses with bustles. She said they were dreadfully uncomfortable to sit down in, but it was better to stand up all the time than be out of style."

"Speaking of dresses, I suppose my maternity frocks must still be around somewhere."

"Right where I can lay my hands on them any time you're ready."

"Stand by," I said. "Pinky, what would we ever do without you?"

By Christmas morning I was feeling fine after the first hour or two, during which John had entertained me by snuggling beside me on the living room couch, together with Teddy, Pretty Baby and the white rabbit, and reciting his own version of Santa's visit with toys and the 'rainy deer.'

Mr. Jerome arrived around noon with Eunice, who was wearing a diamond big enough to strike mere mortals blind.

"One little question," I teased. "Surely you aren't going to go on calling him Mr. Jerome?"

"Paul," she said, turning to him with a smile that transfigured her whole face.

"It happens to be my first name," he returned serenely, "not that I have encouraged its indiscriminate use."

"*I* wouldn't dream of calling you anything but Mr. Jerome," I assured him. "It's nice to know, however, in case the new baby happens to be a boy."

"Don't tell me you're going in for that again."

"We have to do something. The bars don't fizz any more."

He glared at me. "How I ever got mixed up with this madhouse, I'll never know."

"Think hard, it may come to you."

"We are all so happy," said Mrs. Landis tranquilly.

Mr. Jerome glanced at her sharply, then at the rest of us as if he suspected a conspiracy. Then he turned back to her with a smile. "Yes, dear lady," he murmured. "I do believe we are."

Later Eunice and I talked together in the kitchen.

"It's nothing like it was with Fred, of course, but Paul's very good to me. He's—strange sometimes," she added, "but I suppose all men are."

"Undoubtedly," I agreed.

"Other women get used to being married, I guess I can too."

It wasn't the words that bothered me so much, it was the expression on her face. I started to say it could be gotten used to with no pain at all when there was love, that later she would realize how silly she was to have worried at all. Then I stopped myself. As the older girl of the three of us in the apartment, Eunice had never asked advice, she had given it. She had frequently accused Dorothy and me of frivolity. She would probably do so now. Before I could get my tongue working to say anything at all, John came into the kitchen with a collection of Christmas toys, which he proceeded to pile in Eunice's lap.

After the wedding Mr. Jerome and Eunice went to Florida, where they stayed for nearly two months. Even after they returned, we didn't see much of them, but it was natural enough for newlyweds to want to keep to themselves.

In any event my mind was pretty well occupied with a husband who was still fizzing at intervals, a small son whose inventive little mind never slept, and a pair of neighbors who watched us like hawks waiting to pounce.

With the coming of warm weather so John could play outside again, he stopped throwing things in the toilet and started slinging them over the hedge into the Mullyers' driveway. As was to be expected, they reacted instantly and unfavorably. Mr. Mullery's said it was kids like that who were headed straight for reform school.

"Fudge," I said.

"My dear young woman, I assure you I will not have that undisciplined child of yours littering my driveway with his trash."

"So throw it back," I said.

There wasn't after all any great lot of it, and it wasn't even an everyday occurrence, just when John happened to think about it. Toomey and I would push through the hedge and retrieve the stuff when we noticed it, and have another serious talk with our offspring, who had reached a stage in his development when talking seemed to make some impression, at least for a little while.

Then John lost a toy fire truck he was fond of and we couldn't find it anywhere. After it was dark that evening Toomey sneaked over to look in the Mullery's trash cans and came back laughing fit to split, with the truck under his arm. "Vituminol," he gasped. "Two empties in the trash can."

"So they must both be taking it, and goodness knows nobody ever needed it more," I commented.

But Toomey was in a bawdy mood and started speculating on the effect Vituminol might have on our neighbors' sexual life.

"If they knew where it comes from, it would curdle their blood," I said.

"No matter," said Toomey, waving it away. "We could do quite well without their business."

We could indeed; but as Vituminol sales continued to soar, Toomey's mood nevertheless began to sag in proportion. He was growing even more restless than he had during the period of his unemployment. "We ought to take a trip somewhere," he would say, "just the two of us." But when I would mention it later, he would seem to have lost interest.

He started spending a lot of time in the dungeon again but his former enthusiasm for such projects was missing. When I would go there to look for him, I would often as not find him standing quietly beside his workbench staring into space.

"I'm going to paint Peggy red again," he said once, but made no move to set about it. Frequently he reached home late for dinner without seeming to realize what time it was. "I got held up," he would say vaguely. "I had some things to do at the plant."

And then the telephone calls started. I'd have known that voice anywhere, even if she hadn't wanted me to, which I was convinced she did. Ava Brazeale, who had come to work when Eunice left to get married, was a willowy brunette who took considerable care with her makeup and clothes but seemed, I had thought, too languid to get much work done, much less set off in pursuit of anybody. "Isn't Toomey there?" she would inquire in a slow sultry voice. "Oh, it was Toomey I wanted." As if *I* had no right to answer the telephone in my own home!

Toomey was faithful, I would have staked my life on that; but ever since Adam had got bored enough to bite down on an old sour apple, men hadn't got over being susceptible to feminine wiles. After three and a half years maybe it was our marriage Toomey had decided didn't fizz any more. This Ava snake didn't seem at all his of tea but maybe his tastes had changed since our second courtship days. He certainly never seemed to mind returning her telephone calls, and it seemed to me they talked much longer than should have been necessary for purely business matters. I hadn't yet stooped low enough to eavesdrop but I was getting closer to it all the time.

My imagination, the scope of which had been commented upon by experts, was still in dandy working order. When Toomey drove off to work in the morning, I thought about all those hours he would be spending in *her* company, more *waking* hours, in fact, than he spent in mine. And while in my opinion the bedding hours were the critical ones, and they remained eminently satisfactory, I still fretted. But did nothing. What was there to do?

A family named Appleton with four children moved into the house the other side of the Mullerys which had been vacant for a long time. Both the Mullerys were practically apoplectic but John was delighted to have playmates living so close. They were nice children too, girls eight and ten, a boy five, and another girl about John's age. Mr. Mullery threatened to have the law on them for cutting across his yard to get to ours, said they were killing his grass. Mrs. Mullery watched their every move, and John's from the vantage point of her living room window.

One afternoon the wretched woman came bursting into my kitchen with her apron draped around my otherwise naked and loudly wailing son. She was almost, but unfortunately not quite, speechless with indignation. She had caught this monster of depravity running around in his own yard *stark naked before all those girls*!

Three girls to be exact, with a brother of their own. If seeing a naked boy was any novelty to them, I'd miss my guess. "Hi, kid," I said, and tipped my erring son a wink, whereupon he stopped crying and started grinning. It was, after all, his latest and proudest accomplishment, managing to unbutton his clothes and slip out of them, and he was finding it twice as intriguing as throwing things over the hedge.

"Hey, Mrs. Landis." The Appleton boy, Jimmy, had come to the screen door. "Can John come out and play some more?"

"Tell you what," I said. 'You kids gather up John's clothes and bring them in, will you? Then you can all have cookies and milk. O. K.?"

"Yes, ma'am!" He gave me a gap-toothed grin and ran off the porch yelling at the others.

I had almost forgotten Mrs. Mullery but when I turned around, she was still there. "Well, what are *you* staring at!" I demanded. "Surely *you're* seen a naked boy before!"

As she went waddling off I tried to make myself look at her legs but I couldn't. I had a dreadful feeling they might not be legs at all but something slithery and scaly and awful.

I picked up my erring son and kissed him on the nose. "You're a ringtailed tooter," I said.

He patted my face, beamed, and said, "Pretty Mama." This kid was going to get along fine, no doubt of that. He was Toomey Landis to the life.

And that, of course, started me fretting again. If that hipless, bustless, practically voiceless female imagined for one three-thousandths of a second she was going to take Toomey away from John and me, she had better start imagining something else! Was that why she had taken Eunice's job in the first place, just to have a chance at Toomey? With me pregnant, and a period of prolonged abstinence in the offing, she probably figured the time had come to make her move. She could never get Toomey, never in this world, but she could spoil things. Only I wouldn't let her. The next time she called—

That was when it struck me that the last time she'd called had been several days before, maybe a week, maybe more. But did that comfort me? It did not. When they went underground was the most critical time of all.

"Miss Brazeale hasn't called for awhile," I remarked that evening at dinner, in a breezy voice that surely wouldn't fool him for a minute.

"Miss Brazeale doesn't work for us any more."

"Oh," I said. His voice had sounded pretty grim. Maybe they'd quarrelled.

"You knew what she was up to, I suppose. Why didn't you say something?"

"Goodness," I said virtuously. "I never even listened."

"Why didn't you look after me better? You know how naive I am where women are concerned. Look how easy I was for you to catch."

"Yah!" I said, and we were off on another one of those philosophical discussions with which we whiled away the hours.

But there was still something wrong. "Toomey," I said to him after we were in bed, "why don't you tell me what's really bothering you?"

"Does it show that much?"

"Then there is something. About business?"

"Good old Vituminol, and don't think I'm not grateful but—how do you feel about the patent medicine business, baby?"

"It's fine for the bank account but otherwise not inspiring."

"You feel that way too?"

"Well, we never really believed in it, did we? Any more than *they* did. Yasmina and Dr. Modesta. It was just a—well, a sort of lark that got us out of a very tight corner. What I'm trying to say is, it fizzed fine, but when the fizz is gone, what's left?"

He hugged me so tight I could feel my rib cage collapsing. "Baby!" he exulted. "What did I ever do to deserve you!"

"Think back," I advised. "Surely there was something."

"We've paid off our half the investment," he said. "Maybe I could sell out to Mr. Jerome, if you're sure you wouldn't mind."

"You're the breadwinner. Choose your own tools."

"That's what's kind of crazy. I don't really know what I want to do. I like to work with my hands, machines and things, but I don't know where I could get a job, or even if there's some way I might set up for myself."

"So think it over."

"I don't know how much my half share of Vituminol would be worth, even if I can sell it, but if I can, I'll give half of it to you to stash somewhere out of reach, and I'll see what I can do with the rest of it."

"No," I said.

"Because it's too risky?"

"More so than you think, but with my half, not yours. I'm half Broadbent, remember? Maybe I'm afraid of money, but I don't want to let it become too important to me. And it might, with a lump sum like that put away somewhere we're not supposed to touch."

"It wouldn't be too different from the quilt, would it?"

"Yes, it would. The money in the quilt was more like a savings account for a special purpose. It was on my account Mama was trying to avoid an open break with my father; but if it had come to that, she intended to use it to see me through college. When I decided not to go, the money was still there for whatever I needed it for."

"Including tiding us over a rough stretch. That's what worries me now, honey. I'm not the most practical fellow in the world, and no telling what may happen if I break away from Jerome. I may land us right back in the soup, and that wouldn't be fair to you or the babies."

"Pooh," I said. "Our babies have gypsy blood."

I was an idiot, an absolutely feckless creature with more brain cells than I'd ever begin to use, and it was all Yasmina's fault. All that business of knowing the value of what I had while I still had it was going to ruin me yet.

"I'm such a mess, Vicki. Sometimes I can't imagine why you put up with me at all, but thank goodness you do." He pressed his lips to the hollow of my throat and presently began the familiar ritual of our passion.

"Eunice is going to have a baby too," I said later. "She told me today."

"Really? I wonder how Jerome feels about that."

"She says he's terribly pleased."

He was silent for so long I thought he'd fallen asleep. Then he said, "You weren't really worried, were you, about Ava?"

"In a seething rage," I assured him. "Not that I would ever have let her have you. I'd have turned her into a spider."

XXXVI

As it happened, it was neither I nor John nor the Appleton children who finally did the Mullerys in but a two-months-old almost-beagle called, at John's insistence, simply Puppy.

John's devotion to Puppy was complete and unwavering. He even undertood housebreaking chores, suffering all the pangs of conscientious motherhood at the little creature's occasional lapses.

July had been unusually hot and dry, and by the end of that month, when I was also in the later stages of my pregnancy, I was feeling graceless as a water buffalo but with absolutely none of that beast's legendary patience. Along with everything else, the Mullerys had kept up a barrage of complaints all summer, the latest centering around a maple tree in our back yard. It was an old tree that had been there for years. John's swing was attached to one of the lower limbs, and Mrs. Landis enjoyed sitting out there in its shade to read or knit.

The Mullerys had enjoyed its shade too in other years, for the tree stood just inside our back fence; but now they claimed they wanted to start a flower bed in that portion of the yard, the plants they had decided upon naturally being those which required a lot of sun. Mr. Mullery finally came up with a claim that not only was our fence on his property but at least two inches of our tree. He said both had to come down or he was going to sue.

I began to communicate with Yasmina at more frequent intervals, hoping that even now she wasn't past putting some kind of hex on the Mullerys, but calling to her attention it wouldn't do to turn them into toads because John liked toads. He also liked frogs, birds, squirrels, grasshoppers, fish, rabbits, and even the common house fly. He'd lie on his stomach for hours studying an ant hill. I didn't want to look out the door one day and see him petting some bird, beast or insect that might be one of the Mullerys.

It was while I was mulling this over for about the ninety-third time that John summoned me into the living room to witness the result of Puppy's latest indiscretion. "I tell he and tell he," declared John, on the verge of tears, "but he do it anyway. Wight on the wug!"

On the point of going after the culprit with a rolled-up newspaper, I suddenly stayed my hand. With people like the Mullerys cluttering up the world, why waste my powder on a little boy and his dog?

"He so *bad*," quavered John, his lower lip vibrating like a tuning fork but all the while hugging Puppy so tight the breath was about to be squeezed out of him.

I sat down in the nearest chair and pulled them both onto what was left of my lap. "Puppy's only a baby," I said. "He doesn't mean to be bad but he forgets."

A thumb strayed toward John's mouth, the other hand still clutching puppy by the ruff.

"We'll just have to keep telling him," I said.

"So he be good Puppy and we like him?"

"Oh well, we like him anyway, don't we? But he's got to stop peeing on the floor."

"You like Puppy when he be good?"

"Love him when he's good, love him when he's bad," I declared airily.

At which John sat up and extracted his thumb. "You like he when he ba-a-a-ad!"

Aha, my hearty. Gives you something to think about, doesn't it? I found myself smiling. "Why not?" I said. "I love *you* when you're good and love you when you're bad."

It was too much for him to digest all at once. He frowned and shook his head. I kissed him, patted Puppy's head, and said, "Let's all go out in the yard where it's cooler. If I'm nice to your baby, little John, maybe you'll be nice to mine. There's always that to think about too."

Once in the front yard Puppy made straight for his favorite outdoor comfort station, the hedge. He couldn't have had so much as a teaspoon of ammunition left in him but he used what he had. And Mrs. Mullery pounced, and said it would kill the hedge.

"Which," I said scathingly, "is undoubtedly exactly on the property line."

"Certainly," Hands on hips like the Irish washerwoman, mouth pinched together like a badly-done buttonhole, pale eyes squinting into the sun.

Stand by, Yasmina. She was there all right, I could have reached out and touched her. "Exactly on the property line, would you say?"

"Certainly." But to my astonishment she stepped back a little and seemed pale.

"And how wide *is* that line? Say a hundredth of an inch? So it seems to me that at least half your precious hedge is on our land, and Puppy has my permission to pee on our half whenever he feels like it."

And she took it! That was the unbelievable thing. She stood there and took it without a word, then turned and went trotting back into her own house. Just before she slammed the door I remembered to take a quick glance at her legs in case I never got another chance. They seemed in no wise remarkable, which was more than I could say for her actions. A strange feeling began to come over me. Maybe Mrs. Mullery had sensed Yasmina's presence there beside me. Or maybe it was—something else.

Toomey came home from work that evening looking tired and, for him, depressed. He'd talked to a lawyer who, while deploring the triviality on which the complaint was based, said Mr. Mullery would probably be able to make a case. If he won, we would have to move the fence back; and since the tree could scarcely be moved, or a few inches sliced off the offending side, it would probably have to go. "Heaven help us," said Toomey, if they ever find out about the dungeon."

"Toomey, did your mother have this property surveyed when she bought it?"

"I don't know. I was only twelve years old at the time so I wouldn't have thought of it, and probably she didn't either."

It occurred to me that I was speaking pretty learnedly about a subject I knew very little about but I went on to tell him about the affair of the hedge. "'Property line' seems to be the key phrase, at least it doused her like a bucket of cold water."

He frowned a little. "Something they've just found out, you mean?"

"Could be, or maybe they've known about it all the time. People so eager to accuse other people of things aren't always so simon pure themselves." And I was sure it wouldn't have bothered the Mullerys a bit to take advantage of a woman and a twelve-year-old boy if they thought they could get away with it.

"At least they know something now," I said, "but they think *we* don't. Or did, until I said the naughty words this afternoon."

"She could have had a sudden stomach cramp, I suppose, but it might be worth looking into."

"I *know* it's *something*," I said, "and so does Yasmina."

"In that case," he said, "I'd better look into it. I'll try to locate a surveyor tomorrow."

Not on the morrow but a few days later a surveyor appeared and, as it happened, completed his work and left while both the Mullerys were away from home. The verdict: Our property line ended almost seven feet beyond the hedge, smack dab along the Mullery driveway, placing more than half their garage on our land.

Armed with the surveyor's report and accompanied by his lawyer, Toomey went over to negotiate. Mr. Mullery blustered and threatened but there was no real force behind it. He said he was going to get another surveyor but he never did, and a few weeks later he put the property up for sale.

"Now," said Toomey, "I remember why I extended the dungeon walls so far. I was looking for that property line."

"Undoubtedly, but I'll bet *they* knew where it was all the time. They simply wanted more room for their new garage so they took it, figuring you'd never find out. Somehow though, and believe me I can't figure out why, I can't help feeling a little sorry for the poor miserable creatures."

I was conscious of ending that on a rather breathless note, and Toomey shot me an anxious glance. "Are you feeling all right, Vicki?"

"Just a twinge. Nobody starts having a baby in the middle of the morning."

But a couple of hours later there we were, rolling along on our way to the hospital. "So much pleasanter than last time," I commented. "No rain, no snow, no sleet, not even dark, and you're not a bit nervous, are you?"

"Of course not. I'm getting to be an old h-h-h-hand at this business."

"I noticed. That's why you're wearing one black shoe and one brown one. I think I kind of like it."

The baby was a girl, and we had not definitely decided on a name. Another boy we would have called Paul for Mr. Jerome and David because we liked it. We didn't, however, fancy Paula for a girl, Mrs. Landis threatened to go into seclusion if we inflicted her name on a helpless infant, and I felt sure Yasmina's reaction would be much the same.

"Julia Mary?" suggested Toomey.

I hesitated only for an instant. "Why not?" I said. "We'll probably call her Julie. How's my other baby? Does he miss me?"

"He was a little tearful last night but I told him I missed Mama too so why didn't he come in and sleep with me."

"Oh Toomey, I'll bet you didn't sleep a wink. Puppy too, I'm sure."

"*And* Teddy, *and* Pretty Baby. All the troops get called out in a crisis. It wasn't so bad though." He shrugged in self-deprecation. "John patted my face and told me I was pretty. Oh yes, and he loves me when I'm good and loves me when I'm bad, and Puppy loves me when—but you get the drift." He looked up, smiled winningly, and said, "Well, here we are again."

It was The General, looking very generalish indeed.

"Any time my corns start hurting during a dry spell, I know I'm in for trouble." She looked as intransigent as ever but I thought I detected an amused glint in her eye. "There are two other hospitals in the city, Mr. Landis, both of which are admirably equipped to handle your problems."

"Don't you worry a thing about it," Toomey said warmly. "We wouldn't dream of taking our trade away from you."

She glowered at him. "Just you stay away from that nursery then. You frighten off the other paying customers."

"Yes, ma'am," said Toomey cheerfully.

Mr. Jerome's roses arrived next afternoon, with the gentleman himself trailing them by less than an hour. Alone. Eunice was visiting her father, he said.

"She's getting along all right, isn't she?"

"Quite," he said, pulled up the only chair in the room, and sat down.

"I'm lucky this time," I said. "Last time you didn't come."

"No," he said, his expression as sardonic as ever.

"I was surprised you even knew I was married, or was having a baby."

This time the silence was longer. Then he said, "Surely you didn't expect me to lose sight of you, did you?"

"I thought you might be glad to, after all the trouble I'd caused you."

"Tell me about the baby."

"She's lovely. We've named her Julia Mary."

He still didn't smile but I thought his expression softened a little. "Then that's all right," he said.

"Yes, thanks to you."

"Nonsense," he said brusquely, and stood up. "We'll be over as soon as you get home with the baby," he promised.

"Please do, and give Eunice my love."

He suddenly bent over me and kissed me gently on the forehead. He said, "You're a good girl, Victoria."

Before I could find my voice again, he was gone.

XXXVII

If it had originally been Mr. Mullery's intention to shove his real estate problem off on some unsuspecting purchaser, he evidently changed his mind because, shortly after I came home from the hospital, he approached Toomey with an offer to purchase the disputed strip of land. Toomey refused. He said if the Mullerys had ever made the slightest effort to be satisfactory neighbors, he'd have given them the land but under the circumstances he positively wasn't going to sell it to them.

"They aren't going to be any more satisfactory if they have to tear down their garage," I commented.

"I made him a counter offer for the entire property."

His idea was sound enough, as most of his ideas were once you stripped away the wrapper and got down to essentials. Owning both properties would give him a free hand in correcting his own architectural blunders and reestablishing the boundary line as set out in the deeds. He then planned to tear down the Mullery house as well as the garage and put up a bungalow there for Mrs. Landis and Pinky.

We'd had discussions along those lines before. While Mrs. Landis and Pinky had never seemed unhappy living with us, and we certainly had no complaints, they would naturally prefer a place of their own, and one with no stairs to climb now that they were getting older. Pinky's rheumatism was especially troublesome, in spite of which she insisted on doing the same amount of work she always had, and would doubtless continue to do so long as they lived with us.

Mr. Mullery had, not unexpectedly, refused Toomey's offer but he might have second thoughts in the matter. If he continued to refuse to sell to us, Toomey thought we might be able to acquire the property through an agent. Mrs. Landis proposed paying for it herself if in the meantime she could sell two of her rent houses, which seemed possible now that real estate was beginning to move again. Toomey said it would be a good investment for whoever bought it since Mr. Jerome has assured him real estate prices had no way to go but upward.

"When did you see Mr. Jerome?" I asked. "I never did hear from Eunice, you know. I've called the house several times but the housekeeper will only say Mrs. Jerome isn't there and she doesn't know when she's expected."

"Eunice isn't coming back, Vicki."

You don't mean—"

"The marriage is over. Jerome didn't want you to know until after you'd recovered from having little Julie."

"It isn't as though I was critically ill with something," I said tartly. "I do remember now he acted rather strange when I asked about her. What on earth happened?"

Toomey shrugged. "Jerome doesn't say a lot about it, of course. Apparently Eunice never much took to the physical side of marriage, and when she got pregnant she claimed the doctor told her not to indulge any more. Jerome got in touch with the doctor, who denied it. Shortly after that Eunice took off and refuses to come back."

I had never thought of Eunice being a prude. A little more straight-laced than most girls I knew perhaps, but I suppose I'd just figured marriage would wipe out a few of her misconceptions just as it had mine. Still, there was what she'd said at Christmas, and now that I thought about it, she hadn't been anywhere near as crushed by Fred Currier's defection as I had expected her to be. "Where is she?" I asked. "Surely she wouldn't be visiting her father this long."

It seemed, however, that was where she was and where she planned to stay. "She doesn't even like him," I said. "I suppose she must have her side of it too, about Mr. Jerome, I mean, but they can't separate, Toomey, if they're going to have a baby."

I wrote to Eunice next day. Toomey said we had no right to meddle in their affairs, and ordinarily I would have agreed with him, but this once a little meddling seemed to be in order. "Tell Mr. Jerome," I said to Toomey, "if that's why he's been avoiding us, it isn't necessary. If he needs a special invitation, give him one."

Mr. Jerome seemed to be in his usual form when he came to supper a few evenings later, exuding his customary charm for John and Puppy, Mrs. Landis and Pinky. Even Julia Mary allowed herself to be held by him and petted and admired.

"You're certainly handy with babies," I commented.

"An old art is never entirely forgotten." He spoke calmly, laid the baby back in her cradle, and walked with me back to the living room. "I intend to have my son," he said then.

"Of course you must," I agreed warmly. "Eunice will come back, I know she will."

"Whether she does or not, I intend to have the child."

Was this then to be a child of contention, as I had been? "Eunice is just upset," I said. "Sometimes a woman gets that way when she's carrying a baby."

He looked exasperated. "How much do you know about Eunice's background?" he asked.

"Just what you pick up from living with somebody a year or two. Her mother's been dead for several years. Her father—well, she sent him money when he needed it but they never got along. Then he married his housekeeper, who wasn't a very nice woman, according to Eunice. She felt terrible about that but she still sent him money. The marriage broke up, I think. He has a small farm but not apparently a very good one if he couldn't make a living from it."

"He didn't make a living from it," said Mr. Jerome in

measured tones, "because the fat, dirty old reprobate is too lazy to do a lick of work. All he does is sit there stinking to high heaven, with tobacco juice trickling down his whiskered chin, and figure out how he can use Eunice to get enough money out of me to support him the rest of his useless life."

"But that isn't Eunice's fault."

"Eunice has got religion. A malady of her youth, I gather, recurring in its most virulent form. Not any of the rational varieties, of course, but good old time hysterical mindboggling fundamental religion, and all she can think about is repenting her sins, the greatest of which is me. And the old man, fully aware of which side his bread is buttered on, keeps egging her on."

"That doesn't seem like Eunice at all."

"Apparently you didn't know Eunice any better than I did. God knows I should have suspected there was something wrong with a woman who was still a virgin at thirty, but I was just flattered all the way to hell and gone that she'd saved it all for me. Bah! A woman who stays untouched too long ices over."

"You ought to be able to thaw her out," I said deliberately, "with all your experience."

If looks could achieve instant disintegration, I would have disappeared in a puff of smoke. "May I call to your attention that the kind of persuasion you're talking about requires a certain amount of physical contact. Eunice isn't having any."

"She'll come back to you," I said, trying to believe it.

"Of course she'll come back," he said cuttingly. "She didn't take much money with her, and I'm not sending her a cent. She'll have to come back when the money's gone because the old man will kick her out."

"You be nice to her when she comes," I said. "You still have a chance."

"Eunice's chastity is quite safe with me, for now and ever more. I only want the child."

I excused myself and led my son away to be put to bed.

"Gwanpapa mad," he said soberly.

"Not at you," I assured him. "He's had a disappointment, that's all, and he isn't taking it well."

He didn't know a disappointment from a hole in the ground but he was terrific absorber of moods. "Give Gwanpapa a cookie," he said.

"A very good idea. I'll do that."

"John's compliments," I said, when I handed Mr. Jerome the cookie a few minutes later. "He invites both of you to come kiss him goodnight."

He stared at me for a long moment before he stood up and followed Toomey out of the room. If only he would swallow some of his stiff-necked pride, there might be hope. If Eunice would only help him a little. If.

"So there's nothing to be done," said Toomey, after Mr. Jerome had left.

"It's the way girls are raised," I said. "Sex is the wrongest thing in the world until a girl gets married, then all of a sudden it gets to be right. Maybe the older a girl gets the harder it is for her to go into reverse and become the perfect little bed partner her husband expects her to be."

"But, baby, men have their obligations too."

His expression was perfectly guileless but I didn't trust him in the least. "They have a choice in the way they fulfill them," I snapped.

"I know, sweetheart," he said contritely.

What was there about this cunning creature that every time you aimed for the solar plexus, you found yourself patting his head? "It's got nothing to do with you," I said. "With us. It's just that I can understand how Eunice might feel."

That didn't seem to make as much sense as it should.

"I'm going to write her again tomorrow," I said.

"If you must, sweetheart, but you can't change the way other people feel."

I remembered all those discussions we used to have in the apartment, all the searching and groping, the misgivings, the misconceptions. Suddenly it came to me what had been missing from The Book—the way people feel about each other.

"*You* changed *me*," I said.

"Oh well," said Toomey agreeably, "that was different."

XXXVIII

In life there is growth. Some call it progress. Puppy became dependably housebroken. Baby Julie thrived and was loved by John almost as much as he loved Puppy although she wasn't as yet half the fun. He was conscientious about calling my attention to feeding times and diaper changes too. Some day he was going to be as good a father as Toomey.

With the first frost the leaves began to turn and then to fall. John accompanied us now on our pilgrimages to the woods and the apple orchards, deigning to point out a number of wonders we might otherwise have overlooked. To travel with a child is to see the world as it must have appeared to the first man on the dawn of creation.

Eunice had answered my letters with the briefest and chilliest of notes, saying that while she appreciated my interest, it was obvious I didn't understand the problems involved and any decisions would have to be made by her. It didn't sound like Eunice, at least not like the Eunice I had known. Then one morning she telephoned that she was back in town and wanted to see me. I invited her over for lunch.

She had sounded all right on the phone but when she came in, I saw that her color was bad and there were deep shadows under her eyes. "I don't really blame you for taking his part," she began in her old forthright manner, but there was a set to her lips that bothered me. I wondered when and where I had seen that expression before.

"I mean, after all he's done for you and Toomey," she said.

"That has nothing to do with it," I said, trying to conceal my irritation at her last remark. "We're fond of both of you, and you can't possibly have got over loving each other this soon."

"Love," she said witheringly. "Yes, I remember only too well what you said in your letter but I certainly don't agree with you."

I remembered then where I'd see that set of the lips before, on my sister-in-law Orpha; and it bothered me more than anything Eunice had said so far. "If you didn't want that kind of love," I said, "I don't see why you wanted to get married at all."

She simply sat there with that mulish expression on her face, not saying a word.

"You were so good to me," I said. "Always so good to me when I needed you. I only want to help you now."

"I thought he'd be over all that foolishness by now. He's certainly old enough to be.

"He was beastly, Vicki! There's no other word for it! He said I would learn to—*enjoy* it. Then later he said I wasn't even a woman. I guess not, like all the other women he's had!"

That struck an extremely sensitive spot of my own, that I had once become infatuated with him, that even now I could respect him and be fond of him, knowing what I did about him. "Those other women," I said carefully, "were before he knew you. He didn't marry any of them, he married you. It's you he loves."

"You don't know anything about it!" she flung at me furiously. "Toomey's such a *boy*!"

I knew now how Yasmina must have felt in those seconds just before she blew. "God in heaven," I said, "surely you don't imagine Toomey or any other man ever came to his marriage bed a virgin. I've always known there were other girls, and I can't say I enjoy thinking about it, but that was all before me, the same as Mr. Jerome's other women were before you. Those are facts of life, dammit, that you must have known when you married the man, so why don't you come down off your high horse and make your marriage work?"

Eunice was staring at me, her eyes wide with astonishment. "You don't have to remind me what a sinner I was," she said when she was able to speak. "But I have to stop sinning now, not just get deeper into it. Don't you see that? It makes me feel dirty just to think of him ever touching me again."

"You came back to him," I said inexorably. "If you hated him that much, you wouldn't have come back."

"I had to come back," she said, speaking quite calmly now. "I ran out of money and he wouldn't send me any, and I certainly can't be expected to get a job in my condition."

I knew then that further words would be wasted. "Let's go to the kitchen," I said. "I'll fix something for lunch."

Obediently as a child she got up and followed me.

"You love Toomey too much," she said querulously. "It isn't right to love a man so much."

"How is one to know," I wondered aloud, "how much love is wise and how much is foolish and what is the proper blend?

She was in no mood for my homely philosophy but I noticed with some surprise that our argument had not spoiled her appetite for lunch. She ate heartily and, by the time she had finished, had begun to act more like her former self.

In November Mrs. Mullery began to announce to everybody she saw that they were selling out and moving to Florida. "*Nobody* would spend a winter in *this* climate," she proclaimed, "if they could afford to go anywhere else."

That *they* could do so was, of course, due to the fact that Mr. Mullery had finally accepted Toomey's original offer for their house, having probably received no other. During those last weeks the Mullerys became almost amiable.

We continued to see the Jeromes every two or three

weeks, occasionally at their house but more often at ours, where the rest of our household could help relieve the rather stilted occasions. Mr. Jerome maintained a studious politeness toward Eunice but there was no detectable interplay of emotion between them, nor was there any mention of the coming baby.

Then almost before we knew it, we were putting up the Christmas tree, and John was telling Puppy and the baby about Santa Claus coming down the chimney with a sackful of toys. Never a fear about the poor old chap getting roasted in the fireplace. "We had a baseburner," I remembered to Toomey. "You had to keep the doors tight shut every minute or the poisonous gasses would escape into the room and kill you plumb dead. I always wondered how Santa would ever get out of that stove even if he did manage to get down the chimney."

"Such a literal child."

"Quite so. By the way, what are you getting me for Christmas?"

"How about another courtship?"

"It's getting so," I objected, "I can hardly tell where one leaves off and the next begins."

"How about a celebration then?"

"Celebration of what?" I demanded suspiciously.

"Well, I *was* going to save it for Christmas."

"You won't last that long unless you tell me. You've been jumpy as a bug on a hot stove lid for a week."

"O.K., since you've dug it out of me. We're taking over PureSilk and starting it up again." The beam was positively blinding.

"Who's *we*?"

"A group Jerome got together to finance the deal, and they're going to use my patent. Darling, it's going to be sensational!"

The same group, he said, would take over Vituminol and put a manager in charge of it, releasing Toomey to oversee the setting up of the machinery for the new hosiery line. His half-interest in Vituminol would also entitle him to a part interest in the new combine. "I could have had a vice-presidency," he said, trying his best to sound casual about it, "which would, of course, have meant a bigger salary."

His voice was questioning, and I had seen that same look on John's face, even on Puppy's, a mute plea for understanding of words which were not spoken. "You do what you have to do," I said. "Just make it fizz."

He gathered me to him in an enormous hug and kissed me hard. "Why can't you kick up a fuss now and then like other wives?"

"I'd make a lousy vice-president's wife. What else did you get me for Christmas?"

Eunice's baby was born in January, a little boy who died within a few hours of his birth. The child, Mr. Jerome told us, had been badly deformed, but Eunice was not to be told. "She blames herself anyway," he said.

"But she mustn't," I said.

Mrs. Landis simply reached for his hand and held it in both of hers. "Each of us must be allowed to pay in our own way," she said gently. "Otherwise we can never stop punishing ourselves."

She had paid by sitting beside her mute and damaged son through a winter of days, helping him to live again. "Perhaps there can be other children," she said.

I saw that Mr. Jerome was looking at her hands, his face expressing the same surprise I had experienced when seeing them, really seeing them, for the first time. They weren't at all the kind of hands you might expect from seeing the rest of her; not fragile at all but large and capable looking. She had, after all, been playing the piano for a good many years.

Mr. Jerome regarded those hands now with a twisted smile. "All the king's horses and all the king's men," he said.

"Poor Humpy Dumpy," chimed in John.

"Poor Humpy Dumpy indeed," returned Mr. Jerome heavily. "Come here and sit on my lap, young John. We haven't had a talk for a long time."

He had become that human, that like the rest of us he

yearned toward warmth and affection, someone to cuddle when he was hurt. Someone small and warm that he would never have of his own. I felt the tears gathering behind my eyes and remembered some chores in the kitchen that required my immediate attention.

When I went to the hospital the next day to visit Eunice, I found her perfectly calm. "The baby was deformed," she said, "but don't tell *him*."

She never referred to him as Paul any more, it was always "him"; but the fact that she was attempting to shield him as he was shielding her might, I felt, be construed as a hopeful sign.

There always seems something especially poignant about a woman lying in a maternity ward after she has lost her own child, but Eunice didn't appear to be grieving. Perhaps, as Mrs. Landis had suggested, the child was her penance and she now could quit flagellating herself.

On my way out of the hospital I ran into Mr. Jerome, who was just arriving. "She'll be glad to see you," I said.

His expression was sardonic. "Duty must be the chilliest word in any language. Come with me for a walk, Victoria. I'll see Eunice later."

It was snowing, as it had been snowing that afternoon he had driven me home from the office for the first time. We walked along briskly but in silence, coming at length to the Fall Creek bridge, where we paused to look down at the partially frozen stream, and to look out across the city.

"I was born just over there," he said, "to a woman named Tillie Jerome. She had no idea who my father was but she wanted me. Can you understand that?"

"Of course. Women do want their babies."

"Eunice never did. No, my dear, she did not, so there's no use fooling ourselves. At first I thought it was *my* baby she didn't want, but the truth was she wanted none at all. She only thought if she gave me a child, I wouldn't bother her any more."

"She would have loved it anyway, if it had lived."

"Perhaps." His gaze had returned to the dark ice-clogged

water. "My mother was such a warm person," he said, "very pretty and very brave. I was adopted after she died, by a man who may have believed he was my father. We got along well enough, I suppose, certainly he gave me a start in the world I would not otherwise have had; but after he died I took back my own name, my mother's name, and felt as if I had crawled back into my own warm skin."

"The way I did," I said, "after you helped me get back Yasmina."

"And then you took on Toomey."

"And then you came back and took on both of us."

"And helped myself more than I could have possibly realized. That first evening in your kitchen, it was so warm and friendly. Maybe that shouldn't have surprised me as much as it did, but there were all the classic elements for friction. The husband out of work and finances tight, Toomey having been too stiff-necked to accept a personal loan."

"We had to borrow from Pinky," I said. "She'd have felt crushed if we hadn't."

"And that was another thing; a high-spirited young couple living not only with a mother-in-law but another older lady entirely unrelated to them, and a pan-banging toddler to boot. But not a sign of friction or ill-will. Instead there was all that affection and warmth. I felt like a dog that crawls in and puts his nose to your fire, then that feels so good he keeps wriggling the rest of him in, inch by inch, hoping you won't notice and send him packing."

"There was never any danger of that."

"I know that now. Then, however, I was encountering for the first time a simplicity I hadn't found anywhere else in the world, one that wasn't dependent on money or anything at all but human affection.

"That was what first attracted me to Eunice; I believed I saw those same values in her."

"They were there," I said, "only they got overlaid with something else. Not money. I still don't believe she married you for that."

He gave me a wintry smile. "Neither do I. What Eunice wanted was the impossible, a passionate lover who always gets himself in hand somewhere short of the dastardly act. Hardly a role for an aging roué, even a reformed one."

"She might be different, after this."

"You don't believe that any more than I do."

"But if you still love her?"

"That's finished," he said shortly.

When a thing is finished, don't try to string it out. When he had said that, he had not meant that he was finished with me, only with our relationship, although I had not understood that then. "You won't disappear again, will you?" I asked.

His expression softened. "No, dear," he said gently, "I won't disappear."

"Because you mean the world to all of us. Toomey, me, John, everybody."

"Well, now, I can't run away and leave all that, can I? And I certainly have plenty of work to do. Helping revive PureSilk and poking my golden thumb into some other promising-looking pies. Dandling my grandchildren on my knee. You aren't vexed because Toomey turned down the vice-presidency, are you?"

"No. Toomey must do as he sees fit to do."

"You won't suffer from it in any case. Most of what I have will eventually come to you."

It was a moment before his meaning began to sink in. "No!" I cried in alarm. "You can't do that. It would kill Toomey not to take care of us himself! He wouldn't even let me go back to work as much as a day, beans and cabbage or not."

"I never saw anybody get into such a tizzy about inheriting a little money. Do simmer down. I'll just have to hang on for a few more years and give it to your children."

"You hang on anyway but leave your money somewhere else. It's you my children need, and so do I."

And then I remembered, and so did he.

"Maybe the poor little scrap's better off," he said, but his face had gone bleak. "I'll see Eunice through until she's well again and decides what she wants to do."

"Yes," I said.

He saw me into my car, then said he was going back to visit Eunice for awhile.

"Come to our house for supper," I said. "It doesn't matter if you're late."

"Thank you." He seemed to hesitate, and suddenly I felt the intensity of his loneliness, like the agony of a wild thing wounded to the death and alone. "Coming to your house has become like—coming home—to the home I never had."

He remained standing there as I drove away, a strangely poignant figure in the gathering dusk.

XXXIX

Like a child who has rediscovered a once beloved toy, Toomey could scarcely be induced to take time away from his machines to eat and sleep. On his scale model in the dungeon he was experimenting constantly with things he called cams to produce different patterns. "Look at this one," he would enthuse, presenting a swatch of intricate design for Mr. Jerome's approval.

"Women won't wear it. It would make their legs look knobby."

"Men will. And what about women's underwear? And sweaters?"

"Ah yes," says Mr. Jerome, beginning to kindle, as John pokes an inquisitive head between them, demanding, "Me see!"

And is shown, for if there is one trait those two possess in common, it is that they are never too busy or too impatient to instruct my ever-inquisitive son, whose "Me see" now echoes through the house from morning to night in his rage to see and smell and taste and touch everything in his reach before another sun goes down. "Me see," he would demand of his grandmother as she sat knitting or sewing. "Me see," he would cry, pushing up a chair to the kitchen table to watch me mix a salad or roll cookies. "Me do!" he would exclaim enthusiastically, and be given a bit of dough and a rolling pin of his own.

"Like father, like son," said Forster Jerome.

"Like Granpapa too," I said, and he was pleased.

"That's what Henrietta says."

It was Henrietta all the time now, and I'd even heard him calling Mrs. Pincus Alice. There had been a new ease in his manner ever since our walk in the snow.

"Am I keeping Eunice away from here?" he asked me once.

"No," I told him honestly, "she wouldn't come anyway."

I supposed it must seem to her that I had let her down, but to believe as she would have me believe was not possible, and I wasn't much good at pretending. She was now sharing an apartment with one of the girls she had worked with at PureSilk. I had telephoned her once or twice but it was hard to keep a conversation going with so little help from her, and I had finally given up.

Mr. Jerome told us he had instituted proceedings for a divorce. "Not very chivalrous of me, I suppose, but I intend to provide adequately for Eunice."

A week or two later he told us, one afternoon as he was leaving, "By the way, you young people are on your own this evening. I'm taking Henrietta and Alice to dinner and on to the opera."

"How thoughtful of you," I said. "Mrs. Landis loves the opera but she seldom gets to go any more."

"I shall see to it that she does. In case you haven't noticed, Henrietta is—superlative."

"Oh, I've noticed, believe me, but the first time I met her I was sure she must be the Mad Hatter's twin sister. I couldn't understand how a nice sensible girl like me kept getting tangled up with so many sheer idiots."

"After you'd already got tangled up with me. Poor Victoria."

"All because I got into the wrong building by mistake."

"You had nothing to do with it. It was all Yasmina's doing."

There was a teasing light in his eyes. He might even be right. On the other hand he might just be remembering the shock of that first meeting to both of us. I refused to indulge him by inquiring. Instead I said, "I love you dearly, Paul."

"I am a much better father than a husband," he said, smiled mockingly, and bowed himself out.

But he *could* be a good husband, I thought, to a woman who cared about him. And understood him—only what woman could? Mrs. Landis and Pinky seemed to get along with him splendidly but they were constitutionally uncritical of everybody. The three of them, I'd noticed, certainly seemed to enjoy each other's company; and with a Mrs. Brownlee from down the street to complete a bridge foursome, they played for hours on end. In fact, Mr. Jerome seemed to be spending about as much time in our house as his own, including the occasions I'd come upon him unexpectedly, sitting quietly in the living room listening to Mrs. Landis play the piano.

By spring the Mullery house had been razed and construction on the new bungalow was about ready to start. The garage had been left standing for the time being to store building materials and tools.

PureSilk officially reopened the first week in May, and most of the former employees were called back to work. "Eunice wants to work at her old job," Mr. Jerome told us. "It's all right with me, although she doesn't have to work unless she wants to."

What else was there, I wondered, for a girl who had rejected marriage and motherhood? She had not contested the divorce, which would become final in another month, but I knew that Mr. Jerome had made a liberal settlement on her. How a divorce would fit in with her religious principles I couldn't quite reconcile, but then hardly any of her views during the past several months had seemed exactly logical to me.

When John and I returned from a walk one late spring afternoon, Mrs. Landis met us at the door with the announcement that my sister Margaret had called to tell me my father had died that morning.

It was like a message from another world. By now I even had trouble remembering my father's face, which shamed me, because he had once held me in his arms as Toomey held his children now, answered my flow of questions as patiently as Toomey dealt with John's. I went inside and sat down in the nearest chair.

"Are you all right, dear?" Mrs. Landis's face swam before me, looking anxious.

"Yes," I said, "I'll be all right."

"I shouldn't have broken it to you so abruptly."

"I'll be all right," I said again, but I wasn't feeling in the least all right. You ought to feel sorrow when somebody tells you your father has died, but I wasn't feeling a thing.

"When my husband died," said Mrs. Landis, "I was shocked at first because I was not as sorry as I felt I ought to be. What I had to learn to understand was that death doesn't change a thing a man has done, or would do again tomorrow if he were alive. Respect your father for what he was, Vicki, but don't try to endow him with qualities he never possessed, or castigate yourself for those that grieved you.

"The baby will be perfectly all right with us," she went on practically, "now that she's on the bottle."

It took me a moment to realize she was looking ahead to the funeral, assuming I would want to attend. But why go to see him dead when I would never have gone again to see him alive? Even as I questioned, however, I knew that I would go, because somehow it seemed necessary.

"Thank you," I said, and kissed her cheek; felt her fingers trailing down my face and knew they were tracing the path of my tears. You can cry a little, can't you, even when you're not sure what you're crying about?

XL

It was the first time I had been to that cemetery since my mother's funeral, and I found that I remembered little of that occasion except driving away afterward. I saw now that Papa had, after all, done the best he could by both his wives. The two adjoining lots had been treated as one and spaced evenly for three graves, with his in the middle. Against the marker that read YASMINA BROADBENT rested a glass jar containing garden flowers which still looked fairly fresh. I wondered who had put them there.

Papa had only known her as Yasmina, not ever—I felt sure of that—as Julia Mary. I remembered the way he had always called her Minnie, probably not considering Yasmina a proper name for the wife of a Christian. Maybe not, but it had been a delightful name for a princess, or a witch.

Suddenly I remembered something Mr. Jerome had once said: "If I ever found myself married to a woman like your mother and prevented by moral or religious convictions from taking to drink, I would certainly blow my brains out." I found myself smiling. Papa had undoubtedly had his troubles too.

Margaret and Bob had five children now, the youngest about John's age. At their insistence we agreed to follow them home from the cemetery and stay for supper.

"I wish you had brought your children," Margaret kept saying after Toomey had trailed Bob out to the barn to observe the evening chores.

"I wish we had now," I said. "John would love seeing the farm."

"It's been so long since we've seen each other."

"Was Justine still living with Papa?"

Margaret nodded, grimacing. "They weren't getting along at all well but Justine has never bothered abut getting out and trying to find a job. I suppose she'll have to now."

"Unless Papa left her something."

"He never made a will as far as we know, so it will be share out even, the ten of us."

"I don't want anything from him," I said.

"You're entitled to your share same as the rest of us, not that it will amount to much."

Something over a hundred acres at present day prices might bring as much as eleven or twelve thousand dollars, to be split ten ways. Was it for this all the battles had been joined? I started to mention Yasmina's quilt, then stopped myself. It might only cause bad feelings and there had been far too many of those already. Besides, it had been a private matter between Yasmina and me. As had been so many other things that must now remain so.

"Your mother was wonderful," Margaret was saying. "Just simply wonderful."

I was not sure how our conversation had veered to Yasmina but I was relieved.

"I'll never forget that first day she walked into our house," she said. "It was summer and she was wearing a lavender voile dress with lace at the throat and wrists, and a sailor hat trimmed in purple velvet with a bunch of purple violets on the brim. She was absolutely untouchable. We stood there and gaped at her, even Mildred, who was almost sixteen and considered herself quite a young lady. She looked us over that way she had, so straight and steady you were sure she could see right through to the back of your head. Then she said, 'My name is Yasmina. Your papa must have told you I was coming.'

"We managed to nod, and Mildred finally found her tongue and her manners and introduced herself and us. Yasmina took of her hat, laid it aside, smiled at us, and said, 'I've never been a housekeeper before so I don't know very much about it.'

"We didn't believe that, of course. All ladies knew about keeping house. But we would help her, we told her, and she laughed and said, 'we'll get along fine then.' "

"Did you believe she was really a witch?" I asked.

"No," said Margaret judiciously, "but then I didn't exactly believe she *wasn't* one, either."

That started us off, and presently we were laughing together like a pair of fools. "Remember the bread she shot?" I asked.

"And the shivareering."

"And the love potions."

"And Mrs. Rosetree."

"And The Stuff."

"And the way she talked to God."

"Women!" said Toomey, coming up behind me. "Take your eyes off them for a minute and they start gabbing instead of doing their chores."

"Yah to you! Supper's almost ready."

"Where did the flowers come from?" I asked, remembering that homely bouquet leaning against the headstone.

"Nobody seems to know for sure," said Margaret, "but there are nearly always flowers there. A lot of people still have a feeling about her."

She would have liked that, I thought. She wouldn't want them ever to forget that once there had lived among them a witch named Yasmina.

"You're very quiet," said Toomey on the way home, thoughtfully adding, "for you."

"I was thinking," I said.

"About Yasmina?"

"Yes, and about men and women and love and Lysistrata and babies, and what could have happened to me, and what did, and how lucky I am."

"That's quite a bit of thinking."

"And how much I love you."

"Then what are you doing way over there? Pretty soon, I suppose you'll be wanting twin beds." He put his arm across my lap and pulled me closer to him.

"Too rough on the carpet," I said. "Besides, you're always so nice and warm."

"Too bad John missed a trip to the farm. Maybe I ought to take back a cow for him."

"Please don't. It would be unsettling to find teats and horns and a tail scattered over the laundry room floor."

"Hush. Your washing machine will be back in service any day now, better than ever. You're too pretty to be slaving over a hot tub anyway."

"True," I murmured.

"Peggy sounds great, doesn't he? After that overhaul I gave him?"

"Purrs like a kitten," I agreed.

"I suppose I really ought to be thinking about trading him in."

"No," I protested. Automobiles did wear out, no doubt, but Peggy was part of us. He'd seen us through our original courtship and marriage, to say nothing of several courtships since, borne me faithfully to the hospital for the births of my babies. At least half his innards hd been replaced over the years by Toomey, aided lately by John. How often had I seen those two bright heads together puzzling over Peggy's vital parts, John reaching for tools as fast as Toomey put them down, Daddy patiently asking for pliers and then a wrench. "No, John, that's a screwdriver. There's the wrench over there."

"How can you think of such a thing?" I demanded querulously.

"Oh, I suppose he'll wear out sometime," said Toomey, sounding relieved. "Although," he added gallantly, "you never have."

"With an easy life like mine? Especially now that we're over all the bumps and the going is easy? Why should I wear out?"

It was past eleven when we got home but the living room lights were still on. We found Mr. Jerome sitting in the high-backed chair, his head back, his eyes closed. Mrs. Landis was at the piano, playing softly, but she looked up when we came in, stopped playing and swung around to face us. Mr. Jerome opened his eyes and sat up. "So you finally got home," he commented. "What have you been doing all this time?"

"Necking," I said.

"You didn't have to wait up," Toomey pointed out.

"On the contrary. Your mother and I have something to tell you. She won't be needing the bungalow."

"So we can talk about it tomorrow," said Toomey, yawning.

"Henrietta and I are going to be married."

"You—are—*what*?" Then Toomey simply let himself go and allowed the couch to receive him.

I was surprised too although I wondered why I should be. "Well, why not?" I said, trying to give Toomey time to recover his voice if not his usual aplomb. "I'm so happy for both of you!" I went over and kissed Mrs. Landis on the cheek.

"What about you, young man?" demanded Mr. Jerome, turning to Toomey.

I sat down beside Toomey and began to stroke his arm and speak to him in a soothing voice. "Your mother was awfully nice about us, darling. We really can't let her down."

"Who's letting w-w-w-who down?" he demanded belligerently. "Just g-g-give me a minute to c-c-catch my breath, can't you?"

He stood up, swaying only a little, walked over to his mother and put an arm around her, offering Mr. Jerome his other hand. He said, "Congratulations, sir. You c-c-couldn't find a nicer g-girl. Just see that you treat her right."

"You may depend upon that," Mr. Jerome assured him solemnly.

"Alice will be coming with us," he continued. "With my housekeeper, that'll give us our own foursome for bridge."

"Do help yourself to my household," I invited. "Anyone else you fancy? Toomey? John? The baby? Puppy perhaps?"

"Not just now, thank you. And you might try to be a little more respectful, now that I'm going to be your father-in-law."

"I do try," I said.

"Well," he said cheerfully, "I'll be getting along now. I'll call you tomorrow, Henrietta."

"Well," said Toomey, looking after our departing guest.

"You don't really mind, do you?" Mrs. Landis's eyes were dewy and her voice sounded tremulous, as befit a prospective bride.

Toomey's face as he gazed at her was a study in tenderness and devotion, and I could see him gathering all his forces to put into his answer. "No, Mother," he said gently. "I only want you to be happy."

The only place to take a battered warrior is to bed. I took him by the hand and gently led him away.

"You are prepared, I trust," I heard him murmur a few minutes later.

"Naturally," I said, "like always." Well, nearly always. You understand how it is, don't you, Yasmina? I can't always be careful, can I? Anyway, you don't start a baby every time. And even if you did—Yasmina, this is absolutely no time to think!

XLI

Mrs. Landis came down to breakfast next morning while John was having his, and I was keeping company with my third cup of coffee. She still had that dewy look about her, the same soft tremulousness about her mouth. "Toomey isn't really upset, is he?" she inquired a little anxiously.

"He's recovering nicely," I assured her. "It's just that it comes as a bit of a shock the first time you think about your mother going to bed with a man."

I saw the delicate color wash into her face. "I suppose we must look terribly silly to you young people," she said.

"Not at all. What I can't figure out is why he didn't have sense enough to propose to you in the first place."

"I'm afraid I—rather discouraged him then," she confessed, her color rising even higher. "I thought I'd better accept him this time before he made another mistake."

"Very wise. And I might say you're an inspiration to me. Growing older may not be as dismal as it's cracked up to be."

"Oh, it isn't." And then, after a moment, "I thought you might have seen this coming on."

"I suppose I should have, but at first I thought you were just being kind to him, then later I suppose I thought he was being nice to you, although it was certainly out of character."

"He's soft as pudding inside. I once read about some kind of jungle flower that folds right back inside itself the minute anybody touches it."

"That's Mr. Jerome," I agreed, "if you can manage to think of him as a flower." And then I had another thought.

"You must have thought we were pretty silly too, thinking you needed a bungalow because you were too old to climb the stairs."

My gaze fell upon my son, sitting there shoveling down oatmeal. He actually liked the stuff. "Granmama's going to marry Granpapa," I told him.

He was used to having blockbusters fired at him by now. He gave me a winsome smile and went on eating.

"I suppose he has been rather naughty sometimes," said Mrs. Landis, and I knew she wasn't referring to her grandson.

"The first time I saw him," I said, "I was absolutely certain he was a white slaver. When he booted me out five months later I was equally certain he was God. I suppose the truth must lie somewhere between."

"With the bad people so good sometimes and the good people so bad sometimes, it's hardly worthwhile trying to sort them out, is it?"

"At least you've had experience handling rambunctious boys."

"So have you now, dear," she returned, smiling conspiratorially. "And isn't it fun?"

"Never a dull moment," I agreed, reflecting that we didn't so much help each other around this house as aid and abet.

Toomey, of course, adjusted splendidly once he'd recovered from the initial shock. He was back to wheeling and dealing in no time at all. "Now would be a good time for us to consider a little househunting," he said, "or maybe a little housebuilding."

I'd been having some ideas along those lines myself. John was getting old enough to have a room of his own but there were only two bedrooms downstairs. Even having the upstairs rooms available wouldn't do much toward solving the problem because we couldn't put small children to sleep upstairs alone. A house all on one floor and big enough to accommodate us all would be wonderful but there was one drawback. "What about the dungeon?" I asked.

Toomey smiled a little wistfully but said he'd have to move out most of his equipment anyway while pulling in the dungeon walls to where they belonged, so he could just as well set them up in a new placc.

He was quite right, of course, and I appreciated his resolution, but I couldn't help feeling a little regretful too. You get used to living on the edge of a crisis, I guess you kind of hate to give it up. At least Toomey had said no more about replacing Peggy with a new model. After all, the Wonderful One-Horse Shay had lasted a hundred years.

Any remaining doubts I mights have had about the upcoming marriage were completely dispelled when I walked into the living room one morning and found Mr. Jerome holding a skein of knitting yarn on his hands while Mrs. Landis wound it into a ball. It seemed almost ludicrously symbolic, the indomitable man presenting himself bound and helpless before the gentlest of women.

Not entirely helpless, of course. He still had his tongue. "What's Toomey smirking about now?" he demanded.

"Ask him," I suggested.

"I did. He mumbled something about remembering he was a man."

Mrs. Landis stopped winding yarn. "Vicki, dear, it isn't? You're not—again?"

"In a word—yes."

"One would think you actually enjoyed having babies," growled Mr. Jerome.

"Yes and no," I said. "What's bothering me just now is this morning wedding you two are planning, mornings not being my best time just now."

"Then we'll change it, won't we dear?" Her glance went back to Mr. Jerome, practically bathing him in gentle light.

"By all means," he agreed. "And now would you mind getting on with your winding, Henrietta. This isn't all I've got to do today, you know."

She winked at me, picked up the yarn ball from her lap, and resumed winding.

When we returned to our happy home after seeing the newlyweds off at the Union Station for a wedding trip, we found that somebody had parked a car in the street, partially blocking our driveway. Uncomplainingly Toomey pulled into the Mullery driveway which was still intact. We squeezed though a break in the hedge, and went into the house.

I changed John's clothes, and he and Puppy went out to the front yard for a romp. Toomey got a bottle of beer from the refrigerator, and I put on water for tea. We kicked off our shoes and prepared to relax.

About twenty minutes later came a horrendous crash, followed by a child's blood-curdling scream, some wild barking, and then another scream. Only the thought of my beloved firstborn lying broken and close to dying in the street gave me strength to stagger to the door, with Toomey right behind me.

"Mama!" shrieked John. "Daddy! Come see!"

Unmistakably alive and miraculously unblemished, he dashed back down the steps, and we followed him.

" 'at ole car go BOOM! Right in a HOLE!" He was dancing up and down with excitement, and pointing toward our recently acquired and now demolished property. Puppy was running in circles, emitting short excited barks.

"What—?" began Toomey, but that was as far as he got. There lay poor Peggy, fallen on his side and moaning low. And sinking, right through the Mullery's driveway, down into the dungeon. We watched with bated breath until the death throes were over and all was still. "Whee-e-e-e-e!" exulted John.

Toomey's face had gone pale with shock and horror, but he pulled himself heroically together and demonstrated for all posterity mortal man's ability to rise above disaster. "As I was saying, honey, we really must build a new house and buy a new car. And have a new baby."

A belated awareness of my condition wiped away the horror and replaced it with tender concern. "Sweetheart," he asked anxiously, "you're not upset, are you?"

"Me? Upset? Perish the thought!"

XLII

Children are pieced together like quilts, a nose from here, a chin from there, a quirk of the eyebrow from somebody else. My own eyes are set into John's face with the slight squint that is Toomey's, between what are definitely Toomey's grin and Toomey's hair. Like Yasmina he claps his palms together to applaud a job—usually his own—well done. Julie, named for one grandmother, behaves uncannily like the other but physically resembles Margaret's second daughter. All my children were born with a fine crop of black hair, which in the case of Felicity, promptly rechristened Flissy by John, was replaced with hair equally black but considerably more susceptible to brush and comb. Yasmina's hair, beyond a doubt, but strangers invariably exclaim, "How much that baby resembles her grandfather!" And Mr. Jerome basks fatuously in the recognition, his eyes double-daring me to expose the fraud.

Yes, I still think of him as Mr. Jerome although I sometimes call him Paul, as almost everyone does now. It does not seem in the least strange to me that my baby should be thought to resemble him, for his assimilation into our family circle has been natural and complete. My children adore him, although in his oddly ungrandfatherlike manner he exacts of them behavior that would put them off anyone else. No child ever comes tearing into a room and catapults himself unceremoniously into Granpapa's lap. He walks up quietly, places a tentative hand on the gentleman's knee, and is then invited to the gentleman's lap for a spot of cuddling and conversation but no riotous behavior. When Granpapa takes them for a walk, they hold his hand and stroll sedately, with none of the ridiculous cavorting and shouting that accompany similar excursions with me or their father.

And Henrietta? Well, she quietly blossoms, and spoils the irascible creature rotten, aided and abetted by Pinky—Alice, that is—who is obviously loath to consider him even a little lower than the angels.

There is a textile mill now, another of those pies Mr. Jerome couldn't resist sinking his golden thumb into. Under his patient tutelage Toomey has become a vice-president in spite of himself, and is discovering that weaving is almost as fascinating as knitting. The non-run hosiery line has been well-received and profitable. Toomey's present enthusiasm is for the new nylon yarns, for which he envisions a glowing future in fabrics as well as hosiery.

Vituminol continues to flourish, as does Abner Wagon, whose original Stan Stupid series has led to a syndicated comic strip published in newspapers throughout the country. Most of the original Vituminol staff have stayed on, and Eunice, who took back her maiden name, still works at the mill and has never remarried.

For almost a year we have been living in our new house, a sprawling affair with five bedrooms all on one floor. Even allowing a room for each child, we are left a spare, but that may be remedied in time.

John and I, in the process of raising my children and his, have become secure in the knowledge that both puppies and babies *do* get housebroken, and all of them grow and thrive and become boon companions. John is still a dependable type like his father. Yes, I have learned that too, that Toomey is always beside me even when it doesn't show.

But now the time has come when John, almost six, must start to school. "It won't ever be the same again," I sniffled into Toomey's shoulder only a few nights ago. "He'll start growing away from me."

"Now, honey," he comforted, "*I* never have."

Nor has he. His home is still his castle and his proving ground. At this very moment the sewing machine, its innards laid out neatly on the floor, awaits the magic touch of the genius, only one of our three cars is in condition to take to the road, and God alone knows what is going on in Dungeon II. Still, he doesn't gamble or chase women or drink to excess or use offensive language, he's wonderful with the children, and he's still terrific in bed.

All that comforted me usually but not now. "He won't even be six until October," I mourned. "It would really be better to wait a year."

"Why don't you tell him that?"

And hadn't I tried! Betty was going to school, Bobby was going to school, Jeanie was—But, protested my aching heart, *they* were already six. "I won't let him go," I vowed. "I'm going to hide him."

Sure I would let him go, Toomey assured me. I was his sweet girl, wasn't I? His brave wonderful girl? Hadn't I once pushed a full-grown man into a fish pond, brought a wicked old bootlegger to heel, and practically single-handedly scuttled the miserable Mullerys?

"Your mind's wandering," I said presently, "and that's not all."

"My sweet bawdy baby."

So all too soon the day of reckoning arrived. Consider my little family at breakfast on that fateful morning, singlemindedly shoveling it in. Nothing ever affected their appetites, that at least they had in common. Should an earthquake rip through our kitchen and slice our breakfast table smack in half, there they would sit on either side of the chasm, calmly chewing away.

Toomey kissed me goodbye. "Coward," I flung at him, but he grinned back at me with all the goodwill in the world. "Can't be late, baby. Got a meeting this morning."

I saw Julie contemplating her empty cereal bowl. "Fill up on toast," I said brutally. "No, don't cry," I hastily amended. "Mama isn't mad." We observe certain customs in this household, one being that no child is ever allowed to cry uncomforted. I simply didn't feel like comforting anybody right then. I had to put the finishing touches to my eager schoolboy.

We left Julie and Flissy sitting tearfully on the front steps; tearful, I hasten to explain, not because John was going to school but because they were not. Mrs. Hamaker was standing in the doorway sneakily touching her apron to her eyes, and Puppy was howling dismally at the gate. Better there, I thought unfeelingly, than at the schoolhouse door.

At last I was alone with my son, free to prepare him for his first day at school. What came over me then was pure panic. What on earth was I going to tell this child of mine? Not about being on time for the school bus because there wasn't one. Probably nobody was going to chase him with a worm, but if they did, he would only want to pet it. There certainly wasn't any use telling him not to sit on the floor in his white bloomers.

"Mama," he said, tugging at my hand, "you won't forget to feed Puppy, will you?"

His face was shining brighter than the sun. Despite my eyes, it was Toomey's face, with all Toomey's joy of living beaming from behind it. "No, darling," I promised, "I won't forget. I'll feed him as soon as I get home."

"Mrs. Hamaker said there'd be popovers for lunch." He skipped a little.

"Sure thing," I said. At least he would be home for lunch, and that was less than four hours away. And he was such a splendid little boy, so intelligent and self-reliant, quite a big boy really.

The minute we entered the schoolhouse, however, he started shrinking. "He looks so little," I whispered to a Mrs. Reeves I'd met once or twice before. She looked at me so stonily I wanted to disintegrate her on the spot. After all, how could a woman who was entering her fourth child, a husky girl half a head taller than John, in first grade be expected to understand how *I* felt?

"It doesn't get any better either," she whispered back,

the stony face dissolving into a sniffle. "They keep looking littler all the time."

The teacher was pretty, I noticed, and young. Much too young and frivolous-looking to be a teacher. How could a mere strip of a girl like that be expected to know anything about comforting little children?

When it came time for the mothers to make themselves scarce, I was suddenly seized with a mad impulse to clutch my doddle-headed infant to my bosom and head straight for the hinterlands. Then I saw the look on John's face, and once again it was Toomey's face with Toomey's heart and soul behind it, aware of everything I was thinking and chuckling a little inside but nevertheless full of compassion. I tipped him a wink, saw his hand fly to his mouth to stifle a giggle, and fled.

Back home again I fed Puppy, comforted my no longer tearful daughters, verified popovers for lunch with Mrs. Hamaker, then went off to commune with my unrigged sewing machine. And with Yasmina.

Here's to your brave new world, I said, *which is pretty much the way you hoped it would be. Toomey shaves every morning, and sometimes in the evening too. He can't help being a man and I wouldn't have him any other way. With him and me it is the way you always said it could be if relations between a woman and her husband were the way they ought to be. And he still fizzes, Yasmina. I hope he always will.*

Your grandchildren are healthy, bright and happy. Full of the devil on occasion, but they give love freely and receive it as naturally as flowers receive the gentle rain from heaven. I think I may have another one or two just to watch them grow.

You don't have to worry any more about having given me the wrong father, for it was you who made it possible for me to acquire another who suits me to a T. Except for your conditioning he would have scared me into a running fit before I ever got to know him. Probably Henrietta would have too. Maybe even Toomey.

What I have, Yasmina, is a family; pieced together like quilts and children, I know, but the fabric is beautiful and strong and the stitches true and enduring. After all, a family has to start somewhere, doesn't it? I intend to hang on to all of mine for dear life, even when, like this morning, I have to let go a little.

We may even decide to have a family crest. What would you think about a fish pond with a tented quilt over it? And Peggy parked at the side with a love philtre for a radiator cap?

As for us, Yasmina, you and me, all I can say is: What in tunket is coming next?

PRICE: $2.50 LB783

NICOLA
By Dorothy Daniels

Lovely Nicola Maneth had one burning ambition—to become a prima ballerina assoluta. She would allow nothing to stand in her way, and she would use any man to achieve her goal, including Austria's Emperor Franz Josef himself!

Despite the Emperor's patronage, Nicola's ambition created powerful enemies, both backstage and amidst the dazzling decadence of the Imperial Court.

Only one man could protect her from those who plotted her downfall—and the passion she felt for him threatened to destroy her career!